W9-CKI-777

Between Two Shores

Center Point
Large Print

Also by Jocelyn Green and available from Center Point Large Print:

Wedded to War
Widow of Gettysburg
A Refuge Assured

This Large Print Book carries the Seal of Approval of N.A.V.H.

Between Two Shores

JOCELYN GREEN

CENTER POINT LARGE PRINT
THORNDIKE, MAINE

This Center Point Large Print edition
is published in the year 2019 by arrangement with
Bethany House Publishers, a division of
Baker Publishing Group.

Other Scripture quotations are from the
King James Version of the Bible.

This is a work of historical reconstruction; the mention
of certain historical figures is therefore inevitable.
All other characters, however, are products of the
author's imagination, and any resemblance to
actual persons, living or dead, is coincidental.

The text of this Large Print edition is unabridged.
In other aspects, this book may vary
from the original edition.
Printed in the United States of America
on permanent paper.
Set in 16-point Times New Roman type.

ISBN: 978-1-64358-120-0

Library of Congress Cataloging-in-Publication Data

Names: Green, Jocelyn, author.
Title: Between two shores / Jocelyn Green.
Description: Center Point Large Print edition. | Thorndike, Maine :
    Center Point Large Print, 2019.
Identifiers: LCCN 2018058570 | ISBN 9781643581200 (hardcover :
    alk. paper)
Subjects: LCSH: Large type books.
Classification: LCC PS3607.R4329255 B48 2019b | DDC 813/.6—dc23
LC record available at https://lccn.loc.gov/2018058570

To Ann-Margret

FOR EVEN THE SON OF MAN CAME
NOT TO BE SERVED BUT TO SERVE,
AND TO GIVE HIS LIFE AS A
RANSOM FOR MANY.

—MARK 10:45

PROLOGUE

"I told you, I'm not staying." Catherine Stands-Apart drew back from her sister's touch and planted her feet wide at the edge of their mother's grave. The freshly turned soil pushed between her toes. "I only came to say good-bye."

Bright Star put her fists on her hips and frowned. She had thirteen summers to Catherine's ten but acted as though she held all the wisdom and authority of a council full of clan mothers. "You can't leave. This is our home."

Catherine's gaze traveled across the burial ground and past cornfields to the rows of shaggy birchbark longhouses. The Mohawk village of Kahnawake was tucked between wooded hills and the southwest bank of the St. Lawrence River, opposite the island of Montreal. Beside the village was the French fort of St. Louis, where a black robe baptized Mohawks into the Catholic faith and a garrison of soldiers watched for any British who might try to attack Montreal by coming up the river.

"*Yah.* It *was* my home." Catherine and her sister had been born here, along with their little brother, and had lived in one of the few European-style homes suited to just one family. They had stayed there even after the divorce that sent their French-Canadian father away. He had lived nearly two miles from the village ever since.

"You know we can't stay alone in the house without Mother," Bright Star said. "We must move into the longhouse with our clan. They are our family, too. We have many mothers."

Defiance swelled in Catherine, and she shook her head, beaded strands of hair clinking together. She had one true mother, named Strong Wind, and Strong Wind was buried here in the earth as of two sleeps ago. Despite all their efforts to revive her, she had died of the spotting sickness, along with four others from the Wolf Clan. They had caught the illness from the soldiers at the fort. *Smallpox,* the French called it.

Catherine rubbed the burning from her eyelids, then peered up at her sister. "You are my family, but you will marry within a year and start your own."

"What about our brother?" Bright Star asked. Joseph Many Feathers, who preferred to be called by his Christian name, had only four summers and ran wild in the village.

"He will stay with you in the longhouse with

10

everyone else." Catherine was fond of Joseph, but in only one or two more years, he would follow after his uncles and learn to be both hunter and warrior, gone from Kahnawake for months at a time. "He won't miss me."

Bright Star's heart-shaped face drew to a sharp point at her chin. "He will. You are his sister."

But Catherine felt like she couldn't breathe every time she thought of living with five or six other families under one roof. She wasn't used to the closeness, or the noise, or the smoke from so many fires. "I told you, I am going to live with our father. He needs me."

"He chose his path."

A sigh rose and fell in Catherine's chest. "He did not choose for that steel trap to take off his hand." If he had both hands, he would have been able to hunt and trap for his family, and maybe Strong Wind would not have divorced him. "You have all these people, Bright Star. Papa has no one. If you had seen him today when I told him the news about our mother—"

"You should not have done that."

"He deserved to know. And I miss him."

He missed her too, he'd said. He needed her. She was old enough now to help him with cooking and laundry and anything else. *"Come live with me again,"* he'd pleaded. *"You're as much my daughter as you were Strong Wind's, aren't you? You have just as much French blood in your veins as Mohawk. I would never take you away from your mother,* ma chère, *but now— must I live alone to the end of my days?"* That didn't seem fair.

"His blood runs in my veins, and I choose to live with him. *Awiyo.* It is good." Her eyes were the same blue as her father's, a sign they belonged together. Once Catherine was there to help, he wouldn't drink so much anymore. Life wouldn't be nearly as hard for him.

Beyond Bright Star, women stooped in the fields, black heads shining in the sun as they harvested corn. Children ran shrieking through the stalks to chase away the crows that swooped and squawked overhead. Catherine would never do that again if she lived with Papa. He had a different idea of how to live. He said she could help him run his trading post. She could help him with so many things! She would not forget Strong Wind by living with him, but perhaps she could forget this twisting pain of looking for her mother around every corner and never finding her.

Sweat beaded on Bright Star's brow, and her dark eyes glittered. Bits of corn silk stuck to the fringe of her buckskin dress from her own labor in the fields. "Your place is here, with your mother's people. Don't you remember what our mother said about that man you want to live with? He is selfish. He cares only for himself."

"*Totek*! Be quiet!" Catherine clapped her hands over her ears. She did not remember Strong Wind saying those words and did not want to. If she could bring any memories back, it would be of her mother singing to her or telling her stories. But all she could recall of her mother right now was the way she had looked with those blisters all over her skin. They had been everywhere. Her arms, her hands, her face. It was horrible and terrifying. Catherine had to leave this place, or she would go mad with seeing the sickness in her mind every time she thought of Strong Wind.

Bright Star pulled Catherine's arms down to her sides. "You are who your *mother* is, not your father. This is the way of things. What you want to do, it is not done."

Catherine turned away, weary of her sister's constant disapproval. It was a weight that bowed her head like a tumpline attached to a bundle of furs. She would be glad to shed this burden by moving away from here. But she could not convince her feet to leave the spot where her mother's body rested. Not yet.

The noise from the fields grew shrill and gleeful with children's voices. Women laughed and sang. Joseph burst from between two rows of cornstalks, a gourd rattle in his fist. Catherine waved at him.

He ran to her, his brown body naked save for a breechclout. Damp black hair clung to his neck.

13

"We are supposed to chase the crows! I am very good at scaring them away. See?" He shook his rattle and shouted at the sky. "I am fierce, yes?" He grabbed her hand, and the dirt from his palm rubbed hers.

"*Tohske' wahi*. Very fierce," Catherine said. "I need to tell you something. You and Bright Star are going to live in the longhouse from now on, and I am going to live in a different house. With Papa."

Joseph wrinkled his nose. "Where? Why?"

He was too young to remember much of Papa, and Papa never took pride in him, which Catherine could not explain. Fathers prized their sons. But her father wanted *her,* though she was neither male nor firstborn. She was special somehow. That was why Strong Wind had named her Stands-Apart. But Papa preferred her Christian name, Catherine. So did she.

Joseph tugged her hand. "Where are you going?"

A gust of wind swept over her, smelling of cooking fish. "It's not far. I can come back to visit you. *Hen'en*, everything is fine."

He looked at her with large black eyes that seemed to measure what she'd said. Then a shadow flickered over his face, and he squinted into the sky. "Crows!" he shouted, releasing her hand. He scrambled back into the field, shaking his rattle. "*Wahs*! Go away, crows! *Wahs*! No corn for you!"

14

Bright Star crossed her arms and bent her head toward Catherine, her thick braids swinging. They were many shades of brown, like walnut shells, the same as Catherine's hair. Porcupine quills fanned tall and straight from the back of her head. "You say you will visit? Maybe I will not want to see you, a sister who rejects her people." Her voice quivered like a bowstring pulled too taut. She used her words like arrows. "Well were you named Stands-Apart, for you stand too far apart from us. Go away, then, and stay there."

Something ripped inside Catherine. She stared at the mound of dirt that covered Strong Wind and wanted to fling herself upon it, arms open wide to soak in the summer sun baked into the earth. She wanted, one last time, to pretend that warmth was her mother's embrace. She wanted to feel loved again. Right now, she felt alone and shamed.

So she pointed her toes away from the grave to put Bright Star, and that pain, behind her.

PART ONE

Here is Canada, surrounded on all sides. . . .
Only peace can save the colony now.
—Major General Louis-Joseph de Montcalm,
senior field commander for the French and
Canadian forces in North America
during the Seven Years' War

Of all our enemies, famine is the most fearsome.
—Pierre de Rigaud, Marquis de Vaudreuil,
governor-general of New France

CHAPTER ONE

Lachine, Island of Montreal, Quebec
Late August 1759

Catherine Duval was used to waiting.

Outside the old settlement called Lachine on the south bank of the Island of Montreal, she sat on the end of the dock, her empty *bateau* bumping the pilings beside her. With her petticoats and silk skirts pooling at her knees, she dangled her bare feet in the river and looked across its mile-wide expanse toward Kahnawake. Clouds hung low and full in the sky, a lid on the simmering humidity. She unpinned her straw hat from the mass of hair piled upon her head and fanned herself, cicadas ticking away the time.

They would come. Bright Star had brought the news to Catherine's trading post yesterday that clan brothers who had just returned from fishing on the Ottawa River had seen the *coureurs des bois*. The trappers, untethered to any official fur company, were nearby and would be in Lachine today. Her sister could be as prickly as porcupine quills, but she was reliable.

The first strains of boisterous singing floated

down the river, signaling the trappers' approach. Shaking the water from her feet, Catherine stepped back into her moccasins and retied the satin ribbons of her hat beneath her chin as she stood. She arranged herself into a posture of confidence and authority. Hands folded, chin high, back straight. With five and twenty summers behind her, she knew how to manage these men even without her father at her side. In truth, it would be easier without him. His gruff manner tended to impact profit.

After waiting with her for merely an hour this morning, Gabriel had declared that the men weren't coming, for he gave Bright Star's report little credit. *"I'll find my own way home,"* he'd told Catherine, and ambled toward Montreal's city gates, nine miles away, on an errand he did not divulge. When he was finished, he'd hire someone to row him back across the river.

No matter. Catherine had been acting on his behalf for years, for he had no head for market rates and no talent for negotiation whatsoever. She knew that, deep down, he was grateful for her help. That she meant more to him than he admitted. This was the truth she circled back to when she longed for a family of her own. She'd been engaged once but was abandoned. There had been other suitors, and she'd even thought she'd loved one of them, but nothing came of it. So she had bound up her dreams of a family into hard knots and cast them into the river to be stepping-stones to the other side of disappointment.

A chirping bank swallow became a blur of black and white as it fluttered out of a burrow in the riverbank, briefly claiming Catherine's attention. One bateau headed toward her. At roughly twenty-four feet long, it was bigger than a canoe and built for carrying heavy loads. But it was only a single vessel, when before the war it would have been the first in a line of one hundred or more, returning from months spent in the west trapping beaver, muskrat, fox, and wolf. Lachine would have been teeming with merchants vying for their wares.

"*Bonjour, mademoiselle!*" the steersman called out when he spied her. She recognized Denis and Emile from years gone by, but not the two other men with them.

"Bonjour, welcome!" She returned their smiles. "I see you have left all the other trappers behind!"

The bateau cut through the river, the blue-grey water ruffling as it parted. A dragonfly perched on the bow. "*Oui, ma belle,* and where is all your competition?" Emile laughed as he drew close and threw her a line, which she tied to the pilings while all four men climbed onto the dock.

Catherine lifted her hands. "In the militia, *monsieur*, fighting a war. Some might say you ought to do the same, unless you are younger than sixteen or older than sixty and very good at hiding it."

"Ah!" Creases fanned from Emile's eyes and framed the grin on his leathered face, though she knew he was no more than five years her senior. "Some might. Some might. But then who would be left to bring you furs each year? Who are we to allow a little war to interrupt your business?" He winked, for this war was far from little.

What had begun as a squabble between English and French governors over who controlled the Ohio River Valley had since blown into a full-scale war for much more than that. Now all of New France and New England hung in the balance. The battles had spread beyond this continent, too, to Europe, Africa, the Philippines, and South America. The whole world, it seemed, was at war for a chance for empires to gain new lands.

"Come, then," Catherine said after learning the other two men were named Stephen and Philippe. "You must eat."

Ignoring the ache in her empty stomach, she led the men onto the grassy shore, where she had a basket of food waiting. They were made from one mold, these burly men, the same mold that had formed her father. About five feet six inches tall, muscled and stocky, ruddy-faced, independent, carefree—and thirsty. She knew they had been living on dried peas and corn, hard biscuits, and if they'd been lucky, a little salt pork. The corn cakes she offered from her own kitchen came dear, but if she had learned one thing from the famine of the last two years, it was that hunger was a distracting and irritating companion. Business was best done without it.

While Philippe and Stephen traded ribald jokes, Emile said nothing as he ate. Denis tipped his canteen to his lips, then wiped his mouth with the back of his hand. Swiping his toque from his mud-brown hair, he swept an appraising glance over Catherine. She wondered if he noticed that her gown hung looser this year over stays that cinched ever smaller about her waist.

"Not eating?" he asked.

"This is for you," she assured them.

For the last two years, the fields around Montreal had been blighted black. This year, the grain was ripe but the barns were still empty, as all the farmers held muskets, not scythes. So while she had no desire to deal with hungry men, she had learned to keep her own wits and composure whether the emptiness in her gut scraped dull or sharp.

"The forts along the Great Lakes must still be in French control," she ventured once the men had eaten.

Emile mopped his face with the end of his faded red sash. "As far as we know. If the British take them, we'll just go farther north or west to trap."

"In that case, you won't bring your furs here anymore. You'll need a closer outlet. In fact, I'm surprised you came this summer at all, since you must have known Louisbourg was taken by the British and Quebec is under siege." New France was hemmed in from the east. Even if the Montreal merchants were not serving in the militia, they may not have come to Lachine for the annual fur trade anyway, because they had no way to export their furs from the coastal cities to Europe. No doubt this was why only Denis's team of coureurs des bois had come.

"But here you are, just the same," he said. "Still trading with the Dutch in Albany? Isn't that the headquarters of the British army now?"

"It is. So we trade with the merchants at Schenectady, on the Mohawk River, twenty miles north of Albany." Even during times of peace, trade with Albany was forbidden for French-Canadian citizens, but the government turned a blind eye to Kahnawake Mohawks engaged in it. Since Catherine was half of each, arrest seemed half a risk, depending on how authorities wanted to view her. The three French sisters who ran the post before Catherine's father took it over had been deported back to France.

"And how do the French soldiers at Fort St.

Louis feel about your smuggling goods to and from the enemy?" Emile asked.

She smiled. "The soldiers garrisoned at the edge of Kahnawake wouldn't agree with me, I'm afraid, but I don't consider the British, and certainly not my business partners in New York, the enemy."

Emile's laughter suggested he didn't agree with her either, but these men would not report her, for they were also breaking the law by not fighting.

Just as Catherine lived between Kahnawake and Montreal, between Mohawk culture and French, she lived and worked between two sides of a war. She remained neutral, uninterested in choosing sides. Successful trades happened because they needed each other. She sent fur to New England, and her porters returned with British trade goods: linens and kettles in peacetime, good rope and muskets in war. Ironic, perhaps, but a good trade nonetheless.

A sticky breeze that smelled of coming rain stirred the lace at Catherine's elbows. "This is not the first war my trade has weathered, and it won't be the last. My porters are very discreet and adjust their routes to avoid the dangerous areas along the way. They are the best."

"Better than us?" Denis teased.

She laughed. "You are the *very* best for coming this far when you must have known there would be few merchants left in the market."

"All I need is one merchant, ma chère, to make it worth my while. And that one merchant is you. Come now, mademoiselle, and make me glad we came to see you."

She could afford to, and proved it with rum and coin.

Denis and Emile were happy with the payment, and Stephen and Philippe did not mask their surprise. They didn't know, she guessed, that the Dutch merchants paid twice as much for her furs than what she could get anywhere else.

Catherine smiled at the confusion on their faces. "You haven't fleeced me, I assure you. The British have given up their own trapping, content to obtain furs through trade with New France. The war only makes them scarce and thus more valuable."

Thunder rumbled in the distance as the men loaded a dozen ninety-pound bales of fur into her flat-bottomed bateau. Satisfaction brimmed just beneath her calm. She was sure her father would be pleased. That was, whenever he decided to come home.

By the time Catherine arrived at her own dock, the threat of rain had blown past with no more than a few sprinkles escaping the clouds. The air was a thick, damp blanket about her as she secured the bateau. Their other vessel, a birchbark canoe, remained tethered on the opposite side of the dock.

The chemise beneath her bodice stuck to her skin as she climbed onto the dock and eyed the bales of fur in the bateau. They would need to be taken into the storeroom of the trading post before nightfall. If Gabriel returned by then, he could manage the task. With a tumpline strapped around his brow, the weight of the bale would be carried on his back. If he didn't do it, she would wait until the cool of the evening and take care of it herself.

Purple pickerelweed waved to her where the river met the shore. She snapped seeds from the blooms and ate them as she passed, walking up the riverbank toward their two-story fieldstone house. Behind it was a smokehouse, long empty, and a wooden shed full of tools grown rusty with age. The trading post stood apart from the house by twenty yards or so, a one-story building with two rooms: a public room in front for trading, and a storeroom in the back. A wide creek flowed behind it. Bees hummed among goldenrod and black-eyed Susans, which added sunshine to the grey stones.

Stepping inside the post, which smelled of animal skins and pipe tobacco, Catherine found Thankful at a puncheon table at the back of the trading room, driving an awl into leather for a pair of moccasins. Bright Star sat across from her, sorting beads by color into glass jars. The two women were bent over their work, one head crowned with a plain white cap, the other uncovered, dark hair parted neatly down the middle of her scalp and plaited into braids that shone with bear grease.

Catherine's pleasure at seeing Bright Star turned to caution as she gauged the weather in the room, for Bright Star was one who brought it with her. Removing her hat, Catherine inhaled the smell of her sister's presence and the uncertainty that always came with it.

"What is it like in New York?" The question from Thankful stayed Catherine where she stood. As Bright Star talked about her trading trips, Thankful's hands slowed in her work. The young woman had never asked to return to the British colonies herself, content with stories of the land that had once been her home. Her blond hair, blue eyes, and fair skin hinted at Dutch ancestry, but none of her blood family was alive to ask.

Catherine approached them. "Time for another trip to Schenectady," she announced with a smile. "You were right, Bright Star. The coureurs des bois came to Lachine."

Bright Star's countenance clouded. "You are surprised?"

"Not at all." Catherine waved her sister's defensiveness away with forced nonchalance.

"You have pelts, then." Thankful's voice lilted as she pulled sinew through the soft leather, binding a tight seam. The young woman had seen sixteen summers, and she'd been sewing for at least half of them. Her long tapered fingers seemed made for needle and thread.

"A dozen bales of them. If the porters are ready soon, we have time to make one last trip for the season." It would take nearly a month to complete the journey.

Bright Star rose from the table. "I need some time to prepare. After three sleeps, I'll be ready and will return with help." She paused. "Gabriel was pleased, I assume."

"I'm sure he will be, yes." Catherine smoothed a wrinkle from her skirt, feeling like a child again beneath her sister's stony gaze.

"He was not with you," Bright Star said. "He left you alone to deal with four rough men."

"He didn't think they were com—"

"He didn't believe me." Bright Star spoke low. "He never believes me. No wonder you doubt me, too."

"I don't doubt you."

Bright Star held her tongue until the silence between them crackled with tension. At length, Bright Star broke it. "So what did he do instead, while you waited and then made the trade for him?"

Thankful bent over her work with greater concentration.

"I'm not his keeper, Bright Star. As you are not mine." Catherine had meant the statement to be a release, but as soon as the words slipped out, she could see she had chosen them poorly. Frustrated, she made an awkward attempt to close the matter. "Thank you for your help here today." She hung her hat on a peg on the wall.

Feeling Bright Star watching her, Catherine moved to the secretary that held the ledger book to record the day's transaction. As she flipped to the correct page, her thumb grazed over records of previous items traded to and from Mohawk, French, and British agents. When she spotted entries for scalps, she swallowed hard and thanked God that practice had grown rare. Enemies were more valuable alive now, except to the Mohawk warriors who prized the scalps and kept them as proof of their victories.

Movement caught her eye, and she looked up to peer out the window. Through leaded panes, she watched two blurry figures lash their canoe to a piling at the dock opposite her bateau full of fur. Her pulse quickened. They'd followed her from Lachine. They knew she was without a male chaperone and had come to steal the small fortune she'd left unguarded. Her father would—

They didn't even peek inside her bateau. Forms small in the distance, they marched from the riverbank toward the post, though it had already closed for the day. Slowly, Catherine exhaled.

"Soldiers?" Thankful guessed. "Do they know? Are they here to arrest you?" Though Thankful was now a grown woman, sometimes Catherine wondered if she was still prone to her childhood fear of being abandoned.

"More likely they need something we have, which puts us at an advantage," Catherine responded. "Any problem can be solved with fairness, neutrality to all parties, and the right transaction. True in trade, true in life. And true in war."

Bright Star's molasses eyes sparked. "They do not walk like men who have come to accuse." Her hand went to the hunting knife that hung around her neck, its beaded leather sheath a burst of color against the stroud tunic she wore layered over a deerskin skirt. "No one is getting arrested today."

Catherine adjusted her fichu. "We've nothing to hide. You don't need to stay," she told Bright Star. "You may go home if you'd rather."

Bright Star shook her head, and the shining silver hoops dangling from her ears bounced against her jaw. "Not yet. Your father hasn't returned from Montreal." She spoke as if Gabriel Duval were not her father, too. As if Bright Star had not been born of the same union between a French trapper and a Mohawk beauty.

The door banged open, and the two men clomped through it, bringing the sharp odor of sweat and damp wool with them. A warm gust of wind swirled in, a maple leaf scraping across the floor before they wedged the door shut again.

"Here to trade, *messieurs*?" Catherine's tone was even as she appraised them. The younger man was clearly Canadian militia, wearing his own clothes from the toque slouched on his head to his moccasins. The elder, a professional soldier, wore a grey-white *justaucorps* with blue turnback cuffs adorned with six buttons each. Beneath that, his jacket was blue and his breeches grey-white. White stockings and the silver buckles on his shoes caught what little light there was in the post. In both men, their eyes looked too large for their faces.

They were hungry. So was she. So was nearly everyone in the whole of New France.

The elder soldier removed his black tricorne hat trimmed with gold braid, revealing black hair fading to grey and queued in the back. "Bonjour. Do you live in that house?" He pointed to the home she shared with Thankful and Gabriel.

Her eyes narrowed as she observed the bedrolls and packs on the soldiers' backs. "If you have something to trade, let us do business. Otherwise I suggest you take your leave before night falls." She crossed her arms. An unladylike gesture, to be sure, but she'd rather be seen as the proprietor than a lady just now.

"You misunderstand," the officer replied. His lips were thin beyond detection, his mouth a moving slit in his face as he spoke. "I'm Captain

Pierre Moreau, Régiment Royal-Roussillon, and this is Private Gaspard Fontaine, militia. And you are?"

"Marie-Catherine Duval. This is Bright Star."

Private Fontaine removed his hat and brushed a hand over his rusty hair. Younger than Moreau by at least twenty years, his upturned nose lent an even more childish air. "And the blond beauty?" His straight, small teeth could not quite be called white. "What's the matter, too shy?"

"I'm Thankful Winslet." Crossing her ankles, she offered a polite nod. "Pleased to meet you."

Moreau's eyebrow flicked. "Thankful. That's a Puritan name, isn't it? British. Do you know what the penalty is for harboring the enemy?"

Speaking in flawless French, Thankful's voice remained steady as she pulled her needle through the soft leather. "I am no enemy, Captain. My family was taken from our New Hampshire home by Abenaki Indians when I was seven years old. My parents did not survive the march."

Moreau frowned. "The Abenaki are French allies, as are the Mohawk. So you have more reason to resent us than most, *n'est-ce pas?*"

"I was ransomed."

"I don't understand." Impatience strained the officer's voice.

Catherine lifted a rumpled bolt of British stroud from a shelf and unwound a few yards of fabric before smoothing it. "The government in

New France has inspired many raids on British colonies. The Indians capture any number of British civilians to bring back north with them. Many times, they will keep women and children to adopt into their own families, usually to replace loved ones they recently lost to battle or disease."

She paused, rewrapping the fabric around the bolt and tucking it back onto the shelf. With a tug, she pulled another bolt free and repeated the process. "But some captives are sold to Frenchmen or -women. This is what we call 'ransom.' Once a captive is ransomed, he or she stays and works in that location like an indentured servant for several years, until the money spent on the ransom is considered paid off by labor. At the end of that time, the ransomed captive is usually free to leave New France." With a shove, she wedged the bolt back onto the shelf.

Moreau looked down his hawklike nose at Thankful. "You've been here for more than six years. Why are you still here, when you could go?"

"There is nothing for me in the British colonies now," the young woman answered.

Fontaine hooked his thumbs through the straps on his shoulders. "But—were you not christened with a Catholic name once you were baptized into the Catholic faith?"

Catherine bit the inside of her cheek. The truth

was that the girl remained Protestant, though that was illegal in New France, and Thankful's conscience did not allow her to lie.

"We have many names," Bright Star said, likely surprising the Frenchmen with her mastery of their language. All three women spoke English just as well, but there was no need to divulge that right now. "I was named Thérèse when I was baptized by the Jesuits, but I prefer the name my mother gave me on the night of my birth: Bright Star."

"What does it matter what we are called, when God alone can judge the heart?" Catherine asked. "So she wishes to be called Thankful, the name her parents gave her. It is all she has left of them. It is a good name. Show me the man who would deny her that, and I will show you one who grasps for what is not his to take."

The quiet that followed her speech stretched into a long, airless moment. Fontaine's mouth pulled to one side, and Moreau thrust his chin forward, but neither proved willing to speak his mind.

Finally, Thankful cleared her throat, a smile on her lips. "Call me Mademoiselle Winslet, if it please you. That is, should you have need to call me at all, which I don't suppose you will."

Captain Moreau's chest lifted as he pushed his shoulders back. "That all depends on who lives in that house." He fished a limp document from his waistcoat and marched to the counter, where he dropped it on one side of a scale. "We're here under orders. We are to be billeted here."

Glancing at Thankful, Catherine moved to the counter and parsed the script on the paper. "Why here?" she asked. "If it's Montreal you wish to defend, you'd be better off crossing the river again to stay within its walls." It was a city of women, children, and old men now, for every able-bodied man had been called away to defend Quebec.

Moreau drummed his fingers on the counter, a signet ring catching the light. "Our objective is not to defend the city."

"The river, then," Catherine guessed, though the rapids between here and Montreal's main port were too dangerous for most British vessels to attempt. "The St. Lawrence is already guarded by the garrison at Fort St. Louis, not two miles from here, adjacent to Kahnawake. Surely those barracks would better suit you."

"Already full," the private replied, his attention drifting to the muskets and powder horns hanging on the wall behind the counter. He carried no weapon of his own. Militiamen never did. They were handed what they needed just before an expedition and gave it back right after.

Captain Moreau cleared his throat. "There are three hundred of us recently detached from our units to come here, and the fort is overcrowded as it is. We're here to oversee the wheat harvest on the farms of the Montreal Plain. It is said it will amount to more than one and a half million *minots* of wheat." That was almost two and a half million bushels.

"And who is to harvest the wheat?" Bright Star asked. "All the Canadian farmers are serving in the militia and are miles away from their crops." The only people who had no trouble bringing in their harvests were the Indian villagers, where the women tended the crops.

"You see the problem." Fontaine scratched the side of his nose. "Quebec has farmers but no food. Montreal has food but no farmers. So we must—*you* must—harvest the wheat yourselves. All women, children, and elderly. We are here to supervise the harvest in the neighboring farms. And we are to be billeted at that house for as long as it takes to send the wheat up to Quebec."

Catherine tilted her head, considering this. "What about the wheat brought from France this spring by the purveyor general? We heard Monsieur Cadet brought fifteen transports full for the army." It had been an astonishing feat, bringing them across an ocean dominated by the British Royal Navy. More so, since Joseph-Michel Cadet was a butcher from Quebec who had risen to the challenge of provisioning New France's colonial government.

"Those transports carried enough for twenty

thousand rations for two months. But there are thirty thousand soldiers, sailors, warriors, and civilians to feed." Moreau's voice was low and matter-of-fact. "Monsieur Cadet's provisions barely lasted until the end of July. Your soldiers are starving, mademoiselles. Civilians, too. This harvest has always been part of Cadet's plan. The situation is critical, but you can help. In fact, we must insist. Resisting would be breaking the law."

Bright Star looked to Catherine, but it was Thankful who laid her moccasin aside and stood. "If it is help you need, you shall have it. You don't need to threaten us."

Moreau plucked the weightless orders from the scale and returned the paper to his waistcoat. "A wise response, mademoiselle. Now, you will take us to the house at once."

Defiance rose up in Catherine. She was as willing to help feed the hungry as Thankful, and yet she chafed at the demand for her house. "The house is otherwise occupied. Pitch tents if you must, but you will not evict us from our home."

Fontaine shrugged his arms out of their straps and set his pack on the floor. Reaching into an outer pocket, he pulled a plug of tobacco from a paper bag and tucked it into his cheek. Sitting on a barrel of rum, he stretched out one leg and crossed his arms. "We may do whatever we say. How many live there now?"

"Three."

Moreau laughed. "Bah! And here I thought you would tell me a family of ten slept within those walls. That's plenty of room for everyone. We've suffered tighter quarters than that, by far. I won't sleep outside when it rains every other day here. We'll learn how to get along. Consider it proof of your patriotism, ma chère."

Two strange men living with two women and a sixty-year-old, one-armed man? Catherine balked. Patriotism had nothing to do with it.

Bright Star pursed her lips and gave a tiny shake of her head. In Mohawk, she said, "I do not trust them."

"You don't trust anyone," Catherine hissed, irritation edging her tone. "I can handle this."

"Of course you can," Bright Star lashed back. "You manage everything so well on your own."

"You make it sound like a weakness to take care of one's own affairs," Catherine murmured.

"Weakness is dismissing good counsel because you're so convinced of your own strength."

"*Totek!*" Raising her palm, Catherine halted the conversation. This was not the time to air lingering grievances.

"If you are quite finished . . ." Moreau cleared his throat. "You really have no choice in the matter of our lodging." He leaned on a display table, and it wobbled on its uneven legs, sending tallow tapers rolling to the floor. "We need a place to billet."

Catherine scooped the fallen candles and stacked them like cordwood on a silver platter. "And I have one for you. Not our home, but another. It is smaller, but if you're used to cramped quarters, you'll do fine. You'll be out of the rain, comfortable and dry, and you'll have the place all to yourselves. Better for all of us, no? Collect yourselves, messieurs, and follow me."

Thankful caught Catherine's eye as Fontaine hoisted his pack onto his back once more. "Not your house, surely?"

"It was never my house." She led the men outside.

Catherine escorted the soldiers through a thicket of oaks, maples, and pines. When they emerged, a small wooden house came into view.

Fontaine spit into the grass. "It's a cabin."

"It will do." Moreau asked her to show them in.

How she had loved coming here the first few times. Visiting had been like trading secrets. *"You won't be empty for long,"* she had whispered into the barren rooms, filling them with expectation. In her imagination, she had fancied she heard the house whisper back, *"Oh, the joy you will find here, if you can only endure the wait."*

Lies, both of them. But by now she'd grown used to the truth.

Two rockers swayed on the porch as she opened the front door and bade the soldiers enter. A breeze lifted the edges of the curtains inside before they hung limply once more at the windows. She had sewn them herself, and Thankful had embroidered flowering vines along the edges.

Fontaine's footsteps echoed as he trudged from one room to the next and up the stairs before coming back again. "You'll be wanting the bed, then," he muttered to his superior.

Moreau eased his pack from his shoulders and lowered it into a corner. "Naturally. You have a bedroll, Fontaine, and a roof over your head. You've nothing to complain about." He turned to Catherine and gave a small bow, then straightened. "This will serve, mademoiselle. Thank you."

"Then I'll take my leave. Good evening, messieurs."

"What's this?"

Catherine turned to find Fontaine pulling something white from between the windowsill and the wall. An envelope.

" 'Catie,' " Fontaine read. "Is that you? You have mail. From the wall." He chortled but held it out to her all the same.

She crossed the room to retrieve it, then bobbed in a curtsy and walked away, vaguely registering that Moreau was issuing instructions about beginning the harvest in the morning.

Closing the door on his voice, she tucked the envelope into her pocket. She'd seen the handwriting and recognized it. No good could come of reading the letter inside, this she knew. The sentiments it contained belonged to a different time, long buried. She had no business resurrecting them.

Catherine marched away, memories of the cabin and the promises it represented trailing her like cobwebs. Stepping over a gnarled root, she steadied herself on a sugar maple trunk scarred from last winter's tapping. Light lanced through the leaves in spears until she broke free from the woods.

Bright Star, a bale of fur on her back, ducked into the trading post. She came out a few moments later, tumpline in hand.

Catherine intercepted her on the way to the dock. "I'll take over from here."

"In that?" Bright Star scoffed with a derision that seemed to go deeper than Catherine's tight bodice and burdensome skirts, down to the person she'd become to fit them. Catherine suspected that her sister would not spend time in her company at all were it not for the trading work that tied them together. "There are only three left. I will do this and then go. I'll return with the porters for the journey when they're ready."

Catherine nodded, and the sisters' paths diverged.

Her house loomed large as Catherine strode toward it. Made of oyster-grey fieldstone, with two chimneys thrusting from the roof, it was more reminiscent of Gabriel Duval's privileged roots than of the youthful rebellion and wanderlust that compelled him to forsake propriety for the adventure of trapping and trading.

Once inside, Catherine stepped out of her moccasins and climbed the stairs. The door to her chamber made no sound as she closed it.

A tread on the stair signaled Thankful's approach. "Catherine? Are you all right?"

"Yes," she replied. The envelope weighed nothing, and yet it was a burden to be rid of. She drew it from her pocket and tossed it onto the mahogany bureau.

"If you're certain . . ." Thankful said, still outside the door.

Catherine wiped her palms on the apron over her skirt. "Quite, thank you. I'll be down for supper in just a bit." A breeze billowed the mosquito netting draping her canopied bed.

Retreating footsteps, then silence. Her hands did not tremble as she picked up the envelope and beheld the firm hand that had spelled her name. *Catie.*

Only one person had ever called her that.

CHAPTER TWO

October 1748
Eleven Years Ago

"That's it! That's my house!" Heedless of rocking the canoe, Catherine pointed to the dock stretching out into the river, beckoning her to come home. Autumn had touched the trees with fire, and the sight of it set her joy ablaze. Had it only been two years since she had seen this place? It felt like five. Or ten.

Behind her, Monsieur Bonneville grunted as he pulled on the paddle. "Congratulations. And do you suppose your papa will be pleased to see you? To hear that you have been expelled from Madame's school?"

Without turning to face him, she could see his small, close-set eyes and the one long black eyebrow above them, which the students called his pet caterpillar. A chill tickled her skin, but only briefly. It was time for her to be home. King George's War was over now, and there was no more danger of border raids between native allies of the French and English. Papa would be surprised to see her, but he would recover.

She'd been gone so long, and he hadn't written to her or visited, not even to mark her thirteenth year. Or her fourteenth. Was it possible that he had even missed news of the peace treaty, secluded as he was in the woods? She had clamored for every scrap of information to be had inside Montreal's walls. In any case, surely by now he'd had time to miss her.

"My Catherine," he would say when he saw her. *"Daughter. How you've grown. Enough learning to be a proper lady. The war is over, the danger is past. I need you home with me."*

Catherine grinned with anticipation. She didn't even care that river water soaked her silly slippered feet and her gown. Aside from the shoes, she could tolerate the clothing now, petticoats and corset and all. How changed she was, at least on the outside.

Madame Bonneville's School for Young Ladies had made certain of that straightaway. Catherine could still feel the stinging humiliation of being stripped naked by Madame Bonneville and her spinster sister on her first day at the school. They weighed her, measured her, took note of her in ways that made her burn with shame. Then came the scalding hot bath, the scrubbing with sand and soap. It was as if they meant to take her golden skin away so that it could grow back pale and fair. With her own hair piled high and powdered white, Madame cut off Catherine's

45

braid and flung it to the floor as though it were a snake. *"Only savages grow their hair to their knees."*

Catherine knew exactly what they were doing. Hadn't she seen the same thing done before at Kahnawake, when a white person was adopted into the clan? The terrified white girl had been stripped of her British gown and underpinnings, then scrubbed in the river to wash all the white away. When she emerged, it was as a Mohawk. She was dressed in deerskin and adopted as one of the People.

Catherine looked down at the silk gown she wore. She'd been scrubbed that day two years ago and countless days since. She had watched her deerskin and stroud burn. She was layered with French undergarments, and her hair had been pinned, not braided. But she had not become one of them.

The canoe slowed its glide, and she looked up, heartened to be so near home. Kneeling in the bottom of the vessel, she reached out and grabbed a piling, pulling the canoe close before leaping out onto the dock. The sodden slippers she let fall from her feet and into the water, where they floated like pale green leaves before sinking beneath the surface. She was home at last. She was free.

Catherine took off running toward the riverbank, leaving Monsieur Bonneville in her wake.

The land greeted her with the moldering smell of autumn. Before she even had the chance to shout Papa's name, there he was.

He was so still as she ran to greet him. His face held no recognition.

Leaves shook on their branches all around her, waving their colors like banners. Her lips curved in what she hoped was a winsome smile, waiting with trapped breath for the moment he would see her for who she was. She was his, and his alone. He was her papa.

He frowned.

She faltered. "You are surprised," she said at last, excusing his disappointing reaction.

His fist clenched as he took her in from hatless head to the toes peeking from under her hem. "You aren't wearing shoes."

Curling her toes, Catherine bit her lip, her pulse skipping beats. She wanted love, she wanted joy. She needed to belong to someone again. Bewildered, she said, "It is me, Papa. Catherine Stands-Apart."

His hand came across her mouth so fast, she heard the strike before she tasted blood. Her mistake: speaking her Mohawk name.

"What is the meaning of this?" He projected his shout beyond her, and she realized Bonneville was finally near.

"Monsieur." Bonneville dropped a bag of Catherine's clothing on the ground. "Your daughter has run away from the school three times now. Once, we pulled her from the port before she attempted to swim. This last time, we chased her on horseback all the way to Lachine and caught her just as she was about to steal a canoe."

"I was going to return it later!" she protested.

Monsieur Bonneville ignored her. "As you are aware, the third time results in permanent expulsion, without refund of fees already paid. I am here to deliver your daughter back into your keeping."

"You what?" A hint of rum rode Papa's breath. So that was why he had struck her. It was the drink that did it, not him.

Catherine licked the corner of her swelling lip. "If you knew what it was like, you would have come for me yourself. Besides, the war is over! They signed a treaty for peace. New France and New England won't be raiding anymore!"

Papa jabbed a finger at Bonneville. "We had an understanding. We signed papers. You were to train the Mohawk out of her until she was as civilized as any of your pureblood French girls. Did you forget the sum that would have been your reward? As you have utterly failed, you will take her back and keep her until you succeed."

Catherine stared at him in disbelief. It was the war that had compelled Papa to send her away, nothing more. He had sent her inside the walled city of Montreal to keep her safe. And now the war had ended. There was no more reason to stay in that place, where she felt crammed into a shape that did not fit.

"Oh no." Bonneville waggled his eyebrow. "Catherine has caused more than enough trouble to prove it cannot be done. We are casting our pearls before swine, monsieur, when we attempt to refine a half-breed. Not only has she thrice run away and been caught, but her health is not up to standard, either. She sank very low this past winter with tuberculosis, costing us more for her medical care than anticipated. We are through with this project. Good day to you." Without a glance at Catherine, he retreated back toward the dock.

Stunned, Catherine grasped her father's hand. She'd heard wrong. He would explain it when he was calm. Sober. "Papa," she whispered, "I can help at home . . . at the trading post . . ."

He yanked his hand from hers. "Then do so." He turned from her and walked away.

The wilted lace at her elbows moved in the wind, but she did not feel it brush her skin. She felt nothing. She was so full to the brim with emptiness, she feared she would choke.

Papa disappeared with a bottle, and Catherine wondered if she had driven him to drink. She would just have to make her presence worth--while for him, because there was no question of leaving again. There was nowhere else she belonged.

She rubbed a linseed oil–soaked rag over the tea table in the parlor, drawing satisfaction from the polished result. Whatever Papa said, he did need help here. The house was filthy. And how had he been eating when she was not here to prepare the food?

"I saw him hit you." English words.

Dropping her rag, she turned to find a young man in the doorway. Thin as a bean, with large brown eyes and sunny blond hair tailed at his neck. Cheekbones pushed beneath his skin. He looked older than her, but not by much. He had fifteen summers, if she didn't miss her guess.

Pointing to her lip, he approached her. His movements were graceless as he scooped up her rag, wadding it in his fist and transferring it back and forth between his hands. His palms grew greasy with oil and dust, but he didn't seem to mind. The earnestness in his expression reached out to her.

Catherine wiped the back of her hand across her mouth. Papa would be repentant tomorrow. "It's nothing." The English language was the one useful thing she had studied in Montreal.

"He shouldn't have done that." He extended

the rag, and she sensed he was offering more than just her dusting cloth.

She took it. "Who are you?"

Curling up on just one side, his smile was tentative but warm. "I'm Samuel Crane. I didn't mean to startle you, and I didn't mean to spy. Duval can be difficult to ignore. We so seldom get visitors here, even to trade, and when I saw you—" A lump shifted in his throat. "He shouldn't have done that," he said again.

Heat pricked her cheeks and neck. "But why are you here?"

"Same as you, I guess." A shrug lifted his shoulders. His toe scuffed at the fringe of the Persian rug on which he stood.

"You're British," she guessed.

He nodded. So this was what the enemy looked like. But no, now they were at peace once more.

"How came you to be here?" she tried again.

"It's a common tale." But his resistance to share it proved fleeting, and he told her that Kahnawake Mohawk had raided his family's Massachusetts home during the war, along with several of his neighbors'. "The war that just ended with a treaty that returned all conquered land to its original owners," he added. "The war that accomplished nothing for either France or England." The bitterness in his tone was undeniable. The raids she'd been cosseted away from had turned Samuel's life inside out.

"Go on." Suddenly exhausted, she sat on the needlework-cushioned chair, wiped the rag over the Vincennes porcelain tea set in the middle of the table, and invited him to sit next to her.

He folded his long limbs beneath the scalloped table and ran a hand over his hair. Sawdust came away on his fingers. He picked up a cup and cradled it in his hands, his attention fixed upon it as he told the rest of his story in luke-warm tones. She suspected agony rode beneath the surface.

His parents had been killed in the raid. Samuel was captured and marched to Montreal. His brother, Joel, older by four years, had been at a neighbor's home during the raid. The captives had been split into small groups for the march north, and Samuel never saw Joel, had no idea where he was now, if he had even survived.

If Joel had been seen by the Mohawk raiders, Catherine suspected he had been killed on sight. Men usually were. The fact that they had kept Samuel alive meant they saw something in him that made him valuable. Sometimes all it took was personal bravery.

"I was almost adopted into the Kahnawake people, but Monsieur Duval ransomed me before that could happen. He learned I was a carpenter's apprentice and found it worth his while to put my skills to use here. I cook some, too, and do whatever he bids. It's been two years. Six more to go before he will set me free."

So that was how Papa had survived her absence. He'd replaced her with a boy who could do much more than she. Doubt screwed tight inside her chest. Papa's need for her wasn't what she thought. Yet she could hardly blame Samuel Crane for that. And after all, she was still Gabriel Duval's daughter. Nothing would change that.

The thoughts loosed her compassion for Samuel. "I'm so sorry," she told him. "You must miss home terribly." That, she understood.

He rattled the teacup back onto its saucer and glanced at the case clock ticking in the corner of the room. "No more than you, I suppose."

Utterly confused, Catherine searched his eyes. Had Papa already told him that Kahnawake was her home for the first ten years of her life? Or perhaps she'd misheard him, and he'd merely said that she had missed the home she'd now come back to. "What do you mean?"

Samuel kneaded his hands together. "I thought—I thought Duval ransomed you, too. You speak English, you're cleaning his house—"

"No, no, I am his daughter."

A hint of laughter lit his face.

The hair on the back of her neck stood up. "Did he never mention me?"

Samuel's eyebrows shot high. "Duval never

53

mentioned having a child at all. I assumed he was an old bachelor. Are you really—"

"Yes, I am his." Hurt and shame sharpened her tongue.

"I didn't know." Samuel dropped his gaze. "I saw him hit you. Fathers don't hit their daughters."

Catherine pushed back from the table, and Samuel rose just as quickly.

"I would be your friend, just the same," he said, pleading. "I meant no offense. Please don't go. Can't we be friends, you and I? Or are you not staying?"

"I am staying."

"Good." His shoulders relaxed. "What is your name?"

She could not believe that in two years' time, Papa had never said it. Sighing, she told Samuel her name was Marie-Catherine Stands-Apart, daughter of Agnesse Strong Wind as much as of Gabriel Duval. She was born of the People who had raided his family's home. He took this in with interest but laid no blame upon her for what the Kahnawake raiders had done. It was a credit to his character.

He laid his hands on the back of her chair. "Tell me more."

Though the gesture surprised her, she allowed him to seat her and watched as he built a fire in the parlor's hearth. As the flames snapped and popped, the chill fled the room, and Catherine explained to Samuel Crane who she was beyond her names, desperate to be known. In the telling of her tale, perhaps he would come to understand who Gabriel Duval was, too. He had been a loving papa, once. A father who didn't hit his daughter. He would gentle toward her again.

When she was born, she told Samuel, Papa had called her Marie-Catherine, and her mother named her Stands-Apart, even though Catherine found herself mostly standing in the middle, keeping the peace between parents who often argued. Until she couldn't.

As Samuel tossed a pine knot into the fire, Catherine marveled that she was sharing so much with someone she'd just met. But after two years of being shamed for who she was, voicing her past felt like gulping spring water while half dead of thirst.

"One year, Papa returned from a trapping trip with one hand gone from an accident with a steel trap. It didn't heal right, so more of his arm had to be taken by a surgeon's knife. He didn't go trapping or hunting after that, but he didn't feel welcome in my mother's house, either." Pausing, she looked up to read Samuel's face. "Do I bore you?"

"Not a bit." He urged her to continue. His attention quenched something inside her that had shriveled during her years at school.

55

Catherine's petticoats and skirt clung to her ankles, still wet and cold from the river. Burying her toes into the rug, she looked through the window at a willow tree. The wind moaned through it, stripping bright leaves from its branches. "I was ten when my parents divorced. I didn't understand why or what it meant. All I knew was that Papa was being sent out of the village alone and that he couldn't even hunt his own food. My mother died before a full year passed, so I decided to go live with him rather than move with my siblings into the longhouse of my aunts. He needed me."

The case clock chimed, but Catherine barely heard it. "It's less than two miles from here to the Mohawk village of Kahnawake, so I often went alone to visit my siblings. My little brother was always happy to greet me, but my sister only showed me her back."

Samuel rubbed a smudge of dirt from his thumb. "Why?"

"She thought I should have stayed. She said I could not have both Papa and her, too, and that I'd made my choice." Catherine ended her tale by explaining where she'd been these last two years and why. "Now I'm home at last. For good."

Samuel's unaffected manner put her at ease. "I'm glad of it. It's been lonesome here. Do you know, this is the longest conversation I've had in two years?"

She answered his cautious smile with her own. "I should finish cleaning now." She made to stand, and he came immediately to pull out her chair for her. "Such a gentleman, monsieur," Catherine teased.

"Oui, oui, mademoiselle," he countered with a grin, and pretended to doff a hat. "Welcome home, Catie. I'm glad you're here."

"Catie?" she repeated.

"Do you mind if I call you that? It suits."

She didn't mind at all.

CHAPTER THREE

August 1759

The letter Fontaine had found in the house had to be five years old. Years ago, the words might have had consequence, might have changed the course her heart and life would take.

But that time was past. Her course was set, and it would not double back on itself. Catherine could read the letter out of sheer curiosity now, immune to any emotional pull it might have had before. It was an artifact from a bygone era, nothing more. Besides, it might put to rest the question that had once dogged her: Why had he not returned?

Catherine unfolded the letter and noted the date. It was the last time she'd seen Samuel.

My beloved Catie,

I have just seen you safely back to your house after telling you good-bye, but I can't bring myself to let you go just yet. You could have begged me to stay, but you didn't, and the trust you place in me, the patience you've already displayed, endears you to me even more.

Catherine looked up, anger simmering in her veins. Any trust she'd put in this man had been woefully misplaced.

Believe me when I tell you that if it were up to me, we'd be together right now. But honoring your father's wishes was the right thing to do. Just as the cause of our current separation is worthwhile, too. We both know it, and yet I must remind myself of the truth over and over so I don't lose heart and abandon my plans altogether.

Ironic, Catherine mused. Apparently he had lost heart, or at least his heart for her, and abandoned *their* plans together. She clenched her teeth, then told herself to relax, for none of this was new information.

It won't be long now before we are together again. Please know that though leaving for now is the right thing to do, being apart from you pains me more than I can say. When you see the moon, think of me, for I will be thinking of you. Though worlds apart, it seems, the same moon shines down on both of us, and that thought brings me comfort.

I am bungling this letter. I've half a mind to toss it into the river, for I realize I am no poet. Instead, I'll hide it away in our house, the home we will share when I return, and you'll find it only if you're meant to.

Catherine skimmed the rest of the page for the answer to her question. Did Samuel know then that he would abandon her? She found nothing to indicate he did.

Samuel had left after their engagement in order to find his brother, Joel. It was something he needed to do before he could marry her and settle permanently in Canada, and she had agreed.

When he didn't return, and when no letter came month following month, nightmares had haunted her. Sometimes she saw Samuel struck by an arrow, sometimes injured by a steel trap in the woods. In her dreams, she watched him drown in the river. She watched him bleed to death from hatchet, musket, bayonet. Saw him scalped. The means varied, but the end was the same. He was dead. It was the only explanation her mind could conjure. It was Thankful who had shaken her from those dreams, cried with her, prayed for Samuel's safety.

Until one day Bright Star had gone to Schenectady and learned through the merchant there that Samuel Crane was alive and well.

That was when Catherine had ceased praying for him.

She crumpled the letter and tossed it into the fireplace. Twice now, she'd taken sides for a man. Twice, her heart had broken apart for it. She would not suffer the same mistake again.

The soreness easing in her chest, Catherine unpinned her braid from the coil that wrapped her head. It dropped almost to her knees, as long as Strong Wind's had been. Ever since her escape from the Montreal school, Catherine had refused to cut her hair—to honor the mother whom she missed so dearly.

She knew what Strong Wind would say now. A man like Samuel, one did not need. A man like that, a woman was better off without.

Snoring from Gabriel's bedchamber the next morning announced his safe return. After scratching a note explaining the arrival of Fontaine and Moreau and the orders that called her away, Catherine slipped it beneath his door and joined Thankful outside. A one-armed man would not be required to harvest, surely. It was well that he slept, for he tired easily lately.

Her moccasins grew dark with dew as she and Thankful walked. They wore their simplest cotton gowns and their oldest aprons, along with wide-brimmed straw hats.

Pierre Moreau met them, smelling of the camp coffee he must have brewed for himself that morning. Fontaine trailed three paces behind him, reeking of too much rum. The younger man squinted toward Catherine, though the sun remained low in the sky.

"Ready for work, I see." Though slightly wrinkled, Captain Moreau's uniform was spotless. "Where is the other woman? Bright Star?"

Catherine tied her hat's ribbon more snugly beneath her chin. "She won't be joining us. She has her own cornfields to tend."

"I thought those savages were supposed to be our allies." Fontaine winced, as though his words were too loud for his ears.

"And so they are." Catherine hooked her arm through Thankful's elbow and walked down the slope toward the dock. The river lapped gently against its bank, reflecting a pale blue sky. "Many of their warriors have fallen in service to New France, including Bright Star's husband." She made no mention of the children her sister had lost to the spotting sickness, though the disease could be blamed upon the French, as well. "I daresay they will not risk losing their own harvest to feed your soldiers, too."

Moreau waved a hand, dispelling the conversation. "We are already late. Come." He climbed into the canoe first, then helped Thankful and Catherine into it before Fontaine untied the rope holding it to the pilings. The vessel rocked as the private settled into it.

As Catherine and Moreau began paddling, the captain cast a glance downstream. "The current is strong here. Is that because of the Lachine Rapids? How close are we to them?"

"Not close enough to be concerned," Catherine replied. "They begin a few miles east of here. You must have portaged them, didn't you, when you came from the north for this assignment?"

Captain Moreau's uniform jacket pulled at the shoulders as he dipped the paddle. "We came into the city of Montreal first. A tavern owner advised us to cross the island by foot and then cross the river well upstream of the rapids, so we did. Cutting across the land, we were never close enough to the shore to see the rapids."

Catherine nodded but made no effort to continue the conversation.

Once they'd paddled the mile-wide expanse to the Island of Montreal, it did not take long to find a farm in need of workers. The island was mostly farmland, aside from the walled city of Montreal hemming in more than five thousand souls. The population they had lost to the militia was more than compensated for by refugees from Quebec. The city could barely hold them all.

Just as Moreau and Fontaine had said, women and children from the city had gathered amid the chest-high wheat, some in sturdy cotton dresses, and some looking wholly out of place in bright silks with voluminous lace at the elbows. Some of the children were so young that they could not be seen above the stalks. Peppered among them to supervise were three other officers in blue and white uniforms and a dozen militiamen.

"Women!" Moreau shouted, and the feminine voices quieted. "The situation in Quebec is desperate, or else we would not call you to the fields. Your husbands, brothers, sons, and fathers will starve if we do not supply them with food."

A knot of women tightened and whispered loudly enough for Catherine to hear. "Do you believe it is as bad as all that in the capital?" asked one.

Two straw hats dipped in solemn acknowledgment. "And not just for the soldiers and militia, heaven bless them."

Catherine edged closer to hear the haggard-looking woman say more.

"We lived there until we finally had to flee south," she continued. "With the failed harvests of the last two years and the British blockade cutting off supplies from anywhere else, we were fairly devoured with hunger last winter. Workers and artisans were so weak they could barely stand up, let alone work. Squadrons of soldiers went into the countryside to gain what food they could at the point of their guns."

A chill cycled down Catherine's spine despite the damp heat. When Captain Moreau held up his hands to still the murmuring, she returned her attention to him.

"At present, Quebec has provisions for two weeks more, and those rations are less than half what a healthy man would normally consume," he said. "Work not because of my orders. Work so that they may live. Decrease your own consumption, too, that we may send what you spare to the soldiers."

At this, Thankful bowed her head, peeking beneath her brim at Catherine. They had already been rationing their food. For the last three winters, wheat had been so scarce that bakers had mixed in horse feed and dried peas to make it last longer. City officials distributed it only on certain afternoons, and only to those who had special tickets. The bread queues fairly writhed, so desperate were those in line to get their shares.

Moreau wasn't finished with his speech. "If we fail, Quebec falls. This field is a battlefront as much as any. Prove yourselves worthy for a short time, and you'll share the victory."

Catherine bit back the reply that sprang to mind. If Quebec fell, the war would soon be over, and that would be an end to four long years of fighting, starving, killing, scalping, and dying. New France would belong to Britain, and the British government would send food into Canada to feed its subjects. Would this be a worse fate than prolonging the war for another harsh winter or even longer?

Most would call her disloyal for such thoughts, so she kept them to herself. But she could not imagine the British colonies as full of devils when she'd done business with them for a decade, and when a British-born girl such as Thankful lived and worked by her side. Even so, she did not wish harm to come to her countrymen, so she would harvest along with the rest.

She scanned the faces of the other women to measure the effect Moreau's speech had on those assembled. Stirred by patriotism or not, they submitted to the organizing that followed as Moreau and the other officers divided them into groups, farmers' wives distributed among them.

"See how Fontaine sips from his flask already," Thankful whispered. "No good can come of that. I don't trust him."

Neither did Catherine. She'd seen what traders' rum did to many Mohawk men of Kahnawake. They turned violent to get it, and more violent still once it filled their bellies. It was the reason Catherine used only female porters to carry goods between here and New York. The women didn't drink. She wouldn't even carry rum in her post if it weren't for Gabriel's insistence. *"It's good for business,"* he justified. *"Take away the rum, and business dries up just as fast."* But she knew he favored it as much as the Mohawks. When he drank, she and Thankful steered clear, for it rendered her father unpredictable at best.

"Captain," Catherine called to Moreau when he was close enough to hear, "Private Fontaine does not seem quite fit for duty today, does he? He looks to me like a wolf with full access to a herd of sheep."

The captain's gaze swung to Fontaine. "He's not himself lately. I trust you will keep this in confidence, but he lost his brother not two weeks ago in Quebec. They say it was illness, but I suspect that if he had only had enough food . . ." Moreau spread his hands in a helpless gesture.

Thankful covered her mouth, then clasped her hands at her waist. "How horrible. His assignment here can't be easy for him."

"I thought he would be even more motivated than most to see our objective through." The captain's eyelids drooped as he made a scuffing noise with his teeth.

Half turned to the field as he kept himself apart, Fontaine's knuckles were white on the flask as he nursed his drink. Catherine didn't condone it, but at least she understood where it came from. Her own father searched for solace deep in his cups, as well, and always found remorse at the bottom.

"It is not malice or mal intent you observe, but grief," Moreau went on. "Still, now is the time, more than ever before, for him to fall back on his discipline and training. If I must send him back across the river this morning, I will."

After a brief but volatile conversation Catherine couldn't help but overhear, that was exactly what Moreau did. She was not without sympathy for Fontaine, but having him gone eased her spirit so she could better concentrate on the work.

Once the women learned the rudiments of cutting grain, they fell into a rhythm. Across the field, those who could spare the breath sang old songs to which the coureurs des bois and *voyageurs* paddled.

À la claire fontaine m'en allant promener
J'ai trouvé l'eau si belle que je m'y suis
    baignée
Il y a longtemps que je t'aime, jamais je
    ne t'oublierai.

The voices filtered through the wheat like a far-off dream: *I've loved you for so long that I'll never forget you.* It was a melancholy ballad of love and loss. Catherine did not join in, though she knew each word of that and every other folk song. Gabriel had been a coureur des bois himself and had filled her childhood with his songs.

As a young man, Gabriel had been training to be a barrister in Montreal and had recently married a Frenchwoman named Isabelle when the feeling of suffocation grew too much for him. His wife of less than two years waited at home while he broke away from all expectations and responsibility. He paddled along rivers and creeks with corded arms that grew sun-bronzed and strong as timber, trapping without the sanction the French government had given to the voyageurs officially tasked with the fur trade.

When Gabriel returned from one of his months-long absences, he'd found Isabelle laboring to bring their first baby, a girl, into the world. She named the baby Marie-Catherine. Isabelle's dying wish to Gabriel was that he promise to raise the girl properly—in silks and lace, with finishing school and balls. He promised, but the baby died soon after her mother.

Of course, Catherine had no idea of any of this as a child. Only when she found an old sketchbook of Gabriel's filled with images not of Strong Wind, but of a young bride with upswept curls, did she pull the truth from him bit by bit when rum had loosened his tongue. Only then did she see the twisted root of her name. Her father had named her for the pureblood French daughter once lost to him. In the Mohawk culture, such a practice was normal. The replacement for the lost family member was often named for the deceased loved one. In essence, the replacement became the original.

Once Catherine understood this, she knew why Gabriel had worked so hard to train and punish the "savage" out of her. But before her parents' divorce, all she knew of her father was that he brought music and laughter with him every time he returned from a trapping or hunting trip, and that she felt her family was complete when he was near. She'd been his favorite child, or so she fancied. Bright Star always favored their mother, and Joseph, born while Gabriel was away, never did bond with his father.

Catherine swung the scythe across the grain to the rhythm of the folk songs. Chaff hung in the air and dusted her throat, but she smiled at the memories of an age gone by. The days when she had been Stands-Apart were honey-thick with joy and light. She had been loved by both parents and loved them in return with abandon, though Gabriel was so often gone.

She stretched her lower back for a moment before drinking water from her canteen. The morning spread thin and long, and progress seemed slow compared to the work yet to be done. Blisters bubbled on her palms. Thankful worked parallel to her, some distance away. Behind them, old men forced gnarled hands and stooped backs into service as they bound stalks into sheaves and hoisted them into carts.

Catherine's thoughts circled back to her father. After his trapping accident, Gabriel no longer played his fiddle and had not been able to train his remaining hand to sketch. Early attempts resulted in frustrated rages drowned in rum or brandy. He couldn't—or wouldn't—paddle his own canoe or hunt for the family again. But she loved him still, the papa who singled her out among the children, her name, Marie-Catherine, like a song on his lips.

But he never danced with her after his accident. And he only sang when he was drunk.

Catherine wrestled those thoughts down. As difficult as Gabriel was to live with, he was her father, and she would not abandon him. She would never be the refined, sophisticated, purely French daughter he wanted. But as she stood between two empires, could she be a bridge in her family, too?

"Is that your father?" Captain Moreau asked as he handed Catherine out of the canoe and onto the dock that evening. Thankful came right behind her.

Catherine shielded her eyes from the sun as she angled toward the sound of slurring song. "It is." She sighed.

Moreau tied the canoe to the piling, then

joined the women on the dock. Though he had not put blade to wheat, he had raked up the fallen stalks with the older men and exuded the musky odor of labor and late summer sun. With his handkerchief, he rubbed the chaff from the grooves on his brow and straightened his tricorne hat. "I should meet him and explain my orders."

As they closed the distance between dock and house, the air soured with the smell of rum. Catherine's face flushed in shame. "Another time, Captain," she suggested. "When you are rested and have eaten, perhaps."

Chest swelling with an unreleased sigh, Moreau agreed and took his leave.

Gabriel pushed himself out of his chair and leaned awkwardly against a porch column. No longer singing, he just stared at them. Grey hair, once thick and brown, hung to his shoulders in unkempt strands. He hadn't even pinned his empty shirt sleeve, so it waved in the breeze, a white flag of surrender to the hardships that had befallen him. The pinched expression on his face, however, was anything but submissive. Catherine knew that look. It held a fight.

"Do you think he's as angry as he looks?" Thankful whispered.

"I'm certain of it." Gabriel was unused to being alone all day with no one to tend his needs. From what he'd shared of his privileged childhood, his whims had too often been catered to, breeding a selfishness that discarded responsibility in favor of freedom. But then, Catherine had spoiled him, too, she supposed, and she had no doubt he felt affronted by her absence, orders notwithstanding. "He won't be reasoned with in this state. Go on, I'll see to him myself."

Thankful bowed her head and began a wide circle to the back of the house while Catherine approached the porch.

"I'm hungry." Gabriel insisted he couldn't prepare his own food but had no trouble opening a bottle with one hand. A jug dangled from his thumb now, and she judged its weight by its sway. A just-begun jug of rum meant he was still depressed and seeking comfort. A half-drunk jug meant he had mellowed. If he stopped drinking at this point, he could still be talked to, would still listen. But an empty jug loosed him from all inhibition and sometimes from time itself as his mind meandered the paths of his pain.

He stumbled down the steps toward Catherine, dropping the jug to grasp her outstretched hand before he fell. Not one drop of rum spilled into the grass.

"Will you eat if I feed you now?" she asked, her own stomach cramped. She held him steady for a moment before releasing him.

"I saw you with that man down there." The alcohol on his words was overpowering. "You chose to take care of him instead of me today?"

Catherine looked into his red-veined eyes. "That was Captain Pierre Moreau of the Régiment Royal-Roussillon. He's a professional soldier, one of the *troupes de terre* that arrived from France. Remember, I told you about him in my note. Did you read it?"

Gabriel cocked his head. "Liar. You can't read or write. What else are you hiding from me?" He yanked her hat from her head with such force that he dislodged the pins, and her hair came tumbling down.

Catherine's heart drummed. All else fell silent to her ears as she focused only on the labored breathing of her father. She should not have been standing so close to him. She should have remembered what he could do in this state, what he had already done in years past.

"Go to bed. You need to rest." She took a step back from him. "I'll bring you something to eat in a bit."

Gabriel's hand shot out and latched on to her forearm, fingers digging into her flesh. The strength in his one hand and arm was preternatural. "I don't like coming home and finding you not where you should be. A woman should wait for her husband, not move into another man's lodge. Have I been gone so long, Strong Wind, that I mean nothing to you?"

He was crushing the veins beneath her skin. Her fingers tingled, then began to lose feeling. With her free hand, she pried his fingers loose until she could twist from his grasp.

She turned to leave, but before she could take two steps, her head was yanked from behind as Gabriel pulled her hair. Balance lost, she fell backward and tried to spin around to catch herself. She collided with the porch railing, pain searing her temple, and then crumpled on her side on the stone steps.

"Clumsy woman." He shook his head, and she wondered if he was thinking of Isabelle, whose long lines in his sketches had been the very essence of grace.

Catherine touched the wound and found it already swelling. Her ribs throbbed, but she doubted it was anything more than a bruise. She'd made a mistake in trying to talk with him.

Gabriel sat on the step beside her, pressing his hand between his knees. "I couldn't have you walk away from me, see? Don't leave me. You can't leave me, do you understand?"

She pushed away from him, her gut filling with the weight of a pile of rocks. She was ashamed of him, and just as ashamed to be bleeding on the ground at his feet. How often had Strong Wind suffered this humiliation? A few times, after the accident? Several? Strong Wind would say Catherine had chosen the wrong side when she left Kahnawake for Gabriel.

It was a thought Catherine banished with practiced speed. They would reconcile once he was sober.

"I'm not leaving you," she told her father. "Trust me. There's nowhere I belong but here." The truth of it was bitter on her tongue.

His silver-stubbled chin trembled. He made to stroke her hair, but she flinched at his hand, and he blanched.

Stiffly, she retrieved her hat, then rose and helped him do the same. "To bed with you now." She kicked the empty jug aside and led him into the house. He hadn't meant to hurt her.

A floorboard creaked beneath her moccasins, the sound so familiar that she scarcely heard it. Matching her pace to Gabriel's shuffling steps, she led him past the front parlor and up the stairs to the second floor. She followed her father into his chamber and watched his stooped form settle into the bed.

After pulling the edge of the sheet up over Gabriel's chest, Catherine unfurled the mosquito netting from the frame surrounding the bed until it dropped to the floor on all sides.

"Don't go. Have you no pity?" Gabriel pleaded. Wisps of hair fanned onto the pillowcase. "It was no accident, Strong Wind. He pushed me.

Your brother *pushed* me to the ground, knowing that trap was right where I'd fall. He always hated me, never accepted me into the Wolf Clan."

Catherine had the accusations memorized by now. According to Gabriel, her uncle could not accept that a white man had married his sister, and deliberately set out to hurt him. How much truth lived in that story, she didn't know.

"You can't blame me for no longer being able to hunt and trap," he went on. "If it weren't for your brother— But I'll speak no more of it if you'll stay."

Shaking her skirts to create a breeze, Catherine felt as though she were overhearing his last conversation with Strong Wind. She hated when he spoke to her this way. Those words were not meant for her ears but clearly haunted him still.

He stared through the netting at her.

She licked her dry lips. "It's me, Papa. Your daughter."

His face pinched. Then, "Yes. So it is. Sit next to me then, Marie-Catherine. I need you. I always have."

"I know, Papa. I'm here." She stayed until his jaw grew slack.

CHAPTER FOUR

The kitchen was empty when Catherine entered. In the waning light of day, the whitewashed stone walls took on a honeyed hue. A heat-laden breeze pushed through the window near the ceiling, rustling through dried herbs that had all but lost their scents. The hearth was cold, the pot on the crane still empty, the crock of flour nearly as barren.

She tossed her hat onto the broad oak table between drying hazelnuts waiting to be shelled and what was left of the golden bread she'd made out of corn earlier in the week. Gabriel hated the bread, calling corn no fair substitute for wheat, but in times like this, even he could not refuse to eat it.

Gingerly, she washed her scraped and blistered hands before lowering herself onto the bench. The bread crumbled as she pinched a piece from the half-eaten loaf. It was grainy on her tongue as she pressed it to the roof of her mouth. Savoring the flavor kept her from eating too fast.

Memory pressed at the edges of her mind. Strong Wind shelling dried corn into an elm bark cask, her long hair making music as elaborately beaded strands clinked together. Joseph Many Feathers, a baby asleep in the cradleboard on his mother's back. The board was intricately carved and padded with down and furs. *"You mustn't worry your little brother will replace you,"* Strong Wind had said, smiling at her. They could hear children chasing each other between the longhouses, laughing. *"Your little brother will grow up and move into the longhouse of his wife, in a separate clan from ours. But my two daughters are both a part of me, neither one better nor more important than the other. Like two hands of one body."* She'd lifted hers then, wiggling her fingers. *"I need you both. And you need each other."* The girl who had been Stands-Apart had nodded, soothed by the reassurance that she belonged.

Catherine stepped on the heels of her moccasins to remove them, peeling the recollection from her mind as she finished eating her portion of bread. Pushing back from the table, she pulled a pewter cup from the sideboard and drew water from the urn in the corner to slake her thirst. Since the last of the bread would go to Gabriel when he woke, she reached low into the barrel against the wall and measured out dried beans to soak overnight for tomorrow's supper.

Movement outside the window caught her eye. Moments later, she heard a persistent scraping against the outer wall. Leaving hat and moccasins

79

behind, Catherine climbed the stone steps leading out of the house to investigate.

Blackbirds wheeled overhead as the evening air sat heavy on her skin. The setting sun lit the clouds from beneath, painting their bellies pink and gold. Rounding the corner of the house, Catherine stepped around a tree stump and beneath the canopy of a willow. There, she stopped.

His back to her, a man was filling gaps in the house's stone wall with fresh mortar. It was a task that needed doing, to be sure, especially before winter arrived on bitter winds. But who—?

Her heart slammed into her rib cage. She knew that six-foot frame. She knew the lines of those shoulders, the tilt of his head in concentration.

"Samuel?" she whispered.

Turning, he met her gaze.

Catherine did not remember lowering herself to sit on the tree stump, but there she was. Samuel Crane knelt before her, bucket of mortar and trowel abandoned. He was not as she remembered, but he was undeniably the man who had left her and never come back. She knew every contour of his face—the angle of his square jaw, the planes of his cheekbones, the straight line of his nose. His hair, tailed at the neck, was the very color of the wheat she'd cut that day. She remembered the feel of it in her fingers. Soft as corn silk.

"What's this?" he asked, accusation in his tone.

Catherine looked down and saw only her fists balled in her lap.

"Right there." He brushed a fingertip against the inside of her forearm where purple bloomed against her skin. He searched her face, settling on the lump at her temple. "And there. Your father did this to you?"

Catherine pulled her hair over her shoulder, a dark veil to conceal the evidence. Anger surged through her with a force that almost scared her. "How dare you pretend to care about a bruise on my arm when it's obvious how little you care for me at all?"

"Who did this to you? It was Gabriel, wasn't it?"

She didn't want to hear the sympathy in his voice, that particular brand that was edged with steel. She laced her arms at her waist and looked away. "I have nothing to say to you."

She stood, grateful her skirts hid the shake of her legs and that her hair covered the aching side of her head. Still, she felt exposed, as if he could see straight through to the secret places where she hid the truest parts of herself.

Samuel rose. As he brushed leaf matter from his threadbare breeches, she took in her own disrepair. Her apron was yellowed from scything wheat, and the cotton dress it covered was rumpled and damp beneath the arms. With no hat to cover it, her hair streamed as free as if she were still a child at Kahnawake. No Englishwoman would allow a man to see her hair down like this. No full-blooded Frenchwoman, either. Strands lifted on a breeze, dark brown ribbons separating from the plaits that had woven them together. She caught him watching with fascination, or perhaps just recollection.

His presence threatened to unravel her, too. He shouldn't be here, not now, not after so many years. Not during a war, for pity's sake, when French soldiers could see them together and have grounds to arrest them for treason.

Samuel stepped into the gap between them. "I have so much to say to you."

Her lips mashed into a thin line. "You've had five years to say it. I'd say the time for talk is past."

"Catie." He touched her elbow, brow etched with confusion, though she could not imagine why her reaction surprised him.

"Stop." She pulled away.

"Catherine Stands-Apart." The way he said her name made it sound like a sentence.

"Yes, I do." She took another step back from him.

A few days' beard could not hide the flush in his cheeks. "Catherine. I do not expect your forgiveness or even your understanding. But I need you now."

I needed you a long time ago. Desperately. But to confess it aloud would bring nothing but humiliation. It had not been a good trade, their romance. Samuel Crane had gotten what he wanted. She hadn't.

"I need you," he said again, urgency sharpening his tone. "Put aside your own feelings and remember there is a war on. I need your help."

"Most here would call you the enemy," she reminded him.

"Not you, though," Samuel said. "Never you. You don't pick sides like that."

"Exactly."

"Well, now I'm asking you to. Pleading. If you can't choose Britain or France, choose me, or the memory of me you hold most dear. There's something I must do. You're the only one who can help me."

His words ran over her like water over a rock. "I do not have ears for your talk," she said in the tongue of her mother's people, then remembered he could not understand it. With the ease of turning a page, she flipped back to his language. "I will not listen to your speeches. Do not speak to me. Go, and I'll forget you were here. I've done it before."

She watched the arrow hit its mark as the light snuffed from his eyes.

Good, she thought, for he'd wounded her, too, so much that she had grown tough with it. The suffering he'd caused her had been a test of endurance, like walking over hot coals as a child without giving voice to her pain. She had proved her courage then and grown fleet and fearless to run barefoot, even over rocks and sticks. Now it wasn't just her feet that were protected by old scars.

She spun from Samuel to walk away on soles that still served her well.

"Catherine . . ." he called after her.

Her long hair billowed freely in her wake. "Leave," she said over her shoulder, not slowing her pace.

He caught up to her, carrying the scent of damp stone and pine on his shirt. "I intend to. But I can't go alone."

CHAPTER FIVE

October 1749
Ten Years Ago

A stab of anticipation poked hot down Catherine's throat. The autumn wind whipping her skirts carried a sharp tang of crushed mint as she hastened to Samuel's workshop behind the house.

His hand stilled on the shaving stand he'd been sanding. "Well, Catie, you look fair to bursting with news. Good trade at the post?" His breeches rode high on his stockinged calves, as he seemed to grow an inch each month since he'd reached his sixteenth year.

The fire crackled. She pressed her hand against her pocket and felt the letter beneath the fabric. "This time, the news is for you."

The easy grin on his face faltered. He pointed to a block chair by the hearth, where she took a seat. Subtle light twinkled over the workshop walls, glinting off metal tools hanging on their pegs, polished to a shine. Chisels and gouges, gimlets, augers, hammers. Saws for every purpose: crosscut, rip, dovetail, miter, fret and coping, veneer.

Sitting on a barrel opposite her, Samuel wiped a cloth between his hands. Then he waited. She had grown to expect this of him. During the last year, she had learned the steadiness of his manner and drew a certain calm from it. Though a quiet defiance toward Gabriel was rising along with his height, Samuel never pushed Catherine.

"Sam." She clasped her hands on her aproned lap.

A smile twitched his lips as he brushed sawdust from his faded blue vest. "Still here."

A nervous chuckle escaped her. "I've been working more with the porters who trade for us in Albany. I didn't want to say anything to you in case it came to nothing, but I sent word through them to our merchant contacts there, inquiring after your brother."

The color drained from his face. "Joel." His voice cracked on the name.

"Yes." Skipping the unimportant details of who had tracked him down and how, she pulled the letter from her pocket and thrust it toward him. "He lives, Sam. He sent you this." It had been weeks in transit, but what were mere weeks when the brothers had not seen each other in three years?

Samuel took the envelope and paused before breaking the seal, pulling out the letter. It was not a moment for an audience.

"I'll leave you to it," she said, starting to stand.

"No." His hand reached out and grasped hers. "I want you here." He did not release her as he read. The gentle pressure warmed a place in her spirit that hadn't been touched before.

The wait seemed endless before he spoke again, and yet she did not mind the quiet that cradled the rise and fall of Sam's breath. Surely the news was good, for the merchant had said it was written by Joel Crane's own hand. With a pang, she grasped the pull it had on her only friend.

When at last Sam looked up at her, firelight flared in his eyes. "All this time," he whispered. "He's been alive and well, all this time. Walks with a limp from some injury, but he's well. Joel escaped and hid during the raid, and he's been trying to find me ever since. He petitioned the governor to secure my ransom, in vain, but now . . . He says the town needs a carpenter. That he is in need of me." He laughed, the rare sound a gift to Catherine. "Joel's alive!" He leapt up and hugged her tight. "You found him." There was more life in his body now than she'd ever seen.

"You must go to him." It was an instinct that required no thought. "And I don't mean years from now."

"What are you saying?"

Conviction poured strength into her bones. "This is not your home. You have a family, a community, an entire culture, and it isn't here. I know what it is to be apart from that, to feel the soul wither, to begin to wonder who you are."

"Your years at that school in Montreal."

She nodded. "It was horrible beyond description."

Samuel's situation was not exactly the same. He was isolated and lonesome, mistreated by Gabriel, but not entirely stripped of who he was. The Jesuit priest at Kahnawake had come to convert him to Catholicism, but Sam had refused, and Gabriel had not forced the point, no longer being religious himself. Instead, Samuel practiced French by reading Catherine's Bible, and then they spoke English while discussing it. They spoke of courage, forgiveness, loving one's neighbor, putting another's interests ahead of one's own. This was what filled her mind now. It was in Samuel's best interest to be free.

She and Samuel had forged a friendship, but it was not the blood tie he had with Joel. And she was his captor's daughter.

"This place is not your home," she said again. He had been wrongfully taken in an act of war, but now there was peace between the nations. A peace that Gabriel conveniently ignored. "Before the winter, you ought to be home."

She had already formed a plan.

Moccasins planted wide beneath her skirts, Catherine brought down the ax with a crack, parting the log on the chopping stump. Despite an afternoon of splitting wood, the ache in her shoulders could not rival that in her soul. She hadn't realized until Samuel was gone just how deeply she'd come to care for him.

She dropped the ax head to the leaf-littered ground, hand upon its handle. In the nearby thicket, the tops of pine trees leaned, and bare maple branches swayed beneath a full-bellied sky. It had not been a week since she'd sent Samuel off with a canoe and enough dried meat to get him to Albany. He would need to hire help at the portages between rivers, for he'd not be able to carry his canoe alone, but certainly he'd find Mohawks enough to employ.

Please, God, please help him escape.

Unwilling to trust anyone else, she had sent him without an escort. As she had traveled to Albany with the porters herself, she drew maps and wrote detailed instructions from memory. But were her recollections complete?

"Come with me," Samuel had said at their parting, but she knew her place was here. She'd been touched by his sentiment, but now she wondered if it might have been inspired by fear. Nearly two hundred miles separated Montreal from Albany, which included both rivers and portage between them. Much could happen, especially this late in the season, and Samuel Crane was a young British carpenter, not a

seasoned backwoodsman. As soon as Gabriel had learned his captive had run away, he'd sent word with a passing trapper about Samuel, along with a promise of a reward for his capture. Soon every voyageur south of Montreal would be looking for a British boy traveling alone.

A rustling at the wood's edge drew her attention to a black-haired boy with a small bow and quiver of arrows strapped to his back. Leaving her woodpile, she went to him. Joseph had grown bolder since Samuel left. She'd sensed him watching her before this, but only recently had he shown himself.

"Look!" He lifted a clutch of dead rabbits, a grin nearly splitting his face in two. "I hunted these myself. For you." He thrust them toward her, and she accepted with many thanks.

"*Awiyo*," she said. *It is good.* "These will make a fine stew, just what we need for this cold night. And I have something for you." Reaching into her pocket, she withdrew a handful of the British glass trade beads she kept on her person ever since she'd first seen Joseph watching her. "Some are for you, and some for our sister." Catherine was fifteen summers now, so he must be nine. Which meant Bright Star was eighteen.

Joseph picked out a cobalt-blue bead and held it up, one eye closed. "I will tell her this is the color of your eyes. She will want to make a doll for her daughter and use these beads for the eyes."

Catherine's pulse trotted at the thought. If Samuel could travel so far alone to be with his brother, could she not spend time with her siblings and niece, too? It had been so long, but blood ties were stronger than lost time.

A door creaked on its hinge and slammed closed again. Gabriel stood on the porch, watching them without a word, his expression censure enough. He'd been especially cross since Sam had disappeared.

Thunder poured into her brother's face. "Those rabbits are for you. Not for him." He spilled the beads into a small leather pouch tied to his waist and backed into the trees.

"Wait!" Catherine dashed after him, his offering in her fist. When he saw the quilled moccasins beneath the hem of her dress, he relaxed enough to listen. "Never mind him. Come back to me, please? And next time, see if our sister will come, too. Tell her I will help her make the doll myself."

"*Hen'en!*" he agreed, and disappeared between trunks and boughs and a veil of falling rain.

The drops spilled down Catherine's upturned face, and her thoughts went cold as they veered toward Sam. If she could only be sure he would reach home.

November 1749

The fire struggled to keep up with the cold.

From the parlor, the case clock struck the midnight hour while Catherine stayed awake to throw pine knots into the kitchen's hearth. It was the warmest room in the house, so she and Gabriel had made their sleeping pallets here, her father insisting she take the one nearest the fire. Muscles stiff, she reached over and pulled the bearskin robe higher beneath his chin. A fur hat covered his head to the bridge of his reddened nose.

Catherine's thoughts wandered to her siblings in Kahnawake, wondering how they fared in longhouses that could not be warmer than this. Her brother had returned several days ago, but without Bright Star, who apparently could not spare the time. Catherine knew she must be busy, for she had never seen an idle Mohawk mother. Still, the disappointment stung. In the back room of the trading post, while Joseph looked on, Catherine had fashioned a doll from corn husks she had saved for that purpose. When he spotted Gabriel approaching, Joseph had snatched the doll with a promise to deliver it to their niece and scampered back into the woods.

Tucking her own furs around her, Catherine hugged her knees to her chest and watched the fire, wondering if her gift had made her niece—

or Bright Star—happy. She wanted her sister to forgive her for leaving the People, yet she could not bring herself to apologize for her choice. Fatigue weighted her limbs as she considered that perhaps Bright Star had outgrown her.

Outside, moonlight doubled itself on the snow, casting a pearl-grey pall into the air. Frost etched white ferns onto the windows. But beyond them, an orange glow bobbed up and down. Wrestling back her exhaustion, Catherine rose and squinted at it. A touch of her fingertips to the cold pane, and the glass siphoned warmth from her skin, clearing the frost from her view.

Then she heard a man's voice, unfamiliar, shouting in French from the creek behind the house. In the dead of night, he came bearing a lantern. Remarkably, he did not sound drunk. Without a backward glance at Gabriel, Catherine broke from the kitchen, shoving the door closed.

"Are you hurt?" she called out, forcing her leaden legs to carry her.

"This one is."

The reply lit her pace. By the time she reached them, two Frenchmen had beached a canoe on the bank and hoisted a young man onto the ground.

It was Samuel. He wasn't moving.

She raced to kneel beside him. His skin was mottled with cold, the hollows of his eyes sunken and bruised. One arm was folded tightly across his chest. His leg was in a makeshift splint, the bandages crusted and crimson.

Alarm burst through her. The edges of her vision closed in on Samuel. *No, no! No!* Every frantic heartbeat rebelled against what she saw.

One of the men spoke. They were trappers and traders—she could see that now—broken blood vessels webbing across their cheeks. "Word along the traplines is that a British boy ransomed by your father was foolhardy enough to run away. Figured this was him, even before we questioned him."

She nodded, blame and guilt snatching her breath. "Can you help—help me get him to the house?" she gasped. "How bad is it?"

"He's had better days." The brawnier of the two traders heaved Samuel over his shoulder like a sack of flour, Sam's right leg angling awkwardly in its splint. "My brother Rémy and I were downstream of a rapid when a smashed-up canoe came floating behind us on the current. We searched about for the unfortunate owner and found him in bad shape, washed up on some rocks."

Rémy sniffed, rubbing his nose, then pushed his muffler below his chin. "Femur broken, shoulder dislocated, a blow to his head on the rocks. When he finally came to, he told Nicolas and me that he'd nodded off in the canoe, and when he woke, found himself too close to white water he'd rather not brave, though that stretch isn't as challenging as the Lachine Rapids. He tried to stop being pulled in, but the paddle had wedged between some rocks, and the force of it dislocated his shoulder. Dropped the paddle, lost his balance, capsized."

Catherine reeled. She could see it unfold in her mind as clearly as if she'd been there. In his eagerness to get home, Samuel had pushed himself too hard, forfeiting the sleep he needed. But oh, the cost.

Nicolas grunted as he shifted Samuel's weight on his shoulder. "Couldn't swim with his shoulder injured, naturally. The rapids sent him right over a fall, and the landing on the rocks below broke his leg. If we hadn't found him as soon as we did, his story would have a different ending."

"Very different," Rémy echoed. "We made camp and dried him out right away. I poured some brandy into him to brace him some, and Nicolas popped his shoulder back in place and set his leg. It was a clean break, so it may heal all right. But it'll be up to you now to restore him."

He followed Catherine into the kitchen, laying Samuel on her pallet as directed. Stripping fur layers off her body, she laid them across Sam instead. She covered his ears with her hands to warm them.

Gabriel roused as the traders filled him in. Catherine heard her father exclaim, then lapse into a tone of camaraderie with Rémy and Nicolas. If they exchanged stories or terms for the payment Gabriel had promised for Sam's return, she didn't hear them. Condemnation resounded inside her skull like the clapper of a bell.

She had done this. If Sam lost limb or life, it would be her fault.

And if Sam were going to heal, to live wholly once more, that would be solely up to her, as well.

CHAPTER SIX

August 1759

The bell tinkled over the door as Catherine entered the trading post, Thankful close behind her. When Catherine had found Samuel repairing the chinks in their house yesterday evening, Gabriel was already asleep, and she knew better than to wake him for a confrontation. He had still been abed this morning when she rose and left for the harvest, but now he stood behind the counter in the late afternoon sun, trading with Joseph Many Feathers. Once their transaction was complete, she would ask the questions that had been burning all day.

Joseph's head gleamed bronze where it had been plucked clean of hair save for the jet-black scalp lock adorned with feathers. He wore the usual mix of European and native clothing common among a people living at the heart of international trade. Linen leggings, leather breechclout, ready-made French trade shirt embellished with bloodred woodpecker scalps.

Another Mohawk warrior named Grey Wolf stood looking at the muskets. Turkey feathers sprouted from his scalp lock, and his torso was bare above leggings trimmed with dyed porcupine quills. His frame was spare, and his cheeks were pitted from the spotting sickness that had rampaged again through Kahnawake four years ago, taking his wife with it.

Timothy Laughing Creek, his son of eleven summers, made faces at his reflection in a copper kettle. "Catherine!" Naked except for his breechclout, the boy shoved the kettle back onto a shelf and bounded over to greet her, undisturbed by his own mild smallpox scarring. "I caught a fish today in the river. Very big, very good. You should have seen it."

"And did you save me any to eat?" While she bantered with her young friend, Catherine heard through the open windows the rhythmic chop of blade through wood.

Thankful craned her neck to see through a nearby pane, then whispered to Catherine, "That would be Samuel, don't you think? Preparing fuel for our winter hearths, just as he used to do." Catherine had told her last night that Samuel had returned. Thankful had loved him like a brother when he lived here before. "I must greet him." She tucked a coil of hair back under her hat.

Catherine watched her go, noting the spring in her step. Timothy skipped out along with her. Thankful had only been eleven when she'd seen

98

Samuel last. In the years since he left, she'd grown into a woman he might not recognize.

Gabriel put up a hand to gesture that Catherine should stay, and Joseph turned to see her. Though no one spoke of his real father, it had become more obvious with each passing year that he was fully Mohawk. The shade of his skin, the broad planes of his hairless face, his height. The timing of his birth. Joseph was conceived, carried, and delivered while Gabriel was gone for two years together.

"Catherine," he said, coming toward her, "you trade with me. I will not trade with this one." He looked down his nose at Gabriel, who was a full head shorter than he.

Outside, the sound of chopping stopped, and voices of greeting took its place. Samuel laughed. So did Thankful. They were each happy to see the other.

"Catherine," Joseph prompted. Grey Wolf moved from the musket rack toward the tobacco.

"Yes, of course." She went to the counter. "You've brought something to trade?"

"Nothing but these deerskins." Hand splayed on the pile of animal hides, his black eyes snapped with a meaning Catherine immediately understood. He had not brought any game to her, as he often had in years past. Six years her junior at nineteen summers, he took his role as the hunter for his family seriously. Mercifully, he chose to include Catherine in his family. Lately, however, Mohawk hunting grounds had been disappearing, another casualty of the war.

"We need powder and balls," Joseph said. "Two more muskets."

Catherine reached beneath the counter, pulled ammunition from the shelf, and placed the bag of powder and box of balls on the counter. Suffocating heat pressed her muslin gown to her skin. "Do the French not supply you with arms? You fight for them. You risk your life for them. They should at least give you what you need."

Black flies cut through the thick atmosphere, landing on Joseph's quilled shirt. He ignored them. "They give four Kahnawake warriors enough for two. Two muskets, two coats, two blankets, four shirts, four pairs of *mitasses*, a small pot of vermilion face paint, less than a pound of tobacco, and a few cups of spirits. All of this, we are to spread among four men. Does it sound like enough to you?"

It did not.

His expression turned stony as he transferred the powder and balls into a leather bag and slung it across his chest. "Here is a thing I will tell you, Catherine. I fight not for the French, but for the People. I fight against the British who say this land should be theirs."

"And against their allies, the Mohawk still living among them?" Catherine took up a paper fan and stirred the stifling air. More than a century earlier, the Mohawk people had been settled along the Mohawk River in upper New York State. After the Jesuits established a mission there, they encouraged many to relocate to Canada, away from English influence. Clans thinned as the "praying Indians" moved north. This war now divided them by more than mere miles.

"Sister." Joseph smiled. "You know kinship ties are stronger than all else. Do you not remember that battle I told you of? The Kahnawake warriors defied the French orders. We would not fight our own brothers, though they stood with the British. And they would not fire upon us. And so it will ever be. I will not draw blood from the People. Only the British."

"Only British soldiers, you mean," Catherine added, willing him to agree with her. For it was not just the Abenaki who raided British settlements. The most notorious raid on a British settlement was one Kahnawake warriors had made on Deerfield, Massachusetts, in 1704. More than one hundred civilians were captured. Some died or were killed on the march north. Some had been ransomed. But several of the elderly in the Mohawk village had skin whiter than Catherine's. Their English names had long since disappeared. They'd been adopted as Mohawks and had chosen to stay.

Joseph stood taller, raising one eyebrow in challenge.

"Joseph." Her fan stilled, and she leaned across the counter, her stays constricting her ribs. "You do not mean you'll make war on the innocent. The Great Good God loves mercy."

His eyes narrowed. "The Great Good God is just. No one is innocent, sister. No one. The settlers encroach on Iroquois land, including that of our kin on the Mohawk River. Over and over they do this, so that no treaty can ever be trusted. The war is against them as much as it is against their soldiers."

To this, Catherine had no response. What he said was true, and she knew the Jesuit priests at Kahnawake were keen to remind him of it. From what Joseph had told her, the black robes did not restrict their counsel to spiritual matters, but preached the rightness of Mohawks fighting with one empire against the other.

Grey Wolf approached, two muskets in his strong hands. "We take these, yes?" He reminded her of the number of deerskins he and Joseph had brought.

Catherine agreed, and Grey Wolf handed a musket to Joseph. "How many moons will pass before we fight the English at our very doors?" Grey Wolf asked. "The French say they will keep them away, but did they hold them back at Fort Carillon in July? Did they even try to keep them back at Fort Saint-Frédéric?"

He set his jaw, and Joseph's knuckles tightened on the musket barrel. She read in these two warriors the same frustration they'd been exuding since returning from Saint-Frédéric earlier this month. The French had abandoned the fort without a fight, they'd reported, just a month after they'd done the same at Fort Carillon. Worse, at the same time Carillon—or Ticonderoga, as it was now called—fell to British hands, so had Fort Niagara.

"The French give up land that is not theirs to give," Joseph agreed. "They surrender Mohawk land, hunting grounds we rely on to feed the People. The loss of Fort Saint-Frédéric on Lake Champlain has brought the British even closer to Montreal."

No wonder Joseph and Grey Wolf were here to secure their own muskets. No wonder Captain Pierre Moreau looked hunted, and Gaspard Fontaine preferred rum.

Near the hearth, Gabriel sat on a block chair, rubbing a polishing rag over his boots, oblivious to the unhappy tidings spoken in the Mohawk tongue. On the mantel, a clock ticked away the silence that thinned between them.

Then conversation floated in from the window. English words. Samuel's voice.

Joseph jerked his chin toward the sound. "Who do you quarter?" The words were low and accusing. His nostrils flared, and the cords of his neck grew taut. Her brother was not slow to anger.

"Gabriel has ransomed a British soldier, a military captive. That is all." She kept her tone light. "He speaks with Thankful in their native tongue. Think nothing of it."

The glance Joseph shared with Grey Wolf was wary. Inclining his ear, her brother listened. "They sound well acquainted already." Before she could stop him, Joseph strode around the counter and peered through the window. When he turned to face her again, his features had hardened to flint. "Samuel Crane. You are pleased by this?"

"I am not." The fact that he'd asked her, that he cared about her feelings, brought into sharp relief that her own father had not.

The firm press of Joseph's lips bespoke a compassion, however subtle, that touched her. Then understanding fled his eyes, chased by an anger she'd seen in the young warrior before. In three long strides, he was beside Gabriel, dwarfing him with his height, unleashing a string of choice words. Polishing cloth still in hand, Gabriel stood and shouted back in French.

Catherine rushed between them, a hand on Gabriel's heaving chest and another on Joseph's arm. "Please," she said in both languages, feeling her father's heart race beneath her fingertips. "Please, do not fight here. Let this be one place we come together in peace." For what was a trading post for, if not to be the neutral space between nations and empires and family members, where people's needs were acknowledged and met?

Joseph's gaze did not waver from Gabriel as he stepped backward. "Peace? There is no peace." He turned to Catherine. "I am to tell you the porters will come at first light."

Muskets in hand, he and Grey Wolf departed, ducking their heads on the way out. The door banged shut behind them. Through the window, Catherine watched them stalk toward Kahnawake, Timothy running ahead of them, arms flapping like a goose. Slipping a finger between her chin and the ribbons tying her hat in place, she unstuck the satin from her skin and faced her father.

Gabriel sat back down on the block chair and resumed blacking his boot. "What was that about?"

"The furs from my trade at Lachine," Catherine prompted. "Did you not see the bales in the storeroom? A dozen of them."

He flicked a glance toward the rear of the post. "I had no reason to look."

"The ledger would have told you as much." But she should not have been surprised he hadn't checked it. Without his dominant hand, he left all record keeping to her.

Gabriel shrugged. "So the men came to trade after all, then. Well done." He nodded, an end to his praise. "But why Joseph should be in such a foul temper, I can't begin to understand."

"Can't you?"

He straightened and looked her over, lingering on the bruises he'd caused. "Marie-Catherine, I dare not ask how you came to harm, for I fear I know the answer, and I'm sorry for it. More than I can say. Forgive me, ma chère. You are all I have in this world. You take care of me. I can do better than this."

"Yes, you can." Catherine squeezed his hand, the familiar rush of tenderness for him stifled this time. "But there is another matter we need to discuss."

"Ah. It's Crane then, is it?" Standing, he dropped the rag and pulled a pipe from the mantel.

Catherine took it, filled it with tobacco, and lit it before handing it back to him. "I saw him yesterday, completely without warning. I told him to leave, and he says he can't. Why not?"

Pipe cradled in his hand, Gabriel sent sweet blue-grey smoke into the air and shuffled to the puncheon table in the back. She followed. Chairs scraped the floor as they sat. "I couldn't believe it, but there he was, down by the waterfront." He put the pipe stem between his lips and spoke around it. "Samuel Crane, exactly the way we

106

met before. Only slightly different circumstances, of course."

"What circumstances?" she pressed.

Smoke puffed from his lips in rings, and Gabriel chuckled. "You used to love that," he said. "Remember?"

"Papa, please. Explain what happened, from the beginning."

Reminiscence faded from his eyes, and he cleared his throat. "While you were waiting for the furs to arrive at Lachine, I went to Montreal to hear the news down at the waterfront. You remember our old rival, the merchant Trudeau?"

She did. Monsieur Trudeau had competed with the Duvals for furs before he joined the militia. He had been killed some months ago.

"I ran into his widow, the milliner Yvette, who inherited his business," Gabriel said. "Safe to say, she'll be no threat to our trade. She has no idea how to manage the business. No idea how to do anything but trim bonnets and hats."

"I'll call on her later," Catherine resolved. "She was always kind to me. But what about Samuel?" Impatience laced her tone.

Gabriel inhaled on his pipe once more before responding. "Straight to the point, then. Crane and dozens of others were captured by Kahnawake at Fort Saint-Frédéric and sold in Montreal to help make up for the labor shortage."

"To work like slaves, you mean." She folded her blistered hands on her apron.

"Oh, put away your reproach. It's an ancient practice going all the way back to Rome. Spoils of war. The conquered in battle get to work for the victorious. Regardless, I intend to get my work out of him. Apparently he was sold to the Sisters of Charity first—the ones who run the *hôpital-général*. They needed help building a seven-foot stone wall around their fourteen acres just outside the city walls. That work being done, the nuns were ready to sell him and brought him and several others down to the river gates. Of course I bought him. He left without finishing his last year for me, recall."

Catherine stared at her father in disbelief. "So there were others you could have ransomed, but you chose him because you didn't get enough work out of him the first time?"

"Seems logical enough to me." He waved his pipe at a mosquito. "I didn't bring him back so the two of you could repair what was broken between you, that's certain. I'm no romantic. You of all people should know it."

She thought of the sketchbooks she'd found years ago, containing page after page of his first wife's image. Isabelle dancing, reading, laughing. Isabelle bathing. If he was not a romantic now, he had been once, or perhaps he was just filled with regret for that which he could no longer have. But she knew better than to voice that thought. "No, Papa. There will be no reconciliation between Samuel and me."

Gabriel grunted. "I figured as much. You recovered from being jilted years ago. You're a sensible woman. Strong, like your father. Makes it that much easier to have him stay in the house with us, since he surely can't stay with Moreau and Fontaine."

Catherine crumpled her apron in her fist. "Samuel is staying in our house?"

He set down his pipe and it tipped, scattering half-smoked tobacco on the table. "He wouldn't be very well placed with the Frenchmen on the other side of the wood, now would he?"

Through the window, she could hear Samuel talking with Thankful as if their worlds had never diverged. What would she have given four years ago, even three, to have him so close? Yet now his proximity felt suffocating. She waved her hat to stir a breeze.

Gabriel was still talking, reminding her that the wooden stable Samuel had occupied last time had burned down, and since their horse had been taken by the army anyway, there was no reason to rebuild it. "I wouldn't mind if he stayed in the house he built, but he'll have to wait until after the harvest. Who knows but he would come to blows in close quarters with Moreau and Fontaine, and if Samuel is injured, he can't work as well. And I do intend to work him. He has a year to make up for from last time, plus more for the price I just paid."

Her mind spun. *Years.* No, Samuel would never give such a slice of his life to the Duvals again. He was twenty-six years old now. If Gabriel had his way, Samuel would be working here until he was past thirty. If he hadn't even taken the time to write to her these last five years, he wouldn't stand for staying another seven.

"Why so downcast?" Gabriel asked. "It's labor we can use, and just recompense for what he did. I should think you'd find the arrangement utterly satisfying, as I do."

He was right that her broken heart had mended during Samuel's absence. But now that he was back, she doubted every stitch would hold. "No," she replied at length. "I am not satisfied, not in the smallest degree."

Gabriel's chin jutted forward. "Then it is good you have no say in the matter. Discussion has ended."

Catherine stood, chafed raw by her father's words. If she had stayed in Kahnawake, her voice would be sought after, as Bright Star's was. She would be part of a council of women, deciding which men to put in power. Instead she was here, silenced like a schoolgirl though she was five years shy of three decades on this earth and had saved the trading post from her father's sloppy management.

"Oh." Gabriel lifted his pipe to stay her a moment longer. "Captain Moreau came by just before you arrived. I invited him and his militiaman, whom I have yet to meet, to dinner tonight. It may be in our favor to curry theirs, you know. They specifically requested that both of you girls dine with us. Don't disappoint me by serving that wretched yellow bread, either. We dine at eight. I trust that is enough time."

It was plenty of time, in fact, for there was scant food they could even prepare. "Close the post, then," she said. "And keep it closed until after the harvest, when I can run it again myself."

She did not stay to hear his reaction but whisked out of the humid space and into the open air once more. The sky that greeted her churned with steel-grey clouds. Lifting a handful of skirts, she clapped her hat back on her head and hastened to beat the rain.

"Catherine!" Thankful called, still standing by Samuel and the woodpile. Her face seemed lit from within.

Catherine refused to meet Samuel's gaze. "We have company for dinner tonight."

Thankful hurried to join her. "Let's hope they like soup. Thin soup. And there's the last of the blueberries we can put out, too."

Drops began to fall. Samuel caught up with

them, arms full of firewood, his shirt draped over the pile to keep it dry. "Who are you cooking for?"

Thunder cracked overhead, and rain pelted the ground, drumming against Catherine's straw hat and spilling over the brim. "My father must have told you. Captain Moreau and Private Fontaine?"

"Who are they?" Samuel blinked away the water that streaked his face. Rivulets traced shoulders and arms leaner than they once had been. She wanted to ask how long he'd been in captivity this time that he should have lost so much weight. But of all the questions this man might answer, that one interested her the least.

"A French officer and Canadian militiaman are billeted here, since Fort St. Louis is over-crowded," Catherine explained. "They're staying in the house you built. Why else did you think my father decided you should sleep in ours?"

"House arrest," he replied simply. "All the better to keep an eye on me, I supposed. But why are they here?"

A spit of lightning flashed in the middle distance. In a matter of minutes, the afternoon had faded from vibrant greens and blues to a grey reflection of her turbulent spirit. She and Thankful scrambled down the steps that led to the kitchen, the wet hem of her skirts dragging behind her. Samuel followed.

He knelt at the hearth and set down his burden. The knobs of his spine pushed against his skin as he arched over the firewood, stacking it in the rack, then building a fire beneath the kettle. But what stalled Catherine's breath was the scar tissue mapping his back. His skin pulled against the ridges every time he moved, and she wondered how much it hurt him still. Cringing, she stepped back.

Thankful reached out to steady her. "It's not your fault," she whispered, inclining her head toward Samuel. "It was not your hand that held the whip."

Nodding, Catherine hung her hat on a peg in the wall and twisted a spotted onion from the braid hanging near it. While she chopped it at the work table, Thankful added a sprig of dried thyme to a kettle of beans.

The fire hissed and snapped as the flames sucked moisture from the air. The heat and the rain outside both served to sharpen the smells in the kitchen. Wet stone, onion, woodsmoke.

Samuel pushed his arms through his sleeves and pulled his shirt back over his head. Steam lifted from the rain-soaked linen. "Are you going to tell me now? Why the soldiers are here?"

Thankful responded when Catherine didn't. "They're here to supervise the harvest on the Montreal Plain. They've gathered all the women, children, and elderly men to cut the wheat and bind it into sheaves to be shipped to Quebec."

"Including you?"

"Yes. We began yesterday. Captain Moreau said something about working longer hours from now on than we did today and yesterday, though. Nine hours felt like plenty to me, I must say."

After dropping the onion into the kettle, Catherine went to a burlap sack hanging from the wall and pulled out several old potatoes. Their skin was withered, and they surrendered to her squeeze like a sponge. Once boiled, however, no one would know. Making quick work of the peels, she cut them into cubes and added them to the soup.

Samuel drummed his fingers on the table. "They must be hungry in Quebec, eh?"

"Oh yes," Thankful agreed. "Hungrier than we are, to be sure. I'll set some soup by for you, Sam."

"Thank you."

Thankful's fair complexion bloomed a fetching pink.

But it was Catherine Samuel sought. "I would speak to you later, if you'll have time."

His voice, his very presence, raked her nerves. "You have work elsewhere, yes? Best tend to that. Dinner won't be ready for some time." She stood over the kettle, stirring it unnecessarily.

Her cold reply emptied the room of comfort, and Samuel quietly left.

Thankful solemnly regarded Catherine. "I know this is very hard for you. But just think how difficult it must be for him."

Catherine's lips pulled back in something between a smile and a grimace. "Yes. Quite." Steam rose from the kettle and misted her face. She hung the spoon on its hook on the hearth.

"Do you—do you hate him? Truly hate him?"

Drawing back from the heat, Catherine took a small hammer to the table and began cracking hazelnuts from their shells. "I hate what happened. I hate what he did." And she hated that he'd come back and begged a favor right away, without even the decency to ask how she had fared these last five years.

"That's not the same." Thankful's shoulders relaxed as she spoke above the pounding. "I hate how things happened, too. But after all this time, I can't help being glad to see him again. You understand, don't you? I just wanted to ask you—that is, to tell you—I don't hate him. I hope you don't mind. I just can't hate him."

Suspending the hammer over the hazelnuts, Catherine turned to her. "Are you asking my permission? To not hate Samuel?" Soup dripped from the spoon above the hearth, hissing into the fire.

Thankful sat across from her, working the split shells off the nutmeats. "More like your blessing, I suppose. He could use a friend here.

Think of what he's been through, and now, to be a British soldier living in enemy territory with unfriendly hosts . . . He could use a friend," she said again.

Well, so could I. Silence dropped between them, punctuated by the cracking and splintering of shells until they had enough nuts to serve with dinner, and more to set aside for later. Rain pattered outside. A mosquito buzzed in languid loops, and Catherine waved it away. She could not blame Thankful for choosing to remain neutral between two warring parties. She knew what it was to dwell between.

The soup simmered as she spoke. "I'd never ask you to hate someone on my account, Thankful." Understanding softened her tone.

"No, of course not." Thankful laughed, but her relief was obvious. "Will you give him a chance to explain himself?" It was a valid question and gently asked, full of sympathy for both Catherine and Samuel alike.

Catherine considered her answer before responding. "My wounds were so deep, I would rather not open them again. I have enough scars. So does he. It would be best to leave them alone."

CHAPTER SEVEN

If Catherine hadn't been so hungry, dinner would not have been worth the company. Captain Moreau displayed decent enough manners, but Private Fontaine slurped his soup shamelessly. Catherine and Thankful sat across from the soldiers, pretending not to notice.

Outside, rain rushed in silver streams from the eaves, making a steady purr as it met the ground. A fire in the dining room hearth toasted air that would otherwise be damp and chill. Lace swayed at Catherine's elbow as she brought her spoon to her mouth with her left hand. Her right hand rested in the pleats fanning from the waist of her painted silk gown, the grey-yellow bruise inside her forearm discreetly hidden from view.

Thunder rattled the lead windows in their casings. Hurricane lamps cast a warm glow on the table, the flames leaning when a draft forced its way through a chink in the wall that had yet to be filled.

Too polite to note the disrepair, Moreau swallowed another spoonful and sighed through his hawklike nose. "Fine soup, mademoiselles, and I thank you for it."

Without asking for the bowl of blueberries to be passed, Fontaine reached for it, his sleeve cutting a wide swath across the table. He tipped the bowl sideways, using the serving spoon to roll ripe fruit onto his plate, then snatched the last of the hazelnuts for himself.

"Brandy?" Gabriel presided from his place at the head of the table. He sat closest to the fire, and his countenance had colored from the heat.

"Papa," Catherine murmured with a subtle shake of her head. They had already had a round of rum.

He turned to Thankful and bade her pour, an order she could not or would not refuse. Her brow crimped as she did so, no doubt as wary as Catherine.

Gabriel didn't often entertain, but when he did, he styled himself as a man of means and influence. The means, he still retained from the inheritance left him by his parents. As for influence, he might honestly possess it by now had he stayed the course he'd begun as a young man, finished his schooling, and become a barrister in Montreal. Heaven knew he was shrewd enough. Now all he could do to impress guests was draw attention to his hospitality. Drinking was part of it.

Moreau, at least, declined the offer, and Thankful returned to her seat in a rustle of coral damask.

"Soldiers, we aim to please." Gabriel threw his arm wide to the side. "Consider this your home. I've brought a British prisoner down from Montreal. You'll see him about the property, and should you need anything—wood chopped, water carried, uniforms laundered, that sort of thing—do not hesitate to avail yourself of his service."

"A *prisonnier de guerre*?" Moreau looked more interested than he had for the last hour. "I should like to meet him. That is, if it is convenient for you."

"Now? Certainly." Gabriel motioned to Thankful, and she left the dining room to fetch Samuel from the kitchen.

Wind lashed and moaned about the house. Willow branches rapped on the window. Fontaine sat a little straighter and threw his shoulders back. "What can you tell us about your captive, Duval?"

Catherine set her jaw as her father explained that Samuel's scouting party was captured by Mohawks, and that his particular value was as a skilled carpenter and unpaid servant in general. Was it only two days ago that she thought she had burned all memory of him from her mind?

Samuel appeared in the doorway, a phoenix from those ashes. Freshly shaved and perfectly groomed, he ushered Thankful in before him. They looked like a matched pair, these two fair-skinned, blond-haired English. With ten years between them, they could have been siblings from the same family.

Samuel seated Thankful at the table. A true servant would have remained standing, awaiting further instruction, but Samuel sat opposite Gabriel, the length of the table between them.

"Does he speak French?" Moreau asked.

"*Mais oui*," Samuel replied with a cold smile. "But of course."

Fontaine returned the smile. "And what do you think of Canadian hospitality? Enjoying your stay, I presume?"

Moreau leaned toward Fontaine and growled something in his ear. A lump bobbed in the younger man's throat.

"Let us begin again," Moreau said. "Bonjour. My name is Captain Pierre Moreau, and this is Private Gaspard Fontaine." His thin lips curled around the introduction. "And you are?"

"Samuel Crane." Though he didn't offer rank or regiment, his military posture, even while seated, suggested continued service. "I understand you're here to collect food for the troops. Quebec is on its last rations. Isn't that right?" His French was passable but inelegant. He had lost some of his ease with the language.

Moreau shifted in his chair, eyelids thick.

"Desperate measure, putting women and children to work in the fields," Samuel prodded.

He was so different from the boy Gabriel had ransomed so long ago. But Catherine didn't want to think of those days, or of Samuel Crane's coming of age, or of the man sitting not four feet from her right now.

Light and shadow slipped lower on the wall. If Catherine could move, she'd stoke the fire. Instead, she trained her attention straight ahead. Gaspard Fontaine lifted his chin at Samuel's words but said nothing. In the candlelight, his hair shone bright as sugar maples in autumn. For a moment, the veil of haughtiness dropped from his eyes, and Catherine saw the pain he worked to hide. If his brother had truly died of starvation in Quebec, this incessant talk of hunger and harvest must be vinegar to fresh wounds.

Samuel wasn't finished. "I hear your French soldiers have already stripped your countryside of anything edible. They carried off oxen, pigs, cattle, poultry, peas, vegetables . . . In fact, the word is that for two leagues around Quebec, your French soldiers are causing more damage than the British. Do you deny it?"

Moreau seemed unperturbed but did not respond. He tented his fingers before his chest. "Monsieur Duval, if you can spare your prisoner, we could surely put him to use in the field tomorrow. Your women can help keep an eye on him."

Catherine broke from her reverie over

Fontaine's loss. Samuel, work the harvest? Alongside her and Thankful? He would drive her to distraction. "No one will go to the field tomorrow." She folded her napkin and laid it on top of her plate. "If you cut and bind the wheat while it's wet, it will rot before you can get it loaded onto the boats."

Moreau ran a hand over his face, pulling at the lines already carved between his nose and chin. "A delay," he mumbled. "We can't afford it. Frequent heavy rains around Quebec have prevented the wheat crops there from maturing and made road transport nearly impossible. The army there has completely exhausted local supplies of food."

Gabriel brought his goblet to his mouth, then licked his lips. "Then it is well you are here in Montreal instead. Give it a day of sunshine, and you'll be back out with the scythe. You're welcome to take him then. I can't see the point of him running. Where would he go without getting caught? Every able-bodied man aside from you supervisors is already up at Quebec. He'd stick out wherever he went."

Fontaine wagged a finger at Samuel. "Try anything, and you'll be shot first, questioned later. I wouldn't mind doing the honors myself. Been itching to squeeze a trigger for some time now." His words slurred.

Gabriel pointed with his spoon. "You'd owe

me two hundred *livres* if you did that, private. Crane is my property. I'll let him work for you on loan, but I must insist his ability to serve me remain intact." He let the utensil clatter into his empty bowl. "I don't mean to spoil your fun. It's simply business, you understand."

"Shall we retire?" Catherine asked, heedless of how abrupt it sounded. Fontaine was drunk. Gabriel was not quite, but on his way. She was exhausted from harvesting, cooking, and putting up with these men. The droop of Thankful's shoulders suggested she was, too.

"Shall we? Yes, let's." Fontaine leered at Thankful, obviously enthralled by the golden hair beneath her lace cap and by the curves just beneath her fichu.

"Pretty girl for an Englishwoman, isn't she?" Gabriel laughed.

"Indeed. I'd never guess she came from Puritan stock."

Catherine could practically feel the heat radiating from Thankful's mortified face. A muscle flexed in Samuel's jaw. He'd been protective of Thankful, or had tried to be, when she was a little girl. Now she had a woman's body, a childlike innocence, and a wisdom beyond her years. She was beautiful by any standard.

Gabriel chuckled. "A soldier gets lonesome, does he not? I know too well."

"How?" Samuel stood. "How would you know, Gabriel?"

"Lost his arm in King George's War, didn't he?" Fontaine gestured toward the empty sleeve. "A veteran like that would know a thing or two about camp life, and he's earned the right to say it." He lifted his goblet in a toast to Gabriel. "To veterans, soldiers, and to the women who make war easier to bear."

"Is that what you told him?" It was a whisper, but Catherine's accusing tone seemed to bounce off the stone walls. "You told him you fought in a war?"

"What he told us, mademoiselle, was that his quick actions saved the lives of a dozen men, though none could save his limb." Moreau spoke evenly. The look in his eyes invited comment.

The look in Gabriel's forbade it.

Samuel crossed his arms over his chest. "Gabriel Duval never fought for anything other than his own gain, not for a single day of his life."

The air left the room. The fire sputtered, sending up a spray of spark and ash behind her father's chair. The smoke from the flames might have been coming from the man himself, though his composure barely altered.

"Good night, soldiers," Catherine said into the void. As if of one mind, she and Thankful began stacking plates to clear them away. "I'm sure you're very tired. You must think of tomorrow as a day of rest, a gift."

Willing the party to break apart, she carried her dishes toward her father and kissed him on both cheeks. "Rest, Papa. Thankful and I will put the house to rights and retire shortly, as well. Please rest."

He ignored her, staring straight ahead. Catherine glanced over her shoulder to find Samuel returning his gaze. The tension was choking-thick.

"If you want the truth, soldiers, your gracious host lives to serve one person, and one person only: himself," Samuel said. "He is his own first love, and no human being—and certainly no war—could ever be uppermost in his affections. Gabriel Duval fell into his own bear trap, and that is how he lost his arm."

The silence that followed pulsed unbearably, made more pronounced by the whine of wind through the trees. Her own breathing was too loud, too fast, too deep. Bracing herself for an outburst from her father, she slowly turned to take his measure and wished he were drunk after all, so that he wouldn't remember this moment.

But his face was granite behind his whiskers. "I never told you that. I wonder where you could have gotten such a ridiculous notion."

He turned to Catherine, and she felt the heat

of his ire on her skin. At length he smiled, then laughed. But no one else in the room joined in. He'd been humiliated, and he knew it. Never would he forget, at least not until he exacted revenge.

This wasn't the first time Samuel had defied him.

CHAPTER EIGHT

July 1750
Nine Years Ago

Catherine was going to be sick.

Flying Arrow, the Abenaki warrior towering over her, still wore a mask of red paint from the bridge of his nose to his scalp lock. A necklace of bear claws rested against his chest. The silver armband and the rings in his nose and in his distended earlobes caught the dim light in the trading post, but it was not his jewelry that held her fast. Dangling from his fist was a clutch of scalps. Brown hair, auburn, and long wavy blond that shone three shades of yellow in a shaft of sunlight. A tiny wilted wildflower still clung to the strands.

"Your father is here?" he asked.

If only he were. "No. He has left me to trade in his place." It had been this way for some time now, since she had been expelled from the Montreal finishing school two autumns prior. Gabriel still hadn't recovered from the blow to his pride. At least now, with sixteen summers behind her, Catherine was old enough to run the trading post while her father disappeared to do only-he-knew-what. She hadn't seen him all day.

Flying Arrow grunted. "You are the sister of Bright Star, yes? Of the Wolf Clan?"

She said she was.

"I hear your father is a useless man who does not provide for his own. You should have stayed with your clan. You could be married by now. But I will still trade with you. You with your eyes the blue of trade beads." He flashed a smile, his teeth startlingly white. "You give me those muskets." He pointed to the weapons behind her. "Powder and balls, too. You take these to Montreal, and the governor will repay you, thirty-three livres for each one. These are the scalps of those who were too weak to survive the march."

Bile shoved up Catherine's throat, and she muscled it back down to her churning stomach. She summoned her courage, summoned the blood of her mother's people to flow stronger in her veins. If she didn't conduct this well, she could bring dishonor down upon her siblings or her father, or both.

She cleared her mind. She knew the rules of the transaction and that the governor was as good as his word. The price for English scalps was a fraction of the price to be had for a live captive. Still, taken together, it was a hefty sum. Her father would be pleased at this.

Perhaps he would even be pleased with her.

Catherine wiped her sweating palms on her apron and reluctantly agreed to the trade. She lifted the three muskets he desired from the pegs on the wall and laid them on the counter, then counted out the pounds of powder and balls to go with them. Satisfied, he thrust the ring of scalps at her, and she took them with shaking hands. As the warrior left with his weapons, she lowered the scalps into a leather bag and cinched the mouth of it closed.

Guilt filled her belly. She had not killed those people, but she would take payment for their scalps, as though their lives were as fair a trade item as furs and beads and kettles. Her hands were sticky with their blood. Was this worth her father's approval?

An irrelevant question, for there was no undoing it now. She washed her hands at the basin in the corner and recorded the trade in the ledger. The simple act of documenting transactions was something her father never bothered to do, but it had proven key in understanding which items brought the most profit and how often they were in demand. It was one reason the post fared better since Catherine had taken more responsibility.

But she could not stay here a minute longer with those scalps. Though hidden from view, she could smell them. With no other customers in the post, she could almost hear the screams of those who gave them up.

Snatching a pair of leggings from the shelf, she pulled them on under her petticoats, stepped back into her moccasins, and fled the post, bag of scalps in hand. The bell was still clanging above the door as she locked it.

Propelled by her purpose, she plunged into the stable. The thick smell of hay and leather surrounded her. Needle-thin shafts of light slanted through gaps in the walls. "Hello, Lady. Want to go for a ride?" She rubbed the horse's jawline before saddling her.

"Where do you think you're going?" Samuel stood in the doorway, his hair dark with sweat from working outside all day.

"To the city, if you must know." She would ride the mare east along the St. Lawrence River until she was past the Lachine Rapids, then rent a canoe to take her across to Montreal.

"Alone?" He frowned.

She knew his memory flashed to the time he'd taken a canoe alone, at her insistence. But this was vastly different. A short trip and back again, all in one day. She cinched and buckled the belt under the horse's belly. "If I can paddle all the way to Albany, I can certainly make my way to Montreal."

"But you're with another porter for those trips. You shouldn't just go off on your own."

"My father leaves me alone quite often, if you haven't noticed." Dust scratched at the back of her throat.

"That's not right, either." He hooked his thumb into the pocket of his breeches. "He's supposed to watch out for you."

The comment lit a fire inside her, for it gave voice to a whisper she had felt in her spirit but so far refused to credit. Besides, between Samuel and little Joseph, who still came to leave meat and lurk about, there were enough people watching her.

She tucked the leather pouch into the saddlebag, hoping Samuel wouldn't inquire. Those were the scalps of his countrymen. And woman, she reminded herself, recalling that long blond hair. She looked up to see him still waiting for her reply.

"I'm not a child anymore, Samuel." She fit the bridle over Lady's head. "I'm old enough to be on my own for more than just a day's journey. In fact, I'm old enough to be married."

He squinted at her. "You are not." He crossed his arms, still blocking her exit.

"Yes I am. If I had stayed at Kahnawake, I'd be married by now and might even have a baby of my own. Bright Star married at fourteen and has two children now." She led Lady out of the stall, pushing past Samuel and into the sun. Putting one foot in the stirrup, she pulled herself up onto the horse. Madame Bonneville would have been appalled to see her straddling it this way, but her leggings afforded all the modesty she required. "So I'm old enough to cross the river alone. I've taken Papa to Montreal a million times."

"Exactly." Samuel grabbed Lady's bridle, stroking her mane with his other hand. "He never let you go alone before. I don't think he'd like it if you went without his permission."

Lady twitched her tail to ward off flies. Glancing between the house and the trading post to confirm Gabriel was still gone, Catherine spread her skirt over the saddlebag that contained the object of her mission. "I'm going, Sam."

"Come on, Catie. What's so all-important over there that you have to go right now?" His brown eyes seemed older than his years. They held questions she did not want to answer.

She gripped the reins. "Business with the governor. You can't stop me."

"I don't aim to. I'm coming with you." Before she knew what he was about, he'd pulled himself up and was sitting on the horse right behind her.

"Samuel Crane!" She twisted to scold him. "Now who do you think will be punished?"

"If you're old enough to be a wife, you're old enough to need a chaperone." His grin disarmed her. "At your service."

Fighting back a smile, Catherine faced forward again and urged Lady into a walk when what she really wanted was a gallop.

Miles passed beneath a cloud-tufted sky of lapis blue. The foaming Lachine Rapids raced at their left, fringed with cattails and swamp milkweed and flurries of monarchs. Samuel smelled of wood and sweat, and the heat from his body radiated into hers. Though accustomed to being alone, Catherine didn't mind his presence at her back.

The sun had just passed its zenith when they left Lady at a livery stable and rented a canoe to cross the river. Together they paddled, gliding over the water, and something like pleasure eddied around her. It had been a long recovery from Sam's broken leg last November. Seeing him active again, whatever the reason, felt like victory.

Montreal no longer intimidated Catherine, though it seemed built for the task. The walled city was nothing like the piece of earth she called home on the south side of the St. Lawrence. It was a rectangle about a mile long, a quarter mile wide at its west end, and half as wide at its east. As they approached the landing beach, Mount Royal rose dramatically behind it.

Catherine and Samuel tied up the canoe at the riverfront and entered the guarded gates built into a masonry wall eighteen feet high and pierced with narrow openings every six feet for defending musketry. Here in the lower town, close to the river, buildings were connected and hugged the street line. Sailors and brightly rouged women with loose hair teased each other loudly, mouths parted in garish grins. A few beggars sat in doorways and watched.

Catherine glanced up the hill toward two-story, black-gabled houses of rough-split fieldstone and church steeples topped with crucifixes. The metal symbols of the dying Christ stabbed the sky, catching the sun like bayonets. Montreal was a firmly Catholic city, and no fewer than six religious orders dwelled within its boundaries. Still a Protestant, Samuel glanced at several crucifixes, but he made no remark.

Two massive stone towers cast their shadows over the city while she and Samuel threaded their way between soldiers in gleaming white uniforms, nuns in grey, priests in black, and ladies in a rainbow of silks. Noting their white-powdered coifs, Catherine tucked a loose strand of dark hair into the braid encircling her head. Servants scurried and Indians strolled, taller than the Frenchmen by a head, some naked save for their breechclouts, others in trade shirts and leggings. Everyone shared the road with horses and carriages. Shoppers who could not afford those brought dogs pulling small carts.

Turning east, Catherine led Sam away from

the west-end marketplace toward the military and administrative quarter of town. Many homes they passed hid their backyard livestock from view, but cows, chickens, and hogs all added their scents and sounds to the atmosphere.

"Let me carry that." Samuel reached for the bag of scalps as the street broadened and angled upward.

"No, don't." Catherine jerked it out of his reach, flooded with fresh horror. It was a burden far beyond its actual weight, and she would not surrender it to another.

Samuel frowned but didn't argue, though she could see in the set of his jaw that curiosity pressed him tight. They were surrounded by hoofbeats, street vendors, church bells, European and native languages, but all Catherine heard was the silence buzzing like black flies between them.

Their strides and breath grew shorter as they climbed the slope, her nose pinching at the smell of human waste in the gutters lining the unpaved street. A redoubt on the small hill presided over a storehouse and the boatyard below. When she saw the governor's house—two stories of cut stone spread wide, like a French palace—Catherine's stomach clenched.

Gravel crunched beneath their feet as they approached the imposing front doors. The butler admitted them into an entrance taken up by a grand circular staircase. It was here that Catherine left Samuel while she conducted the trade with a clerk, who decreed those four British lives worth one hundred and thirty-two French livres. She was finished with business before Samuel had been waiting a quarter of an hour.

"Let's go," she told him, and hurried past one of the governor's African slaves. The payment sagged in the bottom of the bag. The coins were heavy and clinked together unless she cradled it close to her chest.

"What did you trade to get all that?" Samuel patted the bag once they were back out on the street.

The air inside Catherine's throat expanded and grew sharp. She didn't know what to say. If she told him the truth, what would he think of her? What would he do? She couldn't bear the thought of losing his esteem. But she'd never kept secrets from him before. She bit her lip before opening her mouth to speak.

"Don't lie to me," Sam told her. "I'd rather not know at all than wonder whether I could trust you again."

Catherine sent a frustrated breath through her nose, and they lapsed into a silence that went deeper with every step they took downhill.

They walked through shadows grown long, stretching out from the limestone buildings lining the street. The bag grew heavier in Catherine's arms as they passed a dress shop and then the milliner Yvette Trudeau's place. In the display window, Madame Trudeau arranged new hats and bonnets in the latest styles. If Madame caught sight of Catherine, she would pull her inside for a visit, and today Catherine could not bear Madame's kind attentions. Not after selling scalps off heads that would never wear hats again.

Samuel's stomach rumbled, and Catherine gladly steered them into a yeasty-smelling bakery and paid for a croissant with the few *sous* she'd brought in her pocket.

"Is this a peace offering? For the secrets you're hiding?" Sam took the croissant before she could answer and began eating as they left the building.

"Is it working?" she asked. Horse-drawn carriages trundled by, and pedestrians thickened on the street. Normally she enjoyed trips into the city. Not today. She was nearly as eager to be home now as she had been as a student trapped at Madame Bonneville's.

Samuel's shoulders lifted and fell, but he ate until only a few golden-brown flakes remained on his fingertips, and those he licked clean, too.

The slope gentled as they neared the city gate through which they had entered. But a crowd slowed their steps to a shuffle.

"What's going on?" Samuel asked a man near him.

"Captives for sale." The man stretched his neck above his cravat, craning for a better view. "Most of them already ransomed, though. The Africans are still there, but they're asking a thousand livres for each of them, on account of the permanent labor they'll fetch. Some English, too."

Darkness overtook Sam's face in an instant. Four years ago he was the captive, her father the man who purchased him. What memories filled his mind now, she could only imagine. She gently tugged his hand, thinking it would be easier to leave quickly.

"Wait." Sam moved to better see the captives, and she followed.

She didn't know what she was supposed to feel. Her mother's people had done this, had taken these British settlers from their homes. Her father's people had sanctioned it and grew rich off English slaves and scalps.

Her hands grew sweaty on the bag of silver. *She* had grown rich from this, too.

The captives were filthy. Two African men of sturdy build stood with heads bowed, looking only at their bare feet. An auburn-haired woman of middling years wore a dress but obviously no corset or petticoats. She'd no doubt been captured in the dead of night, then made to dress in a blind rush. The words issuing from her cracked lips sounded German. To the side of the woman was a girl who could not have seen more than seven summers. Her eyelids were pink and swollen, her face mottled with dirt and grime. But it was her hair that made Catherine's mouth go dry. It was wavy, long. And though it was in need of a wash, she could see it was three shades of blond.

"I want my mama!" the child wailed, and Catherine nearly dropped the money she'd been paid for that mama's scalp. Her chest felt so tight and hard, she could barely draw air.

Samuel uttered an unholy oath against the French and against the captors, then called out to the girl in English that everything would be all right. That she need not fear. His voice trembled as he said it.

"Samuel," Catherine gasped, clutching his arm. "Sam!" Her skin felt cold, and she knew she was holding him too tight. She stepped back from the crowd, and he came with her, bending his ear to her lips. In a breathless rush, she told him what she had done.

"You took money for the scalps?" The way he asked it, the way he looked at her, made it seem like she had personally betrayed him, as well as all that was human and decent.

They were already dead, she wanted to say, but didn't. It was the devil's trade, and she had participated in it. The blood had touched her hands. Papa would have wanted her to—he would rejoice at the money it brought.

"I'll never do it again, no matter what Papa says. But what will become of her? The little girl who lost her parents on the way?" No sooner had she voiced the question than a merchant stepped forward and asked the captor about the girl. Catherine recognized him. "Oh no," she murmured. "Not him."

Sam stared at the man. "Why? What do you know?"

"I've heard stories, that's all. He ransoms little girls, just pretty ones. But no one ever sees them again. Some say . . ." But she could not bring herself to repeat it. The base idea took hold in her imagination, and bile soured her gut.

She might be wrong. Perhaps the merchant ransomed little girls and sent them to the convent to be raised in God's service. She knew that to be the fate of many. Such girls were fairly treated, she supposed, aside from being torn from their families.

She listened to the merchant discuss the price with the captor and overheard that the girl's name was Thankful. The merchant spoke of giving her a new name, something French and Catholic. But Thankful was a good name, one that spoke of a contented life. It was almost

Mohawk in nature, the way it succinctly described the person who bore it. Her parents must have loved her very much.

Catherine's heart beat like a caged bird. The little girl wanted her mama. She was all alone, separated from the place of her birth, struggling to recall who she was, and Catherine knew what that was like.

"I'm going to ransom her." The girl's price was one hundred thirty livres. Catherine held that sum in her hands. "I'm going to ransom that little girl."

Samuel's glance swiveled between Catherine and the child. Then he nodded as if this were the only right thing to do. "What about your father?"

She curled her toes inside her moccasins. She already disappointed him in ways she could not help. Too much "savage" blood in her veins. If Catherine had to suffer his displeasure, she might as well earn it by doing something she believed in. "I don't care if he doesn't like it. I'm going to do it anyway. I'll keep her safe. I'll help her get back to her family somehow. Even if I have to row her to Albany myself."

"Your father will hate it."

"He hates a lot of things. I'll treat her right, Sam. She won't belong to him."

His hands came around her shoulders, and she felt the tension leave her body at his touch.

"You do this, Catie, and it will be the truest thing you've ever done."

She didn't know exactly what he meant by that, but she was as drawn in by his words and the conviction behind them as she was by the little girl. She'd been trying so hard to please Papa that sometimes she felt false. More than anything, she wanted to do something true. She wanted that true thing to be Thankful.

Dusk turned the sky lavender and the river a ribbon to match it. Fireflies blinked all around them as Samuel led Lady. Catherine, in the saddle, held a sleeping Thankful, who smelled of grass and earth and wind.

Was it only that morning that Flying Arrow had told Catherine she was old enough to be married and have a child? She knew now that he'd been right. For though she was not Thankful's mother and would never pretend to be, purpose swelled inside her at the thought of caring for this little soul until she could be reunited with her relatives, and purpose felt akin to joy. Uncertainty drifted far from her, like pickerelweed floating downstream.

Samuel was changing, too. Or perhaps this tenderness had always been inside him but never allowed to surface until now.

The remaining miles home passed too quickly. Outside the stable, Sam took Thankful from

Catherine, but instead of setting her down to walk, he just held her in his long, lean arms. The girl's head flopped onto his shoulder.

"Seems a shame to wake her, doesn't it? I reckon she's been traveling a week or longer on precious little food." He pulled a leaf from the girl's tangled hair. "She's so scared and sad. She has no idea if she'll ever see home again, or if she'd be better off forgetting what she knew so she can survive in this strange land."

Twilight deepened to a royal purple, a velvet drape that covered the entire sky save for the silver crescent cut of the moon. Catherine dismounted and led Lady back to her stall, then took off the saddle and blanket.

Sam stood in the doorway, watching. "But she's so young, she'll heal before most do," he added.

"And you, Samuel?" She thought back to when she'd first met him almost two years ago. He'd had no one to speak his language to him then, to assure him he'd find his way. "Are you young enough to heal?"

His lips curved in a wan smile. "As it happens, just now I feel rather old." He hefted Thankful's weight on his hip. "And getting older all the time."

"I believe that's how it works," she teased, rubbing down Lady with smooth strokes. "But are you . . ." She wanted to ask if he was better now that a few years had passed since his capture and ransom. She wanted to hear that he was fine now, that living on their property was better than being adopted by his captors. Better than being scalped.

The turn of his chin stopped her. How could he be at peace about this, when she still mourned her separation from her mother's people, and it was she who had removed herself from them? A mosquito droned near her ear, and she swatted it away, wishing she could as easily send the ache from her spirit. She tallied the sum of what she had forsaken: customs, traditions, family.

Catherine secured Lady in her stall, making sure she had fresh hay and water, then left the stable, Samuel and Thankful alongside her. "Let her sleep, then," she said, resolving to preserve as much of Thankful as she could. The child would learn French, but Catherine would be sure she kept her English, too. Samuel would keep it alive on her tongue, and they could both teach Catherine better. They would pray in the way they saw fit, never mind the Popish laws. Thankful would keep her name.

Quietly, Catherine relayed these decisions to Samuel as he carried the child up to the house. "I will not strip her of all she is and remake her in another's image. Will you help? With the English and the prayers of your people?"

"With that and more. Whatever she needs."

The earnestness in his dark eyes confirmed the truth of his words. *Whatever you need,* they seemed to say. She believed him. Here was a bridge between them, when before this there had been a river with stepping-stones too widely spaced. This child needed them both.

It felt like they were a family, the three of them drawn together in strange ways, though it was inevitable that they would break apart. At least Catherine could brace herself for when Thankful and Samuel returned to their people.

There was no light in the house when they reached it. Inside, Catherine lit a lamp and led the way upstairs. If Thankful had been awake, Catherine would have given her a bath first, but the day had been long enough. Quickly, Catherine set the lamp on her bureau, pulled a quilt from inside to make a sleeping pallet on the floor, and topped it with a feather pillow.

Samuel knelt on one knee, then lowered Thankful down to rest. She curled onto her side, knees brought up to her chest. On an impulse, Catherine dug in the back of the bureau drawer and pulled out an old doll Strong Wind had made.

"Is that you?" Samuel asked, voice full of wonder.

A smile spread on Catherine's face. "Once upon a time." The doll was a few inches taller than the length of her hand. The body was made

145

of dried cornhusks, the hair of black woolen yarn that reached the doll's knees. Unlike French dolls, this one had no face, and its dress was not silk but soft kid leather, fringed, belted, and beaded with white and blue.

"She should have it." Catherine tucked the doll into Thankful's hand and watched her fingers close around it. "A girl should have a doll. Something to hold on to." Propping a fist on her hip, she cocked her head as she regarded the child. "She should have one that looks like her. I will make her one soon." Satisfied, she covered Thankful with a sheet to keep the mosquitoes off her skin.

"Have you done this before?" Sam waved his hand over the sleeping girl. "You're good at it."

This time, her smile was slower to come. "Thank you," she told him. "I'm glad you came."

The knob in his throat jutted sharply as he swallowed, but then his face relaxed into smooth planes and angles. The glow from the oil lamp turned his hair into spun gold. "I left my tools in the grass. The dew will rust them if I don't take care of them." With a final glance at Thankful and a quick nod, he left her chamber and trod down the stairs.

When she heard the front door open and shut, she went to the open window to watch him go. He hadn't put five paces behind him before Gabriel came out of the trading post wiping his mouth and met him between the two buildings. Gripping the windowsill, Catherine leaned forward to listen.

"You were in my house," her father began. Shadows cloaked the scene, but she heard the hard edge to his tone. "Alone with my daughter."

Samuel didn't respond.

Dread tingling through her limbs, she left Thankful, gripped the lamp, and flew down the steps with it. The door squeaked and slapped the frame behind her. "He did nothing wrong, Papa, I swear it." She launched the words ahead of her, praying they'd ease his suspicion.

Gabriel turned, the whites of his eyes gleaming, and the night air chilled the sweat on her skin. "Where have you been? What was I to think when I came home this afternoon to find tools on the ground and the horse gone?"

Was this a protective instinct? Perhaps she should have been grateful for this sliver of sentiment, but as she marched toward him, defiance swelled and buzzed in her head until she felt drunk with it. "Where have *you* been?" The question slipped out without thought or measure.

A hard slap across her mouth told her she must have spoken in Mohawk. She touched her tongue to the blood in the corner of her lips but stood her ground, crossing her arms.

"I told you," he snarled. "Save that savage talk for the customers in the trading post."

Samuel moved as though he would step between them. His lean body grew taut, arcing like a fishing cane. Catherine caught his eye and jerked her head. This was not his fight.

"I saw Flying Arrow today." Gabriel's voice, low and cold, splashed over her. "He told me about the trade. That's good money. I didn't see the scalps in the post, so you must have them."

"I don't." Catherine willed her voice not to shake. Fireflies throbbed and crickets chirped in a high-pitched whine. The air pulsed and thrummed in rhythm with her thudding heart.

"You took them to Montreal, then. That's where you two have been?" A moth pinged against the lamp's glass chimney, then fluttered before Gabriel's face. "Fine. I'll take it now. The money they brought."

Catherine shrank beneath his scrutiny. Her father was not a tall man, but his displeasure could dwarf her, make her feel like a child again. The lamp wavered, and the small flame bobbed as she withdrew into the corner where the stable met the house.

Gabriel neared. "You did take them to Montreal, did you not? The both of you?"

Sam's lips drew thin and pale. "Yes, sir. We did." In two strides he was beside Catherine, his right shoulder overlapping her left. When his fingers brushed hers, she clutched them. His hand was callused and dry and strong.

"And you traded the scalps for cash?"

Catherine pushed a strand of hair from her face. "Yes."

Gabriel held out his hand, palm up. "Then I will take it now. Or did you suppose you would steal it from me? Keep it all for yourself?"

"Of course not!" Heat washed over her. Wishing she could tear the extra layers of fabric from her body, she tore the truth from her lips instead. "The money is gone, Papa. I used it to pay a ransom. For a child."

Shock registered in his eyes. He glanced at Samuel, then appraised Catherine once more, interest kindling in his expression. For hadn't she merely mimicked her father's actions in ransoming a British colonist? Gabriel had benefitted from the arrangement, yes, but she'd always suspected a streak of compassion had urged him to purchase Samuel from his captors.

The sky had deepened to the grey of wet river rocks. It felt hard and cold and too close. "A boy?" Gabriel asked. "With a trade or skill?"

Samuel gave her hand a firm squeeze, and she was grateful, once again, for his presence.

The oil in her lamp ran out. The light guttered, then dimmed and died. "A girl," she said at last.

Gabriel knocked the lamp from her hand. "Another girl! What on earth do I need with another girl, when the one I have is so insubordinate? This is your Mohawk blood. We must help you remember who makes the decisions in this household." He reached back toward something hooked in his belt. A switch, perhaps, or a rod to be laid across her back.

Sweat rolled down Catherine's temples and slicked her palms as she jerked free of Samuel's hold, steeling herself to make no noise. It was another test of endurance, and Strong Wind had borne no coward. Women of Kahnawake did not cry out when babies left their bodies. Neither would Catherine cry out when her blood left hers.

Turning her back, she squeezed her eyes shut and expelled the air from her lungs. Pulled it back in through her nose.

"You wouldn't." Samuel's voice, muffled by the rush in her ears.

Bracing herself against the house and stable, she heard the crack before she felt a searing across her flesh. Biting down on the pain, she whirled in shock to face her father. Her dress flapped open to the summer air, and her skin felt warm and wet.

In the dark, the whip looked like an eel slithering from his palm.

"Stop." Samuel threw back his shoulders. "You can't do this. She's not livestock. She's not your slave!" His voice cracked on the word, betraying the boy inside the young man.

Gabriel mocked him for it. "But you are." He flicked the whip and smiled.

Horror at his meaning filtered through Catherine. He was a shell of the father she loved. Rum had stolen his senses, while pain and fear had chased away hers. She had no idea how to reach the good that still remained buried inside him.

Sam held up his hands in surrender but blocked Catherine from Gabriel. "You've been drinking, monsieur. You'll hate yourself in the morning when you realize what you've done." His French was broken here and there, but the meaning was still clear. "Put it down, sleep it off."

Gabriel roared. "*You* don't tell me what to do! You were bought with a price, and then some, thanks to your foolish attempt to run away! I own you!" He snapped the whip at Samuel, who tried to catch it with his hand, but it was too quick. His palm glistened darkly where the lash had striped the skin.

"Papa, don't!" Catherine cried. "I accept my punishment, but let him go. He's done nothing wrong."

Her father angled toward her, waving his abbreviated arm through a band of mosquitoes. The end of his unpinned sleeve dangled limp. He growled. "You care more for his flesh than for your own? What were you doing in your chamber alone together? Have you defiled yourself?"

"No! No, Papa, he didn't touch me!" Blood trickled down her back.

"You lie!" He reeled the whip back over his shoulder.

Catherine turned her face to the wall, gritting her teeth. She heard a menacing snap, then another, but felt nothing. A sharp intake of breath sounded in her ear. Sam's arms braced on either side of her. He stood at her back, absorbing the blows that were meant for her.

A scream struggled up her throat but collapsed when another crack split the air.

Sam fell to his knees. With one yank on her waist, he pulled her down, too, and arched himself over her curled-up form. His limbs shook as they covered her. "Stay down," he whispered, while his blood spilled instead of hers.

CHAPTER NINE

August 1759

Dawn lifted the fog from the swollen St. Lawrence River, but not the fatigue from Catherine's body. After Samuel humiliated Gabriel at dinner last night, she had slept only fitfully, one ear tuned for any hint that her father might take his revenge. He hadn't. Not last night, at least.

The soil was a sponge beneath her feet as she made her way to the dock. There would be no harvest today, no working in the field alongside Samuel, and for that Catherine was doubly grateful. As she waited on the dock for the porters to arrive from Kahnawake, she felt confident Moreau and Fontaine would remain abed since the wheat was too wet to cut. The French soldiers would call it treason to trade with New York. Catherine simply called it business.

The fleece of clouds thrown across the sky glowed orange. A kingfisher burst from the cattails near the shore to dive after some prey in the water. Then, almost noiselessly, a bateau glided in from the west carrying Bright Star, four Mohawk women, and Joseph, though he had never been part of this trade before.

"Good morning," Catherine greeted them as they rowed near enough to hear. The women's hair shone with grease, their neat plaits embellished with ribbon and feathers. Around each neck hung a sheathed knife atop their stroud tunics, and beneath each buckskin skirt were leggings. Greetings were brief, for they all knew what to do.

Instead of coming alongside the dock, they beached their vessel on the shore and climbed out. The four women aside from Bright Star each had shoulder bags decorated with beads and moose hair, which no doubt held rations. Working together, all six Mohawk turned the bateau over and carried it above their heads to the creek behind the trading post, shell and metal jewelry making a kind of music as they moved.

"Thank you for making one more trip this season," Catherine ventured once the bateau was situated on the creek shore, ready to shove off as soon as it was loaded. "I understand this is a busy time of year with the harvest." But she also knew these women would earn good money for this job, and the communal fields of corn, beans, and squash would be tended by many others in their absence. This income would mean much to their families at a time when there was little security to be had. "I know the current war makes the trip riskier."

One of the women, Chases-Clouds, pulled out her tumpline and tapped it against her leg. Copper hoops glinted in her ears. "We've done it before," she reminded Catherine. "We angle westward in New York to stay out of the fray."

Truly, they were all capable and experienced, so Catherine had no qualms about sending them, especially with Bright Star along.

The women trod the path from the creek to the trading post thirty paces away and into the storeroom, where they attached their tumplines to the ninety-pound bales of furs. Catherine did so, as well, so that each woman need only carry two bundles from the trading post to the bateau. A series of small creeks and portages would take them from here east to the Richelieu River, which would lead them south toward New York State.

Once the vessel was loaded, Catherine stood on the bank to give final instructions to the women while Joseph kept watch for any unwelcome visitors who might disrupt their plans.

Catherine coiled her tumpline and dropped it into her apron pocket. "You remember the route."

Fair Flower recited it as easily as though it were a list of items to buy at market. "Richelieu River, Lake Champlain, Lake George, portage, Hudson River, Mohawk River, Schenectady.

We know the way as well as I know the veins mapping the back of my hand."

As she spoke, Silver Birch and Sweet Meadow watched Joseph admiringly. Little wonder. Since war and disease had come to Kahnawake, there were three unmarried women to every single male, and Joseph had yet to be paired with a bride.

A dragonfly with glassy-paned wings perched on the edge of the bateau. "Yes, good," Catherine said. "And the name of the merchant you'll deal with?"

"Van der Berg, the elder or his son. We've done this before, Catherine." Clearly eager to begin a long day, Chases-Clouds beckoned the other women into the vessel. Fair Flower, Sweet Meadow, and Silver Birch climbed in and took up their oars. Chases-Clouds and Bright Star pushed the vessel farther into the creek, and then Chases-Clouds climbed in.

Bright Star waded back to shore.

"What are you doing?" Catherine's gaze darted between Bright Star and the other porters, who pushed their oars against the creekbed until they were in deeper waters.

"Not going." Creek water streamed from the fringe on Bright Star's leggings and into the grass.

Joseph joined them, his chiseled face revealing nothing.

"Not going?" Catherine repeated, but the departing bateau was answer enough.

Shadowy half-moons hung beneath Bright Star's eyes. "Those women have navigated this route more than once. They know the portages, the path, the merchants. They know what prices are good and what to bring back, which most likely will be a combination of oysters, rope, and weapons. Van der Berg knows these women as well as he knows me by now. I trained them myself. They will not disappoint. Trust them, as I do." A sentiment rarely expressed by one so bent toward suspicion.

"Are you ill?" Worry snaked through Catherine as she studied her sister. Sickness took more of the People than anything else, it seemed.

Bright Star's cheekbones angled sharply beneath her skin. "Staying suits me." The lines on her brow seemed permanent, aging her well beyond her twenty-eight years. It was not just sun and wind but grief that had drawn them there.

How lonely she must be, mere months after her late husband's death in the war. But it was not a subject they spoke of. Catherine wished she knew what thoughts lay behind those brown eyes. Did Bright Star miss Red Fox terribly? Was she numb to it by now? Had she been hardened to loss long before this? A sister should know these things.

Mosquitoes hummed between them. "Bright Star, I think you should go." There was time enough to catch the bateau and jump in, and surely her sister would benefit from doing the work she loved. A change of pace and scenery, a task to complete—these were good medicine. A fact already proven.

As Catherine beheld her sister, she saw the woman of seven years ago. Bright Star had been twenty-one then and had already lost to illness her first husband and both children, a daughter and a son. Death was no stranger to the People, but this was a staggering blow. Clan mothers had encouraged Bright Star to order a raid on New England so she could adopt captives to replace her children. Grey Wolf would have raided. Any warrior would have. When Catherine had learned of the idea, she had railed against it. *"How could you take children from another mother when you know the pain of losing your own?"* In grief-drenched fury, Bright Star had pointed to Thankful and hissed back, *"How could you possibly tell me not to, when you have taken one yourself?"* She had collapsed to the ground and rubbed dirt in her hair. *"I don't want any others,"* she had said then. *"I want Raven and Gentle Breeze."* But children of her own flesh, she could never hold again.

That was the summer Catherine had finally gathered the courage to bridge the gap between them the only way she knew how. *"I need your help,"* she had told Bright Star. *"Our porters no longer want to make the trip to Albany, but I still want to trade with the merchants there myself. Come with me?"* And Bright Star had. Together they had reinforced ties between nations strong enough to weather war. In the process, Bright Star grew stronger, less overshadowed by her loss. Once connected in New York, the sisters had traveled north to collect furs from the Abenaki at Odanak on the Saint-François River and from French traders at Trois-Rivières and Quebec on the St. Lawrence. Eventually, they competed with fur companies every August at Lachine. Samuel kept watch over Thankful while Catherine was away. That arrangement lasted two years.

Then Samuel left, and Catherine had stayed home with Thankful while Bright Star led teams of porters on the voyages without her. Red Fox, her new husband, allowed it. He could tell she was good at the job, and the job was good for her.

All of this flashed through Catherine's mind as she said to Bright Star, "Purpose suits you."

"Sister." Joseph rested his lean hand on the tomahawk at his hip. "She has one."

Birdsong filled the air as the sky tempered from orange to pink. Catherine cast a glance at the porters as they glided around a bend. "What do you mean?"

"Samuel Crane has come back, has he not?" Bright Star fingered the end of her braid. "Joseph told me. And so, I think I will stay."

A breeze ruffled the feathers spiking from Joseph's scalp lock. He jabbed two fingers toward the house where Samuel slept. "You said yourself, his presence does not please you. Did you speak true?"

Catherine watched the willow branches sway for a moment before responding. "I did."

Joseph drew himself up even taller, his face full of all the wisdom a young warrior could possess.

Bright Star rubbed a thumb over knuckles worn raw with work. "I will tend to my harvest here at home."

Exasperated, Catherine threw an outstretched palm in the direction of Kahnawake, imagining dozens of women bending themselves to the fields, their children laughing and running among them. It was one field, one harvest for the entire community. "There are others who can tend it."

"And who will tend to you?" Joseph's voice was low, his words those of a provider and protector.

Bright Star nodded. "Samuel wants something from you, yes? What will he do to get his way? You may not know him as well as you think."

"And you do not know him at all."

Bright Star crossed her arms, the familiar judgment infusing her posture. "Are you defending him now?"

"Of course not." It was irrelevant now, Catherine supposed, that Bright Star hadn't spent more time becoming acquainted with Samuel after he proposed. But old insults were easily recalled.

"Then let us defend *you,*" Joseph added.

"You may not need us at all." Bright Star's voice was flat and controlled. "Isn't that why you left Kahnawake? You never depended on your community. You've always been too busy chasing your own interests."

Catherine could not hold her tongue. "I chose to be the one our father could depend upon, when no one else in the world would, and you make it sound like selfishness."

"My sisters!" Joseph sliced his hand between them, cutting off the age-old argument. "Enough talk of years gone by. There is nothing new to say. We have troubles enough for today. Catherine, Bright Star and I both stay home. If you do need us, much better that we are in Kahnawake rather than somewhere we cannot be reached."

Catherine stood on the soft earth of the bank, composing herself until she could speak without further provoking Bright Star. "Joseph, will you not go fighting with the French?"

His lip curled in a crooked frown, a boyhood expression he'd never outgrown. "There is dissension among the People. Our French Father does not abide by his agreements, so there are some who do not feel bound by treaties already broken. You know they are giving away our hunting grounds without a fight. This fall and winter we will be shot at or captured for hunting on our own land." He pushed his shoulders back, lifted his chin. "I do not wish to fight with the French right now. When I fight again, it will be with and against whomever I please. This is what suits *me.*"

Catherine nodded her understanding and escorted Joseph and Bright Star to the lane that would take them back to Kahnawake. "I'm grateful for your thoughtfulness," she said. "But don't let your concern about Samuel Crane keep either of you from whatever you'd rather be doing."

Joseph paused at the edge of the lane and looked down at her. "You do not understand. Gabriel's way of looking out only for himself—that is not our way, Catherine Stands-Apart. Tell us if you have a need, and we will meet it."

"Which would be far easier if you'd never left." Eyes flashing, Bright Star turned and walked away.

When Joseph and Bright Star departed, their words remained with Catherine. Their protective sentiments surprised her. Bright Star's bristling manner did not. Even so, Catherine couldn't imagine how her siblings might help her deal with Samuel's reentry into her life. This was a struggle for her alone. Unable to sort her feelings just yet, she resolved to restore order where she could.

Propping open both the front and rear doors of the post, she invited fresh air and light to sweep through the space. The whitewashed stone walls smelled damp after last night's rain. Combined with the heat, the sharpened odors of deerskins, rum, and tobacco made for an overpowering experience.

Fists on her hips, she tallied the disarray from Gabriel's shift yesterday and set to work repairing it. Before doing anything else, she swept dust, grass, and leaves out the door. Mud spotted a few places near the wall where rain had seeped in and mixed with dirt tracked onto the floor. Stroud cloth, the most prized British linen, had been unfolded and then shoved back between the shelves in wrinkled heaps. Catherine shook out and refolded them, the stripes facing out for easy perusal. Two red stripes, a triple band of blue. Alternating red and blue. She was lucky they hadn't been knocked to the floor and soiled.

Two new jars of honey told her someone must have traded with her father in Catherine's absence. The ledger held no record of it, but a survey of the shelves showed fewer candles. She made a note.

A gust of wind knocked hanging pots and kettles together, filling her ears with the rustic chime. Casks of rum squatted near the cold hearth opposite a case devoted to bags of tobacco. After making sure the containers were all sealed tightly, she turned her attention to the bowls of trade beads on the counter, sorting out those that had been misplaced. There was satisfaction in the straightening. If only she could organize her thoughts as easily.

A shadow stretched to meet her. Catherine looked up to find Gaspard Fontaine, toque in his hands, standing in the door. He appeared to be sober, and repentant at that. Retying the apron strings behind her waist, she moved to a felt-covered tray and rearranged the knives it held. "Bonjour. May I help you?"

Clearly, he was not here to trade, for he'd brought nothing save a guilty expression. "I've been a rogue, mademoiselle."

Her hands stilled. Lacing her fingers, she gave him her full attention. A hint of coffee carried on his words, but nothing else.

"I'd like to blame the rum. I'd like to blame what compels me to drink so freely. But my mother raised her sons better than that. She'd be appalled at my behavior as your guest, and so

164

would my brother. I must apologize." He sank down onto a cask and bowed his head.

Catherine remained behind the counter, guarded. "Your brother," she repeated, an invitation for him to tell her more.

When Fontaine looked up, the pain in his grey eyes was unfeigned. The corners of his mouth pulled down. "Did Moreau tell you? I thought he might have."

"He mentioned you had a brother in service at Quebec, but that he passed away. Quite recently."

He slid a glance to the fireplace. "Did he tell you he starved to death? Oh, the doctor called it something else, but the truth is, he didn't have enough food to live on, let alone recover from an illness." His tone took on a hatchet's edge. "This wheat you're harvesting, it would have saved him. Instead, his body was in the ground before I was even allowed to pay my respects. News was sent to my parents, mere words on a page. I'd have told them myself, but I can't get leave."

Gone was his arrogant façade. His face was wiped clean of mischief. For the first time, Catherine felt she was seeing a glimpse of who he really was.

"I'm sorry for your loss. Truly." She thought of his parents receiving the letter and could only imagine how much they longed for the comfort their son might offer in person.

"My parents are old. I was the 'miracle' child of their advanced years, like Isaac for Sarah and Abraham. Augustin was much older than me. He used to take care of them, with his wages and more. Now it's my turn, but I can't until the war is over. And do you know what's really troubling? Sometimes I can't even remember what we're fighting for."

Catherine skirted the counter and lowered herself to a cask opposite him. She could see Fontaine floundering without belief in his service to New France. "I hear this war is different from the last one," she tried. "They say when it ends, the victorious empire will reign over the defeated nation's colonies. All of New England and all of New France ruled by just one king. The combined resources of this continent—"

"Pardon me, mademoiselle, but I do not give a fig for empires and conquests and trade routes. I only want to live in peace with my family once more, with food enough to eat without also having to supply the armies of France from our meager yields. And as both King George and King Louis live an ocean away, I don't suppose it very much matters which one of them says this land is theirs. Besides, no matter who wins or loses, Augustin is still dead." Licking his lips, he thumped the cask beneath him with two fingers. "Rum is the only thing that dulls the pain."

Sympathy argued that the grieving young man was no threat. But experience persuaded Catherine that no man filled with rum could be trusted.

"Do you understand?" he asked. "Will you forgive me?"

"I do understand. And I do forgive you. But you would honor me best by refraining from all but a moderate drink with your supper. If you cannot stop there, I'd request you stop before you even begin."

He blinked. "Stop drinking—altogether?"

"If necessary. I won't abide drunkenness."

Fontaine stood, shoving his hat into place over his coppery hair. "Does your father know?"

His smile brought the blood to Catherine's cheeks. He'd called her bluff before she even realized her mistake, but her father's habits were not a subject she wished to discuss. Escorting Fontaine to the door, she stood in its frame and watched him walk away.

CHAPTER TEN

Catherine lingered in the doorway of the post, gaze drifting from the hemlocks that swallowed Fontaine from view to the clouds feathering a sky almost low enough to touch.

"Catherine." Samuel called to her as he crossed from the house, his voice still low and thick from sleep.

She ducked back inside the trading post.

He followed. "Catherine, wait." He closed the door, casting shadows where there had been light.

"Open the door, Samuel."

He lost no time in striding over to her. "Listen to me. I need to get out of here. I can't stay, do you understand?" He stood so close, she saw the stubble on his jaw, felt the heat radiating from his body. "I must leave, and I need you to help me escape. You know I can't do it alone."

Her teeth clenched. "It's not something I'm likely to forget, though I've tried." She stepped away from him and stood behind the counter, a kind of barricade against his entreaties. But there was far more than space between them.

Samuel rested his hands on the counter. "If

you hadn't brought me back to health after my failed attempt to escape, I'd have died. But you wouldn't let me, and for that I'm grateful." Sun seeped through the shutters, slanting across his face. "I don't wish to escape for my own sake this time. I must deliver information to the British that would drastically alter the course of the war. It would speed its end. Isn't that what we all want?" He moved his hand toward hers, and she dropped her fists to her sides. "I need you again, Catherine."

Indignation built inside her. It reared up with the force of a breaker until she was helpless to hold it back. "How dare you," she seethed quietly, and watched his eyes widen. "What? Do you pretend to be surprised that I'm angry with you? I'm livid." She gave vent to it, voice growing stronger with every syllable. "You waltz back into my life—"

"I'd hardly call being captured by the enemy and purchased as a slave *waltzing*—"

"After five years without a word, you just appear and expect me to act like you didn't dice my heart to pieces. Not only that, you're asking for my help, manipulating me, preying on old sympathies." Pulse pounding at her temples, she spilled every ounce of emotion she'd bottled and corked and sealed. "You offer no hint as to what kept you away, not even the faintest glimmer of what happened to you after you parted ways

169

with Bright Star in New York. Did you even get home? Did you find Joel?" She hated that she cared enough to even ask the questions.

Samuel blanched. "Joel?" His hands splayed wide atop the counter as he leaned forward. "You're asking about *Joel?*"

"He's the reason you left me, isn't he? Of course I want to know about him!" Catherine whisked to the front window, slamming the shutters open. Light streamed into the post, gilding everything it touched. "Which you would know if you had read a single letter I sent!"

"You assume I received all your letters!"

They were yelling at each other and over each other in a way they had never done before. Their voices ricocheted against the walls, and when they paused, the kettles rang and reverberated with their anger.

Catherine crossed her arms. "How can you ask me for help when you haven't the decency to explain why you never came back?"

He turned from her, staring at the muskets on the rack until he calmed. "I thought you'd be married by now and away from your father, you and Thankful both. I didn't think this would still matter so much to you." His tone dulled. "I didn't imagine *I* would still matter to you."

Whirling from him, she stared through the lead panes of the window toward the St. Lawrence River and wished she were there instead. The idea that Samuel pitied her was a fire that burned her pride to ash. "I moved on," she said to the glass. "But since you came back, bitterness beats a drum against my chest until I fear my skin may wear away. I don't ask for your love or affection, Samuel, but I deserve to know what happened." Her words turned to fog on the window, and she rubbed it away with her thumb.

"That you do." With a labored sigh, Samuel made his way between barrels to sit at the puncheon table in the back. "I found Joel." His face grim, he gestured to the empty seat across from him.

Pressing a hand to her stomach, she summoned her composure and joined him.

Samuel studied a knot in the board, tracing its lines with a callused finger. "He was married when I finally reached home five years ago. He said he'd tried sending more letters through the merchant in Albany and your porters, but . . . I don't know what happened. Any number of things. It doesn't matter. But when I got home, I was overjoyed to find him, my family. You know how long I'd waited for that moment." He looked up.

"I do." She nearly held her breath, anxious to hear the rest. A breeze swept in from the open back door, blowing strands of hair from the thick knot at the nape of her neck.

"I required too much of that joy." He inhaled

deeply, hesitating for a moment. "I expected it to cancel out the sorrow that surged for my parents. When I was home and they were not, I felt their absence more sharply than I ever did in Montreal. Visiting their graves brought back scenes I didn't even know I still carried. Fond recollections, yes, but also horrific ones of the night they were massacred. I did not handle those memories well." He turned his face away from the sun, and shadows masked his features.

Catherine's palms grew damp on her apron-covered lap. Her mother's people had done this. Their blood ran hot through her veins. "What did you do?"

"Anger filled me. I was so consumed with rage, it scared me. I was afraid it would affect how I saw you." He glanced at her, suffering reflecting in his eyes. "I didn't blame you for what happened to my parents. I didn't blame Bright Star or Joseph. But in the back of my mind, I felt it would be a relief to hate the Mohawk people, the Abenaki people, all the nations who raided New England settlements. I wanted to give in to hate, because it was the only emotion stronger than sorrow." His tone took on an unfamiliar edge.

She bowed her head, submitting to this raw confession. She had asked for this story. She would not stop him from telling it just because her throat stretched tight around its pain.

Samuel clasped his hands, kneading them. "I did pray. I tried to focus on what was good in my life, and that was you and Joel. I made that my rescue from hurting. But joy was never meant for that purpose. If we don't know sorrow, joy holds no meaning at all. We need to feel our losses so we can deal with them. But like I said, I didn't know that then, and I pushed for too much from Joel to fill the hollows made by grief." He squinted at her. "Does this make any sense?"

She told him it did. "Sorrow and joy are two sides to the same blade."

Exhaling, he nodded and stretched one leg out before him, brushing her skirt beneath the table. He pulled back, shifting awkwardly. "One day I asked Joel to go ice fishing with me, just the two of us. He didn't want to take the weekend away from Lydia, but I applied pressure in all the right spots, and he finally gave in." A muscle worked in his jaw. "Joel and I used to go ice fishing with our father, and I wanted to have one last time with him before I left. I was already tired of waiting for you, and winter had just begun, stretching unbearably before me. You have no idea how I missed you, Catie. I could scarcely endure it."

Warmth kindled in her middle, and she focused on anything but his face and the tenderness in his voice. "So the two of you went," she prodded.

"Aye. And only one came home." Something

rippled over his face—regret or guilt. Likely both. "The ice wasn't strong enough. It was too early in the season. I should have known that, and maybe I did, but I rushed our trip because I was selfish. I wanted time with him so I could hurry back and live my life with you."

Catherine's mouth went dry. She had no words.

"The ice broke, Joel slipped under, and I could not save him fast enough. I have no idea how long he was under. Minutes? An eternity. Still, he wasn't gone when I pulled him out, not yet. I prayed that my brother's life would be spared and his bride would not become a widow. Joel trusted the ice because I told him to, and it broke beneath him. His death was my doing entirely."

"Samuel." Catherine grasped his hand while searching for more of her voice. "I'm so sorry," she managed at last. How much did the river remind him of his brother's death? What demons of blame did he confront each day he lived near the water? A thin shaft of understanding pierced her thoughts. Samuel's love for her had compelled him to take risks that resulted in Joel's death. Had staying away from her been his penance?

An ache spread from the center of her chest until it filled every part of her. She wanted to tell him it was an accident, that he could not take on that guilt, but her lips refused to frame the words. She struggled to master herself. Of all the possibilities she had imagined for his absence, this had not been among them.

Samuel's smile was faint but full of meaning. "I have accepted it, just as I have accepted my parents' deaths. Before Joel died, I asked his forgiveness, and he freely gave it." A lump shifted in his throat, and the years that had divided them collapsed. This was no stranger before her. This was Sam.

"I wish you had told me," she whispered. "I wish you'd written." Her thoughts lunged toward what might have been if she'd but known the truth, and she struggled to bridle them before they galloped away with her. "Why didn't you?"

Samuel looked as though he'd been struck. Releasing her hand, he wiped the expression from his face. "Enough storytelling for today. I am sorry, Catie, for any suffering I caused you."

She looked at him through a cloud of dust suspended in the air, her fury having ebbed away. In its wake, she felt exposed, confused. "You didn't have to stay away all this time."

The flat line of his lips suggested otherwise. "Let us speak no more of it. None of it can be changed. What we can discuss is what to do next."

A protest gathered and died on her tongue. Already he'd circled back to talk of escape and her role in it. How easily, how quickly, he turned from reconciliation. How foolish she'd been to lean toward it.

She needed fresh air. The wind, the river, sky. She rose, and so did he. "I believe we're finished here," she told him, snapping a guard back in place over her heart.

"We're not," he countered. "We need to talk about getting out of here. Did you not hear what I said? The war may hinge on the intelligence I've gained, but no good will come of it if I don't carry it to the right people. I need your help. So sit back down, and let's formulate a plan."

"No," she said, angered by how suddenly he'd shifted from sharing the sorrow that had parted them to pushing his agenda. "We're done."

She left the post, forcing Samuel to follow her. He simmered beside her as she locked the door, and there she left him, for she could not bear to be near him a moment longer.

Glancing at the river, she crossed back to the house, Samuel's story hanging heavy on her. But this was a burden she'd asked for, and she could not shrug it off.

Thankful emerged from the house and smiled as Catherine neared the door. "A day without harvest." She put a hand to the small of her back. "What will you do with it?"

Behind her, she could hear Samuel begin to chop more firewood. She saw his face and form without looking. She didn't want to. "I won't stay here."

It did not take much persuasion for Thankful to agree to join her, and even Gabriel made no objection. So as Catherine guided Thankful through the muddy streets of Montreal, the noise and press of people shoved Samuel to a corner of her mind where she struggled to keep him confined.

Though she had come to the island to trade and harvest earlier this week, she'd been miles west of the city. Only now, inside the walls, did she see how choked it was with women, children, and refugees from Quebec. Hunger sharpened their elbows as they jostled against the crowd of their own making.

And the crowd was entirely human. There were no horses, for they too had been enlisted in military service, and without horses, there were no carriages or wagons. Gone were even the dogs that had pulled small carts for the poorer class. They'd begun disappearing last winter, after all the cows and hogs had already been butchered.

"All these people!" Thankful murmured, clutching Catherine's arm for balance. Small valleys in the unpaved road brimmed with rain-water and mud. "How does the city sustain them?"

The smell of unwashed bodies ripened in the

humid air. Catherine held a kerchief to her nose as they turned at the corner. "I don't know," she replied. "There's a labor shortage with the men gone, but surely the women and children who have taken their place cannot fill those positions. I imagine they live largely by charity." How long that charity would last, she couldn't guess.

"Here we are." Thankful slowed as they came to a shop window. "Shall we?"

Catherine opened the door, and the bell tinkled overhead as they entered the millinery. Hats and bonnets of every type topped stands lining the paneled walls. Feathers, ribbons, and lace trimmed straw or satin brims. "Madame Trudeau? Yvette?" she called. The jasmine scent pervading the shop proclaimed the owner's favorite perfume.

"Coming, coming, ma chère!" Yvette, twenty years Catherine's senior, bustled into view, pulling a length of ribbon from around her neck and stuffing it into her pocket. "Catherine and Thankful! What a delightful surprise, do come in." She embraced and bussed both of them, her face wreathed with a smile despite the black mourning gown she wore.

Catherine pulled a small jar of honey from her apron pocket. "This just came to our post, and I thought you might like to have it."

Yvette's mouth rounded before breaking into

another grin. "It's my one weakness. You're sure you can spare it?"

"We have its twin at home," Thankful assured her, then glanced at the ceiling as footsteps sounded on the second floor. "You have company?"

The hint of a sigh swelled in Yvette's chest. "We all do, my dear. My 'guests' include three women—one a widow like me—and four children ranging from four years of age to eleven. They came earlier this summer when the British laid siege to Quebec."

Catherine stifled a gasp. Manners prevented her from asking how Yvette could afford to keep them all, but she knew it must be a strain.

"That's very kind of you, madame." Thankful placed her hand on Yvette's shoulder.

"Ah well. We learn to adapt, do we not? Please, if you have time, sit and visit with me for a spell." Clutching the honey to her bosom, Yvette led the way to a trio of chairs clustered around a thin-legged table that held a mirror. This was where patrons sat to try various styles of hats while sipping tea.

Yvette's silk rustled as she placed the jar on the table and eased into a chair. "Would you care for some light refreshment?"

"No, thank you," Catherine assured her. Surely Yvette needed every morsel to feed herself and seven houseguests.

Light fell through the nearby display window, casting shadows of the latest styles on the floor. Movement caught Catherine's eye. Two russet-feathered chickens bobbed toward her, their claws sinking into the Persian rug with every halting step.

"Ah!" Yvette flounced up from her seat, cheeks pink. "My other houseguests, Maude and Lucie. Shoo! Shoo!" Swishing her skirts at the hens, she shepherded them out of the room and into the stairwell at the back before closing the door. They clucked in protest from the other side.

Yvette chuckled. "Do forgive me, mademoiselles, but I've lost so many hens from our yard to thieves already, I decided to bring my last pair inside. We need them to keep laying eggs, you see."

Catherine smiled at her hostess, hoping to put her at ease again. "Of course. And what do Maude and Lucie think of their fine accommodations?"

Yvette pursed her lips to one side and clasped her hands. "They do not fancy it, I'm sorry to say. Too many people, not enough sunshine. And I daresay not enough food, or at least not the diet they want. My other guests have them marked for a stew, but I can't give them up quite yet. But let us speak of other things." She curved her lips into a smile that seemed slow to come.

Thankful stepped toward the window, her

180

youth and grace a perfect fit for the display there. "Oh, this is charming!" She picked up a peacock-colored bonnet trimmed in ribbon and feathers, a stark contrast to the ruffled white cap she wore. "Look how you've done this trimming! I can barely see the stitches."

Lowering her voice so as not to embarrass Thankful, Catherine leaned toward Yvette. "I ought to show you the beadwork she's done at the post. See her hands? Made for detailed work."

Eyes sparkling, Yvette mouthed a silent, "Oui!" To Thankful, she said, "*Merci*! I confess that one is a particular favorite of mine." She patted her fading auburn curls.

Thankful turned the hat in all directions to inspect the workmanship in the sunshine before trying it on and observing the effect in the mirror. "I'm surprised it hasn't sold yet."

"What a kind thing to say, dear. But it's difficult to sell anything when most days the shop is closed so we can all go and work in the harvest. Not that I mind doing my part, mind you," Yvette was quick to add. "If we can help feed those soldiers, all the better. Even when I'm open, folks aren't as interested in new bonnets as they once were. Times are hard." From upstairs, voices volleyed, growing shrill. Yvette shook her head. "Hunger steals people's patience. So does worry, and they have plenty of that, for they have no idea whether their houses still stand."

Catherine waited for the muffled shouting to subside. "I understand you inherited the management of Monsieur Trudeau's business, God rest him."

Yvette's smile slipped. She twisted her wedding band, and it spun too easily on her finger. "Oh my. You and your father will have no more competition from the Trudeaus, that's certain. I have no idea what he did or how to begin making sense of his books. His notations might as well be ancient Greek to me."

There was no way Yvette could live on what she was—or rather, wasn't—earning from her millinery. "If I may be so bold," Catherine began, "I might be able to offer some guidance."

Surprise lifted Yvette's thin eyebrows toward her hairline. "You would do that for me?"

Catherine reached over and squeezed her hand. Her skin was papery and dry, and moved too easily over her bones. "I've not forgotten how you took me in more than once when I was a child, failing at Madame Bonneville's School for Young Ladies."

Thankful returned the bonnet to its rack and returned to her embroidered seat. "Do tell!"

Catherine smiled. "You know that I was at a boarding school between the ages of twelve and fourteen. I was a terrible pupil. I didn't even like hats."

"No, you most certainly did not." Yvette

laughed. "But"—she grew serious—"they should never have denied you food for making mistakes."

"They did what?" Thankful's porcelain brow furrowed. Outside on the street, a woman paused at the display window for a moment before moving on.

"They had many methods for trying to civilize me," Catherine said. "One day, my class came here for a lesson in the latest styles of wigs and bonnets, and I'm afraid I wasn't an enthusiastic student. I couldn't answer questions correctly when it came time for review. Madame Bonneville declared I should have no dinner that evening for my 'savage' and 'rebellious' ways. But when our lesson was over and we lined up to file back into the street, Yvette slipped two croissants and an apple into my pocket, along with a note that said I should come back and have tea with her any time I could get away. So I did."

Tears lined Yvette's lashes. "You'll never know how glad I was every time you came."

Crossing her ankles, Catherine leaned toward Thankful and said, "Yvette didn't even mind when I forgot the manners I'd been taught. But being here made me want to remember them. If Madame Trudeau had been my teacher instead of Madame Bonneville, I wouldn't have run away."

"Three times," Yvette added. "Wasn't it? How I worried over you. But you're here now, and you've brought Thankful, and you've absolutely brought the sunshine with you. I can almost forget there's a war on when I see you dears."

She was lonely. Catherine could hear it in the warble of her voice. In a city and house overflowing with people, the widow still felt alone. And, if Catherine didn't miss her guess, afraid.

"Show me Monsieur's books, Yvette, and I'll decipher what I can."

When Yvette hastened away to retrieve the ledgers, Thankful whispered, "That was your aim for this visit all along, wasn't it?"

Catherine nodded. "I can't abide the thought of her falling into ruin. I'll advise her the best way I know how and check on her again after the harvest. Discreetly."

"Of course." Thankful's lips bent in a conspiratorial grin. "Your father doesn't have to know."

"If we can all just weather this war to the end, life will return to normal." Catherine pressed a hand to her stomacher, trying to assuage the ache behind it. "Food supplies won't be stretched so thin because the armies will go back to France, and the refugees can go back to their own homes."

Thankful dropped her gaze. "That is, if they have homes to go back to."

CHAPTER ELEVEN

If she had been asleep already, she wouldn't have heard the knocking on her chamber door.

"Catherine." Samuel spoke so low and soft, she wondered at first if she'd only imagined it. She'd been doing far too much imagining since he'd told her two days ago what had happened with Joel. How would their paths have altered if Samuel had only shared that with her right away? Would she have gone to him in his grief, though the war had already begun, or could she have convinced him to return despite the guilt that filled him? Was Samuel truly disinterested in rebuilding the relationship they'd once shared? Was she? Questions wore a ceaseless circuit in her mind, and she wearied of them. They led nowhere.

Meanwhile, all he wanted was her help to escape, not that they'd had much chance to revisit that topic. They'd been busy with the harvest, and with all the French soldiers hovering about, it wasn't safe to talk there. When at home, she closeted herself away, trying to ignore reemerging feelings for Samuel now that she knew it was Joel's death that had kept him from returning. She was warming to him too easily, too quickly. She didn't want to, and being near him only made it worse.

So during her evenings, she worked on decoding Monsieur Trudeau's books for Yvette. It had proven too much to accomplish during their visit the other day, so Catherine had promised to examine them at home and return the records to her friend along with written observations and advice.

Samuel knocked again, and she turned on her bed toward the wall, teeth clenched, and focused on the crickets' song instead. Just because she paid him no mind during the day didn't mean he could enter her bedchamber after dark, no matter how desperately he wanted to speak with her.

The squeak of a hinge told her that Thankful had opened her door, for Gabriel was snoring still. "Samuel?"

"Oh. I didn't mean to disturb you, Thankful."

"Do you need something?" Her voice was muffled, but Catherine could tell she'd stepped into the hall. It was not difficult to picture her in her wrapper, golden hair in a plait at her back.

Samuel's sigh was audible. "I do. I need to talk to her, and there is never a free moment during the day, though surely she could carve out some time if she had a mind to."

"Well," Thankful began, hesitating, "it's quite a shock, having you here. She missed you fiercely. We both did."

A beat of silence passed.

"I'm sorry for the pain my absence caused. I'd like to settle things with her, but how can I when she ignores me?"

A pause followed before Thankful spoke again. "Have you considered that we felt ignored by you for five years?"

"I'm sorr—"

"I didn't say that so you'd apologize. I said it so you'll recognize where she's coming from. You'll need to give her time."

"Time I do not have." The urgency in Samuel's voice was clear even through the door.

Catherine's heart bumped hard against her chest. How much longer could she put him off when he was living under the same roof? He remained as relentless as he had ever been. Stifling a groan, she drew back the mosquito netting and left her bed, threw on a robe, and went to the door.

When she opened it, Thankful offered a fortifying smile and slipped back into her own room.

Slowly, cautiously, Samuel neared. "Does this mean you're ready to talk to me? Or at least hear what I have to say?"

"Not here." Gabriel slept soundly most nights, but what if he stirred and heard their voices?

Unwilling to risk it, she led the way downstairs and out the door, not bothering to look back as she walked, barefoot, to the river.

Bats sprayed from a tree, swooping to catch mosquitoes in their flight. At the end of the dock, she sat, arms wrapped around her knees. Samuel lowered himself beside her, his shoulder brushing hers. A galaxy of fireflies twinkled around them.

Catherine glanced at him. "You want me to help you escape south, to the British headquarters at Crown Point or Albany, but that's not going to happen."

"Not true."

"Very true," she countered. "I sent a team of porters south two days ago. It was the last to go this season. You missed it. So, you see, we have nothing to discuss."

"I don't want to go south, Catherine. I need you to take me to Quebec."

A charge went through her at the word. She lowered her legs, toes skimming the water, and turned to face him. "Quebec! But why?" Surely there was no more dangerous place on the continent for him than that city. All of Canada's military forces were concentrated there, along with their native allies.

He bent his head toward hers, though no one was near to hear them. "I learned some things in Montreal, and more from overhearing

Fontaine and Moreau talking. I need to get the information to General Wolfe."

She stared at him. "You're a spy." Her tone invited him to refute it.

His chin jerked away from her. "I never set out to be. But what I know now cannot be wasted. It could end the war, Catie. I tried to tell you."

Narrowing her eyes, she measured the set of his jaw, the conviction in his voice. "What kind of information?"

Loons called to one another in the span of Samuel's hesitation. "A proper access point for Quebec City, for one. Wolfe has been jabbing at the city for months with nothing to show for it. If he doesn't get a foothold soon, winter will freeze him out of the water, and he won't be able to try again until next year."

Moonlight wrinkled on the river. Water lapped against the bateau, and the rope that tied it to the dock creaked as it stretched and slacked. Catherine pulled her braid over one shoulder so that it coiled in her lap, and she threaded her fingers through the plait. "You want me to help you tell the British general how to attack the capital of New France."

"And soon. Before the wheat harvest has a chance to fortify the Canadian and French troops inside the city. You heard what Captain Moreau said, didn't you? They're running out of food. The time to attack is now, when their morale is low, their bodies are weak, and they may agree to a quick surrender rather than a drawn-out fight and siege. The sooner I can go, the better, but I need your help to get there." Pleading rasped his voice. "Please. You're the only one I trust."

Clutching the dock, she felt the board's rough edge bite into her palm as she leaned on it. "What makes you think I'll do as you ask and not deliver you into the hands of your enemy?"

"Because I know you. We are older, and much has changed, but not the core of who we are. So yes, I still trust you with my life, as I did before."

His hand found hers, and at once she was whisked to years gone by. She knew these hands. She knew the texture of his skin, the sweep of his thumb over her knuckles. She even knew he would squeeze them tightly before he released her.

"I hurt you," he murmured. "I'm sorry. If it eases anything, you were not alone in that pain."

Time grew languid and lazy, pulsing fireflies the only indication that it advanced at all. There was nothing but breath between them, and yet they remained worlds apart. "Then tell me." She licked dry lips. "How did you recover?"

If he had not, wouldn't he say so now that they were together again? Her blood throbbed in her temple, her ears, the hollow of her throat.

He squeezed her hand and let it go. "I put aside my own desires."

She turned her face away to hide her reaction. Indeed, he had put aside Catherine completely.

"And I ask you to do the same," he pressed, "for I know the idea of helping me unsettles you. But this place we find ourselves in now is far bigger than the story of two ill-fated lovers. There is so much more at stake." He cupped a firefly loosely between his hands, and its glow seeped between his fingers. "Think of what this war is costing your people. The Massachusetts Bay Colony alone has four times the number of white residents as in all of New France."

The number stunned her. She'd had no idea the populations were so vastly unbalanced.

Setting the firefly free, Samuel watched its flight. "You won't win, and the longer the war drags on, the greater the sacrifices for all of you. Not just the soldiers, but civilians, too."

Yvette Trudeau came to mind, along with the refugees in her home and on the streets of Montreal. Catherine could not deny that this war demanded much of New France's people. She wound her braid around her wrist, pondering. Wind cut across the river and swept over her, ruffling the hem of her robe.

Samuel shifted on the dock beside her. "It's time to end it."

"In favor of Britain, you mean." Fatigue pulled at Catherine. Sliding back from the edge of the dock, she stood.

He sprang up beside her. "You say it as though you're loyal to the French empire just because your property falls inside the line marking New France from New York. But you've said it a thousand times if you've said it once—that line is blurred and faded. It means nothing to you. You're a woman in the middle. You take no sides."

The dock shook as she put it behind her, Samuel following. "And if I take no sides, why do you think I'd choose yours?"

"Think, Catie. What would another year of war do to Canada? Already its people starve. Yes, this wheat harvest may help, but then what? A British victory is inevitable. In the meantime, Canada suffers. What do you think will happen when Britain wins?" They reached the riverbank, and Samuel captured her hand to stop her. "All of this land becomes her responsibility. King George will not let his people starve. The blockade will lift, food will be sent, the suffering will end."

Catherine's mind whirred feverishly while dew-kissed grass cooled her feet. Were these not her very thoughts just the other day? She set her jaw and pinched a mosquito from her arm.

"Better that we end the war with one battle." Samuel held fast to her hand, infusing Catherine with his intensity. "And with the information I've gleaned, it's possible. Likely, even, if not certain. Listen." Bowing his head toward hers, he cut his voice to a whisper. "The wheat we harvest is destined for Quebec. All you need to do is volunteer to take some cargo yourself. You know the waters north as well as you do south, do you not?"

She did.

"And I am your father's slave. I will help you row. When we get near Quebec, I'll slip away and into British lines. It's simple. It can work. But only with your help."

Catherine teetered on the brink of indecision. She could almost feel herself being taken in, but whether by logic or some unnamed longing, she could not say. At last, she spoke. "You ask me to betray my country."

The excuse felt hollow, for it was true that she felt no more loyalty to one empire than to another. Nonetheless, if she were caught assisting a British colonist, the charge would be treason.

"No." Samuel's tone approached a growl. "I ask you to save its people. I ask you to help stop the suffering before more of your countrymen and women starve. Will you?"

With Samuel's face so near, she felt a current of energy jolt through her. He did not release her hand.

Part of her thrilled at his need for her. It was that portion she could not trust.

• • •

It was dusk when Catherine approached the edge of Kahnawake the next day, nerves buzzing like flies on horseflesh. Bright Star had said she was staying home from the trading trip in case Catherine needed her. But would she regret her offer after this visit?

As was her custom, Catherine entered Fort St. Louis adjacent to Kahnawake. Inside the stone wall, a cluster of soldiers in blue and white uniforms looked up from a card game as she passed the barracks. Others sat outside, polishing buttons and boots. Ignoring their stares and remarks, she headed for the Jesuit mission church.

Shells jangled quietly from the fringed deerskin dress she wore. Gabriel hated Mohawk garb, but she had not dressed to please him. The meeting she sought with Bright Star would have a better chance of going unnoticed if she were not bedecked in French silks and lace. But that was only one reason. When she dressed Mohawk, it was easier to remember her mother.

A single long braid hung loose behind her, brushing her back as she walked toward the steepled Church of St. François Xavier. Though she held her chin high, she looked away whenever anyone approached. There were those who would recognize her as Gabriel's daughter and think her a fool for choosing him.

The mission inside the fort and the village of nearly sixty longhouses sat against the river, hemmed in by fields of corn, squash, and beans. Beyond the fields were wooded slopes that led toward bluish peaks. The crests were powdered white, a portent of the coming winter.

The silver hoops in Catherine's ears tickled her bare neck as she swung her attention from hills to village. Though she hadn't yet reached the boundary of the mission, she could hear the women of the Wolf Clan talking and laughing as they worked together. Singing carried on the breeze. The shrieking of children gaily scaring crows from the corn soared above it all.

In the garden between the church and the priest's home, purple bee balm mingled with black-eyed Susans and sunflowers. Grazing her fingertip over a velvety petal the color of sunshine, Catherine's mind turned inward. What would her life have been like if she had stayed with Bright Star after Strong Wind's death? She might be married and widowed by now, as Bright Star was. She might have children, or she might have mourned them and laid them in their graves already, as her sister had. Even so, she would have family. Every woman in a clan was called mother. She'd belong, even though she was only half Mohawk. After all, they adopted white British settlers without a drop of Indian blood into the village completely.

A priest emerged from the church, engaged in a heated discussion with Grey Wolf. Timothy Laughing Creek walked behind his father, a tricorne hat trimmed with gold braid set rakishly atop his head.

"But the Six Nations have undisputed rights to those lands." Grey Wolf slapped the back of one hand into his palm. "They are our hunting grounds, and the French army just gave them away, when they promised to keep the British far from here."

The priest raised his hands. "I do not pretend to understand the workings of military strategy."

A scowl darkened Grey Wolf's countenance. "I understand a lie. And so do you. I say those who lie cannot be trust—" He spotted Catherine and stopped.

The priest followed Grey Wolf's gaze, then hailed her with a brown-spotted hand. "Catherine? Catherine Duval?"

Timothy pushed the hat back on his head so he could see and ran over to her. "Guess what I found!"

She tapped his hat. "I believe that what you found, someone else has lost. Captain Moreau?"

"I found it outside a cabin. On the porch, but still. If he wanted it, he would have been wearing it."

In Kahnawake, most items were for communal use. Personal belongings were kept beneath a person's sleeping ledge inside the longhouse. From Timothy's perspective, he hadn't stolen this hat, but that wasn't how its owner would see it.

"Care to trade?" She pulled from her pocket a small handful of glass beads, which he was pleased to accept.

When Grey Wolf called his son to his side and strode away, the priest gave her his full attention.

"Father. It has been a long time." She nodded to him, holding Moreau's hat in her hands.

"A very long time, indeed." His clerical collar stuck to his sweat-filmed throat. "Have you come for confession?"

She never had, and she never would. Uncomfortable at Kahnawake, and with a river between her and the many churches of Montreal, she'd grown more familiar with Thankful's view of God, Protestant though it was. A God she could talk to anytime, anywhere, without needing a sachem or priest.

"I've come to speak to Thérèse Bright Star," Catherine told him. "But I'd rather not disturb the village. Do you suppose—that is, I cannot recall if you walk among them." The question beneath the statement was whether his presence would be more welcome than hers.

"I do. Will she be expecting you?"

"She will come when you tell her I'm here."

"Of course she will." He bowed to her and

197

strode away, the hem of his black robes sweeping the dust behind him. Catherine watched his slightly stooped form retreat, then ducked inside the church to wait.

It smelled of incense, old hymnbooks, and wine. Glass flasks hung empty now but would be filled with fireflies for vespers, their light a fair substitute for oil the church did not have. Wampum collars decorated the altar, reminders that this was no ordinary Catholic parish. Few Kahnawake had left behind their old religious traditions completely, preferring to mix their beliefs of the Great Spirit or Supreme Being with the priests' teachings of Jesus. Many Kahnawake refused to restrict their worship but gamely added Jesus into the same category with ancestors and a great number of inferior deities.

"Catherine?" Bright Star stood in the doorframe, hair smooth and shining. The day's last wan rays paled around her. "There is trouble?"

Tricorne in hand, Catherine moved toward her and led her outside with a word of thanks to the priest. "Shall we walk by the river?"

The quiet clinking of shells and beads accompanied the sisters as they made their way through the gate in the stone wall surrounding the mission. Only when they reached the pebbled bank did Catherine speak. "I've been talking with Samuel."

The hawk feathers tied to the ends of Bright

Star's braids fluttered in the breeze. "What does he say of his mistakes?"

As concisely as she could, she unrolled for her sister the story of Joel's death and Samuel's reaction to it all those years ago. "He could have come back. I would have welcomed his return. His guilt need not have kept him away," she finished.

Bright Star folded her arms. "But you understand his dilemma. You could have returned here, too. Was it your guilt that kept you away? Or the shame from a choice poorly made?"

This was what came of confiding in her sister. "How can you ask that, when you were the one who told me to stay away?" Irritation edged Catherine's tone.

Her sister's response was a dense and reproachful silence, her mouth a straight line on her face.

"I didn't come here to argue about our past," Catherine said tightly. "Samuel Crane needs to leave."

"So let him leave." Bright Star's feelings about Samuel had never been veiled. It was clear she had no sympathy to spare for his choices. Just as she had none for Catherine's.

Frustration building, Catherine tapped Moreau's hat against her leg. "I want to, but it's not that simple. The French soldiers staying with us shackle his ankles and make him harvest wheat during the day. He might escape at night, but he wouldn't get far without help. Besides the fact that he doesn't know the land and the river, his English accent will betray that he's not French straightaway."

Bright Star swatted at a mosquito on her arm. "What is this thing you are saying? And what is it you do not say?"

"He wants to go to Quebec. By river. His plan is for me to volunteer to carry some of the harvest by bateau to Quebec, and he, as Papa's servant, would help me row."

Bright Star bent and scooped up a smooth stone. She turned it over in her hand, rubbing her thumb along its rounded edge before tossing it into the water. Ripples expanded around the place it sank, unseen. "That is his plan. What is yours?"

"I want him gone." The words sounded foreign to Catherine even as she said them, but they were no less true for that. "Having him so near is not good for me." She'd made her peace with Samuel's abandonment, but his return eroded her progress. He was quicksand. The more she struggled, the more she sank into memories and feelings that were better left untouched.

Bright Star's lips cinched, drawing faint lines around her mouth. "Gabriel will not be pleased his slave has slipped through his fingers a second time. You would risk this? You would travel alone with this man, though it may cost you?"

A sigh swelled in Catherine, then broke as she whispered, "This is why I came to talk to you. I don't want to be alone with Samuel, especially not for such a journey." Either she would change her mind about helping him and leave him stranded, or old longings would return, only to be denied again.

Her sister's gaze was frank. "You want him gone. He can't go alone. But you don't want to be the one to take him. Is this correct?"

Catherine shaped her hand around one corner of the hat. "I need him to leave as much as he wants to go."

Bright Star's eyes flashed. "He has hurt you?"

"Not in body."

"But in spirit, his presence brings you pain." Slowing her steps, Bright Star looked toward the lowering sun. "What will he do in Quebec?"

Catherine stilled, planting herself by the river that could take him there. "His aim is to help end the war completely, if he can reach his general soon enough with critical information. I confess, I favor the idea of the war being over, regardless of the victor."

Her sister's smile was rueful. "France wins. Britain wins. The result for the People will be the same. We will be discarded like a used-up weapon. Do you not agree?"

"Then better to have it over with soon and stop losing your warriors to the fight."

Bright Star cast her a sidelong glance, then resumed walking along the river with the grace she'd inherited from Strong Wind.

"Do you miss him terribly?" Following her, Catherine edged toward the subject of Red Fox, unsure if her sister would welcome it. Bright Star was not in the habit of sharing her feelings. At least not with Catherine. "You could tell me, if you've a mind to," she added, chafing against the silence.

"I miss many people." Bright Star rubbed at a spot on her sleeve with a concentration Catherine saw right through. "Red Fox was a decent man. He provided as well as any husband could. But he was not a replacement for Thunder, the husband of my youth. I did not expect it of him, either. It would have been unreasonable. Unfair."

The air sat like warm, wet flannel on Catherine's skin. "I understand. Just as you could never replace Raven and Gentle Breeze with captured British children."

The instant sharpening of Bright Star's features took Catherine's breath away. "So you have told me, many times." She spread her hands wide, palms up. Empty. "And so, childless I have remained, even after two husbands. Yet you have your British captive, when you've never been married once."

The heat prickling Catherine's scalp had

nothing to do with the weather. Bright Star knew full well that Catherine had sent letters in search of Thankful's family every time they went to Albany together. The search was fruitless. "Do you fault me for this?"

The question was a door between them. Catherine beckoned to Bright Star to walk through it, to share whatever resentment or sorrow she bore alone. Instead, her sister turned and walked away, slamming the door soundly shut.

Feeling punished, Catherine followed. "Silence cannot be your answer to everything."

Bright Star notched her head over her shoulder. "And giving free rein to your tongue and feelings should not always be yours."

Was it any wonder they still had not bridged the chasm yawning between them? And yet her sister was here, her very presence testament to her earlier offer of aid. She was a riddle Catherine always failed to solve.

At length, Bright Star's voice lifted from the hidden places of her thoughts. "I have a thing for you to consider."

Catherine hastened her step to walk alongside her.

"It has been some time since we have been to Saint-François and Trois-Rivières. Perhaps I could strengthen our friendships with the People there, then continue toward Quebec, as close as it suits me. I could bring some wheat so they will let me pass. If Samuel is dressed as a white Indian, people would not question us. They will be too happy to get the food. It would be up to Samuel to get himself where he desires to be when we part ways."

By the time Bright Star had finished her astounding proposal, they stood between the walled-off fort of St. Louis and the Kahnawake village of longhouses. Smoke from the cookfires drifted, carrying the smell of fish and corncakes and drying meat. Dusk softened the points of trees on the hills behind.

"You would do this for me?" Catherine asked.

"I said only *perhaps*. I said it is a thing to consider, nothing more. But first, tell me this one thing. Do you trust Samuel Crane enough to send me alone with him?"

Catherine pressed her sister's hand between hers. "I trust him, and I trust you. It is myself I do not trust."

CHAPTER TWELVE

June 1754
Five Years Ago

Fireflies winked at Catherine as she made her way to the creek, the grass beneath her feet a carpet of cool silk threads. Hair unbound, she hung her towel on a rhododendron bush and waded into the water in her shift, a bar of soap in hand.

Faint sounds of celebration rang out from Kahnawake, made louder as they carried on the creek. Singing, shouting, drumming. Last night her sister of twenty-three summers had wed a new husband, this one twice her age, and the celebrations continued still. Being there last night had been enough for Catherine, though. She'd been invited, and yet she didn't feel as though she belonged. Red Fox was a warrior, brave in battle, and had the scars to prove it. Rumors of a new war against the British colonies were as many as the grains of sand beneath Catherine's toes. Both Red Fox and Joseph, now fourteen, had already been raiding British settlements on behalf of France.

Meanwhile, Catherine continued to nurture trade with merchants in Albany, and the two people she held most dear were British captives she could not imagine life without. Neither could she forget that the horrors that had brought Thankful and Samuel to her were French-sanctioned and carried out by Indian allies. Standing in the creek between two banks, she felt the pull between New France and New England, between Kahnawake and Montreal, between her father and her siblings.

Wading deeper into the water, Catherine sank below the surface entirely. Even submerged, she could feel the drumbeats from Kahnawake beat a tattoo on her chest. Only when her lungs screwed tight did she rise again for air.

Then she saw him. Naked save his breeches, Samuel jumped from the bank into the creek with the grace of a dog falling in. Her laughter drew his notice.

Smiling, he moved toward her, and she to him, until they were only a few feet apart. Behind him, night's curtain unfurled slowly, blotting a lavender twilight from the sky. But it did not hide the fact that Samuel had grown into a broad-shouldered man six feet tall who had nearly reached the end of his bondage. Neither was Catherine the girl he'd first met, the one starved for her father's love.

Standing up to her ribs in the water, her wet hair

hanging in front of her shoulders and floating on the creek's surface, she felt no shame at all and wondered at it.

"Thankful is asleep?" Sam asked.

Taking a handful at a time, she scrubbed her hair with soap. "Yes. It went easy with her tonight, and with my father, too. But my sister, I'm afraid, will be very tired come morning."

Samuel turned toward the noise of celebration. "I wondered if they were making ready for another raid."

"Not this time."

With languid movements, he sluiced water over his limbs and chest, then scooped sand from the creek bed and scrubbed his skin. "You don't seem pleased for her."

Catherine rubbed the soap along her arms. "She longs for children more than anything. Red Fox may give her many things, but I suspect he may not give her this. She would scold me for saying anything about his age, though. She would say that *I* am old to be unmarried, with twenty summers behind me."

Samuel rinsed sand from his shoulder. "Does she love him?" Crickets chirped from the grassy bank.

"No. Love did not keep my parents together, so she says she would rather leave her match to the clan mothers to decide."

Samuel dunked his head under the water and

came up again, blinking. "And you? Will you marry for love or in a match your father will make?"

Suppressing a laugh, she swished a hand through the water, pushing a raft of bubbles away. "He would offer no dowry. Besides, he needs me here. He wouldn't want me to leave him."

"You speak of Gabriel's wishes. I'm asking about your own."

The far-off drumming echoed the hammering of her pulse. "What I wish is irrelevant."

"It is relevant to me." Samuel stepped closer, until the ends of her hair swayed up against his chest. His fingers entwined in the inky strands, slowly tugging the bubbles free. "Tell me, Catie."

"*Konoronhkwa.*" *I love you.*

His lips slanted to one side. "In a language I can understand."

So forceful was the beat of her foolish heart behind her shift, she wondered that he could not hear it. "You have a little more than a year left before your ransom will be paid off."

"Tell me what you want."

Swallowing, she took a step back. "You will be free to leave, to go back to your brother and the land where you were born. You can do what I cannot. You can belong somewhere truly, in body and spirit."

Samuel's gaze drilled into hers. "Tell me what you want." He stepped closer, and the water lapped between them.

"War is coming. We all know this. You will want to be on the side you believe in, not the side that has taken so much from you." She paused.

"If you don't answer my question, I shall have to answer it for you." His hand came around the back of her neck, and she nearly dropped the bar of soap.

Catching her breath, Catherine curled her toes into the sand to anchor herself in place while the rest of her seemed weightless in the water, ready to drift into Samuel. Darkness thickened as night finally dropped its hem. Fireflies throbbed, and the bold rhythms from Kahnawake seemed to pull to the surface all the longings she'd meant to bury.

"My wish is that when you have the freedom to go, instead you will stay," she said. "With me."

Samuel bent his head to hers. "Need a carpenter, do you?"

"No, Samuel," she said in English to please him. "I just need you."

His lips met hers, and his strength wrapped around her, lifting her feet off the sand. Without thought, she gave herself up to the pleasure of wanting and being wanted in return. The soap slipped from her fingers, and her hands swept over his water-beaded shoulders and up into his hair. *"Konoronhkwa,"* she whispered against his ear, then kissed his cheek, his mouth.

Maybe it was the night, or the silver glow of the moon. Maybe it was the Mohawk wedding dance thrumming against her chest and through her veins. But what she felt in that moment was instinctual. Something primal and pure and fierce. If this was a love match, she wanted it. She wanted Samuel with a strength of desire that made her bold and left her weak, all at once.

Her long hair swirled and tangled around them in the water. *"Je t'aime,"* he said, and she believed him, his many kindnesses standing tall in her memory. She couldn't name the date it had happened, but over the years they had grown together, bonded by more than mere circumstance. When she laid herself down to sleep at night, it was his face she most wanted to see come morning.

Samuel's hands dipped into the creek and found the hollows of her waist, pressing her muslin shift to her skin. His touch was possessive, but tenderly so. With her fingertips, Catherine traced the scars on his back from her father's whip. Sam was her protection, her shelter, her joy and hope.

"I require no dowry, and I have nothing to offer save my unending devotion. But if you would have me, Catie, I would be yours, as long as we both shall live. And I would count myself favored and blessed."

"I would have you," she heard herself say, and watched the smile bloom on his face.

He kissed her lips once more, but held her firmly apart when she yearned to mold herself to his embrace. Taking her hand, he stepped back, putting air and water between them. "I will speak to your father, and we will wed soon, for I see no reason to prolong it."

And it would be for love. At last, she would belong to another in a way she hadn't truly felt since her mother's death. She would know what it was to be cherished.

CHAPTER THIRTEEN

August 1759

Bareheaded, Captain Pierre Moreau was waiting for Catherine when she returned to the house. He flinched at the sight of her, and she felt the blood mount in her face. "Captain Moreau." She extended the tricorne to him. "I believe this belongs to you. It made its way into Kahnawake."

He stepped closer, peering at her through the half light of evening as he took the hat and tugged it onto his head. "Is that you, Catherine? I didn't recognize you. Why are you dressed as a savage?" Perhaps it was only surprise in his voice, but she could not help but hear suspicion or disgust. "Why did you go to the Mohawk village?"

She spoke quickly, anxious to retire before her father saw her. "I went to Kahnawake to visit with my porter about some trade. Now, if you'll excuse me, I'd like to retire."

Moreau climbed onto the porch and barred her entrance to the house. "The woman we met our first day here. Thérèse Bright Star. You resemble her, do you know that? Aside from your blue eyes and scent of lavender soap. As I recall, she carried a strong animal odor about her person. Do you dress like them because you find that French gowns intimidate? I imagine there *is* a benefit in lowering yourself to their level when you visit. As Christ did when he came to earth."

Catherine bristled. "If you please, Captain. I will see you in the morning for the harvest."

"Stay a moment. I've been meaning to speak to you about that British military captive your father purchased. Crane, isn't it? There's something about him, the way he carries himself. Not submissive enough for a defeated man or prisoner. I get the distinct impression he'd rather not be here."

She didn't bother to hide a laugh. "Hardly a secret, I should say."

A chuckle puffed through his nose. "I suppose. In any case, with the harvest being so paramount to Quebec, I must be vigilant and at least raise the question. Do you have any reason to suspect he may try to slow down the harvest, interfere in some way? I've been waiting to speak to your father about this, but he doesn't seem to be here. So, if you please, what is your assessment of Crane's character?"

Catherine schooled her features into a show of innocence. "The fact that he isn't happy to be in our service isn't a stain upon his character. In fact, what kind of man would be just as pleased to be enslaved to an enemy host as he was to fight for his country? Show me a soldier like that, and I'll show you a double-minded man who can't be trusted."

Her pulse thrummed in her ears. She'd said too much, too quickly.

"Hmm." Moreau narrowed his hooded eyes at her, mouth quirked as though unconvinced. "This entire business of ransoming military captives and allowing them to walk about is something I'm still getting used to. I know it's common enough here, but it's unheard of in France. Prisoners belong in prison, and that's all there is to the matter. I daresay I'd rest easier if such were the case here, too."

The evening air cooled and colors dimmed, muting a patch of flowers next to the porch. Catherine's hands turned clammy at the mention of prison. It was a filthy place where inmates wasted away. Vermin had more to eat there than the men crammed into the cells. She reached down and plucked a flower by the stem, rubbing the petals between her fingers.

"I did wonder, since you mention the harvest," she began. She must tread carefully here and not give herself away. "The transportation of the wheat to Quebec. Will you require the service of my porters? They are more than capable of rowing the waters with bateaux full of precious cargo."

Captain Moreau's mouth pulled down in lines that bracketed his chin. "You're kind to offer. But no, ma belle, my orders tell me that schooners are coming to take the grain away in bulk. Can you imagine how many bateaux it would take to carry all the wheat and flour?" He laughed shortly. "I do thank you for the offer. But once the wheat is cut and some of it milled, we'll be on our way and require nothing more of you people."

Catherine's heart sank like a stone in deep water. If they weren't using bateaux and had no use for porters, how could Samuel escape unnoticed? "When do you suppose that will begin? The shipment of the harvest via schooners."

Turning, Moreau looked toward someplace unseen, his beak-like nose in sharp relief against the door he blocked. "Next week, if all goes well, and no more rain delays us." He pulled a timepiece from his pocket and buffed his thumb over its face. A nervous gesture, as if every moment must be counted. "No, it will be next week no matter what. The men in Quebec cannot wait longer, and I'll not have their deaths on my conscience."

Slurred singing snapped Catherine's attention toward a rustling in the woods. Gabriel stumbled out from among the trees, bottle in hand. Fresh from drinking with Gaspard Fontaine, no doubt. He cut short his song when he spied her.

"Let me by," Catherine told Moreau, but it was too late. The flower she'd picked dropped to her feet.

"Halt!" Gabriel yelled. "What's this about?"

Catherine longed for the shadows to shield her as her father covered the distance to the porch.

He appraised her. "The very likeness," he muttered. "Why would you do this to me?" He swayed up the stairs, and Moreau caught his elbow to steady him, tucking his timepiece away.

"What do you mean, monsieur?" the captain asked.

"Dressing exactly like Strong Wind. Her mother," he said to Moreau, who now looked on with understanding. "Yes, she's half savage. And fully bent on reminding me of the greatest mistake of my life, it seems."

The empty bottle thumped to the floor as he dropped it to grab her shell necklace in his fist instead. With one yank, he broke the string that looped around her neck, and shells clattered across the porch. Catherine's hands flew to her ears to remove the silver hoops before her father could grab those, too.

"You're a half-breed?" Moreau spoke the term lowly, as if it were foul language.

To Catherine, it was exactly that. She could not count how many times she'd heard it whispered behind porcelain-white hands, accompanied by girlish giggling. Invariably, recognition

216

followed, as if her deficiencies suddenly made sense in light of this revelation.

Frustration burned through her. "I am *your daughter.*" Her father always seemed to absolve himself of his role in bringing her into this world.

The blur cleared from Gabriel's eyes long enough for Catherine to see in them his disappointment in her. A shake of his head told her the rest. She was his daughter by a technicality. But she was not her namesake, Marie-Catherine, the perfectly French daughter he'd had with Isabelle. She was a substitute child.

"Come now, Monsieur Duval," Captain Moreau cut in. "You've been too much in your drink tonight. I have a matter to discuss with you, but I can see you're in no state for it."

The door opened and Samuel stepped out, stubble shadowing his jaw, candlestick in hand. He looked from Moreau to Gabriel. When he saw Catherine, his eyes warmed. It was not the first time he'd seen her this way. *Stunning,* he had called her then. *Regal.* And he had crowned her hair with wildflowers.

"Like what you see, do you, Crane?" Gabriel's speech seemed to slosh from his mouth. "Take my word, you were right to leave it alone the first time. Savage blood is no good in a wife. It's barely tolerable in a daughter." His head swayed to look at Catherine again.

Humiliation washed over her. It was the drink

insulting her, she told herself, but the lie was getting harder to believe. If the papa she loved was still within the man Gabriel had become, he was locked away tight, and she despaired of finding the key.

Jaw tense, Samuel put himself between Gabriel and Catherine, the taper's flame bouncing light across his face. Moreau shifted to let her pass, and she quietly stepped over the threshold. But she could not bring herself to shut the door on the conversation unfolding outside.

"Have a care, Gabriel," Samuel ground out. "You may not remember what you say come morning, but the rest of us will. Surely you don't mean to belittle your own daughter."

He should not defend her like this. She did not want his kindness when it changed nothing.

"Oh, don't act like you care overmuch," Gabriel snarled. "If you did, you'd have married her years ago, as you promised. You'd be living in that little house you built for her, but I venture that Moreau and the private were pleased enough to find it empty."

"Married her?" Captain Moreau's back was to Catherine, so she couldn't read his expression, but his tone belied his shock. "That house was to be yours and Catherine's?"

Gabriel scuffed his boots closer to Samuel, sending a spray of shells from her necklace into the dark. "You did well to stay single, to my

218

thinking. But you've no right to interfere with family affairs."

Samuel and Gabriel continued to spar, one voice escalating, the other steady, but Catherine no longer made sense of the words. For Pierre Moreau had turned and was staring at her, thin lips parted in unspoken questions.

Or accusations.

He knows, a voice whispered in Catherine's mind. She countered it with logic and reason. What could Moreau know now? That she was half Mohawk. That her father regretted her birth. That she and Samuel had once loved each other and planned to marry, but that Samuel had broken the engagement. What sort of conclusion could he draw from that?

She closed the door and leaned against it. Moreau could believe Samuel loved her and would stay for her sake. Or he could believe she loved Sam still and would help him escape for his sake.

Either way, the captain was wrong. There was no love between them.

Catherine had no idea why Gaspard Fontaine loitered about while she and Thankful labored over the washtubs, but he was decidedly out of place.

"Something troubles you, sir," Thankful tried. Clouds floated across the early morning sky like downy feathers. The air was sweet and clean, even if the smells from the boiling kettle were not.

"Does it not trouble you to be breaking the Sabbath?" he asked. "Or do Protestants and half-breeds not bother to keep the day holy?"

Catherine had expected the term to be repeated now that Captain Moreau had learned her blood was mixed. But hearing it slung like dung, she had half a mind to shove her bar of lye soap into Fontaine's mouth. Instead, she replied with convincing calm. "Our work in the fields has prevented us from doing laundry any other day of the week. Our clothes would stand up on their own if we didn't wash them today, yours included." She gestured toward his trousers and linen spread to dry on the grass.

"If it's worship you want, there are Jesuit services at Kahnawake this morning and evening," Thankful offered. Or he could do as she and Thankful had learned to do, and worship wherever he was.

"So I hear." Private Fontaine tucked a plug of tobacco inside his cheek. "The captain insists on our going, although between you and me and these fetid garments, it's not our souls that are uppermost on his mind. He means to talk to our Mohawk allies." Squinting one eye, he spewed a brown stream into the grass. "There is news from Quebec."

Catherine let the wooden stick lean against the side of the boiling kettle while she stepped away from its wafting heat, giving Fontaine her full focus. Thankful followed suit.

Fontaine edged closer, dropping his voice low. "Moreau paces at night. He says General Montcalm received a shipment of wheat from us on the twenty-third, but in order to make it last until he receives the next, he had to cut rations. The daily allowance of bread for soldiers, militiamen, and warriors is down by a quarter. The civilian ration has been cut in half. In place of the missing bread, the fighters are given an extra shot of brandy per day." He grinned, his stained teeth betraying his own penchant for drink.

Catherine winced. Thankful closed her eyes and murmured a prayer.

Crossing his arms, Fontaine nodded, clearly enjoying their rapt attention. "Word is, Canada's survival depends on the rest of the wheat reaching the army no later than September 15, for at that point, they'll be completely out of their stores. Moreover, news from the south is that the British plan to invade and burn whatever wheat they find before it can be shipped out. You wouldn't happen to know anything about that now, would you?"

"Of course not!" Thankful backed away.

He turned to Catherine. "And you? Don't you have plenty of British friends down in

Albany?" He paused. "Don't you have a very good British friend right here? Someone other than Mademoiselle Winslet, that is. Someone all too ready to fight. Or burn, as the case may be." He cocked one eyebrow high.

Catherine measured his stance, his tone. He was making sport with them, nothing more. "The only thing burning right now is the fire beneath this kettle of soiled clothes," she said. "Do you truly suppose any of us would be so foolish as to torch the food we've been harvesting?"

A dark laugh possessed him. "The truth is, I don't really care. Captain Moreau certainly does, though. He hasn't slept in three days. My guess is he suspects that if any British come to raid and burn, Samuel Crane would prove most willing to help. But me? I sleep like a baby." Fontaine ended his speech with a shrug. If Catherine didn't know about his brother's death, she'd think him shockingly callous.

Before she could form a response, Moreau hailed Fontaine. The captain's face was haggard, the dark bands beneath his eyes visible even from this distance. She did not envy the responsibility that stooped his shoulders.

"Time for church. Or more war-making, depending." With a bow and a smile, the rusty-haired private sauntered toward Kahnawake.

Neither woman spoke until the soldiers were well away, and then only in somber acknowledgment of Fontaine's news. Men starving, or men coming to burn the wheat—either scenario was unnerving enough on its own, but even more so was Moreau's suspicion. It seemed that here, on the Duval property, he saw werewolves where there were none. Now he went to mass with an eye to ally himself with the Wolf Clan. If it was warriors he sought, he would find them there. He would find Joseph.

Veering from that thought, Catherine stirred the laundry in the boiling kettle while Thankful spread shirts and petticoats to dry on bushes in the sun. "You took Samuel the salve for his ankles, yes?"

"I did, and he was grateful for it," Thankful said over her shoulder. "He said to tell you so."

Steam rose from the cauldron and seemed to collect beneath the brim of Catherine's straw hat. She lifted a shirt into the washtub. The shackles Samuel wore at Moreau's insistence had cut through his trousers and chafed his ankles until the skin broke in angry red lines. Though he'd made no complaint, the raw wounds required attention.

"You could have taken it to him yourself." There was no reproach in Thankful's tone as she took over Catherine's place at the wash kettle. "Unless it pains you too much to be near him."

Catherine plucked the bar of soap from the wooden bench on which the washtub sat and set to scrubbing the collar of her father's shirt. A strand of hair slipped free of the braids beneath her hat and hung straight as a pin beside her face. "He causes an ache I would rather go without." And he was still waiting for an answer she was not ready to give. An answer she had not yet formed.

Thankful was quiet for a moment as she prodded stockings and aprons boiling in the kettle. "I would not be surprised if your presence affects him the same way."

Finding the only sleeve Gabriel had use of, Catherine scrubbed the inside of the cuff with renewed vigor, the lye stinging her hands. "You jest."

"I do not."

Plunging the shirt into the rinse tub next, Catherine sent Thankful a sidelong glance. The young woman's face was flushed beneath her hat, flaxen tendrils of hair coiling from the steam. She fed another pine knot to the fire beneath the kettle and stirred the laundry again, one fist pressed to the small of her back.

"You don't look at Samuel, so you cannot see the way he looks at you." Slowly, her stick circled the kettle. "You don't talk to him."

"I have spoken with him, just not always in your presence," Catherine told her. "I'm not ignoring him, and I'm not angry anymore."

Thankful lifted her shoulders. "I'm glad of it,

but that's not enough. You have the opportunity to forgive him, and it would do you both more good than I can say. But Catherine, he feels more than guilt. Regret, I'm certain of it."

"Has he told you?"

"In all ways but in words."

Shaking her head, Catherine chuckled and spread her rinsed garments on a bush to dry. "Words are most important, *mon amie*."

"Sort it out before it's too late." Even beneath the shade of her brim, Thankful's eyes were bright with conviction, especially since Catherine had shared Samuel's story of Joel's death. "It's a chance to close up old wounds and heal. For your own sake, as much as his. Don't you see what a gift these short days could be?"

These days, a gift. Only Thankful would say such a thing with war raging on either side of them, with soldiers starving, women and children blistering to cut the grain that might save them. But of course, the battle Thankful referred to was the one within Catherine.

Returning to the washtub, she rubbed at apron stains until her knuckles grew raw. Catherine had spoken with Samuel briefly yesterday. It was during the harvest, while they paused to drink from the water bucket that was being passed around. She had assumed he'd press her for his escape, but instead, he'd spoken of hers. *"Leave Gabriel, Catie. He mistreats you, uses you as much as he ever did. Break away from him. We'll leave together, and you can make a new path for yourself."* It was far too similar to a previous proposal he'd made and had not honored.

Samuel's words did not close old wounds, but reopened them. She felt weak near him, when she needed to be strong. It was true that she felt scant love from Gabriel, but he was her father nonetheless. And who was Samuel Crane? He was a phantom, here now, but not for long.

"I believe you've rubbed that spot clear away, and half the fabric with it." Thankful's gentle voice pulled Catherine from her thoughts.

"So I have." Smiling, she transferred the apron to the rinse tub and swished the linen about. At length, she added quietly, "I will work to forgive Samuel."

Thankful dropped the laundry stick in the kettle and threw her arms around Catherine, pulling her into an embrace that smelled of woodsmoke, lye, and sunshine. "God be praised!"

Laughing, Catherine returned the embrace with hands still dripping rinse water. "Come now," she said, releasing Thankful. "We're nearly done here."

Movement flickered at the edge of the woods.

"Bright Star," Catherine called out.

"Go on," Thankful offered. "I'll finish this."

Thanking her, Catherine went to meet her sister beneath the canopy of a towering sugar maple, its leaves curling and unfurling in the warm wind. The beaked hazelnut bush tucked beneath it had dropped more husks to the ground, so Catherine scooped them into her apron pocket before pulling her hat from her head to use as a fan.

A rare smile curved Bright Star's mouth as she swatted the folds of Catherine's skirt and petticoats. "You would not be so hot if you wore one dress instead of three." She bobbed in a playful French curtsy, showing off her cool, soft deerskin. Her sheathed hunting knife rested on her uncorseted chest.

"But you have not come to judge my dress," Catherine prompted.

Scanning their surroundings, Bright Star beckoned Catherine deeper into the shadows that gathered beneath the trees. Joseph appeared, tomahawk in hand, quiver of arrows and bow slung across his back.

"I thought you'd be at mass," Catherine told them, "and instead I find you ready to meet an enemy."

"Always." Joseph looked beyond her. Spotting Thankful, he tucked the tomahawk into the loop at his belt and strode toward her.

Catherine watched as they spoke. Her porters, Silver Birch and Sweet Meadow, would have relished such attention from Joseph, but Thankful did not blush. Catherine wondered if he wished she would.

He'd had only ten summers to Thankful's seven when the girl was ransomed, and he'd made no effort to disguise his fascination with her then. Bringing her wampum beads and captured butterflies, he learned what chased the shadows from her haunted face. Eventually he had noticed that while she smiled timidly for him, she beamed for Samuel Crane. It wasn't until after Samuel returned to New York that Joseph had pursued a friendship with Thankful. She had not been as receptive as he'd hoped.

Bright Star tilted her head, lines tracing from the corners of her mouth to her chin. "See how he looks at her."

"As a brother upon a sister, I should think," Catherine suggested. Though Thankful was grateful for Joseph's provision and protective care, she could not forget that he had participated in raids on New England. The knowledge was a barrier she could not surmount. "She's been more than clear."

A chuckle escaped Bright Star. "What is clear to a woman is less so to a man. But we have not come so Joseph could go courting."

"Of course. I have news to consider." Spying a felled tree, Catherine placed her hat atop the trunk, then pushed herself up to sit beside it, the bark scraping hands already raw from the lye soap. "Captain Moreau says they won't be using bateaux to carry the wheat to Quebec, but schooners. So the original plan will need to be adjusted."

"Catherine." Bright Star sat beside her, feet dangling a few inches above the forest floor.

"I know it sounds dire, but I've been thinking about this, and we can still get him away. We'll need to do it quickly, though. Moreau already suspects Samuel simply because—"

Bright Star held up her hand. "I have decided."

Waiting, Catherine clasped one hand over the other, the sweat from her palm stinging her work-worn skin. A shining brown beetle waddled over a fold of her skirt until she shook it away. "Tell me."

"I have discussed the matter with Joseph. We have decided together. *Jaghte oghte.*"

Jaghte oghte. The literal translation was "maybe not." But in the Mohawk tongue it was plain denial, and it was final, however soft the bearer meant to land the blow.

Bright Star twisted a shell necklace around one finger. "We think it best to leave the matter of Samuel Crane alone."

They did not face each other, but looked straight ahead between the trees, toward the white linen hanging from bushes and branches. The apron Catherine had worked so hard to clean fluttered on a breeze like a small flag of surrender. Fanciful thought. The war raged on, while she wanted nothing more than for it to end.

So did Samuel. But he couldn't affect change from here.

"Joseph persuaded you against it?" Catherine should have expected that he would try. Still, "I thought you would come to your own mind on this."

"There is wisdom in counsel. Joseph knows the war in ways we do not. He knows British soldiers."

Almost as though he'd heard them, Joseph looked up from his conversation with Thankful. Raising his hand, he bade Thankful farewell and with long, purposeful strides joined his sisters inside the wood's edge. "I see Bright Star has told you our decision." He stood before them in a warrior's posture, as if Samuel was the enemy he was prepared to face.

"Samuel is not just a British soldier. I trust him. I know him," Catherine said.

"You knew him," Joseph countered. "There is a difference."

Catherine opened her mouth, but a response was slow to form. It was true she didn't know Samuel the way she used to. But was it possible that the core of his character remained unchanged, as he had said of her? "He's made mistakes. So have we all. But I believe his motives and purpose are for the greater good."

"His motives and purpose are British," Bright Star said. "The People are allied to the French, who would call it treason to aid the British. If I were caught, the consequences would extend to my family, my clan. The French would make an example of it, if not by official sanction, then by individual soldiers just waiting for a reason to take more land away from us."

The truth in Bright Star's words was impossible to deny.

"You share this opinion?" Catherine eyed the bow slung over Joseph's shoulder.

His chin jerked down. "I do not call the French a very good ally to the People. I do not wish to bend to their wishes like slaves. My concern here is the risk to Bright Star if she is caught. This is a dangerous undertaking even for a friend, and Samuel Crane is not her friend, nor mine. Catherine, he is not even yours, or he would not have broken his treaty with you. He hurt you and Thankful when he had it in his power to make both of you happy. Why would we help this man?" Lifting his chest, he crossed his arms and frowned.

Catherine's throat dried. How she loved this half brother of hers, shunned by Gabriel and yet fully devoted to his sisters. In many ways, he was the link between them. If he hadn't told Catherine when Bright Star's first husband and children had died, she would never have reached out to her grieving sister. If not for his encouragement, Bright Star may not have agreed to trade in Albany with Catherine. Now he had placed himself at the crossroads of their well-being yet again. Catherine knew he questioned her out of concern, not contrariness.

"I don't see this as just helping one man," she ventured, "but as aid for a cause. If what Samuel says is true, his information can bring a victory so resounding that the war would end before another winter sets in. This is for peace."

Bright Star slid down from the branch and placed a hand on her hip. "A peace by which his empire stands to gain. Will the British respect our land and customs any better than the French?" Her lips puckered. "I do not trust Samuel Crane enough to expose my neck for him."

"What do I do?" Catherine whispered to herself, barely aware she'd spoken.

"Do nothing." Joseph's tone brooked no argument. "Leave the British man to his captors. It is not your place to save him, so let his path run its course. But you must do nothing to change it." His hand again clutched the handle of his tomahawk.

"Promise," Bright Star prompted.

Catherine forced her lips to bend in half a smile and slid down to stand beside her sister, smoothing her skirts from her waist. But as they parted ways, one refrain echoed in Catherine's mind: *Jaghte oghte.*

CHAPTER FOURTEEN

August 1754
Five Years Ago

Crack!

Catherine sat up in bed, listening. Hugging her feather pillow to her chest, she leaned against the mahogany headboard and stared at her open bedroom window.

A pebble sailed in on a moonbeam and skittered across the floor until it disappeared beneath her bureau. Wide awake now, she parted the netting that surrounded her bed, then went to the second-story window and leaned out, her braid a thick rope hanging over her shoulder.

Starlight glanced off Samuel's cheekbones as he beckoned to her from the ground. With a finger to her lips, Catherine gestured for him to wait. Tugging a light shawl over her shoulders, she stole down the corridor. Snoring sounded from her father's chamber, and when she paused at the door to Thankful's room, she heard no sign that the girl had awakened. Satisfied, Catherine glided down the winding stairs and out of the house.

Samuel captured her hand and brushed a kiss to her cheek as soon as she stepped outside. Moonlight cloaked the moment in silver, an ethereal glow that almost convinced her she was still dreaming.

A dream, indeed, to have the love of this man before her.

"I can't sleep," he murmured. "I had to see you one last time before I leave in the morning. Come," he said. "I want to show you something."

The hem of her nightdress absorbed the dew from the grass as they crossed the yard, moving past the trading post and into the woods. "Samuel." Her steps slowed as the trees blotted the stars from the sky. She had no idea where he was taking her.

"Trust me."

She did.

Blindly, she followed him, her braid swinging behind her, brushing the backs of her legs above her knees. Fallen pine needles and twigs crunched beneath her toughened feet until they came to a clearing where a small wooden house rose up to greet her.

So this was the secret project he'd been disappearing into the woods to work on in his free time this summer. No wonder he'd made her promise not to follow him or ask questions. This was for her. For them. For the family they would begin.

"I thought—I thought you hadn't decided where we would live yet." She squeezed Samuel's hand, the roughness of his palms as endearing as his smile.

He leaned down and kissed her forehead. "I made up my mind. There's plenty of room in your father's house, but you know I can't share a roof with him. Even Joseph agreed with me, which is why he lent a hand a few times himself."

"My brother helped you?" She looped her arms around Samuel's solid waist.

"I caught him spying on me, as usual. When I asked for his help, he gave it. He doesn't say a lot, but I can tell he loves you very much."

Catherine smiled. Joseph had been more accepting of the engagement than Bright Star had been. "I'm glad you could work together."

Samuel raised an eyebrow. "Gabriel wasn't about to try. We're lucky your father is letting me go now and then pay off the last year of my debt after we're wed. He knows I'll come back for you, if not for him. When I do, I'll take you out from under his thumb, too."

"Samuel," she scolded gently. "He doesn't show it very well, but deep down, I know he loves me."

Samuel led her to a pair of rocking chairs on the front porch of their new home. He sat in one and pulled her onto his lap. "He needs you. As

235

he needs me, and even Thankful, whether he'll admit it or not."

Catherine tried not to chafe at his words. "Need and love are practically the same thing, aren't they?" For she loved Samuel and needed him, too. In different ways, she loved and needed her father in her life.

"Ah, but to love someone even when you don't *need* them—isn't that a deeper, less selfish kind of love? To say, 'I love you and will always love you, even if I stand to gain nothing by it.' That's sweeter still, is it not?"

She took in the depths of his eyes, moved by his sincerity but unable to grasp this kind of love. "That doesn't sound like a good trade to me."

Samuel chuckled and kissed her cheek, coaxing a smile from her. "I'll spend the rest of my life showing you what I mean. Now, as to this house, it isn't large, but it will grow as our family does. I wanted you to see it before I begin the journey tomorrow. It's a promise, Catie. A promise that I'll return after I've seen Joel. I need to tell him that what man meant for evil, God used for my good. He's given me you. And then I'll come back."

Catherine had no reason to doubt him, and it was only right that he visit the brother he'd spoken of so often. Yet she was unsettled by the prospect of his absence and the distance he must cross. Dismayed by his inference that he loved her but didn't need her.

"I wish I could go with you. I'd love to meet Joel." Gladly would she help paddle and portage the canoe.

"Your father would never agree to it. Keeping you here guarantees my return." He winked. "Besides, he may have begun the trading post here, but you're the one who keeps it running smoothly. The Mohawk porters will work for you in ways they would never work for him. He doesn't respect them, and it shows."

But Catherine couldn't ignore the foreboding that claimed her. "I can make arrangements," she said, her hand on Samuel's stubbled jaw. She breathed in his scent of sawdust and pine. "Give me an hour of daylight before you leave, and I'll go to Kahnawake to ask Bright Star to stay here and manage the post while I take you instead . . ." Her voice trailed away as she heard herself grasping after him. It wasn't like her.

Neither would it work. Bright Star would never work directly with Gabriel, even if begged. Besides, Catherine had Thankful to think of. The child would hate being left behind by both Samuel and Catherine. Her fear of losing Catherine was beyond all reason until one considered how she had lost her parents.

A sigh brushed Catherine's lips as she surrendered to the original plan. She would stay with Thankful, Gabriel, and the trading post. Bright Star and the other porters would take Samuel as far as Albany, where she would conduct business for Catherine's post, trading beaver pelts for British stroud and kettles. From Albany, Samuel would travel east to the Massachusetts Bay Colony while Bright Star returned to Kahnawake.

"I'll stay," she conceded. She wondered if this was how her mother had felt in those years when Gabriel had left her to go trapping. He had always returned to her, though months stretched long in between. How she wished she could talk to Strong Wind now.

"If anything should delay me, know it's only temporary." Samuel spoke in soothing tones, but all she heard was *delay*. "Come here, to our house, and imagine how it will be once we've filled it with children of our own. I'm coming back for you, Catie. Do not doubt it."

She turned to him, wrapping her arms about his neck, and kissed him with an urgency she could not name, a need she would not admit.

He loved her, and that was enough. He would come back to her. All she had to do was wait.

CHAPTER FIFTEEN

August 1759

Shadows retracted as the morning sun crept higher. A half hour had passed, maybe more, since Bright Star and Joseph had disappeared into the wood, leaving Catherine with their refusal to escort Samuel to Quebec. She understood their reasons.

And yet the matter remained unresolved in her spirit.

Wind sashayed through the branches above her, sending fallen leaves into a swirl that reflected her tumbling thoughts. Suppose Samuel did not take his information to General Wolfe. Suppose there was no battle before the British were frozen out of the St. Lawrence River, and that the wheat harvest was delivered to the French and Canadian troops on time. If what Moreau had said was true, Quebec might survive this winter, but what of the people of Montreal, with all of its grain gone north? And what of next winter? Would the country remain on the brink of starvation, cutting rations by quarters and halves?

The air smelled of warm earth and pine needles,

but Catherine could already feel the season beginning to turn. Another thought gripped her, bringing a chill to her skin. King George's War had lasted four years here in North America, and at the end of it, all conquered territories were returned to their original empires. Four years of fighting, suffering, capturing, dying, for naught. The only difference at the end of that war were the families ripped apart by raiding abductors or death. Across the Atlantic Ocean, France and England had vied for more land. The colonies had fought, along with their Indian allies. People died, homes were destroyed, and relationships ruined. And nothing was achieved.

Would this war be any different? Or, if British victory was inevitable, what would be gained by delaying it?

Unease screwed tight in her middle, its sharp edge wrapped in the usual hunger. The cramping in her stomach had grown harder to ignore. Perhaps she shouldn't, for it represented the hunger so many people now endured. The empires were using the colonists as a puppeteer pulls the strings of marionettes, but another year of war was one more year New France could not afford.

A rhythmic pounding drew her attention to Samuel perched on the roof of the house, hammering new shingles in place of leaky ones.

From the shade, she could watch him unobserved. But she would not allow herself to do so.

Hands still stinging from scrubbing laundry, Catherine retied her hat into place. Flapping her apron against a cloud of gnats, she stepped between pinecones and emerged into the sun just as her father came out of the kitchen, a yoke over his shoulders. Empty buckets swung from ropes on each side. Hat askew upon his bowed head, his left hand and right elbow held the ropes to keep the buckets from swaying too wildly.

Hoisting her skirts in her left hand, she hastened to meet him. "Out of water, are we? I can help, if you like."

"Let an old man be of some use yet, won't you?" His tone was gruff, but the plea behind it sincere.

"Then I shall walk with you."

A grin softened his weathered face. "And I shall be glad of the company. You've been gone so much lately."

So he'd been lonesome. For her. It was a notion both sad and soothing. Glancing at her father as they walked, Catherine noted with a pang how thin his shoulders and arms had become, how narrow his neck. Even his hair had thinned, either from age or the famine, or both. His hat slipped forward, and she pushed it back into place with a smile.

Beneath a sky of peerless blue, they went to

the creek behind the trading post and found the spot where water ruffled over rocks made smooth and round by its flow. On the opposite bank, butterflies opened and closed their black-veined wings on purple wildflowers. Gabriel knelt on one knee, and Catherine scooped clean water into each bucket.

"Ach." Pushing himself back to his feet, Gabriel widened his stance to support the weight of the full pails. "Look at your hands now. Come, let me see the extent of it."

Reluctantly, she turned them up and back again, revealing blistered palms from scythe and sickle, and cracked knuckles reddened from soap. "They'll heal, Papa." She slipped her hands into her apron pockets.

He exhaled the sweet tang of his pipe smoke. "I never meant you for fieldwork, you know. I'm not pleased it's come to this, no matter the bluster I may put on for the captain. The sooner his business here is done, the sooner you and I can get on with ours, eh?" He slanted his head toward the trading post. "We're losing trades with you away at the fields every day." The sleeve on his abbreviated right arm worked loose of its pin and fluttered in the heat-laden breeze.

As she repinned the sleeve for him, Catherine felt how reduced the stump had become beneath the linen. "Business is slow right now, anyway, and likely will be until our porters return from

New York. But I appreciate you heeding my wishes and keeping the post closed while I'm not here to manage it."

His laugh was not darkened by drink or bitterness. "You and I both know I make a muddle of things almost as soon as I enter the place. I don't know where I'd be without you."

The rare praise took Catherine by surprise, but she knew better than to make too much of it. "Thank you for saying so," was all she allowed herself, grateful that this time his words were a balm and not a club.

He winked at her. "I don't say what I should often enough, I own. And what I shouldn't say likely comes out too frequently. That's the drink, you know, don't you?"

Sunshine beat down upon Catherine's hat and shoulders. With only a moment's hesitation, she decided to take advantage of his good spirits. "I do. You're a better man without it, Papa."

Gabriel gripped the rope from which one bucket hung. His opposite elbow steadied the other. "It's a man's right to ease his burdens and wet his whistle. Besides, your mother tried keeping me from my drink for a time, and my body couldn't cope with the deprivation." He licked his lips. "The only thing for it was more rum. It's good medicine, that, and I take it faithfully." The discussion ended, he pivoted to carry the water away.

But when he cast a glance toward Samuel, who was climbing down the ladder from the roof, he turned back toward Catherine, sloshing water into the grass.

She went to him. "What is it?"

His voice lowered. "Moreau told me the Montreal prison is still overcrowded, but as soon as the space allows, he means for Samuel to go. I fought him on it, of course, since Crane belongs to me and has committed no crime. Moreau styles himself a stallion in that fancy uniform, but he's skittish as a colt. If he takes Crane, he'll be stealing my property. I daresay the law is on my side. But if you see Crane saying or doing anything to incite the soldiers, put a stop to it straightaway, or we'll lose more than we already have." He tapped the side of his nose. "Crane is an infuriating fool, but a useful one. Talk sense to him, Catherine, in the way only you can. I'll leave you to it." Bearing his yoke, he trudged away.

Samuel headed toward her, the sun gilding his hair and shining on bronzed arms where his shirtsleeves were rolled to the elbows. She met his gaze across the distance of years and broken dreams, for she stood beside the very creek in which he had proposed marriage.

But it was a question of war that brought him now, and she could no longer put off her answer.

Pulse quickening, Catherine beckoned Samuel

into the dappled shade of birch trees. "I see my father has put you to work on the Sabbath, too."

"The roof, you mean?" He moved his shoulder in a circle, the one he'd dislocated years ago. "I didn't mind. It was easy enough to repair."

If only all things were. "Thank you."

"You're welcome. By the way, you'd be amazed at the view from up there. You want to know what I saw?"

Catherine waited, head tilted.

"Your hands." Smiling, he reached into a pocket and withdrew the jar of salve she'd made for his ankles. "All right, I didn't get a good look, but if they held your father's interest, my guess is you could use some of your own medicine. Let's see."

Resigned, Catherine held out her hands. What a mess of calluses, blisters, and cracks. Whatever vanity she may have owned had dissolved in the laundry tub along with the lye.

"See, that's what happens when you don't spend years toughening up your hands like me." He scooped ointment out of the jar with his finger and gently applied it to her skin.

She sucked in a breath at his touch on her palms, fingertips, knuckles. The slight pressure brought relief to her skin, but her heart pushed hard against her chest. Mastering herself, she chuckled. "I am covered in salve enough for both of us. You might have saved more for yourself."

Replacing the lid, he slipped it into her front apron pocket. "I suspect Thankful may have use of it, as well." Bending, he snapped seed-pods from some pickerelweed, and Catherine's stomach groaned loudly enough to hear. It felt as though it were gnawing at her backbone.

Samuel noticed. "I'd say it's time you pick some seed yourself, but I don't think it would taste very good right now." He nodded at her ointment-coated hands. "Anyone watching us?"

A fresh wave of heat crawled up her neck. She glanced around. "No." She knew what he meant to do. If she weren't so hungry, she wouldn't let him.

"Here."

Wrinkling her nose, she opened her mouth. Samuel dropped some seeds inside, and she kept them there as long as she could, making them last before chewing. The warmth she'd felt before burst into a blazing inferno.

This was ridiculous. Here she was, sweating beneath the noonday sun, unpresentable hands covered in strong-smelling unguent, being fed weeds and blushing over it. The absurdity of it bubbled up inside her, eventually finding release in laughter.

Grinning, Sam helped himself to his own portion of seeds, then gave her a few more.

Was she going mad to laugh at a time like this? She went to cover her mouth with her hand, then stopped herself, but not before she'd smeared her cheek with salve.

Chuckling, Samuel wiped it off with the pad of his thumb. "How I've missed you, Catie."

For a fleeting instant, possibility fluttered. Fire and ice came together inside her, each warring for the upper hand. She had burned for him, and burned against him. She had gone numb in his absence, and his return had left her cold.

"Please," she whispered, all levity sifted away. "Don't call me that anymore."

Samuel studied her. "What then, you who push me away and then eat from my hand? You who stole the whole of my heart and keep it still? What would you have me call you?"

Yours. The word burst upon her mind with a suddenness, an intensity that overwhelmed her. With a violent shift, the gate to her guarded longings cracked open.

"What do you mean, I keep your heart?" She nudged peels of white bark on the ground with her toe. "Not now, I don't. Not for years."

A long moment passed, heavy with things unspoken. "I said too much. Forgive me."

Catherine needed to summon her wits. In their limited time alone together, there was much to discuss. She needed to think. "Samuel," she whispered, "we must talk about the war and your role in it while we have the chance, and not continue talking in circles about our past. But

I will tell you I'm trying to forgive it all. Can you at least tell me why you changed your mind about us? Was it Joel's death that altered our course? Was it the war and your loyalties to the British crown?"

He leaned back against a thin birch trunk. Plucking a leaf from a low-hanging branch, he smoothed it between thumb and fingers. "No. War was no match for our love."

Bewilderment lodged in her throat. Catherine looped her arm around a tree opposite him, pressing her hip to the slender support. Sunlight speared through the leaves above them. "I just wish I understood why you stopped loving me."

Samuel's lips parted. The leaf slipped from his hand as he leaned forward. "Did you not hear me? I never stopped. Whatever happens, believe me: There is nothing wrong with you. You are far too good for the trials you suffer. Find a husband, Catherine, to bring you the happiness you deserve."

She found no sense in his contradiction. "You still love me and yet tell me to seek another man to marry?"

"We cannot resume our relationship now. Too much has happened. There's no going back."

Unconvinced but not ready to show it, Catherine massaged the salve into her hands, coaxing it into her skin. Hurt and hope tangled together. "Why didn't you at least write?"

"Catherine, I did."

A gasp escaped her. "What? When? You mean before Joel's death?"

"And after."

The words burrowed into her and expanded until the pressure grew nearly unbearable. He could be lying. It would be easy enough to do and could not be proven either way. But she knew by his expression that he wasn't. "That's why you reacted the way you did when I asked about Joel."

A ridge forming between his eyebrows, Samuel tapped his thumb against the hammer hooked into his waistband. "I thought you knew. I thought you'd received my letter, and that your lack of reply was response enough."

The air left her lungs. Ache rushed in. Catherine felt hot and cold by turns. Water riffled and purled in the creek, and memory spilled over in her mind. The proposal, the parting, the promise that he'd return. The letter that never came. The empires must have been at war by the time Samuel sent it. *You could have sent another, tried again a different way.* She wouldn't say it. One could drown in should-haves and what-ifs. These were distractions from the chief matter at hand.

But he still loved her. Or had she only dreamed it? She could not—would not—name the stirring she felt. Catherine kneaded her hands. Possessing herself, she met his unblinking gaze.

"Sam, I—"

Footfalls sounded. They were too widely spaced to be Thankful.

Samuel closed the gap between them. "Say you'll help me. You know the way north, and you know I can't get there on my own. I must get there before all the wheat does."

She scanned their surroundings. Gabriel was returning for more water but was still too far away to hear their whispers. "Fontaine said this morning that the last of the harvest would arrive in Quebec by September 15."

"Then I must get there before that date." Urgency tightened his voice.

The knot of resistance inside her broke apart, transforming into an overwhelming conviction that a chance to end the war was worth the risks. Joseph and Bright Star didn't think so, but Catherine had disagreed with them before.

"I'll take you."

CHAPTER SIXTEEN

September 1759

Two weeks had passed since Fontaine and Moreau had come to supervise the harvest, and the fields were now more stubble than grain. Sweat glued Catherine's cotton gown to her skin as she swung the scythe, but this time the sun was not to blame. She couldn't put off the trip to Quebec much longer, but she still needed to talk with Yvette and Bright Star before she left. She hadn't had time to seek them out all week.

Stalks of wheat swished at the slice of her blade. Hundreds of women and a dozen soldiers peppered the field, but it was Captain Moreau who drew Catherine's eye.

He looked well rested. More than that, he appeared in high spirits.

"Good news, Captain?" Catherine asked when he ambled near enough to hear.

A genuine smile warmed his stony face, the first he'd offered her in a week. "Mademoiselle, I admit my mistrust in you was misplaced. You've been nothing but faithful in this work, and I'm pleased to say it's nearly done. The worst is over."

"Oh?" She rested one hand on the top of her scythe. "What makes you think so?"

"News. The English burned their entrenchment at Montmorency Falls after evacuating their troops and carrying off their effects."

Not far away, Samuel paused in his work, and she knew he was listening intently. The falls were just east of Quebec. If the British had abandoned that location, it could only mean one thing. "They're giving up on taking Quebec?" she asked.

Moreau rocked back on his heels. "Their General Wolfe certainly seems to have lost any chance of taking it. What can we conclude from his actions but his imminent departure? Everyone in Quebec is filled with joy. Confidence has replaced despair." Perhaps it was that confidence that loosened the captain's tongue, for he wasn't finished yet. "News here in Montreal is just as encouraging. The British intend to halt their advance toward us at Fort Saint-Frédéric, partway up Lake Champlain."

"That's only seventy miles to the south of us," Catherine remarked. Lake Champlain was part of the trade corridor her porters normally used between Montreal and Albany, at least during peacetime. The route from here to Fort Saint-Frédéric could be covered in less than a week.

"I would to God the distance were greater, but if they stop there, it will do. No one will burn our wheat. We shall survive the winter to fight again."

Catherine ran her thumb along the callused ridge at the top of her palm. "You do seem confident," she prodded. "If what you say is true, we have reason to rejoice, indeed."

"Rejoice, then. My intelligence is sound. It comes straight from the mouths of a British engineer and six soldiers recently captured on Lake Champlain. Canada will not be taken this year." He bellowed the last statement, arms raised in an impromptu hurrah. The field workers paused and turned to stare. "I've kept you too long from your work," he said, clasping his hands at his back. "Carry on. A few more days, and you will be finished with this business entirely. We all will. The schooners will be here soon."

Catherine gripped her tool. They needed to leave. Tonight, if possible.

Ten paces distant, Thankful's scythe slowed to a stop. A gust of wind blew chaff from her straw hat's brim as she pressed a fist to the small of her back. Pink-cheeked from exertion, she signaled to Catherine that she was taking a break to find water.

Watching her go, Catherine felt a stab and a twist in her gut.

Thankful. Could they leave her here, alone with Gabriel, Fontaine, and Moreau? The journey to Quebec was dangerous and treasonous, for few would agree with Catherine's logic. Surely Thankful would be safer here at home. Catherine would deliver Sam and come back as quickly as possible.

Mopping a kerchief across her brow, Catherine calculated how long she'd be away. The distance between Montreal and Quebec was more than one hundred and fifty miles. They would travel by river to avoid leaving tracks. Three miles an hour, ten hours a day. Barring any delays, they'd reach the city in less than six days, and then Catherine could double back alone.

Her hands tightened on the scythe, and she kept swinging, rolling questions and answers in her mind. The schooners would be coming to pick up the wheat soon. How would that affect their journey on the same river?

A burst of female laughter jarred her from her thoughts. When Captain Moreau's voice rose, ordering the women back to work, Catherine cast a glance toward him.

She did not see Gaspard Fontaine.

Neither had Thankful returned.

This morning Fontaine had been fractious and shaky, and he might well be resting somewhere in the shade. Too much drink, she had guessed at first sight, but on the contrary, he reported the opposite was true. *"As there is not enough rum to drown my sorrows, I've decided to face them, at last,"* he had confessed. It would take as much bravery as the private possessed. Gabriel certainly didn't have enough.

Tightening the ribbons of her hat beneath her chin, Catherine scanned the fields, then squinted toward the canvas tent the soldiers had erected for small spells of rest. Women lined up for their turn with the dipper at the buckets of water. Thankful was surely just waiting in the queue. Catherine returned to the task at hand.

But minutes passed, and still Thankful's scythe lay idle.

Unease clamped Catherine's chest. Her own scythe still firmly in her hand, she cut across the field toward the tent. "Have you seen Thankful in the last twenty minutes?" she called as she passed Samuel, whose movements were made awkward by his shackles.

Straightening, he shaded his eyes with a hand and pivoted to take in the fields. "Something amiss?"

She waved his question away. She didn't know how to answer it.

In moments, she had ducked into the shade of the tent. Conversations stilled as women raked her with silent appraisal, from the scythe in her fist to the moccasins beneath her hem.

"Half-breed," one whispered. "But I'd say the

balance is not quite equal. Does she not look more savage than French?"

Catherine would not relinquish her scythe. Given her growing concern, she would have drawn comfort from having Bright Star's hunting knife around her neck. "Thankful," she called, craning her neck to see among them. "Thankful Winslet?"

"Her captive." Another voice. "She collects them, didn't you know? Partial to blondes, it appears. Although in the case of that strapping man in the field, I can't say as I fault her for that. Pity he's the enemy."

"That's quite enough, *mesdames*." Yvette Trudeau stepped from her place in the line, bony fists on slender hips. "You ought to be ashamed of yourselves."

"Yvette!" Catherine went to her and bussed her cheek. "How are you?"

She gave a tremulous smile. "I'm well enough, ma chère, well enough for the times. Can't say the same for Lucie, though." She dusted wheat chaff from her shoulders. "But at least we had our fill for a night. It won't be long before I must sacrifice Maude to the pot, too." Her sour breath spoke of a chronically empty stomach.

"I'm sorry," Catherine said, knowing how fond Yvette had been of her chickens. "And I'm sorry I still have your ledger book. My notes are complete and tucked inside—I should have brought it with me today so I could give it to you."

Yvette waved her hand. "I haven't missed it."

"But it belongs to you. My notes may help make sense of Monsieur's dealings." Catherine dabbed her handkerchief to the back of her neck, grateful that at least the mosquitoes weren't as numerous. Soon they'd be no nuisance to speak of.

The line shuffled forward. Eyes crinkling at the corners, Yvette patted Catherine's back. "I'll tell you what. Come visit me once this harvest is done and explain it to me yourself. We may not have croissants to share, but I still have some tea set by for special occasions."

But Catherine fully intended to be gone by the time the harvest ended, well on her way to Quebec. "I'll be glad to come, Yvette. I may be delayed with other work, but I'll come just as soon as I can."

Yvette touched the back of her hand to her flushed cheeks. "I know you will. And bring Thankful. If she is as good with a needle and thread as you say, she may enjoy helping me with a piece of trim I just can't seem to get right." She winked.

A soldier called above the din to keep the drinks short. A wave of disapproving murmurs followed.

Catherine wiped her palms on her apron and

re-gripped the scythe handle. "Yes, of course. Have you seen Thankful today, by the way?"

A gnarled hand rose along the side of the tent. The seamed face of an elderly man looked up at her from where he sat on a stool. "I think I know who you seek," he said. "She went to help that fiery private, the one with red hair. Although he seems to have lost his fire today." He pointed to a barn.

If Fontaine had laid a hand on her . . . Catherine bid a hasty adieu to Yvette and ran through a shaven field, petticoats tangling around her legs, her scythe a weapon she was willing to wield. The ferocity she felt was nearly overpowering.

The barn door had been left open. On broken hinges, the warping wooden planks hung askance. "Thankful! Fontaine!" She pushed inside.

Dust motes peppered the air. Spears of light stabbed a cracked leather saddle and rusted tools pinned to the wall. There, between untidy mounds of hay, lay Fontaine, with Thankful kneeling over him.

He had her by the wrists.

"Catherine!" Thankful gasped. "He is unwell. Put down the scythe, for mercy's sake!"

Catherine stepped closer, the tip of the curved metal blade pointed at Fontaine's chest. "Let her go."

His teeth were clenched, and his entire body was possessed by tremors and filmed with a sour-smelling sweat. He was already in pain without her inflicting more. Catherine thrust the scythe into a bale of hay and drew near. His eyes were glassy and wild, staring into some unseen place.

"What's wrong?" She pried his fingers from Thankful's flesh, but the marks of his grip remained. "What happened?"

Thankful wiggled her fingers and rubbed a red streak above her wrist. "I went for a drink and saw him in the tent. He was soaked in sweat and holding his head, groaning. His head ached, his stomach ached, everything hurt, he said. I offered to help him to the barn so he could rest here."

Catherine stiffened at the girl's naïveté. "Did you not suspect it might be a ruse? To get you alone and away from everyone else, to a place you would not be seen or heard?"

Sitting back on her heels, Thankful pushed a strand of hair from her cheek with the back of her hand. "You'll call me foolish, but honestly, I didn't."

Catherine bit her tongue before she could lay out the danger Thankful had put herself in. *Foolish* was only one of the words that came to mind.

"I could tell he was ill. I gave him water to drink, but his stomach rejected it." Thankful gestured to a matted pile of hay.

The sound of shuffling footsteps and jangling

chains announced Samuel's arrival before his shadow fell inside the barn. "What's this?" Shackles slowing his stride, he still seemed to hurtle toward Fontaine. One glance at the finger-prints on Thankful's wrists, and he had Fontaine by the shirt, yanking him to his feet. "What have you done?" Though his voice was low and controlled, it was a thin mask to his anger.

The militiaman's pupils were pinpricks, his hair dark with sweat and slicked back. "Don't you touch me," he seethed, but his words seemed to be formed around marbles. "Unhand me."

"You'll tell me why you left marks on Mademoiselle Winslet first."

Fontaine's head lolled as he turned to Thankful, then back again, his expression hardening like cooling wax as he matched Samuel's stony stare. "She's fine. I didn't hurt her." He began laughing, but it was a mirthless sound. "Truth is, I never hurt *anyone,* never *wanted* to hurt anyone, and yet here I am, serving in a war I never wanted to be part of!" He struggled to be free, but Samuel held him by the shoulders. "And now my brother's dead, and I can't figure out a way to go home to my parents without him, at least not without doing something, anything, to make them proud of me. To make all of this worth it, you understand?"

He calmed, and Samuel slowly released him.

Quiet expanded inside the barn. The stalls that

had held livestock had been emptied when the militia took the animals for food. That was how Gaspard Fontaine looked now—hollowed out and spent. Catherine stepped back from him, and Thankful did the same.

Fontaine bent and gripped his knees as though about to retch into the hay at his feet. After a steadying moment, he uncoiled himself once more. "My parents have no reason to be proud of me. Look—I can't even stand upright without a drink. I unburden myself to a Protestant, a half-breed, and a man who, if I had met him upon the field, I ought to kill on sight."

The afternoon sun lit Samuel from the open door behind him so that shadows obscured his face. Even so, Catherine could see the working of his jaw as he listened. "I'm not your enemy now," he said.

Fontaine kicked at the chain between Sam's shackles. "You're a prisoner, fettered with irons, and still you are stronger than me." He held his head in his hands. "I ought to be able to best a man chained," he whispered. "And why shouldn't I? He is the enemy, and I'm no coward. Not anymore." He dropped his hands to his sides, curled them into fists. "I'm no coward!" He made a graceless swing at Samuel and roared when he missed.

Again he attempted to land a blow, but even with his chains, Samuel dodged.

"Fontaine—" Catherine called, but he was in a desperate place she could not reach.

"Stop this." Samuel held up his hands to block the young man's flailing arms. "No one called you a coward."

"But you think it!" Fontaine cried. "And I don't blame you. No, I don't." He pulled an old sickle from the wall and lunged with it.

"Sam!" Catherine pointed to her scythe, still half buried in hay.

He pulled it free. "Out," he told her.

Truly, Fontaine was more likely to injure himself than anyone else with the short-handled, curved-bladed sickle. She tugged Thankful toward the door.

"Stay," Fontaine shouted. "See me best the Englishman!" In awkward, jerky movements, he thrust and parried.

Samuel moved to the far side of the barn, drawing Fontaine away from the women.

"I'm going for the captain." Thankful slipped out the door, but Catherine tarried, unable to look away from the wreck of Gaspard Fontaine.

"You're in no condition to fight," Sam said, scythe raised, blade pointed toward Fontaine. His chains scraped the dirt floor as he moved. "We've no cause for it, besides. Not here. Not now."

"Right here and right now!" Fontaine lunged.

Samuel deflected the blade with the wooden

handle of the scythe. A wood chip split off and spiraled to the floor. Sam's posture was purely defensive, Fontaine's unwieldy and aggressive. Over and again he struck with the sickle, until Catherine feared the scythe handle would be whittled to a shard. Chaff and dust thickened in the air, lining the inside of her throat and nose.

A mouse darted from a cobwebbed corner, scrambling across Fontaine's moccasin. Sweating profusely, he swayed, stumbled, and kicked over a bucket. His blade scraped across his left sleeve and split the fabric as he struggled to right himself. He muttered an oath and wiped one palm and then the other on his *mitasses*, then gripped the handle of the sickle and attacked again. Whether from fever or hunger or lack of drink, he looked almost ready to faint.

It had to stop, even if the only one at risk of injury was Fontaine.

Catherine moved toward him, palms facing out. "You're unwell, Private. You must stop this. If it's a fight you're after, this isn't it."

"This *is* a fight, and I will have it."

"This is cowardice. This is no way to make your parents proud."

He rounded on her, furious, and in his moment of unbalance, Samuel knocked the sickle from his hand. It barely made a noise as it fell on scattered hay.

"Stay your weapon!" Captain Moreau's voice filled the barn to its every corner with a suddenness that took Catherine aback. How long had Fontaine and Samuel been sparring?

"None too soon," she said. "He attacked without cause and wouldn't give it up. He couldn't be reasoned with."

"I can see that." But Moreau's narrowed gaze was not on Fontaine. "Samuel Crane, you have attacked a soldier of the Canadian militia."

"No—" he interrupted.

"Your weapon is in your hands."

Catherine grabbed the tool from Samuel's grip. "You misunderstand, Captain. That's my scythe. I brought it with me when I noticed Thankful and the private were both missing."

"And Monsieur Crane took full advantage of the situation." Moreau peered around the barn. "He's been waiting for the right moment ever since he was brought into captivity. Apparently it was not enough to fetter his ankles." In three quick strides, he was nose to nose with Samuel.

"All I've done is defend myself," Samuel said. "If I really wanted to disable your soldier, don't you think I could have done it? Look at him. Fontaine is ill, in body and spirit, if not in the mind."

Not quite stifling a groan, Fontaine clutched his forearm. Blood seeped from the cut of his own making. "The prisoner provoked me, Captain.

He would have killed me had I not blocked his blows."

Alarm rang inside Catherine. "Captain Moreau, I saw it from start to finish. The facts are simply this: I found Thankful and Fontaine here, and Samuel came soon after. Fontaine snatched that rusty tool off the wall and brandished it like a sword at Sam, who used my scythe to defend himself."

"He bleeds, mademoiselle," the captain boomed. "The prisoner attacked an unarmed militiaman."

"Unarmed!" Catherine burst out. "All militiamen are unarmed until you need them to do battle, as you well know, so this bears no proof of Fontaine's innocence. He took up a farm tool against a shackled prisoner. The scratch on his arm? Made by his own blade when he stumbled over a bucket."

Fontaine collapsed onto a hay bale, leaned his head between his knees, and vomited. The stench carried.

"See," whispered Catherine to Captain Moreau. "See how weak he is. Samuel could have hurt him with little effort, if that was his intention. But he didn't." She rolled her lips between her teeth as soon as she heard her own words. It was no help to Samuel to remind the soldiers he could cause harm any time he wanted.

At length, Captain Moreau exhaled sharply through his nose. "We have lost enough time here. Go. There is still work to be done in the fields." After a few quiet words to Fontaine, Moreau left him there, then sent Catherine back out into the light, where Thankful waited, hands clasped.

"What happened?" Thankful looked past her, into the barn.

"It came to naught, thank heaven." Scythe in hand once more, Catherine began walking back toward the field.

A muffled blow sounded from the barn. As Catherine glanced over her shoulder, her breath stalled. Captain Moreau was leading Samuel away from the waiting harvest. Sam was bleeding from a gash on his temple, and his wrists were bound with a length of rope.

CHAPTER SEVENTEEN

The following day, Catherine still didn't know where Samuel was. After their shift harvesting on the island, she and Thankful shared the canoe with Moreau as they headed home. Catherine refused to help paddle until the captain had answered her questions, but Moreau remained unmoved. If Gaspard Fontaine had not spent the day ill in his bed, she would have interrogated him, as well.

Kneeling in the center of the canoe, Thankful bowed her head into her hands. She was coming undone with guilt. "If I hadn't helped Fontaine into the barn, Samuel wouldn't have come looking," she had moaned last night. "If I hadn't run for the captain, the matter would have resolved itself!"

Frustration swelled inside Catherine. She didn't even know if Sam remained on the island of Montreal or if he'd been ferried back across the St. Lawrence to their side.

At least Timothy Laughing Creek had come to visit last evening, and she had tasked him with ferreting out Samuel's whereabouts. If anyone could accomplish it, he could. Already, he had stolen the key to Sam's shackles and given it to her. Now all that was missing was Samuel himself.

Back stiff from a long day of labor, Catherine leaned forward to reason with Captain Moreau. "Samuel Crane is my father's property. You've stolen him, which is thievery punishable by law." She stared at the queued hair beneath his tricorne.

The captain didn't turn around as he pulled the paddle through the river, cutting a wobbly path toward the dock. "If he is your father's property, then he is your father's concern, not yours."

"What concerns my father concerns me," she protested. He could have no idea how much. "Samuel did nothing wrong. We've all done as you've requested. I insist you return him to our care at once."

A muffled chuckle bounced Captain Moreau's shoulders. "Star-crossed lovers if I ever met a pair."

She bit back a denial. Better that Moreau assumed her interest stemmed from the heart alone. She could not give any hint that her primary objective was a military one. "He's done no wrong," she said again. Sweat itched across her scalp beneath coils of hair and her hat.

Captain Moreau turned his head to the side. "Do not worry about things you cannot understand. War is the business of men."

"War is everyone's business. Have you not been using women and children to supply the army? The whole of Montreal will go hungry again this winter to feed them. Our first harvest in three summers, and we will have none of it." She stopped herself before pointing out the labor shortage, overcrowded conditions, and above all, the loss of husbands, sons, and fathers.

"We must all sacrifice for the greater good, mademoiselle." The captain's tone grew dagger sharp. "Perhaps it is the savage in you that carries on so. A true lady would have better comportment. You must stop. Your father and I have discussed it, and we've reached agreeable terms."

"Terms?" Catherine peered beyond Moreau's frame to find they were nearly home. Grey clouds billowed across the darkening sky. They'd been kept in the fields later this evening, and would be each day until harvest was complete. She had to find Samuel. If they were going to leave, they must do it now, or the plan would unravel.

Moreau switched his paddle to the other side of the canoe. "He is kept safe, where he can cause no further harm. Monsieur Duval is aware of the location and perfectly at ease with the arrangement, which includes keeping that location in strictest confidence, even from you. Especially from you. The moment the last of the harvest is safely on board the schooners, I'll release the captive back into your father's care. It won't be long now, I assure you."

A hard bump jerked the canoe as Moreau collided with the dock's pilings. Catherine reached out and grabbed one, then held her skirts out of the way and climbed out. "You paddled, so you can tie her up," she said to Moreau.

She helped Thankful step out of the canoe, then hurried toward the bank. "Did you hear that?" she whispered. "My father knows where Samuel is."

Doubt shadowed Thankful's blue eyes. "But will he tell you?"

"I mean to find out." Catherine looked over her shoulder and watched the captain make his way toward the cabin for the night. As she and Thankful neared the house, she spotted her father. "There he is, headed for the back door." She paused, studying how Gabriel walked holding his hand out before him, palm up. "Something's wrong."

When Catherine and Thankful reached him, Gabriel was in the kitchen, pulling out drawers using only his forefinger and thumb. Even in the dim light, a crimson trickle was visible down the side of his hand.

"Papa!" Catherine cried. "What happened?" She lit a taper.

Straightening, he angled to see her. "Home at

last, are you? It's merely a scratch, but I suppose I could do with a bandage." He turned up his palm to show her, and she plucked a small shard of brown glass from his skin.

While he sat at the table, Thankful filled a bowl with water from the urn in the corner, then brought it along with a sponge and length of linen. "Will it need stitching?" She leaned over to see.

Sitting beside him, Catherine set to work cleaning Gabriel's hand and examining the wound. "I don't think so, thank goodness. Papa, tell us how you did this."

"Don't concern yourself." His casual reaction to the injury echoed Moreau's sentiments.

Catherine huffed. "I am concerned. At least tell me where it happened so I can sweep up the remaining glass. What did you break? A bottle?"

"An empty one." Gabriel winced as she dabbed his skin with the sponge.

Thankful locked her gaze on Catherine, mouth buttoned tight.

"Where?" Catherine asked again. She unrolled the linen and wrapped it around his hand.

He shrugged.

She knotted the linen strips together. "Where is Samuel?"

Gabriel flexed his hand and smiled. "Can't say. But find one, and you'll find the other."

Whistling, he pushed back from the table and sauntered away.

A queasiness gripped Catherine's stomach. Whatever urgency she had felt before ratcheted up tenfold. She pushed the straw hat from her head so it hung at her back.

"What do we do?" Thankful cradled her elbows in her palms. "This is all—"

"It's not your fault." Catherine's thoughts raced her pulse. "Gather a change of clothing for yourself and for me, and meet me in the trading post right away."

Eyes wide, Thankful hastened out of the kitchen while Catherine snatched the bag of shelled hazelnuts, extinguished the lamp, then left the house and crossed the yard. Drying grasses tugged at the fraying hem of her skirt.

She fished the trading post key from her pocket and unlocked the door, nearly kicking over the water bucket as she entered. Moments later, Thankful joined her with a bundle under her arm. When she moved to light a taper, Catherine stopped her. "No light."

Even in the shadows, Thankful's surprise was clearly written in her expression. "What are we doing?"

Catherine moved between tables, barrels, and shelves. "Carrying basket, please."

To her credit, Thankful brought the Mohawk-fashioned basket without repeating her curiosity.

The container was tall, about as wide as her back, and with a tumpline to loop around one's forehead. With few words, Catherine set Thankful's bundled clothing inside along with the bag of nuts and explained what else she wanted to fill it. Into the basket went powder horns, shot pouches, bullets, a brass bullet mold. Flint and steel for starting fires, fishing nets, and hooks for repairing its lines. A quiver of arrows, a bow.

To this, Catherine added capes and blankets, men's clothing fit for a journey, and canteens. Bandages would be prudent. She would make those from old petticoats tonight. Lightweight trade items would be useful, for whomever they might meet along the way. Glass beads, tobacco, mirrors, utensils.

She recorded none of this in the ledger.

"I need a musket," Catherine murmured. "No, three." After setting the weapons in the basket stocks first, she turned to Thankful. "That's one for you, as well."

Thankful's lips parted, but she made no sound.

"We need to go. As soon as we find Samuel, we're leaving." Catherine untied the ribbons on her hat and added it to the basket.

Thankful did the same. "For New England?" Her tone was flat, but Catherine could not help but wonder if it harbored a hint of longing. For all Thankful's loyalty, wouldn't some part of her want to return to the land of her birth? The land of her mother's people?

"We go north." Catherine gestured toward the puncheon table, and they both sat. "You know Samuel is in danger," she began. "He needs to get to Quebec. He thinks he can end this war and the suffering it brings. Bright Star has decided not to take him, but he cannot go alone. It's up to me. To us, for I won't leave you here with my father and Moreau and Fontaine."

Thankful took time to digest this news. "I want to help him, if we can find him. Do you have some idea where he could be?"

"Timothy will find him. Whether tonight or tomorrow, we'll be ready for the moment when it comes."

Slowly, Thankful nodded. "I do not wish to fire a musket."

"Neither do I. But if trouble comes, we must prepare for that, too. If you could at least carry it, the show of force may serve our purpose just as well. Besides that, the musket may be useful for trade."

"With whom?" Thankful laced her trembling fingers to still them.

"Whoever has something even more useful for us. But I pray for a quiet journey, with only birds and fish for company." Outside, darkness descended, obscuring lines and shapes from view. "We travel between two empires at war.

We must be ready to transact in a way that benefits both parties."

Crickets filled the quiet that followed. Thankful had never been a porter, had never been farther than Montreal since she arrived there as a child. She was faithful, but she would also need courage.

"We only need six days to reach Quebec, and then we can come straight home again."

"Six days," Thankful repeated in a whisper. "But it must be done, and my place is with you." Reaching to a shelf behind her, she pulled down patch leather, an awl, scissors, and sinew. "For repairing our moccasins along the way." After inserting the items into a pouch, she dropped it into the basket. But a quake in her voice belied her misgiving.

Catherine reached across the table and grasped her hand. "With all that I am, I will see you back home safely."

A high-pitched voice split the air outside. *"To takyenawa's! Anyon' oksa!" Help! Hurry!*

"Timothy." Catherine stood, knocking over her chair. In the dark, she cut between tables of wares until she was at the door and outside, dread coiling in her middle. The swish of Thankful's skirts said she was right behind.

Starlight gleamed on Timothy's bare torso and pumping arms as he raced toward her. Kneeling, she brushed back his midnight-colored hair. "What's wrong?"

"A barn is on fire at the farm east of here, this side of the river." He panted and leaned his hands on his knees.

"The abandoned Langlois place," Thankful said. "It must be. But that's where Moreau has stored a portion of the wheat until the schooners come for it."

Catherine's mind reeled. Moreau had said the danger of British raiders coming to burn the harvest was past. Was his intelligence wrong? All that grain burning, when men were dying for want of it!

Timothy shook his head, chest still heaving. "I don't know about wheat, but a man is trapped inside. I heard him."

Catherine's insides turned to lead. "Run to the cabin through the woods. Tell Captain Moreau his harvest is burning!"

The boy spun and ran, the soles of his bare feet pale flags against the night.

Ducking back into the trading post, Catherine grabbed two hatchets and handed one to Thankful. Hoisting fistfuls of skirts above their ankles, they ran together toward the fire.

Smoke stung Catherine's eyes, but her feet felt nothing as they carried her over the ground. Behind her, twigs snapped and cracked. Thankful coughed but did not lag far behind.

Pushing through a copse of silver birch, Catherine saw it. Flames lapped at the sky from the old wooden structure Monsieur Langlois could not afford to rebuild in stone. Moreau had been so wary of fire all this time. It was hard to believe he would trust the harvest to a fire-prone structure, no matter how much credit he gave the reports that the British had halted their advance.

All of this passed through her mind in a fraction of a heartbeat while she moved toward the blaze, hatchet growing slippery in her sweaty grip. Timbers creaked and cracked like cannon fire. In a shower of sparks, a chunk of the roof collapsed.

"No!" Thankful cried.

A solitary figure came around one side of the building.

"Samuel?" Catherine ran closer.

But it was not a white man she saw. This one had brought an ax and was cutting a hole in the barn door.

"Joseph!" Catherine hurtled toward him.

Sweat beaded on his bronze head and rolled down his face. "Timothy told me before he told you. But I could smell the smoke myself." A cloth tied over his nose and mouth muffled his voice.

Samuel shouted from inside, but his words were mere sounds beneath the roar of the fire.

Catherine raised her hatchet, slamming the blade into the wood planks of the door, then struggled to wrest her weapon free again.

"Get back!" Joseph shouted. "I will do this thing for you. You will only hurt yourself, or me, or the man you came to save. Stay back, you and Thankful both." In the fire's orange light, his eyes were veined red.

Tendrils of hair curled about Thankful's stricken face, while loose strands hung at Catherine's neck. An explosion of sparks outshone the stars, then turned to ash on the wind. The atmosphere was thick with the smell of burning wood. But scorched wheat or flour? She could not detect it.

Perhaps there was no wheat in that barn after all. Perhaps the only object of the arson was the prisoner inside. Either way, surely Captain Moreau would be here soon, after what she'd told Timothy to tell him. Was it Captain Moreau who wanted Samuel dead?

With a mighty heave, Joseph swung his ax into the door again, then pulled it free. Enough damage was done that his hands could find purchase and wrench a piece loose. He kicked in another, repeating the process until the hole was large enough to let a man through.

Catherine pivoted toward Thankful, whose face was white as the moon. With one hand, she grabbed her arm. "We go tonight."

When Catherine turned back, to her horror, she saw that instead of Samuel coming out through the door, Joseph was ducking inside it. The burning barn had swallowed them both.

Thankful dropped her hatchet to the ground and then fell to her knees beside it.

Catherine ran to the barn door opening, choking on smoke and ash. Covering her nose and mouth with the end of her apron, she squinted inside. Beams groaned above her, spitting sparks into her hair, onto her hands and neck. Each was a white-hot quill digging into her flesh.

Half the barn was eaten away by fire already. If any grain had been stored there, it was destroyed. Samuel sat on the floor, flames creeping toward him from three sides. Ankles shackled, wrists bound, he was tied to the post of an empty horse stall.

Standing over him, Joseph brought a hunting knife from its sheath, the blade reflecting a red glare as he bent and cut the rope. Once freed, Samuel struggled to his feet and stumbled toward the door, followed closely by Joseph, who shoved him through the splintered opening. Sam cradled his arm.

"Get back," Sam wheezed, but his legs proved as weak as his voice. Catherine caught him in her arms, and he shouted in pain. Joseph dragged them both away from the building and into the birch trees.

"My shoulder." Samuel grimaced. "It's dislocated again."

"Lie down," Joseph told him.

Catherine turned away. A loud pop, a brief

cry, then nothing. "What happened?" She turned back to Samuel, unlocking the shackles with the key Timothy had spirited from Moreau.

Thankful scrambled to join them, hair slipping from the plait crowning her head, hatchet in her white-knuckled hand.

"Gabriel paid me a visit," Sam said, "which he concluded by breaking his bottle of rum over my head. It knocked me senseless. I must have fallen forward, and my wrists jerked against the post to yank my shoulder out of place." His explanation was peppered with coughs and gasps. Face screwed tight, he grunted with effort. "I can't move my arm. I won't be able to, at least not very well, for weeks."

Ripping her apron from about her waist, Catherine fashioned a sling to keep his arm immobile and close to his chest, recalling his struggle to recover from the shoulder dislocation he suffered years ago.

She glanced at the dark scab slashing across his temple where Moreau had subdued him the day before. "Someone obviously wants you dead." Gabriel was a menace, but he had paid for Samuel in order to work him, not kill him. This was either Moreau's or Fontaine's doing. She looked up at her brother. "He needs to leave."

Joseph grunted an agreement. A scarlet stream twisted down his arm where a shard of wood in the door had snagged him. Catherine tore a strip from her hem and tied it firmly around his wound. *"Nia:wen,"* she told him, her hand on his back. *Thank you.*

They formed a tight knot, the four of them. "Moreau is coming, and soon," Catherine said. "Even if he knows there was never any wheat stored here."

"There wasn't." Sam coughed on the words. "Not one grain."

Catherine nodded. "Even so, he will investigate, or pretend to. He cannot find you again. Nor us." She pressed the key to the trading post into Joseph's hand. "Give this to Bright Star. Ask her to pay the porters for me when they return. And please send some of the oysters to Yvette Trudeau, my milliner friend in Montreal. Do not charge her for them. Bright Star knows where to find her." She paused. "When Moreau comes here, can you detain him? Will you?"

Joseph's black eyes glinted with understanding. He knew what she meant to do.

Please, brother, do not stop me. Do not ask me to choose between your counsel and what my conviction tells me to do.

Joseph's jaw tensed. A breathless moment passed before he exhaled and looked away. "How much time do you need?"

Chapter Eighteen

They could not go back the way they had come. Clouds passed over the moon like a length of gauze as Catherine led Samuel and Thankful in a wide circuit toward home. The carrying basket was packed and waiting, along with the bateau. All they needed to do was carefully time their reaching it.

As they entered a small wood of oak and maple, the darkness intensified. Sounds magnified. The dropping of acorns from branches above. An animal—an opossum, perhaps—skittering through the brush. Insects. Sam's erratic, pain-saddled breathing. Footsteps.

Not her own.

The same instant she heard them, Samuel's uninjured arm came around her waist and pulled her from the leaf-muffled path, and she pulled Thankful with her. Sam had holstered Thankful's hatchet at his belt, and the handle poked at Catherine's hip. Backed against an enormous tree trunk, they stood drenched in shadows, as still as if they were on a hunt, but she felt as if they were prey. Bark pressed into her back through her gown and caught the pins from her hair.

It tumbled down, a black veil over her shoulder.

Heat and tension radiated from Samuel's body. The smell of smoke on his clothes was so overpowering that anyone could easily track them based on that alone. Catherine's flesh seemed at war with itself. Her face burned with heat while her fingers were freezing cold. She listened, straining to filter nature's night sounds from whoever was in pursuit. The hatchet grew heavy in her hand.

A bird whistled. A bird that had no business singing at this time of night.

"Catherine!" It was mere whisper, but she knew at once it came from Timothy. Fleet of foot, he was a shadow racing through the wood. "It's safe, Catherine. Where are you?"

She stepped back into the path and caught his arm.

The boy jumped in surprise but quickly recovered. "The French captain is on his way, and that red-haired man with him. Their muskets are fixed with bayonets."

Would they think Joseph had set the barn ablaze and punish him for an act he did not commit? "Timothy, run to the fire and warn Joseph the soldiers are armed for a fight. Thankful and Samuel and I must hurry back to the trading post. If we continue this way, our path is clear, yes?"

"*Hen'en.* But they will come looking for the captive, won't they? They have a lantern."

"Then we must hurry."

"And I will throw them off your trail." A dim flash of white teeth matched the grin she heard in his voice.

He sprinted toward the smoke and flames, and Catherine led Samuel and Thankful away. She glanced at Samuel, mindful of his injuries.

"Just how much does the boy know of our plans?" he rasped.

Catherine grasped Thankful's hand to be sure she kept stride, and found it as cold as her own. "He knows I wanted to find you. He is the one who alerted us to the fire. He stole the key that unlocked your shackles. But if he is questioned, he'll have nothing else to offer. Anyone would guess you're running south, not north."

"I'm indebted to him, and to Joseph." Sam spoke through gritted teeth. "But the fewer we involve in this, the better."

"I agree." Tightening her grip on her weapon, she hastened all the more toward home.

When they emerged from the trees, a yellow light glowed in the parlor, a beacon. Just outside the wood's edge, she turned to Samuel. "Take Thankful to the dock and get the bateau ready. I just need to pick up the carrying basket I left in the trading post."

"Take Thankful?"

Catherine should have guessed this would concern him. The risks of their journey would begin almost immediately. Samuel's injury meant he couldn't help portage the rapids, so she would have to navigate them from the water. "She's coming with us. You know I can't leave her here with Gabriel and the soldiers. We'll keep her safe. I've paddled through the rapids before." But never at night.

He hesitated. "Would she not be safer in Kahnawake with your sister? She's not made for the wilderness."

"She doesn't speak Mohawk. I don't think she'd be comfortable there."

"I'm not the girl you remember, Samuel." Thankful's quiet, clear voice pierced the growing tension. "I make my own decisions, and I choose to join you. Catherine will need help rowing. I may prove more capable than you think." She tilted her head toward the docks and freed Catherine's hands of the hatchet. "No time to waste."

Samuel made no further argument. He would tend to Thankful's needs, Catherine knew. But it struck her that doing so may also slow them down at a time when he could brook no delay.

Catherine spared only a moment to watch the two of them creep along the edge of the property before she hurried into the trading post. Samuel's face fresh in her mind, she added a razor and strop to the carrying basket, along with shaving soap. After positioning the basket on her back, she placed the leather tumpline on her forehead and turned to leave.

A gleam near the ground stopped her. Bottles of rum seemed to wink at her from the floor. She never touched it, never drank it, never encouraged anyone else to, either. Yet it remained the most popular trade item at the post. In all likelihood, they may need it on the journey, should they meet someone unsatisfied with beads or linens. Ill at ease, she bent and picked up two bottles before stepping back into the night.

"Who's there?" Gabriel's voice sliced through her. He was three yards away, weaving toward her. "Marie-Catherine? Is that you?" The hope in his tone could only mean one thing—he'd slipped into the past again, where he pined for the daughter born to Isabelle.

He stood before her, unmoving. How much of her could he see in the dark? Braids unraveled, her hair fell to her knees, as long as Strong Wind's had ever been. Her gown was French, sleeves edged in lace and skirts full with petticoats, but the strap crossing her brow held a Mohawk carrying basket to her back. Could he suspect she had filled it for the purpose of spiriting his military captive away?

"Papa." She trusted the dark to hide the truth that this Marie-Catherine was as much Mohawk as French and no longer willing to serve him.

"What are you doing out here?"

"Do you need something?" But of course he did. What did he ever want from the post but rum? She wanted to rail at him for his cowardly habit, for using it as an excuse to hurt people, for sneaking into the barn and unleashing his frustration on a man who could not defend himself. Her grip tightened on the necks of the bottles she held, and she bridled the confrontation that sat ready on her tongue. Marshaling her thoughts, she took a different tack. "Another bottle, perhaps? Here." She extended the rum and felt him take it from her.

Catherine had never offered alcohol to her father. If he was already too deep in his cups tonight to notice, she should consider it a mercy. But what she felt instead was a twisting in her gut, a tearing. It was one thing to watch Gabriel drink himself into oblivion, and another to have a hand in it. Men had died from overdrinking. Men had come to harm—Samuel had come to harm—from those who overdrank.

Many more die from war. Starvation, disease, battle. The thought jolted her from her reverie. Samuel and Thankful were waiting, and Moreau and Fontaine may be returning with news that Sam had escaped.

"Something wrong, daughter?" Perhaps he smelled the smoke on her.

At the moment, she was hard-pressed to name

something that felt right. Forcing a smile into her voice, she replied, "I have business to attend to. Go on and rest, Papa. It's getting late." True, every word.

Catherine watched him shuffle back toward the house. The dew-heavy air settled on her skin, and an owl gurgled into the night. Lantern light bobbed in the distance, flickering through the trees. Moreau's voice filtered with it, calling for her father. For her.

Snatching one more bottle of rum, Catherine rushed to the dock, the tumpline digging into her forehead from the weight of the basket on her back. The river blinked and whispered in greeting as she dashed over the wooden planks.

"Gabriel! Catherine!" The captain's shouts bounced off the water, making them seem closer than they truly were. "Thankful!"

Small white hands that had never touched a drop of alcohol reached up and took the bottles of rum from Catherine. Samuel took the basket with one arm. Catherine threw off the last rope looped around the piling and climbed into the bateau.

She signaled to Samuel and Thankful to lower their fair-haired profiles. Catherine's dark tresses cloaked her, blending her silhouette into the sky. She shoved off from the dock, then dipped her oar into the river and pulled.

"Where are they, you old fool?" Moreau's

question to her father raised the hair on Catherine's arms.

Wind cooled the sweat on her face and teased the ends of her fraying nerves. Samuel used his good arm to steer with an oar positioned off the stern like a rudder. As Thankful managed the other oar, the bateau glided noiselessly down the river, straight for the rapids that lay ahead. Escaping one danger, Catherine steeled herself for the next.

PART TWO

*Now was the time to strike a stroke
which in all probability would
determine the fate of Canada.*
—Lieutenant Edward Coates,
British Royal Navy

*Although we lacked neither faith nor hope,
the approach of night redoubled our fears.*
—Marie de la Visitation, Hôpital-Général
de Quebec

CHAPTER NINETEEN

The Lachine Rapids shone jet and silver as they churned between the two shores. Were it not for moonlight gleaming on the foam, there would be little distinguishing water from sky.

"Hold on," Catherine urged, but Thankful and Samuel needed no prodding. Thankful's lack of experience meant it was safer for her to draw her oar inside the vessel and let Samuel steer while Catherine rowed through the rapids alone.

The river kicked at the bateau in the dark. When the bow began to spin in the current's whorl, warning licked through Catherine. She'd misjudged their position, had drifted too far from shore. If they were pulled into the eddies or boils, the river would flip them like a toy boat in a waterfall.

Darker shapes emerged from the river, islands Catherine had hopped across with Gabriel as a child. They should not be anywhere near them now. Calling directions to Samuel, she made deeper strokes with the oar, her stays pinching with every lean and heave.

Water misted her face and hands. Her energy surged, and her oar became an extension of her limbs. Catherine dipped the blade, skimming the surface until the vessel turned toward the river-bank. With shoulders and arms made stronger by sickle and scythe, she dug the oar in and pulled with all her might. She felt a sudden loosening in her movement as her dress tore beneath the arms.

The vessel bucked as it rode the river, and water sloshed over Catherine's feet, soaking her hem. Had she been a fool to attempt the rapids? She let the question roll off her back, for there was no turning back now. All she needed was to get near shore and follow it downstream.

Catherine's pulse roared to rival the river, and the oar grew slick with sweat and spray. Her senses strung tight, she gained her bearings and had Samuel steer the vessel toward the dark line of the south bank, where shallower water flowed more gently.

All at once, the bateau rolled violently to one side. Thankful screamed, Samuel shouted, water poured in, and then almost as quickly, they were righted—but unbalanced. Catherine watched Samuel haul Thankful back into the vessel, pain from the effort wrenching his face.

The sight knocked the air from her lungs. Thankful had not been fully overboard, but nearly. "Are you all right?" she called. "Can you bail water?"

Soaked and dripping, Thankful grabbed the pail tied to the inside of the bateau. Her hair and skin gleamed pale as a ghost in the moonlight. She was shaking.

So was Catherine. She kept a closer eye on the glistening expanse around them, scouting for signs of holes in the riverbed beneath the surface. Her skirts pooled around her shins as she rowed.

By the time the water level in the bateau had dropped to her ankles, they'd reached the shoreline, and Catherine turned to glance farther ahead. From there, it was two more miles until they were safely clear of the rapids. When she turned back to her rowing position, facing Samuel, her heart was still thrumming.

"Both here," said Samuel. Smoke lingered on his clothing, layered over the musky smell of sweat. "Your hats tumbled out of the basket and into the river, but not much else."

"Thank God." Catherine grasped Thankful's hand. "Do we need to stop to change clothing, or can we press on? The farther we can travel by night, the better."

Thankful squeezed her fingers, then bent and wrung out a handful of her skirt. "Don't stop for my sake. I won't be the one to slow us down already. That was the worst of it, wasn't it?"

"I'm sure it was. It is calmer along the shoreline."

"Then allow me to help." Thankful took up an oar.

They soon left the rapids behind, and the river

gentled and grew quiet. The stars seemed almost low enough to touch, diamond chips scattered against night's mantle.

Hours later, Catherine estimated they had traveled more than twenty miles northeast. The sun had not yet awakened, but she knew they had passed into the next day. The rhythmic motion of the bateau and the quiet slip of water over the oars might prove calming if she were not constantly scanning the riverbanks and straining her ears for sound.

Montreal was the nerve center of Canada, Quebec its very heart, and the St. Lawrence River the artery between them. On either side of the watery highway, *arpents* of cultivated land stretched back into woods. Farmhouses and barns drew dark shapes against the sky. Would Moreau or Fontaine be hiding among them in wait? If they had found horses to ride, they could have outpaced the bateau already. Catherine's thoughts bounced from them to Joseph and to Gabriel, wondering how the night had passed for them.

A haunting, high-pitched warbling captured her attention before she saw the loons. Aside from the white at their throats, they were obsidian black, scarcely visible on the river they shared. Hidden, but not hiding. Catherine envied them.

Adjusting her grip on her oar, she resumed the dip and pull that came so naturally to her.

Dawn would soon lay a crimson ribbon atop the river. When it did, they should not be here to greet it.

"There." She pointed. "You see that spot up on the right, a break in the trees along the bank? We'll land there. A cavern lies just beyond it where we can rest."

"You're sure?" Samuel asked.

"It's the best spot we'll find in thirty miles."

The river was mercifully placid here. As it shallowed near the landing place, the current thinned to a silver shine that purled over the rocks near the edge.

With a groaning slide, the bateau bumped up onto the pebbled beach. Samuel climbed out, the carrying basket over one shoulder, and set it on the ground. Thankful followed suit, bringing the bottles of rum, while Catherine lashed the oars securely to the inside of the vessel with leather strips.

"Now we sink it," she said.

Thankful looked at her askance. In the fading night, dark bands hung beneath her wide eyes.

"It's too wide to fit through the passage we'll take," Catherine explained. "Nor will we want to leave it here to signal our presence. We'll pile rocks inside until it's completely submerged. Over there, beneath that outcropping. No one will know we're here. Then tonight we pull it up again."

Keeping one arm tight to his middle, Samuel had already begun filling the vessel as she explained, though the tension in his shoulders hinted at unspoken pain. With all three of them working together, the task was accomplished in less than a quarter of an hour. The bateau slipped beneath the river's surface, hidden further by the shadows of the rock that jutted out over it. The black limestone here was soft and had been cut away by water over the years. The cavern where they would rest had been formed in the same way.

Catherine tucked the rum bottles into the basket, then hoisted it into position on her back. But Samuel took it from her to carry himself, strap across his own brow.

Thanking him, she placed a hand on Thankful's shoulder. How delicate she seemed, still wet with the river that had almost claimed her. Catherine hoped the scare in the rapids would not amplify her every misgiving.

"It's not far, mon amie. Soon we shall rest and dry out. You've done well. You've been brave and helpful." Catherine lifted evergreen boughs from the ground as they walked.

A wan smile cracked Thankful's lips. "I've been terrified, though I desperately want to be courageous for you and Sam."

Catherine had been frightened in the rapids, too, but would such a confession dissolve their confidence in her ability to take them safely to Quebec? She needed to be strong and bold for all of their sakes, including her own. Holding back a large hemlock branch, she let Thankful pass ahead of her. Samuel took the branch and gestured for Catherine to follow her.

"What is courage," he said, "but moving forward in the face of fear? If there was nothing to be afraid of, we would have no need to be brave."

Watery light filtered through the trees, too dim to call dawn but strong enough to show that Samuel's words had brought the sunshine back into Thankful's face. Following Catherine's example, she gathered loose boughs into her arms.

"A rest will do you good," Samuel added. "It will do all of us good." He'd always had a way of bolstering Thankful. His voice was still serrated from the fire, and yet it was the very sound of comfort.

Catherine caught his gaze and smiled her appreciation. He returned it, then looked toward the narrow slit in the black limestone cliff ahead of them. In single file, they entered and passed between dank walls beaded with condensation until the cave opened to a space the size of a drawing room. Several yards above, the sky peeked over the ledge, its color a match for the inside of a clamshell.

After laying the boughs on the soft limestone ground, Catherine covered them with stroud blankets to make sleeping pallets.

"Can you rest?" Thankful asked her.

"Soon." Slowly, Catherine rolled her head from one shoulder to the other. Her muscles were nearly as stiff as her mud-caked skirts. "But first, I'm going to wash." She pointed to another opening on the opposite side of the cavern. "Just through there is a path to a well-behaved little creek."

Thankful smiled. "I'll wash, too. But if you don't mind, I'll sleep first, right after I change out of these wet things. Just wake me if I sleep too long."

"Rest while you can." Samuel's voice was tired but determined. "Go ahead, both of you. I'll keep watch on the river for a spell."

The cavern walls bottled the gentle sound of the water. It whirled around and over them, a lullaby to cover them, though night had broken and day was at the door. In that moment, Catherine could almost believe it was just the three of them alone in the world, though she knew the dangers that awaited outside the cavern, the empires and colonies at war. Perhaps it was the combination of excitement and fatigue that made her weak, for she gave herself up to the simple sensation of being with Thankful and Samuel, the feeling of being needed. Of belonging.

With a smile, she took a change of clothing from the basket and picked her way to the creek she remembered.

A thicket of trees screening her, she peeled the layers from her body one by one. Off came the front-lacing French gown with its stomacher, fichu, and lace-pinned sleeves. Off came the underpinnings of corset and petticoats. With the stripping away of each item, she felt a weight released from her spirit. Wearing only her shift, she waded into the water.

Submerging herself up to her neck, she found the creek cold but not chilling. Water trickled over moss-glazed rocks at the creek's edge with a musical chiming sound. A whippoorwill trilled his relentless song, and Catherine inhaled the invigorating air. She scooped a handful of sand from the creek bed and scrubbed her skin free of smoke and soot and sweat.

Images crowded her mind, pressing from all sides of her consciousness. She saw Gabriel, disappointed in the color of her skin, the length of her hair, the planes of her cheeks that were broader than his. She saw the mesdames of the Montreal school as they tried to scrub the "savage" out of her and then disguise it in silk and lace. Catherine even saw the resentment in Bright Star when she'd learned of Thankful's ransom.

She did not believe in ghosts, but she did

believe in memories. And these laid thick a residue that congealed to her spirit until she struggled to separate who she was from the judgment that came with who she was not. What would they all think of her now? It took no effort to conjure it. They would say she had defied her mother's people and her father's people, both. *Catherine Stands-Apart.*

She clapped another handful of sand to her skin and rubbed until the spot glowed red, then let it return to its golden hue. Here in this creek, behind a black cavern shaped by water, she would shed the burden of others' expectations. She would be the river that set its own course and not the rock hollowed out by continual force. A river that flowed between nations and did not heed a man-made war.

The river that carried Samuel where he needed to go.

Sluicing the creek water from her face and arms, she stepped out onto dry land and traded her filthy, wet shift for a dress of butter-soft buckskin over blue linen leggings. Casting a glance at her soot-stained gown, she ripped the French lace and ribbon trim from the bodice and used it to bind her hair into a knot at the nape of her neck.

Half-breed, some called her. But she was wholly who the Great Good God had made her, and wholly set upon this path.

• • •

When Catherine found him, Samuel was sitting on an outcropping overlooking the river, shielded by yellow birch and eastern hemlock trees. Between the branches, she glimpsed a sky layered with sunrise shades of scarlet, marigold, and indigo. A white-throated sparrow heralded the dawn with its two-toned song.

Catherine lowered herself to sit beside Samuel, nestling between two long birch roots that seemed made for that purpose. "I'll take over. Go rest," she suggested. "Or bathe. You'll find fresh clothing in the basket. I also foraged a bit behind the cavern." Cupped in one hand were oyster-colored mushrooms she'd broken off a maple trunk. In the other she held a bouquet of sorrel, along with a few clusters of bright red ginseng berries still on the stem. She'd eaten her fill already and had set some by for Thankful, too.

He turned and seemed to take in the whole of her with his eyes. In that unguarded moment, his lips parted, then closed as he pinned his attention to the food in her hands.

"I've startled you." She dropped the mushrooms into his palm and set the sorrel and ginseng down between them.

"Yes. Thank you for this." Samuel ran his thumb over the velvety gills beneath a mushroom's cap before popping it into his mouth. He did not look at her again as he ate the rest of the food, down to the last sour sorrel leaf and nearly tasteless ginseng berry.

Twisting the fringe of her dress around her fingers, she wondered if her very presence offended him somehow, as his had offended her. "I'm—" But no. She would not apologize for how she looked or who she was.

"Comfortable?" he finished for her, stealing a glance. He picked up a small round hemlock cone. "And beautiful," he murmured.

Heat climbed into Catherine's cheeks. "Some would call the piecing together of French and Mohawk a garish thing."

"I'm not talking about clothing, but the woman who wears it." He drew back the hemlock cone as if to hurl it into the river, then thought better of it and settled for rolling it in one hand. "You are not pieced together, Catie. You are not half of one thing, half of another. You are wholly Catherine, don't you see? Look." Pointing to the river with the cone still tucked into his palm, he leaned close enough that she felt the warmth radiating from him. "The St. Lawrence River is one river. In some places it foams white, in others it is as still and green as grass, or blue as your ey—blue as trade beads. Its behavior calm and turbulent by turns. The river is many colors and many temperaments, but it is one river."

Samuel took her hand and turned it over, exposing the veins mapping the inside of her wrist. With his fingertip, he grazed a line. "You have French blood and Mohawk blood both. I know you feel they war against each other, but they needn't. You are more than the blood of your parents' peoples. You have courage, compassion, intelligence, strength. All of this makes you who you are."

All of this, she had just realized at the creek. But hearing it from Samuel seemed to crystalize the truth of it. The urge to slide her hand beneath his, to entwine their fingers, brought a heat blazing across her face and neck. Withdrawing her hand, she tucked a piece of hair back under the ribbon meant to bind it. "Thank you," she whispered.

"Thank *you*. For this." He swept his arm toward the river. "You are as brave as you are lovely." His cheeks darkened to rival the shade of the berries on a nearby viburnum bush, but he made no move to stand. He was uncomfortable yet chose to stay.

Folding her legs beneath her skirt, she searched for something to say. Through the foliage overhead, sunlight bloomed upon the ground. "You never told me what happened, Samuel. When you were captured during this war," she clarified.

"You never asked."

"I'm asking now." Strange, she mused, that war was a safer subject than love. "If you don't mind telling me."

Sam frowned. "It doesn't make for good telling." He shrugged. When she said nothing, he continued. "It was the end of July, I think. You lose track of the days when afield. We were getting ready to take Fort Saint-Frédéric from the French, and we knew we could do it." He glanced at her. "You must know the place I mean."

She did. Situated on a narrows of Lake Champlain, Fort Saint-Frédéric was a hub of activity for French soldiers, with an eight-sided blockhouse presiding over a chapel, barracks, a bakehouse, a storehouse, and a windmill. In addition, Iroquois natives, English captives, African slaves, and the Hudson Valley Dutch could all be found there to trade or be traded to places as far as Quebec or even Boston.

"Then you know the fort has been a thorn in our side for decades," Samuel went on, "as the departure point for French raids into New England. This summer, we had our chance to destroy it. Ironic that the French did it for us, burning it upon their retreat. But I've gotten ahead of myself. I wasn't even there to see that."

The story was familiar. Joseph had returned to Kahnawake in early August, infuriated that the French had given up the fort on Lake Champlain without a fight.

"Let me back up a few days. Our General Amherst was getting ready to attack. I was part of a scout of three dozen men sent in advance to collect intelligence that might prove useful. The number of soldiers, condition of the defenses, that sort of thing. I was the leader of that patrol, and I ordered all of us to get close. Closer than some of them wanted to go." He winced.

"Closer than necessary?" She plucked a leaf from the bush beside her and ran her finger along its saw-toothed edge.

"It was necessary to the object of our mission. We needed good intelligence, Catie. I was a provincial, and my superior officer was a pompous wig-wearing redcoat fresh from England, whose disdain for the Americans in his unit was so thick we thought he might choke on it. Wished he would, at times." He chuckled, then grew grave once more. "These officers from England—I respect their decades of service, but the wars they fought were in Europe, not here in the North American colonies. Tactics are different here, as Braddock certainly found out down in Virginia."

"Braddock?" Catherine had heard the name, but couldn't place it in proper context now.

Samuel flicked another scale off the cone with his thumb. "In short: Celebrated English officer came to save the day. Provincial named George Washington tried to explain a new way to fight the French and Indians. Celebrated English officer didn't listen, wound up killed in an ambush, and a chest full of his letters fell into French hands, revealing his next plans. Total debacle."

"And your officer was cut of similar cloth?" She grazed her thumb over the fine hairs on the underside of the leaf, then discarded it and clasped her hands.

"The very same. Bright red, and no give at all. He wouldn't listen to me when I tried to warn him about French native tactics. So when it came time to lead the scout, I was determined to prove myself. To bring back the most accurate information possible."

Closing his eyes, he bent one knee and rested an elbow upon it. The silence stretched so long between them, Catherine wondered if he'd fallen asleep. The sun gained strength, and the rock began to lose its chill beneath her.

"When we were ambushed, the war cries were so terrifying, some of the young men—boys, really—lost their bowels on the spot. The natives all had black-painted faces and scalp locks. They loosed arrows and shot muskets, filling the air with smoke."

Catherine's tongue stuck to the roof of her mouth. "Kahnawake warriors?"

He nodded.

Joseph? But she could not bring herself to ask.

There were many Mohawk defending that fort. Joseph may still have been inside the walls.

"Our attackers were three times our number, with French soldiers just on the other side of the wall. Most of us were taken as captives and sent to Montreal for trade. But first they made us watch the fate of ten of our men." He brought the heels of his hands to his eyes, and his lips pulled tight against his teeth.

"Don't say it," she whispered. "You don't need to tell me." Some warriors, when they came to her post, traded with stories on their tongues. Some were mere exaggerations. She knew now that the ones about the ambush outside Fort Saint-Frédéric were not.

Ten men scalped, mutilated, killed, perhaps in that order. Ten heads cut off and set upon poles to greet the English attackers when they came.

Understanding tugged Catherine in both directions. No defense sprang to her tongue on behalf of the Mohawk warriors, nor did she blame them for participating in the war in the only way they knew how. And yet she could well imagine the horrors that Samuel had lived through, and those his fellow soldiers had not. She had seen the heads on poles, the clutches of scalps. She had sold them herself.

A fine sheen of sweat glistened on Samuel's face. "When Amherst attacked, the French fled. As I said, I was gone by then, but news was easy to learn once we got to Montreal. The French just gave it up, burning what they could on their departure. Their native allies were furious."

"Of course they were," she said quietly. "Their hunting grounds are at stake. The Mohawk fight this war for the French, but not according to French rules."

"I've noticed."

"The Mohawk are fighting because they said they were the friends of the French, and friends fight with and for each other. But the People measure bravery by plunder, captives, and kills."

Samuel allowed a dark laugh to escape. "Then our attackers must have been happy to get at us before the French abandoned the fort."

Catherine drew her knees to her chest and crossed her hands over her moccasins. The porcupine quills and beads were cool and hard under her palms, which had grown damp with sweat. "Yes," she admitted. "I do not defend their practices, Samuel. I'm only explaining how they see it. It isn't the European way."

"It isn't a European war, and both France and England would do well to remember it." His tone was sharp and layered with regrets.

"What happened that day outside Fort Saint-Frédéric—"

"The massacre."

Catherine didn't deny it. Sparrows still whistled on the branches above them, near enough for the spots of yellow above their eyes and black stripes on their small heads to be visible. "It wasn't your fault."

"I still see the faces of my men on those poles. Every night. Sometimes I even see them in the day." His voice pulled taut. "Now the British and Americans are building a new fort on that land, much better than the flimsy blockhouse that burned down. Crown Point, they call it."

Catherine lifted a flat hemlock needle from the ground and pressed it between her fingers until her skin became scented with its oil. "How do you know this?"

"I overheard Captain Moreau telling Fontaine. The British engineer captured by the French certainly had a lot to say. Crown Point will be Amherst's new headquarters. But I'm more interested in Monsieur Montcalm's in Quebec." Rising, he brushed dirt and pinecone scales from his trousers.

Catherine stood as well and noticed the color had drained from Samuel's face. Her gut twisted. She'd forgotten how intensely she could feel on his behalf. But this was how it had always been between the two of them. When Samuel was recovering from his broken leg, her heart had buckled in sympathy. When Gabriel belittled Catherine, it was Samuel who couldn't bear to eat.

He peered at the river once more. "Wake me

if you see anything." Then he turned, and chips of limestone crunched beneath his retreating feet. He pushed a branch out of his way as he brushed past it, and Catherine watched it sway until it slowed to a halt.

An ache throbbed beneath her skull. She turned her attention back to the river, scanning for any vessels, but the pressure in her chest would not relent. Perhaps the tie between them had not been completely severed after all.

CHAPTER TWENTY

By late morning, Catherine was restless. From her perch on the outcropping, she scanned the river in both directions before walking down to where the water lapped the land. Reveling in the freedom of movement her deerskin dress and leggings afforded, she squatted by the river and filled her canteen.

The river was quiet today. A kingfisher dove in to snatch his prey with his long black beak, then soared away again as quickly. Rising, Catherine watched its flight.

Far in the distance, a small white square rose above the surface of the river. Soon it would become two white squares, perhaps three, and they would no longer be small. They were ship sails.

Hastening back up to her screened overlook, she knelt and kept watch until her suspicions were confirmed. Not just one French schooner, but a convoy of them were sailing upstream toward Montreal, no doubt to collect that critical last shipment of grain. At the tail end of the convoy glided a two-masted snow brig.

Catherine willed her pulse to slow. Her bateau

was safely sunk, and she and Samuel and Thankful were hidden from view.

"Catherine?"

She whipped around, jerking a finger to her lips. Thankful halted in a blade of sunlight that flashed on her golden hair. Catherine motioned for her to get down. Bending stiffly at the waist, Thankful hurried to kneel beside her. She had washed and smelled faintly of the lavender sachet that had scented her cotton gown. Without a word, she peered through the viburnum branches at the approaching schooners. In silence they sat together until the snow had passed well beyond them.

"The convoy works in our favor," Catherine said. "No one saw us or the bateau."

Thankful peeked again at the river. "So when all those ships and their crew reach Montreal, the captain will ask them if they saw anyone like Samuel—or us—on the river. And they'll say no."

"Moreau will have no reason to come this way looking for us, especially not when he'll be occupied loading the last several tons of grain."

Thankful tucked her hands into the folds of her skirt. "How long do you think it will be before they come back?" A breeze sighed through the trees, lifting wisps of hair off her neck.

Montreal was little more than twenty miles

from here. Even going south against the current, it would only take schooners about two hours to reach it. They'd need time to load the cargo, but once they headed back downstream, they'd travel at speeds three to four times faster than a bateau, depending on the wind. "A couple of days?" Catherine's voice trailed away. "If there's strong wind against them, longer. In three days' time, we should be near Quebec, going downstream as we are." It would be a race.

"You haven't slept yet, have you? We won't leave again until you rest. I'll keep watch."

As much as Catherine wanted to argue, she knew Thankful was right. Her body cried out for sleep. But a closer look at Thankful made her linger. The young woman was still wearing her stays beneath her fitted bodice.

"Once we start the journey again, you'll be much more comfortable rowing if you wear a deerskin skirt and stroud tunic."

"No, I wouldn't." Her voice took on an edge. "Trust me, Catherine, I really wouldn't. It might be fine for you to wear such things, but not me." She dropped her gaze. Her entire face seemed pinched.

"You didn't sleep well, or at least not enough," Catherine said.

Ducks swam on the water below, some of them dabbling their beaks in the mud. Thankful stared at them as one unseeing. "I journeyed on a river before, once. The Hudson, I think. And then Lake George, and then Lake Champlain. I didn't sleep well then, either."

Realization swept over Catherine. The last time was after Thankful and her parents had been captured from their New Hampshire home. While Catherine and Bright Star had traded up and down rivers and lakes, Thankful had grown roots on the south shore of the St. Lawrence River, and there she had stayed for nine years. Catherine chided herself for not anticipating all that this trip would mean to her.

"So you see, I don't blame you for what happened to my family, but I can't wear Mohawk clothing. Maybe it's similar to why you won't cut your hair. You honor your mother with its length. I honor my parents by keeping my name, my faith, and clothing that looks more like what my mother wore and not like the people who killed her, though I know they were Abenaki." She tucked her knees up under her skirts until they were below her chin. Hugging her ankles, she rocked back and forth while a single tear traced a path to the tip of her nose.

The sight of it peeled the years away until Catherine saw not a young woman but the child within. Terrified, confused, lost in a world whose languages and customs she did not know. That girl had wet the bed every night for two years even after she knew she was safe.

"I'm sorry if I've upset you," Thankful whispered. "I'm thankful for you, and for everything you've done for me. It's just that last night . . ."

"I should have prepared you better for the rapids." Catherine should have steered farther away from them altogether. Guilt pricked her, but it could have turned out so much worse.

"It wasn't just that."

Black-capped chickadees whistled in the pause that followed. "Please tell me," Catherine urged. "If you would like to."

Thankful's rocking slowed. "I don't think I ever mentioned it before, but when I was taken and put in a canoe, my parents had already been killed. I don't know if I saw that happen, because I don't see it in my mind, but I—I think I hear their screams. *'My baby,'* my mother cried over and over."

"She meant you."

"Perhaps." Turning her head, Thankful seemed to study a spider web strung in the crook of a branch. A few dried petals stuck to the silk strands, residue of a spring long past. "I think it more likely she meant the babe in her womb. I don't remember any last words between us, Catherine. Part of me wishes I did, and part of me is glad I don't. I do miss them, though. And I miss the little sister or brother I might have had."

Catherine put her arm around Thankful's

shoulders. "Of course," she murmured. "Of course you do." Moments floated by like leaves on the river, languid and unhurried. "Being in the bateau brings it all back to you, then?" she dared to ask.

A great sigh lifted Thankful's chest. "When I was taken captive and put in the canoe all those years ago, my parents' scalps—among others—lay at my feet. I know they were theirs because I could see the daisies I had wreathed and put in my mother's hair that day."

Catherine had seen those wilted flowers. She had touched the hair that resembled Thankful's in its many shades of gold and bronze. Now was not the time to tell her that those scalps had paid her ransom. That time may never come at all.

Birch leaves trembled overhead, and the papery bark peeling from the trunk whispered secrets in the wind. Catherine offered her canteen to Thankful.

When she finished drinking from it, Thankful wiped her lips and stared at the moisture on her fingers. "There was water in the bottom of the canoe, wetting my feet. I'm sure it was water now that I look back on it. But when I was a child, I thought—it was irrational, but I thought it was their blood."

Catherine ached in sympathy for the traumatized Thankful. "You were just a child. There was nothing rational about that day or the ones surrounding it. Thankful, I'm so sorry this happened to you. If I could take the pain away, I would."

"I would let you." A wan smile slanted on Thankful's pale face. "If my faith were stronger, I would say that I consider the trial a joy. I would say that testing produces perseverance. But if I am honest, I just want this pain to go away. I don't feel it all the time, mind you. But when I do, I'm not thankful for it. It's a festering boil in need of lancing. It's not sorrow. Sorrow to me is a temporary hollowing. But this boil beneath the surface spreads a fever to every part of me. It's anger. It's an unforgiveness that I need to deal with, but I don't know how. Or don't want to." She squinted at Catherine, looking for her reaction. "Disappointed? After all my talk of you forgiving Samuel."

"Oh, Thankful. The hurts I endured by him are nothing compared to losing your family in such a sudden way."

"And violent," she inserted. "Sudden and violent. It was brutal."

It was. Catherine held back the thoughts that sprang to mind. She would gain nothing and Thankful would feel no comfort if Catherine pointed out that the French government encouraged those raids, or that the practice of adopting captives into Abenaki families was how they replaced loved ones lost to war or British raids or disease. The Abenaki might have died out completely if they had not incorporated so many captives into their clans. But even as the words formed in her mind, they sounded like justification, so she held her tongue.

Sunshine warmed the hemlock boughs enough to release their lemony perfume. A finch trilled, and birch leaves fluttered to the ground. "This journey we are on now," Catherine began. "Did you feel you had a choice in coming? Or do you feel I took you captive?"

Thankful didn't respond right away. It didn't take long for the quiet to become unbearable, and Catherine rushed to fill it.

"Listen. You know I do not confess the way the black robes want me to. But I will confess to you now. I thought I was making the right choice for you by bringing you along, but I should have allowed you the freedom to make that choice yourself. I didn't think how hard the river journey might be for you, even without any rapids. I should have asked. Will you forgive me for treating you like a child who cannot think for herself?"

Thankful grasped her hand. "You were thinking quickly, Catherine. I trust you had my best interests in mind. It was the right decision for me to come, but I appreciate you wanting to give me more say in the matter. I forgive you, so say no more about it." She shifted her weight on the rock and looked out over the river. "And now I have my own confession to make. Your ability to forgive Samuel is a challenge to me to forgive the Abenaki. You remember what I said to you about reconciling with Samuel?"

Catherine recalled every word. "You said being with him again was a chance to close old wounds and heal. For my sake, as much as his. Old wounds. Like yours."

"Yes. And now this experience, this journey confronts me with memories and feelings I'd rather not have. But perhaps this will be my chance to work on forgiving the Abenaki. It's not the same as being face-to-face with them, but God help me, I will lance the boil that has plagued me for so long."

"No, you are not in their presence. But, Thankful . . ." Hesitating, Catherine plucked weedlike runners from Thankful's skirt and cast them aside. "In another day or two, the river will take us within a few miles of Odanak, the Abenaki village. It's off the St. Lawrence on the smaller river of Saint-François. We may see some Abenaki."

Thankful hugged her knees to her chest once more. "Then will you pray for me, that my heart cooperates with my will in this?"

Clouds wreathed the sun, muting the midday rays. Catherine did not pray as much as she ought. But for this, for Thankful, she would.

• • •

Samuel colored as soon as Catherine entered the cavern, then recovered with a chuckle. "I forget you're accustomed to seeing men half naked." He stood in the buckskin leggings she'd packed for him, right arm held tight across his bare middle. A forest-green hunting shirt hung limply from his left hand. "It's easier to take off my shirt than to get it back on."

"May I help?"

At his nod, Catherine went to him. She had seen countless men in naught but breechclouts, it was true, so she could not attribute the warmth spreading through her to modesty. She'd seen Samuel in this state before, as well. The night he proposed to her when he found her in the creek, for instance.

Heart rate quickening, she gathered up the right sleeve of the shirt, then gently threaded it over his hand, arm, elbow, and shoulder until she could slide the neck opening over his head. Her fingers brushed his hair, unbound and still wet from washing. Memories pulled at her like strong currents as she retied the sling that held his arm. She was so tired of struggling against them that she almost wanted to let them carry her away.

Samuel took her hand from his neck, pressed his lips to it for the briefest of instants, then stepped away from her. "Thank you."

Shock raced through Catherine at his touch. "You're welcome," she told him, and was surprised at how deeply she meant it. But she did not know what that kiss had meant, or if she had only imagined it. Bewildered, she stood back as he pushed his left arm through the shirt and tugged the hem of it down between his chest and folded right arm.

"I can't tail my hair with one hand," he said.

"I'll do it."

"No, I won't have you brushing and dressing my hair like I'm a child. But will you cut it? Very short all over. I might have done it before this, like our American rangers. It's far more practical."

She agreed and quickly found scissors in the moccasin patching kit. Once they were in her hand, Samuel knelt before her. "I'm not practiced at cutting hair," she told him.

"Bah. You cannot hurt my vanity."

His hair slipped like corn silk between her fingers as she combed through it. The motion, meant to be practical, felt far more intimate. Mastering her imagination, she snipped locks and tossed them to the ground for birds to find and weave into their nests.

Several minutes later, she carefully trimmed over his ears and at his neck, then brushed the loose hair from his shoulders and back. "Finished."

Rising, Samuel thanked her and raked his fingers through his cropped hair. "Do I look like a shorn sheep?" His smile teased her. "More like a wheat field after harvest, eh?"

Catherine couldn't help smiling. "You look—" Masculine. Handsome. "Fine. You look fine." She tucked the scissors back into the kit.

"I wish I wasn't such a burden to you, Catie. I wish I didn't need you so much, but I do."

Need. That was what this was. She could still feel the spot where he'd kissed her hand, and she could certainly still feel his hair between her fingers. But this entire journey was a transaction, a trade, nothing more. He needed her for his escape.

Clouds shifted overhead, and sunshine flared across Samuel's face for a fleeting moment before fading again. Sparrows chirped on branches that swayed in a temperate wind. But here, in this black limestone cavern, there was only Catherine and Samuel, and the shadows and memories that both drew them together and broke them apart.

Need. The irony of it twisted inside her until a small laugh escaped.

His expression furrowed, and faint lines fanned from eyes that were deep, unfathomable wells.

"Ah, Samuel." She resisted the urge to smooth his cares away. "How I once longed to hear that you needed me. How I needed you once, too. More than I should have."

"You thought need was the same as love. Do you still think so?"

Need, hunger, longing, love. Threads of the same fabric, were they not? And yet so tangled in Catherine's mind that she could scarcely see where one ended and another began. Veering from that dangerous territory, she spoke only of the present. "I think you need me to help you, and I need the war to stop. If helping you get to Quebec makes that a possibility, then this is a fair trade." She would not admit it was anything more.

Samuel looked at her for a long moment, a struggle evident in his face. He was weighing something in his mind—either her words or his own yet to come. She waited beneath his study until, at length, he spoke. "I'm tired, and so are you, but who knows when we may have another moment alone. My conscience won't let me rest until I tell you the whole of what kept me away. It was not just Joel's death. There was more." He pointed to her sleeping pallet, and she sat on it while he lowered himself to his.

Catherine crossed her legs beneath her deer-skin skirt. With a tug on the ribbons at her neck, her hair tumbled free. Surprise spiraling through her, she spread the strands out to dry faster.

Samuel's lips twitched into a smile, then back again. "You and I—we were practically children when we met. We were lost, both of us. We saved each other in so many ways. But I'm not your Rescuer, Catie. Only Christ can be that, both then and now."

It would have felt like an insult if he had not cradled the words in the most tender, protective voice she'd ever heard from him. She wanted to argue, to deny that she'd ever placed her entire future, her very happiness in his hands alone. Her words refused to form that lie. Instead she said, "I thought you were going to tell me what happened after your brother died." She would go without sleep for a week to hear it if she had to.

"Aye, but that needed to be said first." Samuel coughed, then studied a set of parallel grooves in the limestone between them. "I've been reluctant to tell you the rest of the story for a few reasons. Not the least of which was my concern that if you knew, you'd change your mind about taking me north." He swallowed hard, clearly uneasy.

Catherine's own nerves followed suit. The ridges on his brow were easily read, even more so now that his hair was cropped short. They spoke of secrets about to surface.

"I could keep this from you until we reach Quebec, but doing so would be living a lie. And

I need you to know the truth now, so we can both honor it."

"Honor the truth," Catherine repeated, suspense mounting. "You speak in riddles. Please, just say it."

He clenched his jaw, and his knuckles went white in fists. His entire body contracted in front of her, as though he would retreat within himself if he could. Then he lifted his chin and met her gaze, though he still seemed to hold his breath.

"Joel's widow, Lydia," he said, exhaling at last. "I married her."

The words echoed and swirled in the cavern, and Catherine could not make sense of them. They were patterns of sound without context. "You said Joel married Lydia before you arrived. She was Joel's wife. That's what you told me."

"And then Joel died because of me. Lydia was widowed. So I married her. She is my wife now."

The silence that followed took on a suffocating texture as Catherine forced herself to grasp what he was telling her. "You married her while I waited to marry you? You saved one woman from widowhood and made a spinster of the woman you loved? Or was that a lie, too? Perhaps you have a habit of promising yourself to whichever woman is within arm's reach."

He looked as though she'd struck him, his chest concave between tight shoulders. "Do you truly think so little of me? I already told you, my love for you never waned. If it had, I would not have pushed Joel to go ice fishing with me so I could hurry back to you."

"You're saying our love killed Joel. And you atoned for that by marrying his widow." Catherine was on her feet, head spinning, unable to say more or think or breathe.

Samuel pushed up and reached out to steady her, but she stumbled away from him. "She would have been destitute," he said through colorless lips. "She had no one else. Her entire family was killed in the same raid that made me a captive. It was Joel's dying wish that I provide for her, and it was the right thing to do. She was with child. We have another—" His voice cracked and broke apart.

"That's enough," Catherine whispered and turned her back on him. It took all her self-possession not to clutch at the ripping inside her chest.

"Catherine, wait. Where are you going? Wait!"

"Wait?" She rounded on him, fury flashing through her. She grasped it, for it was the strength that held her up. "I am done waiting. I will never wait on you again."

CHAPTER TWENTY-ONE

With a stitch in her side from running, Catherine slowed her pace at last. She pulled her unbound hair over her shoulder and let it pool in her lap as she sank against a tree. She didn't care where she was, only that she was away from Samuel Crane. Anger boiled inside her not just against him, but against herself for caring after all these years, and she could not say which was stronger.

A murder of crows exploded from the tree, leaving her with only her thundering pulse. She needed to be alone right now, and yet loneliness was the very demon she longed to slay. Samuel's words replayed over and again in her mind, digging deeper with each repetition. Whatever Catherine had shared with him seemed like a farce, the home he'd built for them a stage set.

Furiously, she plaited her hair, pulling the three hanks tight. She felt betrayed all over again, but why? Samuel had broken their engagement years ago, and she had mourned and recovered from that loss. If betrayal was unmet expectation, a shattered trust, what had Catherine been expecting from him? With what had she entrusted him?

Tying a ribbon around her braid, she secured it with a yank and leaned against the flaking birch trunk behind her. She'd been harboring a tiny ember of hope ever since she had learned about Joel's death and assumed it was the sole reason for Samuel's absence. But he had fanned that hope into a bright flicker, however meager that flame. A look, a touch. No—more. He had confessed that he'd never stopped loving her, and this was the root that continued to trip her. Was it a ruse, another manipulation to ensure she would take him to Quebec? Or had they both been bewitched by danger and fireflies and memory?

Catherine buried her face in her hands and groaned with the weight of her shame. All this time, Samuel had a wife and children, one of them fully his own.

Samuel, a father! She reined in her imagination and hobbled her own desires. How she had longed for him to lead the family they were to build together.

Fatigue pulled on her body, mind, and spirit. She was dizzy with exhaustion and combusting with sadness and anger. No wonder he'd worried she wouldn't take him north if she had known his secret.

Her thoughts came to an abrupt halt. Did she really only give when she expected to get back in equal measure? Did she consider all of life a trade?

It is. The whisper slithered through her. She rubbed the muscles in her shoulders, still sore from last night's voyage, and considered that every action had a consequence, every cause an effect. If that wasn't trade, she would be hard-pressed to give it another name. This was her business, her way of life. Which meant she should have known better. Samuel had allowed her to feel loved in return for her help. Had she agreed to help him solely for the chance to end the war, or had part of her done it for the chance to begin again with him?

Only one answer could explain her reaction to his news.

Bowing her head to her knees, Catherine's fury slipped away. Gasping sobs heaved her shoulders. As much as she wanted to hate Samuel for what he had done, she couldn't. But neither was she ready to face him again. If Christ was her rescuer, as Samuel had said, she needed Him to rescue her from bitterness.

Utterly spent, she curled onto her side on a bed of leaves, dappled shade her blanket, the hushing wind a song. Roots pushed up through the ground, but her body was too tired to protest. In the middle of a prayer, sleep carried her far away.

It was a merciful, dreamless slumber, the kind that made time disappear.

Then crickets pierced her consciousness,

along with something else. A voice calling her name. With a start, Catherine awoke to shadows that told her hours had drifted past. She pushed herself up from the ground and stepped away from the tree.

"Catherine!" Thankful's voice was muffled by distance.

Muscles stiff from her unmoving sleep, Catherine hastened back toward the cavern. It wasn't long before she found Thankful walking near the creek behind it. "Catherine!" she called again, pushing branches out of her way.

"I'm here." Catherine ducked under a low bough to meet her.

Tears streaking her cheeks, Thankful plunged toward her. "I was so worried." She clung to Catherine in a fierce embrace. "Sam told me what he shared with you. I can scarcely believe it myself, so I can only imagine how you feel. I thought you'd decided to leave us." She stood back.

Catherine picked an evergreen needle from Thankful's uncovered hair. "I'd never just leave you. I confess, the notion of letting Samuel find his own way from here did cross my mind. He can walk, even if he cannot row." She shrugged. "So can we."

Thankful's lips tipped to one side. "Ah, mon amie." Understanding filled her voice. "I knew you loved him still. I am so sorry for—for—"

A hemlock cone dropped to the ground beside her. "For all of it."

A wedge expanded in Catherine's throat. "So am I." There was so much she could say, and yet she had no appetite for it. "He should have told me sooner," she whispered.

The creek bubbled beneath an evening growing cool. "And what would you have done if he had?" Thankful asked.

Catherine shuffled through a drift of leaves. "I don't know."

Twigs crunched beneath their moccasins. Thankful's hem caught and dragged them in her wake. "I hate to see you hurting."

"I don't understand why his news has affected me this way," Catherine confessed. "He cast me aside years ago, but I recovered. How could I have been so foolish as to place him at the center of my affections again? I should have known better."

Thankful picked her steps around moss-furred stones. "Loving someone is never a foolish thing to do, Catherine. But now that we know about his family, loving Samuel has to mean something different than it did before. It has to mean letting him go."

"Again." Another tear slid to the end of Catherine's nose, and she caught it with the side of her finger. "I've had practice."

The gathering twilight did not hide Thankful's

red-rimmed eyes, her swollen lids. "Don't be harsh with yourself for feeling sad. And please, please don't be harsh with Samuel for caring for Lydia and their children. He genuinely believed it was the right thing to do, though it cost him dearly to give you up. You may not believe that, but it would be wrong to persuade him to prove it."

Catherine stilled. Arms crossed, she looked up at the cavern where Samuel waited inside. The entrance was partially hidden by trees and shadow, but the echo of the rambling creek bounced off its walls. "He has a family, and it isn't us."

A gentle touch on her shoulder softened the sting of that truth. "They wait and pray for his return." Thankful's voice blended with the water rippling behind them. "We could turn around now, leaving Samuel on his own, and you could put him behind you once and for all. Personally, I would consider it a relief not to face any Abenaki. I imagine it would be a relief for you not to face Sam. Is that what you want? To turn around?"

Options tugged at Catherine from both sides, and she followed each to its logical conclusion. Samuel still needed her help, and she still wanted to speed the end of the war. At least now there was no question that after Quebec, she and Samuel would part forever. With a great heave, she began rebuilding the wall around the remnants of her heart. In time, she knew the pressure would ease.

Leveling her gaze at Thankful, she squeezed her hand. "I'll bear my burden if you will bear yours."

Samuel emerged from the cavern. "I'm glad to see you. I thought you might—"

Catherine cut him off. "I know what you thought." Bending, she picked a clutch of sorrel and forced her feet to carry her forward. "We leave as soon as it's dark."

Shortly after dusk, they were back on the river again. At least while rowing, Catherine could focus her energy on something else. Still, she couldn't ignore him there at the stern, Thankful rowing between them. Catherine would rather steer the rudder herself, but with the rapids behind them, speed was more important than careful maneuvering, and Samuel's shoulder needed more time to heal.

The wood creaked as he shifted his weight. She wondered if he was thinking of his wife. *Lydia.*

Catherine maintained her steady rhythm with the oar but focused on the heavens. Blazoned with colored light, they were a merciful distraction. Where the sky above should be black except for the stars, it looked like a giant warrior had slashed it with his knife. A ghostly green spilled and oozed from the line stretching across the horizon. Shafts of light rippled to a music only they could hear.

Catherine rowed toward the magnificent expanse, and Thankful and Samuel remained silent in quiet reverence. They did not worship the *Hodonäi'a*, as the Iroquois called the Northern Lights, but the Great Good God who created them.

The river lapped gently against the bateau, and somewhere in the distance, a wolf's cry soared, held its long note, then fell. The land on both shores sloped up before dipping again. Slowly up, then slowly down, the howl and the hills were in harmony with the water's ebb and flow. This, too, was a kind of music to Catherine. Time bent itself to a similar pattern, for she could no better track how long they'd been rowing than she could get any closer to that elusive light. So separate from the world of war did Catherine feel, it was as if the moment were sealed off by itself.

And then it was punctured.

Stilling the oar, she paused to look around. "Something's not right," she whispered.

"What is it?" Samuel asked, his profile sketched in charcoal as he turned to scan the banks.

Wind feathered over Catherine, carrying an unmistakable scent. "Behind you. We're being followed."

"What?" Thankful twisted on the plank that held her.

Catherine held up her hand, then pointed to their wake. With the Northern Lights illuminating the night, it was not difficult to see the outline of another vessel on the river, and at least one person paddling it. The lithe figure moved with the strength of a porter and a practiced grace unknown to Pierre Moreau or Gaspard Fontaine. Slowly, but perceptibly, the shape of the pursuer grew larger.

"Who is it?" Samuel's voice was strung low and tight.

"My sister." She was almost certain of it. But whatever compelled Bright Star to race after them now, when Catherine knew she had wanted no part of this plan—that sent cold dread into her spine.

"You're sure?" Samuel pressed. "What makes you think so?"

"Bear grease. Don't you smell it?" Most of the People rendered the grease and used it in their hair or over their skin to protect from mosquitoes. But only Bright Star would come after her. "Something's wrong, or she would not have come to find us."

Tension radiated from the angles of Samuel's posture. "Press on. You said yourself that she did not want you to take me. Neither did Joseph."

But Joseph hadn't stopped them when he'd

had the chance. Catherine squeezed the oar, the blade suspended over the water. The weathered wood had begun to split, and the fractures pinched her palms. "She is my sister. Though she mistrusts you, she would not bring me harm." She glanced from Samuel to Thankful.

"You're sure it's her?" the young woman whispered. "What if you're wrong?"

"I am not. It's Bright Star. I just don't know what drives her. Whatever it is, it's important, and I aim to find out."

Thankful's chest rose and fell in shallow breaths. "Samuel says we should keep going. Look, there's a bend in the river. Once we get beyond it, could we not hide?"

"She'll find us before we would have time to sink the bateau. Come now, Thankful. It's Bright Star. We have no reason to fear her."

The sky glowed with waves the color of algae. Beneath it, Thankful's complexion took on a similar cast.

"Catherine. Row." Gone was the tenderness Samuel had shown back in the cavern. In its place, a stern command.

She set her jaw. "We have held our council, and you both have said your piece. Now it is time you listen to your leader, for like it or not, that is what I am." She directed her words to Samuel. "You asked me to lead you. So let me."

The air thinned and grew brittle between them, but Catherine would not back down. Neither did she call out to Bright Star. Instead, she waited silently for her sister's canoe to reach them, while her heart drummed against her ribs.

The sky writhed like a serpent, its bright green twin wrinkling on the river. If there was one thing the display of Northern Lights told Catherine, it was that the Creator God was vast beyond all comprehension, and she was small. Perhaps even too small to capture His notice. Yet she prayed He would notice them now, and guide her.

"What will your decision cost us?" Samuel muttered, jarring Catherine from her thoughts.

The canoe neared. Bright Star paddled so that her vessel was parallel with Catherine's, the sisters across from each other.

She wasn't alone. Joseph was behind her in the canoe, adding his powerful strokes to the water with his own paddle. No wonder they'd been able to overtake Catherine.

Gaspard Fontaine hunched between them.

Shock beat through Catherine at the sight of him, even as she noticed he'd been gagged and trussed, immobilizing any threat. "What are you doing here?" The question burst from her before her siblings had a chance to say a word.

"This one was following you." Joseph thrust the handle of his paddle toward Fontaine.

"And so you brought him straight to us?" Samuel's voice was flinty.

"Because we were following you, too." Bright Star looked over her shoulder, then continued to paddle.

Catherine looked back, as well. Accompanied or not, the urgency to reach Quebec remained. "But why?" She sliced her oar into the water and pulled back, ignoring the ache in her shoulders. The burn in her belly was worse. Had she made a mistake in allowing them to reach her? Doubts circled, and she fought to chase them away. "Why have you come all this way?"

The gaze Bright Star directed at Samuel was as pointed as her chin. "That one is British. We are at war. Even if we trusted him, who knows what may happen to all three of you because of the risks you take for this man?"

" 'This man,' " Samuel repeated gruffly. "You know my name, Bright Star, and I know yours and Joseph's. The only stranger among us is Fontaine. Tell me how bringing a Canadian militiaman right to us demonstrates a desire to keep us safe."

"Samuel," Catherine whispered at him. "Don't judge them quite yet."

"What would you have us do?" Joseph sat directly across from Samuel, river rippling between their vessels. "If we let him go, he could go back to Pierre Moreau or any of those schooners we passed, and they'd all be on the hunt for you at his bidding. Better to keep him close."

"You didn't kill him," Samuel observed coldly. "You could have. It might have been him who set fire to the barn."

Fontaine's wide eyes gleamed as he stared at Samuel.

"Kill him!" At last, Thankful found her voice. "Surely it needn't come to that."

Catherine's braids hung heavy on her shoulders as she rowed. She searched for meaning between and behind the words that were spoken, and within the words that were left unsaid. What she heard was that Bright Star and Joseph had come to protect her, a revelation which stood so tall in her mind that it nearly overshadowed all else. But beneath that notion she heard more. That Samuel wanted Fontaine dead, and that Thankful considered it murder. Fontaine had heard it all.

Without altering their pace, Catherine slid a glance to the hunting knife that hung in its sheath around Bright Star's neck, swaying against her white stroud tunic as she paddled. Joseph's scalping knife made a dark outline against the French trade shirt he wore. Surely their canoe contained other weapons, as hers did. They distrusted Samuel as much as she distrusted Fontaine. What would happen when they stopped to rest?

"The French are our ally until the Six Nations say otherwise." Eerie light glowed on Joseph's head where it was bald around his scalp lock. The feathers sprouting from his hair shivered in the breeze. "I will not kill Fontaine unless he poses a threat to my family." He turned to Samuel. "I'll kill any man who poses that threat, regardless of former allegiances."

Catherine shuddered at the fierceness in her brother's tone. She had never seen him fight or kill, though she knew he had done both. He had hunted for her and brought her meat when she was hungry. Now he hunted for her in a different way.

"I do not intend to hurt Catherine or Thankful." Samuel's voice held a struggle to keep calm.

"We have no interest in your intentions," Bright Star said. "Only in your actions. What would keep you from hurting her again once you get what you want, especially now that our nations are at war?"

Catherine pulled harder at the oar, her focus fragmenting like the shards of green light moving across the night. Piece by piece, she mustered her wits. Samuel held his tongue, but she would no longer keep secrets. "Samuel can hurt me no further than he already has," she told her siblings. "He is married. He'll return to his wife and children as soon as he can."

"He has told you this himself?" Joseph asked

in Mohawk, and Catherine confirmed it in the same language.

"And still you do this for him." A rare softness gentled Bright Star's expression.

"My aim is to help end the war," Catherine reminded her, and in so doing reminded herself. "I have released Samuel Crane before." She would do it again.

The lack of response that followed was unsurprising. Bright Star and Joseph did not waste words and likely figured there was nothing more to say on the subject of Samuel's family. They were right.

A wolf howled again, and a muffled cry came from Fontaine. Catherine welcomed the distraction. Switching back to French, she asked, "And what does Fontaine have to say for himself?"

Pulling his paddle inside the canoe, Joseph reached forward and yanked the cloth from the young man's mouth.

Fontaine coughed. His head hung toward his chest while he composed himself. "Water," he rasped, and Joseph tipped a canteen into his mouth.

Shifting her weight, Thankful turned toward the canoe. The press of her lips and tilt of her neck betrayed that she sympathized with Fontaine—if not for his actions, at least his discomfort. He appeared little recovered from the last time she'd seen him.

"You have to believe me," he panted.

"No, we don't," Samuel said, and Joseph grunted his agreement.

"Just listen. I did set that barn on fire."

Catherine's attention jerked to Fontaine. Thankful gasped but made no further sound.

"I knew it." Samuel growled. "You couldn't strike me with a rusty sickle while I was shackled, so you thought you'd commit a bit of arson while I was trapped inside. Not very sporting—"

Fontaine cut him off. "Moreau ordered me to do it. Trained a gun on me and said if I didn't obey a direct command, he'd shoot me for insubordination and wouldn't miss me, since I was a useless drunk anyway. I was half out of my mind for want of drink, as you saw for yourself before he arrested you. He wanted you out of the picture, Crane, but didn't want to dirty his own hands to do it. He said if I told the Duvals about the arrangement, it would be my word against his, and who would believe someone like me?" His voice was weak and reedy, but he seemed lucid.

"So you did it," Samuel ground out.

"Consider my options!" Fontaine cried. "I would have been dead on the spot if I hadn't. At least I knew the smoke would signal your location and you'd have some chance of being rescued. And that's exactly what happened."

"Only now you've come to trap me and deliver me back to Moreau."

"No." Fontaine shook his head furiously. "I'm deserting. I swear it's the truth."

Catherine found that hard to believe. "Deserting? In the direction of Quebec, where all the armies are gathered?"

His skin shone with a fever sweat. "We are both headed the opposite way others expect of us. Moreau believes that you headed south to Crown Point on Lake Champlain. So why would he send me north to chase after you?" He paused to catch his breath. "No, I don't give a fig what you're up to. I've had it with Moreau and with this war that never seems to end. It took my brother's life, and for all I know, my parents are starving on the outskirts of Quebec, while I spent the last few weeks surrounded by grain in abundance. No more. I'm going home to take care of my own."

The two vessels glided in tandem over the river. Samuel watched Fontaine in silence, his forearms flexed and tight. Bright Star and Joseph made no commentary, but Catherine knew they were listening to every word.

She considered what Fontaine had just shared, measuring the tale in her mind. "Where is the wheat?" she asked at length.

Fontaine stared at her for a moment before responding. "You know as well as I do. It's being loaded onto schooners at Montreal."

"No. The wheat you took for your family. You would have brought some of it with you, n'est-ce pas? To feed your starving parents?"

"You think I stole from Moreau's storehouses?" A tremor shook his body.

"Didn't you?" she pressed. A man who deserted during war would have no qualms about stealing grain. Fontaine had not shown himself to be scrupled in general.

She could hear his scowl in his voice. "You have trapped me. Neither answer would satisfy you."

A clever evasion. Catherine tilted her head toward one shoulder, then the other, stretching out the tension she carried there.

"All I want is to get home. Gag me, truss me, do what you will, as long as I can reach my family. Why would you think I care any less for mine than you do for yours?" he asked Joseph. "We are not so different, you and I." The canoe rocked, and Fontaine leaned over the side to retch.

"Finished?" Allowing a few more moments to pass, Joseph stuffed the rag back into Fontaine's mouth.

Thankful winced. "How did you come by him?"

"The day after you left, we noticed your canoe missing from your dock," Bright Star said. "Gabriel remains at the house, and we knew you had taken the bateau, so we suspected it was someone who had gone after you, whether one of the People or one of the French. We didn't know which direction your pursuer went, but since we knew yours, that's where we headed."

"He made a fire his first night on land," Joseph supplied. "Made it easy to find him. Easy to capture."

"And the canoe?" Samuel asked. "Where is it now?"

"Lost." Bright Star paddled with steady rhythm as she spoke. "He said he capsized near the rapids and couldn't recover the vessel or supplies. He was soaking wet and trying to dry his clothing by the fire when we found him."

"So he could be telling the truth," Thankful concluded. "He could simply be returning to his family."

"Or he could be lying through his teeth." Samuel exuded frustration. "I'll grant that you found him washed up with nothing. But I'd warrant he didn't have proper supplies for the journey to start with. Except, perhaps, for rum."

Fontaine shook his head at this, protest sounding in his throat.

"I have doubted Fontaine's story, too, Samuel." Joseph put his paddle back in the river. "But if he is lying, why would he confess to setting the fire? Whatever his true motives, I say we let the two men take the canoe, and I will take the women home in the bateau. I'll loose Fontaine's bindings so he can row to Quebec, as Samuel's shoulder is not healed yet."

A knot tightened in Catherine's stomach. Samuel's eyes flashed a warning above his cheekbones. As tempting as it might be to say yes to Joseph's plan, she couldn't ignore its most prominent flaw.

"Joseph. Thank you for wanting to keep me safe. But Fontaine has twice attempted to injure Samuel. We can't be sure he won't try again. Besides that, if Fontaine is unwilling to fight for his own country, he most certainly will not help Samuel serve his, even if he means him no harm. I don't trust him to complete the task I've promised to accomplish myself." She could scarcely believe her own words.

Bright Star turned to face her. "Are you truly so full of conviction or merely grasping for more time with a man you cannot have?"

Heat blazed across Catherine's cheeks, though Samuel could not have understood the Mohawk words. "I've more sense than that, and you know it."

"What about Thankful?" Joseph glanced at her, a protectiveness in his tone. "Would you like to go home? I will see you safely there."

Thankful pulled her shawl tighter about her shoulders, pausing to consider. "What will you do, Catherine?"

Frustration swelled, not at Thankful, but at the sheer number of times Catherine was required to make the same decision. She calmed herself with the knowledge that in less than two weeks, it would all be over and she would be home once more. "I will do what I said I would, and take Samuel to Quebec. Would you like to go back with Joseph and Bright Star?"

Thankful's eyes rounded.

Joseph did not give her the chance to respond. "We will not leave you alone with two warring men. That is not something I will do."

Catherine met the steel in his voice with her own. "I'm going to Quebec, brother. Bright Star, I need you to be home in case the porters return from New York while I'm gone. I placed you in charge of their payment and the delivery of the trade goods they'll bring."

Bright Star held up a hand. "It's your trading post. You're in charge."

Teeth on edge, Catherine calculated time and distance. By her reckoning, it was a month or longer to New York and back, less than two weeks for Quebec. "I'd feel better if you returned now, but if you refuse—I should be back before they arrive, anyway."

"Then so will we," Joseph said. "We're going with you."

Chapter Twenty-Two

The river had grown narrow and felt even smaller since Bright Star and Joseph had arrived with Gaspard Fontaine. Now that the schooners had passed and would soon return, haste pressed the group to row through the night and continue on. All day, tension had strung between the vessels like a trembling fiddle string. But at least Bright Star had brought smoked fish to eat with the hazelnuts Catherine had packed in the carrying basket.

With Thankful now near the bow with her oar on the port side and Samuel at the stern with the rudder, Catherine rowed on the starboard side from the middle, facing him.

"Thank you," Samuel said. "For honoring your agreement to take me north. It would have been easy for you to leave me."

"Not as easy as it was for you to leave me." She bit her tongue, but too late. "I shouldn't have said that."

The top of Samuel's nose and the tips of his ears were rosy from the sun, but the open collar of his fringed hunting shirt revealed the line where his skin paled to its natural color. "It wasn't easy."

Easy enough. But then she chided herself. "You don't need to explain. Best not to try." As Thankful had pointed out, no good could come of it, and nothing would change.

In the canoe, Fontaine bent his head over his knees, moaning about the vessel's motion while Joseph and Bright Star paddled.

Samuel ignored Fontaine's groaning. "I'm not sorry for my choice, Catherine. I only want you to know it was the hardest thing I've ever done. But I don't regret it, and you need to know that, too. We'll both be better off if we're clear on this."

Water insects dimpled the river while dragon-flies winged among the cattails by the shore. Catherine pulled the oar through the water a little faster, until her vessel glided ahead of Bright Star's. "Clear on what, precisely?"

His blond lashes lowered to his flushed cheeks. "There are different kinds of love. I do love my wife. Even though it began out of duty."

"How fortunate for her." The words launched sharp and quick, and again she regretted them. Samuel was drawing a line between them, a boundary that neither should cross, no matter their past. But lingering disappointment clamored louder than logic, at least for now.

"Fortunate?" The bateau rocked as Samuel shifted his weight and leaned forward. "Lydia was not fortunate to lose Joel, her true love, before he'd seen the face of their child. It was not fortunate that when she remarried to save herself from destitution, it was to a younger man still in love with another woman, a man so lost in the destruction of his own plans that he was surely more child than husband. You didn't see me when I was first captured and ransomed by your father, but I was nearly as adrift and useless to Lydia when I married her as I was then."

Catherine's strokes slowed as she listened. She saw him in her mind as he must have been when Gabriel purchased him from his captors. Raw. Devastated. Utterly at sea.

"Lydia knows about you." Samuel's grip flexed on the steering oar. "We had an agreement. She wouldn't expect me to be Joel, and I wouldn't expect her to be you, but there was the baby's future to think of. I could barely look her in the eye for months, Catherine, even after we wed. I certainly didn't touch her—not even her hand—until after the babies were born."

"Babies?"

"Twin boys. I feared they would rip the life right from her as they came screaming into the world. I left the naming to her, and she settled on Joel and Samuel. The younger of the two was too small and wouldn't nurse, and he didn't survive his first month. Baby Joel lived, and it was a mercy indeed that my brother's name-sake was not the one we buried." His voice grew thick. "Lydia had too much to bear. At the time, to my thinking, the wrong Samuel met his end."

"You can't think God punished you by taking that innocent life," Catherine told him. "Babies die so often, at least in New France, that there is no reason to call it judgment. It's heartbreaking, yes, but not divine reckoning."

She saw his memories carry him far away and waited for him to travel back to her.

"You could not have convinced me of that at the time, but I've come around," he said at last. "But baby Samuel's death piled sorrow on Lydia, too, and she certainly deserved no more. We swam through our grief separately for too long, but then we emerged to find each other. Lydia and I saw the burden the other carried instead of only the pain in ourselves. Comfort and patience led to respect, and eventually, to hard-earned love. I don't use the word lightly, nor was it lightly given or received."

A single nod was all Catherine could manage as she moved her gaze from his familiar, beloved face to the shoreline.

"It's too much to ask of you now, perhaps, but someday you'll see beyond your own hurts, too. You've done it before." Samuel leaned back in his seat and looked away. Her chest ached, but she could not tell if it was his pain or her own.

The St. Lawrence was calm and buoyant, but wariness churned, and not just over Samuel's revelations. Facing aft as she rowed, Catherine remained vigilant for any sign of the schooners returning this way with grain. The farther north they traveled, the more fire burned into the branches. Flaming foliage nudged up against a sky of blinding blue.

While Thankful inquired about the pain in Samuel's shoulder, their course bent east and split into a channel threading around the Sorel islands, where bulrushes fringed the marshy shores. Gabriel's voyaging songs ran through Catherine's mind, but she did not feel like singing. Instead, she tried to pray, though her attempts felt as fragmented as the St. Lawrence split by the Île de Grâce, Île à la Pierre, and Île des Barques.

The sun slipped low on the horizon, and cool air dropped like a curtain. The warbling of loons, which Catherine usually found melodic, grated on her. When she spotted a place to beach the vessels for the night, she declared it was time to rest, and no one complained.

Dense shadows spilled from the woods. Fontaine, who had been banned from weapons and tools, was no longer bound and helped Joseph and Bright Star secure the vessels. The carrying basket slung over one shoulder, Samuel went with Catherine and Thankful to find level ground on which to sleep. Tree trunks against twilight walled them in with deep purple and silver stripes. Before the hour was over, all would be painted over with night's ink.

"This looks fine to me." The hem of Thankful's cotton gown dragged behind her, banded with dingy grey. A few curls slipped from the bun at her neck and coiled against her skin.

Catherine was distracted by what Samuel had shared earlier until a scrambling in the leaves seized her full attention. Wheeling toward the sound, she found a French lookout rousing from sleep ten yards away.

Tricorne askew on matted brown hair, he staggered to his feet. "Halt!" The young man could not have been older than Thankful. Filmed with sweat, his boyish face was creased on one ruddy cheek from sleep. "Who are you, and what is your business here?" He leveled a pistol at Samuel.

Catherine's heart pounded against its cage. "Calm down." She held out her hands, palms up, while Samuel shoved Thankful behind him. "We've given you a start, which is no way to wake up. Be at ease, soldier, and we'll talk."

Not that she knew what to say. She should have been rehearsing just such a conversation instead of rearranging her feelings for Samuel! The lookout was disoriented, scared, and alone.

A volatile combination for the only person currently armed.

Thankful receded into the trees while Samuel remained.

The soldier licked his lips as he clenched the gun. "State your business or I'll shoot!" Panic pitched his voice high and raised the hair on Catherine's arms.

"Steady, man, there are women here!" Samuel spoke in French, but his accent was imperfect.

The boy noticed, blinking wide eyes in rapid succession. "You're British, aren't you? A scout, a spy? Stay back!"

Catherine could find no words. She'd led them all straight into harm's way.

Fontaine emerged through a copse of birch, his bright hair capturing the soldier's attention. A torrent of speech tumbled from Fontaine's lips. "Don't shoot! I'm in the Canadian militia, and that man is a British—"

"Put down the gun, soldier," Catherine called to him, diverting his attention. Whether Fontaine intended to betray them or was trying to protect them, she had no idea.

"Halt! Come no farther! How many are you?" The boy's arm quavered in a uniform too large for his frame.

"Calm yourself," she said again, louder, to drown out Fontaine. She stepped closer, though Samuel called for her to stay back.

"You're with the Englishman?" He swiveled and trained the gun on her instead. His composure was nearly gone.

Joseph and Bright Star appeared, knives stark against their tunics. Joseph notched an arrow to his bow.

The soldier blanched. "Ambush!" He wavered, and the sweat-slick weapon slipped from his grip into the leaves. He fumbled for it.

Samuel jerked a musket from the carrying basket, but there was no way he could find the powder horn and shot pouch and load it in time.

"Give me a weapon!" Fontaine cried.

"Catherine, down!" Joseph's voice.

A shot cracked the air. Thankful screamed from some distant place, but Catherine could not look away from the violence unfolding before her. An arrow parted the air, then another. Joseph had hidden himself within the wood's edge, but his arrows launched true and found their mark in the soldier's chest. The boy dropped to his knees, clutching a shaft with his left hand but raising his pistol again with his right.

"Lieutenant!" A second lookout barreled through the trees from the north, his gun gleaming in the twilight. Shouts and shots were overpowered by Joseph's chilling Mohawk war cry.

All of this happened in the span of a single frantic heartbeat. Out of nowhere, Bright Star pulled Catherine behind a boulder and held her fast. More arrows whistled past, each ending with a sickening thud in human flesh. The war Catherine had longed to end blazed around and above her, and those she cared about were caught in its fray.

"Stay down." But Bright Star watched, a vein throbbing at her temple.

Catherine clamped her hands over her ears but couldn't stop the screams from vibrating through her chest. It wasn't Thankful this time, but the soldiers, in terror and agony from her brother's warfare. A horrifying notion seized her, and she gripped her sister's arm. "Will he scalp them? In front of Samuel and Thankful?" The war cry alone surely evoked their childhood captures and their parents' murders.

Bright Star shook her head. "He wouldn't scalp Mohawk allies."

Allies. The word cut through the noise. It was one thing for Joseph to escort her north, as a free and independent agent. But if any French heard that he'd killed French soldiers, they'd make an example of his transgression and hang him from the nearest tree.

When whimpers replaced the war cry, Catherine fought to master her galloping pulse. Smoke and a wet metallic smell choked the air. Bright Star peered around the boulder, then leapt to her feet and hurried away.

Ears ringing, Catherine stood on shaky legs and leaned on the rough stone that had hidden her. Arrows bristled from both lookout soldiers, blood staining their uniforms purple and pooling beneath their bodies. Bending, Samuel wrenched a pistol from one of their clutches. For one nauseating moment, Catherine thought he meant to shoot them, but he didn't. The men expired on their own with gurgling, bubbling breath so loud it seemed to shake the trees.

Only then did she turn and see both Thankful and Bright Star kneeling beside Joseph and Fontaine. The men sat with their backs against trees, heads bowed.

Her sister looked up. "Shot," she said. "Both of them."

CHAPTER TWENTY-THREE

Night stretched out long by the light of a small fire and promised little sleep. With a strip of Thankful's petticoat binding his arm, Fontaine waited while all eyes turned to Joseph. The militiaman had worn himself out insisting he could have talked their way to safety if they'd only let him.

Catherine sat on her heels and cut away her brother's leggings a few inches above his knee. White shards and splinters pushed up from the muscle and tissue. The bone had shattered.

"Did the ball exit?" Samuel knelt beside her. He'd been the one to examine Fontaine's wound and declare the ball had passed clean through his bicep. Fontaine would heal.

Catherine slipped her hand beneath Joseph's calf and felt the dry ground. "There's no blood from that side. It must still be in the wound."

The cords of Joseph's neck were tightly strung. "Get it out." He forced the words through clenched teeth.

"I'll do it." Thankful squeezed his hand. "At least, I'll try."

"You have the smallest and steadiest hands,"

Catherine said. "You're the best one for the job."

Releasing Joseph, Thankful pulled an awl from the moccasin mending kit and, with a prayer on her lips, began to probe. When Joseph's back arched in pain, a tear slid down her cheek. "I'm sorry. I'm so sorry." A hairpin slipped free, and blond tresses tumbled down, obscuring her view.

Bright Star swept the hair back and held it at the base of Thankful's neck so she could see, just as she'd held back Catherine's hair when they were girls and Catherine had been sick.

Joseph's body relaxed as he fell into merciful oblivion. Catherine angled herself so more firelight wavered over the wound. Looking away from the ruined limb, she caught Samuel's gaze and held it. Shared blame and regret arced between them, for she had led them to danger for the sake of his mission.

"I never meant for this to happen," he murmured.

"But it did." She glanced at Joseph, whose expression screwed tight unconsciously. The moan he'd so bravely trapped before now escaped him.

Tears glistened on Thankful's cheeks as she worked. "I've almost got it," she whispered. The awl dug deeper and tilted, lifting the ball so she could pluck it out with her other hand. "There." Her shoulders sagged, her hands dark with Joseph's blood. "I'll need to stitch him, but

I need someone to hold the skin together. After that, it will be your turn, Gaspard."

At the sound of his Christian name, the private looked up, something like gratitude softening his features. "I could have convinced him I was on his side. I could have earned his trust and then tied his hands and feet while he slept."

Ignoring him, Bright Star bound Thankful's hair for her, then stood. "Those bodies should be buried."

Rising from where he knelt, Samuel said, "I'll do it."

Catherine eyed the sling that held his arm and stood, stepping away from Thankful and her patients. "No. You can't."

"I need to do something." He shoved his fingers through his hair, making it stand on end. "I need to help."

"Of course you do." Catherine's nerves unraveled, leaving her raw and sharp. "You always need to help. That's why you took an interest in me when we were young, isn't it? To help me. Then you wed your brother's widow, for her need for help was greater still. In fact, your compulsion to help is why we're all on the way to Quebec, so you can aid the entire British empire toward victory, and in so doing help all who suffer in a drawn-out war."

Samuel narrowed the gap between them. "You make that sound like a character flaw." His left hand curled near the fringe running down the side of his buckskin trousers. "Did you ever consider why my desire to help runs so deep? Imagine hearing a war cry like Joseph's multiplied by twelve but made to sound like a hundred warriors. Imagine the moment they descend upon you in your home, the one place you ought to feel safe. Their teeth are bared, their faces are painted black and red to terrify. Now imagine being made to watch as they kill your mother even as her hands stretch out to you. The last thing she screams is your name. Your infirm father pleads for mercy, until he, too, is murdered before you. Both are scalped and mutilated. I vomited. I was helpless to save them."

Catherine squeezed her fists until her fingernails bit her palms, for she'd rather feel her own pain than his.

Thankful translated this story for Gaspard. "When did this happen?" the militiaman asked, words slurred from the rum they had given him to dull the pain.

Samuel blinked at him, as if surprised he'd taken interest. "I was thirteen. Young, and yet six years older than Thankful was at her capture."

His gaze traveled to the fire, where it rested so long that Catherine wondered what he saw there. His nostrils flared. A branch snapped and sent sparks into the rising column of smoke, and he rubbed the heel of his hand against his eyelids.

"If I could have spared my parents from death or terror or pain," he continued, his voice softer, "I would have, but I couldn't, and it haunts me still. Just as Joel's death does, and his son's, for I couldn't save them, either. So yes, if I can help in small ways or large, I must. You make it sound like a strange obsession to make myself feel important, but don't you see? If all of New England and New France belong to just one empire, there will be no more government-sanctioned raids between the two. I'm not out for revenge against those who killed my parents and Thankful's. But ending this war also protects my wife and children, so I will not apologize for trying. Let me help along the way."

Moths fluttered, drawn by the popping flames. While Thankful finished translating for Gaspard, Catherine swallowed for a second time at the mention of Samuel's family. But she could no longer afford to pine. "So help." She gestured to Joseph. "Assist Thankful. Fashion a splint, do whatever she requires. I'll dig with Bright Star."

After pulling two hatchets from the cache of supplies, Bright Star led the way to the bodies at the edge of the firelight's reach. "We may need the arrows later. I have to cut them out so I don't leave the arrowheads behind." Flipping her braids over her shoulder, she put the hatchets in Catherine's hands, took her hunting knife from its sheath, and bent over the first lookout.

Skin turning cold all at once, Catherine whirled from the sight. Cloaked in shadow though the body was, her imagination supplied what she couldn't see. "How can you do that?"

Crickets chirped, and twigs crackled as they burned in the fire. Bats flapped and squeaked overhead. Light-headed from worry if not from hunger and exhaustion, Catherine lowered the weapons to the ground, then leaned her hands on her knees. When she straightened moments later, Bright Star stood before her. Amber light flickered over one golden side of her, while the other half was hidden in darkness.

"How can I do this?" Her sister raised the arrows she'd harvested, then tossed them to the ground. "I do what needs to be done. I don't have to enjoy it. Do you call me savage for this, and Thankful brave? Come now, Catherine. We are not the only ones with blood on our hands."

That truth struck through her. An apology tipped her tongue, but she let it die. She had known the risk and counted it worth the cost. "I don't deny it." She lifted a hatchet from the ground, and Bright Star did the same. "If Joseph doesn't recover . . ."

"Don't say it," Bright Star hissed. Ash peppered the air, drifting onto her shoulders. "Just dig, but with care. Use the blades to loosen the earth, and then I'll fetch our canoe paddles to scoop the soil away. These will be shallow graves, so near the water, so we'll cover both of them with rocks to keep animals from rooting them up."

A knot cinched around Catherine's throat. The last time she had stood at a graveside with her sister, they'd buried their mother, and since then Bright Star had buried two husbands and both children. Catherine knew better than to say it aloud, but if Joseph did not survive, it would be her fault. She could not bear to lose him, nor could she stand to be the cause of one more death in Bright Star's life.

Bright Star trod the soft ground, looking for a place to bury the bodies. Satisfied, she held the handle of the hatchet in both hands, light and shadow dancing over her heart-shaped face. "I have one more thing to say to you. Samuel's words were meant for your ears, and yours for his. But one thing you said did not fit, and as he did not correct you, I will."

Catherine braced for a scolding.

"You said Samuel took an interest in you because you needed help. Help with what? Living with Gabriel?" Bright Star's eyes narrowed. "No. Samuel must have loved you for other reasons, because you do not need his help. You didn't need anyone's, ever. You were Catherine Stands-Apart, so independent that you broke fellowship with the People. I have chided you for this many times, because that was easier than admitting how hurt I was that you went away when I longed for my sister to stay. But it was not fair to call you selfish. You are the one who helps Gabriel and Thankful. You are the one who helped me live again, when I longed to bury myself just to be near my children. You are still Catherine Stands-Apart, and strong. Now dig."

At last the sun's disc surfaced in the east. The lookouts were buried, Joseph and Gaspard had been tended, and both men were still asleep.

Wind rushed through trees that shivered and gave up their leaves in a blizzard of bronze and gold. Catherine fastened a cape about her shoulders as she stood and examined the sky. "We need to move."

Gaspard was likely just thick with sleep from too much rum, but it was Joseph who concerned her. The bandages ripped from Thankful's petticoats had soaked through three times already. He wouldn't recover here.

"He has lost a lot of blood," Bright Star murmured. "He won't be able to paddle."

Catherine had already considered this, along with Gaspard's injured arm and Samuel's weak shoulder. The men, it seemed, would be cargo for the women to port. "We can manage. We're close to the Saint-François River, and we have allies at Odanak." The detour off the St. Lawrence would add roughly eight miles there and back again, but it was their best option. "The Abenaki have healing herbs, and I'm sure they will not turn us away if we come seeking their help."

Bright Star stood and raised an eyebrow. "They will not turn *us* away. Samuel Crane will not be welcome." She glanced over her shoulder toward where he kept watch over Gaspard while cleaning the musket.

Thunder rumbled. Catherine led her sister toward the river, where they could speak more freely. Spying Thankful kneeling at the water's edge, Catherine joined her at her task. The water stained pink where they scrubbed strips of petticoat that had been used as bandages the night before. Upstream from them, Bright Star squatted and refilled her canteen.

Thankful's knuckles were chapped and red as she wrung out the linen she'd just rinsed. Her thin cotton gown sank limply against her legs without her petticoats beneath her skirt. "What do we do?"

Catherine plunged a crusted strip of cloth into the river and worked a handful of pebbles against it. "Joseph needs more care than we can give him. He will stay at Odanak while I take Samuel the rest of the way. I'm thinking about bringing Gaspard, too."

Bright Star corked one canteen and began to fill another. "He may prove useful to you, since Samuel's French is so accented. I will oversee Joseph's care and keeping in Odanak."

Low-bellied clouds hung heavy in a sky of hammered pewter. Thankful sat back on her heels, countenance wary beneath smudges of dirt across her cheek. "Odanak," she repeated. "The Abenaki? We're going to their village?" The tip of her nose was pink with cold.

"They will not capture you again," Catherine said. "You're safe now, Thankful." But that rang untrue. This entire journey put her at risk. "I know you're afraid, but you would be far safer staying with them than continuing on to Quebec with us."

The hair that had worked free of Thankful's bun hung in greasy strands over her shoulders. "Safe. With the people who raided my home and killed my parents?"

"The past is buried," Catherine began, and then halted to examine her motivation. Was she once again ordering Thankful about for her own good? Or was urging Thankful to face the Abenaki truly in the young woman's best interest?

Large drops made ripples in the river. Catherine blinked the rain from her lashes. "The closer we get to Quebec, the more danger there will be. I know how you feel about the Abenaki, and I understand why. But you said yourself that the best way to work on forgiveness is to face the ones you aim to forgive. Bright Star will be with you. Their hospitality will be generous, I promise."

The rain came faster now, pattering through the silver maple above them with a hum and a whir. Cold streams spilled down the back of Catherine's neck.

Shoulders lifted rigidly toward her ears, Thankful twirled a wet strand of hair around her finger. She bit the inside of her cheek, pulling the skin even tighter across the bones of her face. Her stomach growled, a faint echo of thunder, and she soberly met Catherine's gaze. "I pray you're right."

Before Catherine could form a response, Bright Star snapped her fingers, then gestured for them to fall back, away from the shoreline. She pointed upstream.

Catherine crouched beside Thankful behind a thatch of river bulrush five feet high. The convoy of schooners sailed toward them, white canvas snapping against masts, rigging rattling, bowsprits spearing toward Quebec like bayonets. Loaded with wheat and flour, the hulls sat lower in the river than the last time she'd seen them. Now going downstream, they clipped through the water with good speed.

The sight brought both a lift and a twinge to Catherine's spirit. Those ships bore the means of the French army's survival and the promise of another hungry winter for Montreal. For some to live, some might have to die. This was the truth that sat like a boulder on her chest.

As the last of five schooners came near, Thankful shrank to hide herself more fully behind the shrub. Ducking her head, Catherine peered through the leaves until she saw the cause of Thankful's reaction.

Heedless of the rain pelting his face, an officer gripped the rail, feet planted wide on the forecastle deck as he scanned both banks of the river. She knew the slant of his shoulders beneath the grey-white *justaucorps*, the gold braid on his tricorne hat, the curve of his nose. It was Pierre Moreau, his work done in Montreal. He was looking for something.

Without a doubt, Catherine knew he was looking for them.

By the time Catherine's bateau neared the village of Odanak, with Bright Star's canoe close behind her, Gaspard had quietly finished last night's bottle of rum. Joseph had awakened long enough for Catherine to explain that she would leave him with the Abenaki for better care. His face was tight and his skin beaded with sweat from pain he would never admit to, but the fact that he'd conceded without a fight was confession enough.

After beaching the vessels on the low-lying terrace, Samuel climbed out and squinted up the hill toward the fortified village surrounded by wooden palisades. Bright Star carried the last jug of rum in one arm as she came up next to him. Thankful and Gaspard followed her out.

Catherine steadied Joseph as he pushed himself up on one leg. Jaw clenched, he took Samuel's arm and hopped out onto dry land. Quickly, she scrambled up beside him and supported his weight on one side while Samuel held him up on the other.

As they wended up the wooded path to the village gates, the rain thinned to a drizzle, but they were all soaked through to the skin already. Catherine leaned forward to speak to Samuel. "Remember, you are my captive." Technically, it was true, since her father had paid his ransom. And it was more reasonable to present this clearly than to make Samuel stay behind, alone, while she and Bright Star spoke with their trading contacts. "You belong to me." Heat flashed over her face. "I mean—"

A rueful smile tipped Samuel's lips. "I know what you meant. I'll play along."

Joseph hobbled between them, and Catherine was struck once more by the magnitude of his injury. Infection had invaded the wound and brought intense fever with it. She squeezed the hand that gripped her shoulder and held him firmly around his solid waist, with Samuel's arm crossing from the other side.

Recalling what had happened to her father's arm, she knew that Joseph might lose his leg. If he kept it, he might never recover the use of it, for she had no illusions that the bone could heal from such a smashing. In either case, how could he hunt? Could he be a warrior still, or would he be dependent on others? Her mind choked on visions of Gabriel, who had plunged into depression and drunkenness after his trapping accident. She could not bear the thought of Joseph suffering a similar decline.

He deserved none of this.

"I'm so sorry," Catherine told him, pressing him firmly to her side. Odanak was situated on a bluff, and the uphill climb was taking its toll on him. "If you hadn't followed me, this would not have happened." Her throat threatened to strangle the words.

He sighed through gritted teeth. "A warrior's life is short, my sister. I accept this."

"But if you'd known protecting me would cause this—"

Joseph grunted, features twisting into a grimace. "*If. If.* A useless word. I did what any man would do for his family. I would do it again."

The words were razors against Catherine's ears, spoken by a man who was her kin by half and yet still called her fully his own. Regret and gratitude battled for the upper hand, each as fierce as the other, until she felt filled with nothing else.

Inside the twelve-foot-tall palisades, the village of Odanak, otherwise known as Saint-François, was not at all like Kahnawake. Instead of a stockade arrangement of longhouses, about fifty European-style homes held several hundred Abenaki. Most were made of square log timbers covered with lengths of bark or rough-cut boards. At least a dozen were one- or two-story French-style wood-frame houses with clapboards, and a church was built of stone. All of them were arranged in rows around a central square, which held a Jesuit church and a council house. And yet above houses and prominent buildings, including the mission church, poles bore not flags, but scalps. Hundreds upon hundreds of scalps.

Thankful faltered when she spied them, and Bright Star murmured in her ear. Whatever she said at least kept Thankful moving.

Odanak was the launching point for so many raids into New England that it was notorious among the British and famous among the French, who encouraged their actions. The people who ventured outdoors were proof of decades, if not longer, of successful captures. Their skin was white, red, brown, and black. British settlers, African slaves, and other native peoples had been assimilated into this enclave, marrying and mating between races, and yet all were known as Abenaki. Along with their linen tunics and deerskin leggings or skirts, some wore conical birchbark hats to shed the rain. Nose rings and earrings adorned the men.

Clouds broke apart, and shafts of timid sun spilled down. Reaching the trading post, Catherine and Samuel eased Joseph onto a barrel inside the door. Dust hung suspended in the shadows. The air was thick and musty from the recent rain, sharp with the smell of animal skins. In many ways, it reminded Catherine of home, from the bucket and drinking gourd inside the door to the patterned baskets and beaded collars on display.

"Fawn? It's Bright Star." Her sister hoisted the rum onto a table.

A shuffling sound preceded the emergence from the back room of an Abenaki woman whose long silver-streaked hair was secured by a feathered headband. Her face was creased from age and weather, her eyes deep-set and kind. Greeting Bright Star and Catherine, Fawn's smile piled more lines into her cheeks. She had traded furs with them for years.

Samuel ducked back outside to wait with Thankful and Gaspard while Bright Star presented the situation—and the remaining rum—to Fawn. "My brother has been injured." She gestured to where he rested. "If you agree, I would stay and care for him myself, just until he's well enough to travel. Could you spare a room?" It was understood that with shelter would come food, water, and any herbs and poultices that may help.

"Of course." Glancing his way, Fawn rubbed a thumb over the polished slate pendant about her neck. "Stay here as my guest as long as you need. Catherine, you'll be staying, as well?" She brought a pipe to her lips and puffed.

The sweet tang of tobacco lined Catherine's nose, reminding her of the smoke rings Gabriel used to blow. When she'd laughed, so had he. But those uncomplicated days were a distant, fading memory. Shoving his face from her mind, she focused on Fawn's question. "I have business elsewhere, but if you don't mind, there is another young woman named Thankful who might stay."

"She may if she likes," Fawn said. "What of the yellow-haired man? Who is he?"

"My captive. A ransomed British prisoner of war."

Narrowing her eyes, Fawn cradled the bowl of her pipe in her palm. "He is not another emissary from the British general Amherst?"

Catherine told her he was not. "You've had emissaries here? What did they want?"

Bright Star's expression feigned a casual indifference. "Excuse me, but first, is there somewhere we can take our brother?"

Following Fawn's instructions, Bright Star

and Catherine supported Joseph once more and brought him to a small room at the back of the post. Bright Star spread a fur over the floor, and with a silent grimace, Joseph lowered himself onto it. Animal skins and bunches of corn tied by their husks hung from poles near the ceiling, shrinking the already small space.

"What did she say about the British?" Joseph rasped, and Catherine squeezed his outstretched hand.

Bright Star folded a faded blanket beneath his injured leg to cushion it. "It isn't wise to appear curious."

"My sister, the tides are changing. We must be ready to change with them." His eyelids drifted closed. "Our friends have not all been true . . ."

Bright Star's braids swung as she leaned over Joseph and told him to rest. "I will see you soon and will bring help."

In the front room, Fawn stood just inside the open door, pipe clenched between the teeth that remained to her. In the wedge of light she occupied, her gnarled hands busied themselves grinding hominy with a long wooden paddle in a straight-sided barrel.

She looked up when Catherine neared, and beckoned with her finger. "We have known each other many years," Fawn said. "You know our custom would be to welcome you and your entire company to eat. But this time, it will be a kindness to you if I send you on your way." Taking her pipe in her hand, she pointed with it to a pouch on a nearby table. "There's dried venison to last a few days if you can stretch it, and a few rounds of flat bread. Take that with you, and soon. There are some who would not believe your man is your captive, but assume he is a spy, as they called the other two British men who were escorted here by six Stockbridge Mohicans."

Catherine thanked her for the food and tucked the welcome offering under her arm, dropping her gaze to the corn being ground into meal. "What happened to them? The British and Mohicans."

"One Mohican was killed, but I doubt either army cares much about that. As for the British, they were not slain. Abused, as is our custom, but they live."

Ritualistic torture. It was the only true name for what must have happened. Catherine fought to disguise her recoil.

"Our warriors took them straight to Trois-Rivières, where they are in irons on the French ship there," Fawn continued. "If you don't want the same for your captive, I'll bid you good-bye and peace. Get you gone and in good time, for our warriors love a chase." She poked the pipe back between her teeth and took to pounding the corn once more.

Bright Star pulled Catherine by the elbow, accusation in her grip, for she had always been against this voyage. But her lips formed just one word. "Go!"

Catherine would go, indeed. And their path led straight past Trois-Rivières.

Samuel's arm was around Thankful's shoulders when Catherine emerged from the post with Bright Star. Tears slipped down Thankful's wan cheeks, meeting below her chin. Gaspard slouched against the outside of the post, one knee bent so that his foot rested on the timbered wall.

"Time to go? Can't say I'll miss the place." Gaspard pushed away from the post and took a few steps, but when no one followed, he stopped with an exaggerated sigh and sidled back into the shade.

"Thankful?" Catherine took her hands and found her fingers stone cold. Her urgency to put this place behind her bowed to the need to address this fear. The nine-year difference in age between them expanded until Catherine felt more like an aunt or mother to the young woman. "I believe this is for the best. I think you can do this—stay here with Bright Star and help Joseph get well. But I want to know if you believe you can, for that is what matters most."

"If I can, it will only be by the grace of God." Thankful's voice betrayed her doubt.

"Then give the grace of the Great Good God a chance to do its work." Bright Star's sharp tone belied her impatience. She began again, more temperate. "Thankful, you can assist me here, but that is not why I think you should stay. I think you have something else that needs mending, and it can best be done right here. You do not need my sister for this. You need Someone else."

As Thankful glanced about, Catherine could almost hear the objections forming in her mind. That this was a godless place, though a chapel spiked a spire toward the sky. A place where her terrors had been born and her nightmares lived in broad daylight.

Scalps on poles lining the street lifted in the wind. Grimacing, Gaspard watched them, fists jammed into his trouser pockets. The scalps were old, by Catherine's reckoning, shrunken and without smell. But blond hair fluttered like tattered ribbons.

Thankful covered her mouth with both hands and turned her face into Samuel's chest. His hand came over the top of her head with as much care as if they were family. In the sense that mattered most, they were. He, more than anyone else, understood exactly what she felt.

Samuel lifted Thankful's chin with his finger. "Thankful." His voice held a father's warmth and comfort. "Remember what we have talked about before. God is not hemmed in by church or chapel, He does not belong to priests alone. He is no respecter of the lines drawn between nations, armies, or empires, but lives within you, wherever you are. You cannot get away from Him. He is here, because He dwells in you. Don't be afraid."

A tremulous smile transformed her face. "My faith is weak."

"He is strong. That's all you need."

Thankful reached out and grasped both Catherine's hand and Bright Star's. "Pray for me," she whispered, desperation in her tone. Then she bade Samuel a tearful farewell before hugging Catherine around the neck. "Don't stop praying, even if I am not the subject of your prayers. And I will pray for your safe return."

Agreeing, Catherine bussed Thankful's cheeks and asked Samuel and Gaspard to wait one moment more. She ducked back inside the trading post to say good-bye to her brother. Kneeling beside him, she spoke his name, and his eyelids fluttered open.

"I'm going now, with Samuel and Gaspard. Bright Star and Thankful will take good care of you here, and I'll see you when I return."

Joseph licked his lips. "I do not like that you go alone with those two men."

"A few days, brother, and it will be over."

He grunted. "Thankful is afraid, I think, to be

among the Abenaki. But I will keep her safe. I will make her feel safe if I can."

"I have no doubt of that."

"*O:nen*," he whispered. *Good-bye.*

"*Au revoir*, Joseph." *See you again.* Catherine kissed his cheek and left.

Bright Star remained outside with Samuel, Thankful, and Gaspard. How weathered she looked, but how nobly and tall she still stood.

"Thank you," Catherine whispered. "This is more than I wanted you to bear. Don't wait for my return. As soon as Joseph is well enough, take the canoe home again."

Confusion flickered over Bright Star's features. "You are only days away from Quebec. How many sleeps until you come back this way? Won't you just make your deliveries and return?"

The pouch with Fawn's food still pressed between her elbow and side, Catherine retied the ribbon around the end of her loosening braid. "That is my plan. But who can say what might happen? You do what is best for you."

Her sister lifted her sheathed hunting knife over her head and placed it over Catherine's. "Protect yourself."

Catherine's hand went to the weapon. "I will."

Bright Star's smile was rueful. "Good. But I meant your heart."

CHAPTER TWENTY-FOUR

Gaspard was one more thorn in the briar patch of Catherine's concerns. For now, at least, he was feeling better after drinking the rum, and using his good arm on the rudder as she rowed on the Saint-François River toward the St. Lawrence. Samuel insisted on rowing, too, but the stiffness of his frame suggested that more than a sore shoulder troubled him.

"I'm not any happier about our guest than you are," she said to Samuel. "But what do you suppose would happen if we release him?"

"Oh no. Not yet, you don't," Gaspard interjected. "I told you my parents are outside Quebec, and if that's where you're headed, I'm along for the ride. You don't tell anyone I'm a deserter, and I won't tell anyone you're spies. Look, if none of us hold a flag for King Louis, that means we're on the same side now, right?"

Resting his oar in the oarlock, Samuel challenged him. "Quite a loose interpretation of loyalties."

"It makes sense though, doesn't it?" Gaspard said. "It's only fair. Then we both get what we want. That business with the lookouts—I wasn't betraying you. I was buying time, which you would know if you hadn't interrupted."

Catherine leaned forward and pulled back with her oar. "There are rules to this game, Gaspard. You play the role we give you, at a moment's notice, and you play it so well you convince us both. If we bid you be silent, make no sound. If you play the captor in order to get us past patrols, make us believers."

Samuel jabbed a finger at the militiaman's chest. "Try to harm either one of us or give us any reason to doubt your intentions, and we'll bind you up, discard you like so much jetsam, and be all the more swiftly on our way." With a firm double pat to Gaspard's knee, he resumed rowing.

The young man had little to say after that, and Catherine was more than content with the quiet.

As soon as they reached the St. Lawrence and turned northeast, the river broadened into Lac Saint-Pierre, an expanse twenty-one miles long and six miles wide. Too wide for Catherine to see the opposite shore. White egrets stood on spindly legs in the shallows, and great herons soared overhead, long necks folded, wings slow but sure in their flight.

Miles passed. Gaspard distributed modest rations from Fawn's pouch, and as Catherine ate and rowed, she replayed the events of the last day in her mind. They were painted in a palette of crimson and grey, a shocking contrast to the riot of autumn shades surrounding her now. Scrubbed clean from the rain, the sky doubled its blue on the water. The broad satin sheet stretched before them, trimmed near the shore by maples turned saffron and scarlet. A gust of wind stripped leaves from their branches and sent them cartwheeling across the water, where they swirled in the eddies made by their oars. She drank it all in as though nature's tranquility could be stored up and savored later.

After finishing his portion of dried venison, Samuel broke the silence. "Tell me again what Fawn said."

At once, the peace she'd sensed drained away. Stifling a sigh, she repeated what she knew. "Two British men claimed to be Amherst's emissaries and were escorted by six Mohicans."

"In French, please," Gaspard called. "If I'm going to play a part, I must be privy to the information."

He had a point, and Catherine acquiesced. "The Abenaki would not hear them, but took them prisoner and delivered them to the French at Trois-Rivières. If they had listened, what do you think the British men would have said?"

Samuel pulled his oar through the water. "If they were truly sent by Amherst, my guess is that it was an overture of friendship, or at least neutrality. Amherst is still at Crown Point, but when he sends men north, which I've no doubt he will do, I'm certain he'll want assurances that the natives will not harass them on their way to fight the French."

A hope deferred for the British general. Whatever qualms Joseph had about Mohawk alliances, the Abenaki clearly knew which side they were on. It was no surprise, given their history of attacks on New England.

"Amherst received an answer, but not the one he wanted. What do you suppose he'll do now?" she asked Samuel.

Early afternoon sun caught on his blond hair. "If the emissaries were unharmed, he may try again. If they were tortured or killed, the attempts will cease, and the Abenaki will be a sworn enemy."

"Odanak is a long way from Crown Point," Catherine mused.

"It is. That distance, especially with the coming winter, likely only makes the Abenaki more confident that Amherst's army can't touch them there. British raiders have never reached that far before."

"Does that mean they never will?" Catherine asked.

Samuel paused before replying. "You're thinking of Thankful and your sister and brother. I've seen too much and lived too long to promise you they'll be fine, but I know worrying won't protect them." He paused again. "We can't protect the ones we love. Only God can, and sometimes He doesn't."

Catherine stared across the water. "That fails to comfort me."

"Your comfort is not my concern."

She matched Samuel's stern expression. Beyond him, Gaspard rolled his lips between his teeth, raised his eyebrows, then looked away, whistling.

Her irritation simmered at both men. "That's obvious, Samuel, or you'd never have insisted I bring you on this journey."

His shoulders sloped downward. "I won't deny it. But aren't we all at risk every day, for no reason at all? Illness, an accident, hunger? God can keep us safe on an ordinary day, or not. He can keep us safe in war, or not."

A moment passed before Gaspard spoke. "Well. It's been some time since I've confessed or prayed, but if I get a vote, I vote for safe in war." Bowing his head, he crossed himself. "Or at least safer than we have been so far. One bullet through my arm is enough for me. I am sorry, by the way, about Joseph."

"Thank you, Gaspard," Catherine replied.

"Be glad you still have your siblings," Gaspard went on, the levity gone from his voice. "If I could talk to Augustin just one more time . . . well. I'd give a lot to be able to do that. I could usually tell what he was thinking just by looking at him. A squint meant suspicion. A smile meant he was nervous, and a squeeze to the back of his neck with one hand meant his patience was coming to an end. He gets that—he got that one from our father." Shrugging, he adjusted the steering oar to help straighten their course. "Your siblings are harder to read."

Catherine silently agreed with him. How could she explain the little boy who had matured into her most loyal guardian? The sister who had grown more distant as years went by, at least until fairly recently? "Most of the time I understand them, but sometimes they do surprise me."

"I haven't figured the three of you out," Gaspard admitted. "Are you very close to them?"

Pulling at the oar, Catherine increased the distance that separated her from her brother and sister. "Not close enough."

"Trois-Rivières is just up ahead." Catherine tightened the ribbons binding her braids into a knot at the nape of her neck. After Lac Saint-Pierre narrowed back into the goose neck of the St. Lawrence River, it was only a short stretch to this point.

"It's the halfway point of our journey, isn't it?" Gaspard asked. His freckles blended into sunburned cheeks. "We should see more lookouts from here on out."

The smell of burning coal and hot metal announced the foundry before they neared it. On the opposite side of the river, high on a bluff stained champagne pink with the evening sun, the walled city stood.

"That must be where the British emissaries are being held." Samuel pointed to a French frigate anchored at the port, the name *Atalante* emblazoned on its stern. With the sails rolled tight against the masts, the wind rattled through ratlines and snapped the French flag high atop the crow's nest. The sides of the vessel bristled with cannons below a deck that held precious few men.

On the shore, a French cavalryman paced on his mount, his coat a smear of blue with red collar and cuffs. For an instant, Catherine's pulse skipped. But as he was watching for British warships, a single bateau would not command his attention. Unless Captain Moreau had alerted the cavalry to look for them.

But there was nowhere to go but forward, right past the frigate.

"Do not speak," Catherine murmured to Samuel. To Gaspard, "Remember the plan."

With a purposeful but unhurried pace, she pulled the oar through the river. The frigate was more than five times the length of the bateau. Even its shadow smelled of the prisoners kept belowdecks. Deeply in and deeply out she breathed, willing herself to remain calm. She was a Canadian citizen, after all. There was no reason she should not be here.

"You there!" The voice pinched. "Bonjour, mademoiselle and messieurs! Yes, you in that tiny bateau! What are you about?"

She twisted to see who spoke. A French sailor hailed them from the frigate deck.

"Those men should be with their militia unit!" His white neckstock strained above waistcoat and breeches of huckleberry blue.

"Bonjour! We're following the convoy to Quebec," Gaspard replied, pointing a thin finger. "You must have seen it pass through here, loaded with food. We've come from Montreal."

Shadows hovered just beneath the sailor's tricorne hat, obscuring his eyes but not the curious tilt of his mouth. "Up you come, the lot of you," he ordered. Sun glinted on the silver buckles of his shoes and the musket barrel in his hand.

Stones fell to the pit of Catherine's stomach, but a bateau could not outrun a frigate.

Children ran up and down the docks as she paddled close enough to throw a line over a piling. Samuel climbed out and secured it, and Catherine added trade items to a beaded pouch slung across her body. When she stepped out and onto the dock, Gaspard beside her, the sailor was marching toward them already, the heels of his shoes clipping across the wooden planks. He gripped Samuel's right elbow.

"Don't!" Catherine reached out to stop him from pulling. "His shoulder was dislocated a few days ago. This man is my captive, ransomed at Montreal after being taken at Fort Saint-Frédéric as a prisoner of war. He belongs to me."

The sailor rubbed his thumb over the cleft in his chin, eyeing Samuel from his cropped hair to his moccasins. "And this one?" He appraised Gaspard, whose hair was tailed in the common fashion. "What's your business?"

If Gaspard harbored any qualms about being discovered a deserter, he didn't show it. "I was detached from my unit to help oversee the wheat harvest on the Montreal Plain. I worked under Captain Pierre Moreau while there, but stayed behind to recover after a little skirmish with some natives." He tapped the bandage on his arm. "We couldn't delay the convoy on my account, though. Now that I'm on the mend, I aim to redeem lost time. I'm rejoining my unit, and this man is a carpenter. His skills could be useful to us in ship repair and many other things. And so, if you please . . ." He flourished a hand toward the river in a perfect blend of nonchalance and confidence. A magnificent performance.

The sailor grunted. "That doesn't explain why *you're* here." He squinted at Catherine with closely set eyes. If the lines framing them could be read like the rings of a tree, she'd guess he had nearly three decades.

She placed a hand on her hip. "Do you have any idea how much money it cost to ransom a captive with a trade? Do you have any idea what I can *make* off him? I'm not letting my investment out of my sight. I'll let him serve, but he's coming back with me when the task is complete. Besides, I'm their guide to get there. I've plied these waters as a porter in the fur trade and know the way better than they do." Lifting her chin, she crossed her arms. In her buckskin dress, she knew she looked the part.

The sailor looked east. "The convoy of schooners you mentioned passed by not long ago with the last of the wheat and flour. But those brigs will never be able to sneak past the British gunships. I heard they're gathering a fleet of bateaux to transfer the cargo down-stream." He cast a glance toward Catherine's vessel.

"And we shall meet them there," Gaspard improvised. "We are to rendezvous during the transfer." Truly, he was so skilled at deception, Catherine wondered if he might deceive her, too. Or if perhaps he already had.

"So you're to help with that, eh?" The sailor chewed the inside of his cheek, then swore. "Habits," he muttered, "but when there's no tobacco to chew, it makes for a painful experience. You'd think that if they keep bread from a man, they would give him something else, wouldn't you?"

Catherine clutched the strap of her shoulder bag. "Surely the schooners dropped off some of the wheat here first."

"No, mademoiselle, they did not. No bread, no wheat, no flour. It all goes to Quebec. But you know what we do have here? Shoe brushes. We may die of starvation, but we'll do it with mighty clean shoes and spit-polished buckles."

Catherine took in the sailor's gaunt frame and his shining black leather shoes. "I helped harvest that wheat. If it were up to me, you'd have your share of it, and that's the truth."

"I'm sure it is." He studied Samuel once more. "You know, we have two of your friends in irons, and it's lucky they're alive at all."

"The emissaries who tried to reach the Abenakis?" Gaspard proved he'd been paying attention.

The sailor laughed shortly. "That's what they call themselves. A likely story. They were caught in plain clothes. No uniforms. We could shoot them as spies, and still might." He tugged the sleeve of Samuel's green shirt. "You look like one of them rangers to me. Rogers' Rangers. Those famous short-haired, green-frocked wilderness soldiers, n'est-ce pas?"

"Well, he isn't. As I said, he's my captive,

and we best be on our way." Before the sailor could say anything else, she reached into her pouch. "Since you did not receive the wheat you deserved, please accept these gifts instead." She presented him with small mirrors, eating utensils, and a bag of chewing tobacco. "It's too much for one man, I grant you. But surely you have friends who might be willing to trade for some of these items? And now, we'll be on our way." Satisfied they had reached an understanding, she, Gaspard, and Samuel returned to the bateau, while the sailor watched.

Not until they had rowed well out of sight of Trois-Rivières did Catherine begin to relax. This time, she sat in the stern so she could steer.

"How'd I do?" One hand on his oar, Gaspard tipped a canteen to his lips, then wiped his mouth with the back of his hand. "I was good. So good, I can't imagine how you could have done it without me. Trust me now? Finally? Because that story was very like the one I meant to tell the lookouts before you stopped me."

"You did well." A downy feather carried on the breeze and drifted into Catherine's lap. She rolled it between her fingers for a moment before tossing it overboard. "But he took you for a spy, Samuel. We escaped by the skin of our teeth."

"And came away with intelligence we can use." Seated in front, Samuel spoke in a tone both low and intense. "The schooners need bateaux. Those large ships were useful for transporting masses of grain in bulk, but you heard what the sailor said. They can't possibly sneak by British gunships. They'll need to transfer the wheat into bateaux for the last leg of the journey. Bateaux just like this one. Gaspard may have been telling the truth when he said we would meet them."

She adjusted her grip on the weathered oar so the splitting wood would not bite her skin. "We'll never reach them in time."

"But if we do—"

"We won't. And if we did, you'd be in the center of suspicion again, this time with more than just one sailor to placate. My trading and Gaspard's talking will only go so far."

Gaspard scanned the shoreline. "From here to Cap-Rouge, the lookouts will be multiplied far beyond what we've seen so far."

"How many?" Samuel asked. They skirted a small island thick with pine trees, and the wind whispering over them carried their scent across the water.

The bateau rocked gently as Gaspard shifted his weight on the center seat. "I don't have a number for the stretch from here to the mouth of the Jacques-Cartier River. But between the Jacques-Cartier and Cap-Rouge, I heard there are eight hundred and twenty."

"How many miles is that?" Samuel asked.

"Twenty. With so many men, if they are stationed on both shores . . ." She divided them in her mind by half, then by miles, then feet. "That's a lookout every two hundred sixty-four feet. Can that be right?"

Samuel sliced an oar through the water and pulled. "Aye, I figured the same. That's a lot of nervous fingers on triggers."

Favoring his injured arm, Gaspard continued to row. "I admit I'm not eager for that. But my home is north of Quebec."

The violence of their last encounter with lookouts loomed large in Catherine's mind. Arrows, bullets, screams, and smoke. Bright Star burying bodies. Joseph's ruined limb, and Thankful with his blood on her hands.

A wave of Canada geese flapped loudly overhead, their V-shaped formation undulating against a mottled blue sky. How unconcerned they were with the plights of men, who drew invisible lines on land to claim it, who starved and killed and died to shift those lines around.

Catherine waited for the geese to pass. "Our best chance is to stay together. The river is wide. We'll stay away from the shores and time our voyaging carefully. If we're questioned, Gaspard can supply the same answer he gave the sailor."

Pulling his oar in for a moment, Gaspard

rummaged through the remaining supplies until he found the empty jug of rum he'd already finished. He tipped it upside down, shaking it over his open mouth, and caught two drops on his tongue. Groaning, he returned it to the vessel's floor. "Just as well. When I get home, I'll get there sober, saints preserve me. I must get to my parents, empty-handed though I'll be."

For the first time, Samuel regarded Gaspard with a glimmer of understanding. "I know you lost a brother. I lost mine, too. We all want to get home to the family we have left."

Catherine swallowed the sting in her throat.

CHAPTER TWENTY-FIVE

Once, to be with Samuel beneath a moon such as this was Catherine's own version of paradise. But in no version in her imagination did they share the romantic setting with a deserter groaning again for lack of drink.

Bowed low in the bottom of the vessel, Gaspard trembled between Samuel and Catherine. At least his retching had stopped several miles upstream, but his suffering remained obvious to them. She only prayed it would not be obvious to anyone else. Reaching forward, she touched his back. Heat radiated from beneath the linen.

Samuel looked on, his profile severe with censure. "If fever wracks his mind as it did when he attacked me . . ."

"It may not come to that," she whispered as she rowed. With Gaspard unable to help, she'd tied the steering oar into position, reaching to swivel it and make course corrections as necessary while she helped Samuel move the bateau north.

"I pray you're right. But he may not have his wits at his disposal."

Catherine knew that well enough. "Just let him rest." For the past two days, she had matched their travel to the moon's pull on the tide so the currents could carry them swiftly downstream, well out of view of any lookouts on the bluffs. The river had been two miles wide or greater since they'd left Trois-Rivières. The one time the bateau had drifted too close to shore, Gaspard had persuaded inquiring soldiers that all was just as it should be. All they needed to do now was keep quiet.

Bright Star had excelled at that, even when there had been no risk of danger. The first porting trip they'd made together after the loss of her family, Bright Star had been so silent that Catherine could scarcely believe she was the same sister who had once had so much to say. As children, Bright Star had been the first to grow up and quick to correct Catherine's ways. But she'd also told the best bedtime stories, especially on the nights when their parents argued outside.

Almost as soon as Strong Wind and Gabriel began slinging harsh words by the fire, Bright Star had scooped Joseph and Catherine onto her bed and spun fantastical tales that always began with, *"I have a story you just won't believe!"* And just like that, the ugliness between their parents faded behind adventure, love, loss, and reunion. Joseph was always the first to fall asleep, and then it was just the two sisters. Bright Star brushed the hair off Catherine's sweat-damp forehead and gave her stories happy endings night after night after night. *"Your kids are going to love that one!"* Catherine would tell her, for she'd always known Bright Star was born to mother.

So when the silence had stretched for hours on their first trading trip together, Catherine had been the one to break it. *"Tell me a story?"* she'd asked, hoping to reach back to the place in time when they'd had at least that in common. Bright Star hadn't responded right away. Then, *"I'm all out of happy endings."*

Oars creaked in the oarlocks, and Catherine pulled herself back to the present. By the time she rejoined her siblings and Thankful after this trip, what tales would they have to share? Whatever lay ahead at Cap-Rouge and Quebec, the one thing she knew was that the story of her forced reunion with Samuel Crane would soon be at an end.

The bateau bobbed in the current, and Gaspard moaned again. Samuel offered him a canteen, but Gaspard pushed it away.

"What does he need?" Samuel whispered to Catherine. "What could make him feel better?"

"Aside from being on dry land, I don't know," she replied. "My father has never tried to give up drinking, so I have no experience with this." Her lips tipped up on one side.

Samuel chuckled and shook his head.

Perhaps she ought not make light of Gabriel's

struggle, if one could call it that. "He isn't a completely horrible person, you know."

"Bright Star and Joseph would disagree, and I've seen enough myself to know why." Finger to his lips, he began rowing once more.

While they resumed their silence, Catherine recalled fond memories that tempered her father's faults. Gestures as small as tucking a wildflower into her hair had told her what his words rarely did.

The loons were muffled in the early morning fog. Dew settled a chill onto her skin and made heavy the braid coiled about her head. Not ten miles separated them from Quebec. The closer they were to gaining that city under siege, the more alert Samuel grew, a soldier preparing to rejoin the fight.

Thick mist hovered over the river and slowed their progress. Sounds, though dim, traveled across the water.

Voices.

Samuel's back jolted ramrod straight. Catherine held firm the oar, tilting her head, straining to hear. Before she could distinguish the words, let alone the riverbanks, the bateau jerked and skidded to a stop. In the fog and her distraction, she had accidentally beached it on the shore. She winced at the scrape of the bateau against rock, unnaturally loud in the quiet morning.

Grunting, Gaspard sat up and peered around.

He put a hand to his troubled stomach, but the tremors seemed to have passed.

"What's this, what's this?" A man emerged from the vapors, spying Samuel first. "Are you here to caulk? Monsieur Cadet sent you?"

Catherine could not believe their fortune. No suspicion laced the man's tone as he mentioned the purveyor general of Canada. In fact, it seemed they would fit right in, exactly as Samuel had hoped.

Rallying, Gaspard licked his lips and replied. "Mais oui." As the French soldier introduced himself to them as Richard Martin, Samuel climbed over the edge of the bateau and into the shallows. The river eddied about his buckskin-clad legs as he grabbed the vessel's side with his good arm and pulled it farther onto the beach. Rocks crunched under the bow as it swiveled sideways, becoming parallel with the shoreline.

"There are four other caulkers here already," Martin was saying. "Arrived not long before you, but . . ." He scratched his chin while looking at the bow of the bateau. "You've come from a different direction, it would seem."

Catherine's heart tapped an erratic beat. "The fog did not make you easy to find." She climbed out and stood beside Samuel, feet wet inside her moccasins. Gaspard was slow to join her, his strength clearly not recovered.

"True enough." Martin peered into the thick

mist. "Went right past Cap-Rouge, did you, before you turned around again? Well, no wonder you're later than the others."

Gaspard introduced himself with a false name and explained that Samuel was a military captive skilled in bateau repair.

"We have need of that, for certain." Martin straightened the hat on his head. "But pardon me, young lady, you cannot be here to caulk, too."

"No." The only explanation was the original plan she and Samuel had devised. The one Pierre Moreau had extinguished, the one that had flared back to life in Samuel's mind in Trois-Rivières. "I have many skills, but caulking is not one of them. I came to offer the use of my bateau here, should you need it. It is seaworthy, and I'm a fine hand at rowing, so I'll carry whatever cargo it bears myself."

Martin grunted, then scratched the side of his bulbous nose. "A woman rower."

She stiffened. "I'm a trader, monsieur. Voyaging is part of my business."

His gaze narrowed on the knife hanging about her neck and her buckskin dress. "You savage women are such drudges, doing all the heavy labor while your men go off and hunt, eh? Seems you're bred for strength, if not beauty."

"I am just as French as I am Mohawk, which means I also possess the grace to be embarrassed by your lack of manners. You meet my generosity with insult." She clicked her tongue. "It would seem you've been away from civilized company too long. Or do you simply have no need of aid?"

Martin scratched behind his ear. Behind him, several other men had come to inspect the situation. The fog began to lift its lacy veil, and beneath it, Catherine spied an armada of bateaux dragged onto the beach, away from the tide's reach. A quick count revealed nineteen of them.

"That vessel looks solid," one of the men called out to Martin. "Some of ours aren't anymore and won't be, no matter how much caulk they get."

"What happened?" Gaspard pressed a balled-up handkerchief to his face and neck, dabbing fever-sweat away. What he needed was a bath.

"Holmes happened, that's what," Martin grumbled. "About fourteen miles southwest of here, the British Royal Navy pounced. We had already transferred the wheat from the schooners into the bateaux, expecting the smaller vessels to sneak past the British unnoticed. We were wrong."

"Spotted you anyway, did they?" Gaspard asked.

"A British warship opened fire on us, so we had no choice but to beach at Pointe-aux-Trembles. We saved the cargo, storing some in the local church and the rest in wooden carts, but some of our bateaux did not handle the sudden landings well. Others were damaged by Holmes. He had us trapped there before an all-day rain turned the ground to quagmire. He gave up his attempt to make a landing and drifted downstream. It was a delay we can ill afford."

"So you lost the use of a bateau," Catherine prompted. "Or more than one, perhaps?"

A dark laugh erupted behind Martin. He waved it away, then composed himself. "All right, if you're offering the bateau and your help to row it, we accept. Monsieur Cadet says the men at Quebec have just two days left of food—and I warrant those two days' worth are reduced rations that wouldn't amount to one decent meal when put together. Meanwhile, here we sit on thirty-three tons of flour and five hundred twenty-five bushels of wheat from Montreal. We'll take all the help we can to get it north."

Catherine sat in the shade of a tree and mended the moccasins of those who came to lay them at her feet. Her supply of patch leather already exhausted, she did the best she could with her awl, boring new holes through which to sew the seams together. The sinew in her patch kit had been quickly used, so she had taken to unraveling the fabric of an apron to salvage thread. Strips of it had already been ripped off for bandages for Gaspard, so whittling it further did not trouble her. The change of pace was a welcome relief for her shoulders and arms.

Every now and then, she paused to eat a few

hazelnuts from their dwindling supply, saving the last of Fawn's venison for later. She glanced up to see Samuel caulking a vessel and teaching Gaspard to do the same. The fact that they'd come without the necessary tools had not concerned the men here, as the policy among the French army was to supply men with what they needed only at the moment they needed it. Samuel made use of the tools sent with the four other caulkers and was not questioned. His skills were enough to recommend him, and Gaspard proved a reliable apprentice, though they both had much to lose if their true natures were discovered.

From where she sat, the mood at Cap-Rouge was restless and tense. With the morning fog but a memory, the sun set the red shale cliffs surrounding the settlement ablaze. The V-shaped cape off the St. Lawrence narrowed along the path of the Cap-Rouge River. Maples, oaks, and ash trees moved in the wind, gemstone-colored blurs of ruby, topaz, and garnet. On the north shore of the river, on the heights, lookout soldiers moved back and forth, patrolling for the enemy. From some place unseen, Catherine could hear columns marching, drilling.

Richard Martin ambled toward her and kicked off his moccasins, adding them to the pile beside her. Apparently, his turn drilling would be later. For now he sat cross-legged on the ground, squinting at the men repairing the bateaux.

"He's good, that Englishman you brought. Some of these bateaux were run aground so hard, I thought they couldn't be saved, but he might yet prove me wrong."

Catherine sent him a small smile. "He might."

Martin turned toward the sun-sparked river. "We'll make the final run to Quebec past Holmes' squadron as soon as we finish repairs and get reloaded."

She thrust her needle through a hole in the leather and pulled it through. "And when do you suppose that will be?"

"The night of the twelfth. So the day after tomorrow, we'll hurry to reload the cargo and then set off at dark for the six-mile trip. Tidal conditions will be ideal then, likely the best of the month. You're all right to row at night? Silently, like?"

She smiled. "I'll manage rowing in the dark just fine."

Martin swiped a hand across the back of his neck. "I figure we'll leave around ten o'clock, and then the falling tide will carry us right quick starting about two in the morning. If all goes well, we'll be in Quebec before first light at five thirty. None too soon, but not late either."

Catherine's hands stilled. "But we'll be rowing right past Holmes' squadrons? All nineteen bateaux?"

He raised his hands. "Real quiet-like, though! Just as silent as you please. They won't see or hear us this time. That disaster where Holmes pinned us down won't be repeated. They must have been tipped off by a deserter that we were near, that's all. But on the twelfth, the British won't even hear our own lookouts giving a challenge as we go by. And we've got a whole chain of outposts from here to Quebec, ready to fire on British ships should they harass us." His grin creased his face.

"But why wouldn't the lookouts challenge us and ask for a countersign?" Masking her eagerness, she bent over her work once more. Shifting a finished moccasin to the ground beside her, she drew its twin into her lap and inspected it.

"It's being managed. Monsieur Cadet sent word from Sillery just today. Governor-General Vaudreuil has ordered Bougainville's troops— the lookouts—to remain as silent as possible while our convoy passes by. No challenges." He tapped the side of his nose. "The British will have no idea we're bringing this campaign to a glorious close right beneath their noses. And all they've done so far is make useless attacks." He pushed himself up and stood over her, the breeze pushing the smell of his unwashed body in her direction. "You'll be ready, then? When the time comes?"

"I will," Catherine told him, and he left. As she pushed her needle in and out of the holes in the leather, her thoughts darted in similar fashion, binding together what patches of information she held. New pieces and old aligned.

But with just one tug in the wrong place, it would all unravel.

"Tell me again." Samuel adjusted his grip on the fishing pole. After a warmer than usual day, twilight had brought autumn's crisp tang to the air. All along the shore of Cap-Rouge, other soldiers were catching their dinner, as well. Gaspard sat and watched, his shaking having returned. Rather than stop it with the rum now available, he chose to endure it. Soon he'd be home, and he wouldn't show himself a drunk, an effort Catherine could respect.

Fishing net in her hands, she repeated in low tones what Richard Martin had revealed to her earlier that day.

"You're certain," Samuel prompted. "The plan is to deploy the night of the twelfth."

Campfires cracked and popped along the beach where men cooked their catch and sent ribald laughter soaring above the flames. "I'm not mistaken." Her fingers laced tighter into the net, eager to fill it with her own dinner.

In typical fashion, Samuel didn't speak as he digested the information. A song rose up from a knot of soldiers behind them, while some on the bluff looked down, their silhouettes sketched against a burning sky.

The English search for laurels,
just like our fighters.
That's the resemblance.
The French gather them in heaps,
the English can't harvest them at all.
That's the difference.

"They believe the British will attack at Beauport, if anywhere. Have you heard the same today?" he asked.

She had. "A considerable number don't even believe that. They trust the British to be a scattered lot, all noise, no bite, who can do no damage before winter sends them off the river." They were spies for certain now, though the intelligence had been freely given. The label rattled her conscience. They could be executed for this.

What had Joseph said at Odanak? What had he and Grey Wolf said before, after the French abandoned Mohawk hunting grounds without a fight? Catherine summoned the sentiments to mind. The French had not proven good allies to the People. Ties of friendship had already been broken. *"The tides are changing,"* Joseph had said. *"We must be ready to change with them."* French, British, Mohawk. In Catherine's mind, they were three pieces to one puzzle, but not one of them fit with another.

"They are confident." Samuel's musing was

barely audible. "Too confident, now that they believe themselves so close to their aim. This will work in our favor."

Rocks pointed into the soles of her bare feet as she waited for fish to bite. "I want this over," she murmured, speaking of the war, not just the journey.

He seemed to understand. "We'll speed the end. I heard the HMS *Sutherland* is anchored at Saint-Nicolas, with General Wolfe on board. Where is that? If we can get there, we won't need to go all the way to Quebec."

Catherine cringed. "It's three to four miles from here. Upstream."

His lips parted in surprise. "So we passed it already? How did we miss it? It's a fifty-gun warship."

"The fog, for one. But even if the mist hadn't shrouded everything, we wouldn't have been able to see it. The river is three miles wide at that point, and Saint-Nicolas is on the opposite shore."

Samuel stared out at the water. In the distance, birds swooped, diving into the river and then flapping away with their catch. "Just as well. If we had reached the *Sutherland* first, we wouldn't know about the plans to carry the grain. Now the question is, can we get there? If we leave after dark tomorrow?"

She wanted nothing more than to say what

he wanted to hear. But she couldn't. "It would be unlikely. Rowing upstream is challenging enough, but to do so in the dark, with the moon dragging us the other way . . . Saint-Nicolas is three miles behind us, and three miles across to the other side. Better to work with the tide, not against it, and let it carry us to another British ship, yes? Martin said the convoy would slip past Holmes' squadron between here and Quebec."

"Aye, that he did. But he cannot know exactly where they are. They might have gone back to Île d'Orléans or Point Lévis, opposite the city. Even if we come across them, Wolfe won't be onboard. He's the one who needs to hear what I have to say. He makes his decisions alone."

Another peal of laughter from the beach speared the tension growing between them. "Your ultimate aim is Quebec, is it not?" Catherine reasoned. "So is Wolfe's. You said yourself that Holmes may have returned there. So, too, Wolfe could be moving even now toward the city. If it comes down to a chase—our bateau in pursuit of a warship—we both know we'd never catch him." She paused to let this sink in, scanning for any ears too close. "Aim true, Samuel. We'll intercept the first English ship we come to, and they can send word with better channels than you and I have."

He didn't reply. Catherine stepped away from

him, for she had said her piece and wished to end the matter there.

Slowly, he pulled back with the pole, then jerked it to set the hook. The tip of the willow cane arched.

Having shed her leggings, Catherine hastened to the water's edge and stepped into the river. Bending low, she scooped up a walleye with the net, releasing the pressure on Samuel's pole. It weighed five pounds or near it, she judged, which would make a fine meal for the three of them.

She carried it back to Samuel. Mindful of the fish's strong jaw and sharp teeth, she held it while he removed the hook. He bent his head so that his chin grazed her temple. "Tomorrow, it's our turn to swim," he whispered. "We'll take the bateau. After dark."

Staring at the walleye's cold, dark eyes, Catherine could only pray her counsel had been wise, and that they would not be caught.

Catherine could not stay asleep. Rolling to her side on the fur-topped ground, she bent her arm beneath her head and pulled a blanket over her shoulder. Her body was now firmly in the rhythm of retiring early and rising again before midnight. All the better, she reflected, for by this time tomorrow, she would be back on the shining obsidian river.

Only six miles separated them from Quebec.

Fewer than that, certainly, until they would meet an English ship.

Her thoughts circled back to Joseph, Bright Star, and Thankful. She wore a track in her mind exploring every uncertainty surrounding each fate until she finally brought them to God in prayer. *Please heal them, please protect them, please carry them safely home, be it Your will.* It was a different sort of prayer than she liked, admitting that God's plan might not be hers.

Stifling a groan, she abandoned all pretense of rest and stood. Pulling her stroud blanket about her shoulders, she slipped her feet into her moccasins. Her loosely plaited hair swung at her waist as she passed the guttering fires of the soldiers.

A lone figure already strolled the beach. Even before she could see his face, his gait and frame revealed him. Samuel neared, and her heart twisted with that blade of joy and sorrow.

"Couldn't sleep?" He rubbed at a muscle in his shoulder, belying a soreness he would not admit.

Stars shone in the sky above them like chips of glass thrown across an unending bolt of black velvet. "There's too much to think about. And wonder," she added.

"You wonder why you agreed to come."

"As if you ever would have given up your begging." It was an attempt to make light of the risks she took and the circumstances leading up to their flight. It failed.

He stepped closer. "I'm sorry, Catherine, for what happened to Joseph. I'm sorry the ones you love were ever endangered."

The ones I love. Catherine peered into the deep wells of his eyes and wondered if he knew he was among them, in spite of everything. Her love for Samuel had been through the fire and come out altered, but it remained. There were different kinds of love, indeed.

"I knew there would be dangers." She tugged the blanket more tightly about her. "It was my choice to come. And after you told me about Lydia, it was my choice to stay with you. I don't regret it."

"We'll see if you feel the same way tomorrow, and the next day, and the next. I can't begin to thank you. Nothing I say or do would be enough."

She didn't argue.

The river lapped at the shore, glittering in the moonlight. It was both calming and bittersweet, for it was the rhythmic backdrop behind uncounted memories with Samuel. "After all we've been through," she whispered, "I wonder if I'll ever hear the river again without thinking of you."

He didn't respond. His feet were rooted on the rocks, but his expression showed that his thoughts were cast far away. "You're so natural on the water. You enjoy it. I envy you."

The cold ground leached the warmth from her feet. "What do you mean?"

"All my nightmares take place on the river. Or should I say, took place. Whatever my mind conjures in sleep is only a retelling of what has already happened. The first incident was my accident when I tried to escape my bondage to your father and ended up with a broken leg and dislocated shoulder."

Catherine felt the blood mount in her cheeks. "That was my fault for sending you alone."

He held up his hand. "No more apologies. No more excuses or regrets. Right now I just need you to listen."

Crickets chirped, but slower now that autumn's chill touched the air. It felt almost indulgent to speak like this. For hours upon the river, she had always talked to him with someone else present. Still holding her blanket about her shoulders, she nodded for Samuel to continue.

"That nightmare of being broken and alone before I was discovered—that's nothing compared to the nightly hauntings of Joel's death on the river near his home. When I married Lydia and moved into their house, I had to see that river every day, hear it rushing every spring. I couldn't get Joel's near-frozen, colorless face out of my mind for years. In the dream, his eyes are open and he's reaching up to me from under the ice. I grasp his fingertips and then lose him every time. Every night, I watched him die again." He spoke with little inflection, but his hand curled tightly at his side.

She wanted to reach out and lace her fingers through his. Instead, she said, "How horrible. And this dream has haunted you again on this trip?"

"Yes, at the start." He slid her a troubled gaze. "But it's changed. It's not Joel I watch drown now. It's you."

Catherine inhaled sharply. "I do not believe that dreams are predictors of what will come. Your past is mixing with your fear. That's all."

But Samuel looked unconvinced. "I don't think it's a vision or a prophecy, either. But I'd be a fool not to realize that these last few miles to Quebec may not go as planned. It's a gamble, and the stakes are our lives."

"Shh!" She cast a look about her, senses growing sharp and tight. "We knew this going into it, before we ever left Montreal," she whispered.

He cut his voice lower, stepped near. "I've been running through the possible scenarios in my mind. Gaspard could betray us by accident or by intention."

"We're not leaving him behind." A cloud obscured the moon, then drifted away like gauze.

"I know. But be aware of the risk he adds. And rowing in the dark past French lookouts and British ships . . . Someone could fire on us. You could fall overboard, and if you die on this journey, heaven help me, for I don't know what I would—"

"Samuel Crane," she hissed. "Stop this. It's too late to do anything but follow through." It was not her life she thought of now, but Joseph's. She could not bear the notion of his suffering being in vain. "Think again about those stakes, for they are higher than just our lives. This story is about more than just the two of us. The war needs to end, and if you can speed it, you must."

But his chin hovered above his chest, and she could see that her words had failed to bolster him.

"This is what you were made to do," she tried. "See a wrong and set it right. If bringing fight and famine to a close isn't the right thing to do, then I don't know what is."

Wariness etched his face. "I was not made to be a spy or warrior."

Dismay shot through Catherine. Were these doubts common to any soldier just before a dangerous mission? Did voicing them set them free, or would they siphon his courage away when he needed it most? "Samuel." She gripped his hands, and the blanket slipped from her

418

shoulders. "You were made to love and protect. Tell me about your children."

His gaze snapped up. His hands warmed hers before he squeezed and then released them, crossing his arms over his chest instead.

"You're doing this for them, right?" she pressed. "When the war is over, and you are home again with your family, I'll think of them. I'll be glad to imagine their happiness at your return. Tell me about them."

Tenderness softened his features. "Joel is four now and the very image of my brother, from his green eyes to the small dents in his cheeks when he smiles. He says he wants to be like me, so sometimes I give him a board to hammer without any nails, and he pounds away at it, practicing for when he gets bigger. But the way he loves his mama—" He glanced at Catherine, question in his eyes.

"Go on," she told him. "Tell me."

Samuel shifted his weight, nudging a piece of driftwood with his boot. "His favorite thing is to bring her flowers in his dimpled fists. Never mind if his flowers are really onions he's pulled from the garden, or weeds fit for a road-side ditch. Lydia treasures them all. You should see the bouquets on our kitchen table. They're absurd, of course, and the smell—onions!" His shoulders bounced in quiet laughter. "Lydia tells him they're sweeter than roses, though, and he is fit to burst his buttons with pride."

The smile on Samuel's face was so full and free, it unlocked Catherine's last defenses. She wanted this joy for him, had wanted it for him ever since she'd first thought of him as her friend. He'd suffered enough. She wanted this love to light him up, even though it had nothing to do with her.

"He sounds absolutely charming," she said.

The gleam in Samuel's eye was unmistakable. "That he is, almost as charming as his sister. Our daughter, Molly, reached her second birthday this week. If you saw her, you'd know she's mine. Hair like the sun, curls springing from her head. And her laughter . . . there's nothing more infectious."

"You have a daughter," Catherine whispered tightly, overcome. "And a son and a wife."

"I do." His smile was gentle.

So was hers. "There's your reason for what we're about to do."

A gust of wind swept between them, smelling of last night's cookfires. Stooping, Samuel picked up the blanket Catherine had dropped and draped it once more on her shoulders. "Thank you." Voice hoarse, his hands lingered on her arms for a moment. "Does this mean—that is, do you forgive me?"

Wrapping herself in the stroud, she pulled it tight. "I do."

CHAPTER TWENTY-SIX

It was time.

Silently, Catherine joined Samuel at the shore, hoping last night's conversation had given him the courage he needed now. Hunching low, Gaspard hastened to her side.

A long line of bateaux stretched along the beach. "Which one?" she whispered, searching for their own.

Several of these vessels had already been loaded with cargo for tomorrow night's departure. Theirs was one of them. A group of soldiers would be able to slide it to the water bearing so much weight, but Catherine, Samuel, and Gaspard could not. Neither could they risk the noise of the boat scraping over rocks on its way.

"This." Samuel pointed to an empty bateau, third from the end of the line.

Taking her position by its side, Catherine secured the pins holding her braid in a coil at her neck, then pointed to where Gaspard should be. Samuel stood on the other side, closer to the bow, and grasped the edge. At her signal, they lifted and carried the vessel until they could set it halfway into the river.

Then they hurried back to the other bateaux and retrieved a barrel of flour, rolling it so slowly that it made no noise worth noting. If they were challenged by lookouts, they would say they were an early detachment taking flour to Quebec. After heaving the barrel into the bateau, Samuel and Gaspard went back and each returned with a bag of grain on their shoulders. She helped them ease the sacks into the bateau. It could hold far more, but not without compromising their speed. This would have to be enough.

Clutching the sheathed knife at her chest, Catherine climbed into the vessel, and Samuel and Gaspard gave the final heave into the water.

The bateau rocked as the men climbed into it. At the stern, Catherine dipped an oar into the inky water until it gained purchase on the river-bed. She pushed, sending the vessel forward before clapping the handle into the oarlock to serve as the rudder.

Samuel took an oar near the bow of the vessel, while Gaspard rowed in the middle. In moments, they were gliding away. The angle of the men's oars as they entered and left the water had never been more precise, nor their strokes so smooth and strong. Their movement was as near to silent as they could manage.

They didn't speak, didn't need to. The moon was a silver arc, a celestial bow ready to launch. Stars pinpricked both sky and river, so that they floated in and on and through the shimmering black. This was far easier to navigate than fog.

Resting at Cap-Rouge had restored Catherine's strength, so they put the first mile behind them with remarkable ease. Nerves that had been coiled all day at last began to relax.

Gaspard leaned forward. "Lookouts, north shore," he whispered.

Her gaze swung left, and her heart rate ratcheted up once more. There were not many men standing guard, so thinly spread were the patrolling troops. She saw only two along this stretch, but it took only one to sound an alarm or take a shot. Praying for calm, she steered for shadows overhanging the south bank from the trees that crowded there.

An owl hooted from a low-hanging branch, and she ducked just in time to pass beneath it.

"Look out!" Samuel whispered, but too late.

The bateau clunked into something, jarring Catherine nearly off her seat, though their speed had been slow. A length of rotten tree trunk crossed their path.

"*Qui vive?*"

The challenge clapped Catherine's ears like blocks of wood.

"France!" Gaspard called back. A new wave of energy rushed to her shoulders and arms, and she steered the bateau away from the shore and into the safer middle.

"What regiment?"

"Shh!" Gaspard's bold reply. "Don't make noise! We have flour from Cap-Rouge!"

"We were told that was for tomo—"

"Shh!" Gaspard interrupted. "We won't all go at once, to protect some provisions if some are caught. Do not give us away!"

It worked. The soldier, well within pistol shot range, let them go and wished them Godspeed.

Within another mile, they were challenged once more, and Gaspard gave the same response he had before. This time, he was bold enough to ask the lookout to pass word along to let the bateau proceed with its flour unchallenged. The young man lowered his pistol and complied. Relief flooded Catherine.

Then she felt the tide pulling the current beneath the vessel. Its speed easily outpaced what they had experienced thus far, and a sense of elation vied with the continued need for caution. They were not safe yet and would not be until they were on board a British ship or onshore at a British camp, opposite the river from Quebec.

Faintly, she discerned in the distance the cliffs of the Quebec promontory rising ahead of them on the north shore. "Do you see any lookouts?" she asked.

"A few," Gaspard whispered after twisting to look. "They assume the cliff is all the defense they need."

They were almost halfway to Quebec. She'd been so confident they'd see English ships by now. Were they all amassed at Saint-Nicolas, except for a few staged opposite the city? She leaned forward. "What will those lookouts do if we have to turn away from Quebec to get to the British camp on the opposite shore?"

Samuel turned his head. "Nothing, if they don't see us. And they won't. Look there." A dark shape against the cliffs began to take form, flagged by the white sails at the top. "That sloop is British. All we need to do is row abreast of it, and no one on shore will see us climb aboard."

"But how can you tell it's not French?" She could barely distinguish the masts, let alone read the hull or decode its flags.

"He's right," Gaspard said. "France has precious few ships to spare, as most of them are waging war off France or India. Those that are here would not be wasted guarding impenetrable cliffs."

The bateau creaked. Catherine frowned. The only sound should be from the oars in the oarlocks. The rudder still, she watched Gaspard and Samuel row and listened for the vessel's response.

Another creak. No, a crack. Catherine listed slightly to the right. Then farther still. Her feet suddenly grew cold. Wet.

"We're sinking," she gasped. Samuel's dream

flew so quickly to her mind that she was sure it entered his.

The whites of his eyes shone wide.

Gaspard groaned, complaining of losing the flour. "I intended to take that to my parents. But at least now the lookouts won't see the bateau."

Catherine put her hand to the crack in the hull. The river rushed between her fingers. This vessel was clearly one of those that had been run aground and damaged at Pointe-aux-Trembles. It had been caulked at Cap-Rouge, but the repair was not enough. Perhaps this bateau had not been loaded because it had already been deemed unseaworthy.

"I can swim. Can you?" She looked to both men, nearly forgetting to keep her voice down. "With your injuries as they are, can you swim?"

Gaspard reckoned he could. Rotating his right arm, Samuel winced. "I'll manage it. Let's row straight as hard and long as we can."

They tilted farther to the right as they rowed. Water crept over her moccasins, up her ankles and leggings. It weighted and pulled at the hem of her dress.

Samuel murmured, "'When thou passest through the waters, I will be with thee; and through the rivers, they shall not overflow thee . . .' Lord, we need Your help."

But would He help them? Could they even ask it of Him, as He was a God of truth, and they had used deception in their plans? Surely both French and English claimed to be on the side of right, both nations beseeched God for help. *Creator God, I don't know Your will.* Catherine shoved her right foot to the side of the bateau, leaning left to straighten herself. *Just help me do the next right thing.*

"Aim for the sloop." Samuel pointed. "I see lantern light on deck. Both of you, swim for the light and tell them what we know. Gaspard, they'll protect you, don't worry. And don't wait for me, I'll be slower. Just head for the light. Don't splash about and draw attention, and the lookouts won't even notice."

"Sam." Catherine caught his eye, willing her confidence to pour into him. "I can do this. We all can."

The bateau was breaking apart beneath them. Cold water surged about her waist, and she gasped at the shock that sliced through her. The flour sacks began to sink, but the barrel merely tipped and bobbed.

She reached out for it. "Stay with the barrel." It had started to drift away on the current.

"Swim for the light. I'll be behind you. Go now." Samuel lunged into the river to grasp the barrel's rim.

The pins in her hair dislodged, and her braid tumbled down, floating like an eel on the river's surface. She whipped it behind her, then tucked the hunting knife inside her dress. With her toes, she peeled her moccasins off her feet, filled her lungs with air, and slipped into the river. A quiet splash told her Gaspard had done the same.

Her dress ballooned about her legs as she submerged. Cupping her hands, she reached over her head, then pushed down in an arching sweep. Her arms would be her oars, propelling her through the water.

Something yanked her hard from behind, and she jerked backward. Air escaped her lips too soon. Kicking, Catherine made for the surface to take another breath.

But she could not see any light. Had clouds completely covered the moon, or was she swimming the wrong direction? Panic triggered. Seaweed twined about her toes and ankles. Her limbs tingled with cold as she tried to calm her mind and body.

She would float. She would still herself and rise to the surface on her own. Wouldn't she?

The pressure built in her chest, ribs screwing tighter and tighter over her burning lungs. Slowly, she waved her arms above her head until her fingertips broke the surface. With a few more kicks, she felt the air on her face and gulped it into her lungs.

Something pulled her back under. She was caught, being dragged down.

Her hair. Someone was pulling her by her braid.

Samuel? But it couldn't be him; she had seen him grip the barrel. Was it Gaspard, in a panic that outmatched hers? Her thoughts pitched and yawed as she clutched the thick rope of her hair and strained to yank it free.

It wouldn't give. The river that had carried her so far now wrapped around her. The water turned colder, darker. All she could guess was that she was anchored to the bateau, her braid somehow caught between the splitting planks or tangled in an oarlock.

Catherine pulled in a mouthful of water. She couldn't stop, couldn't breathe, could barely think. She would drown with air just a few feet away.

Desperately, she fumbled to bring the knife outside her dress and pull it from its sheath. Fingers struggling to keep their grip, she brought blade to braid and sawed through it. Feeling her plait unraveling and her body floating free, she dropped the knife, mustered all her might, and flailed up to the surface.

Breaking through, she coughed and sputtered while treading water. She turned until she saw the light on the ship's deck, fully expecting to hear a challenge shouted from atop the cliffs. Before the lookouts had a chance to inquire, she swam.

An oval of light wavered on the river beside the sloop, swinging one way and the other. With the last of her strength, Catherine pushed herself toward it.

"Man overboard!" The call thrilled through her, as did the clatter of a rope ladder being let down over the edge.

Chilled and shaking, she climbed with ungainly movements, her sodden dress tripping her steps. Hands came under her arms and hauled her onto the deck.

Catherine pushed her hair away from her face. Vaguely, she registered that the men were exclaiming that their catch was a woman. She interrupted them. "There are two more men out there, a British provincial escaped from captivity, and a Canadian deserter. You need to hear what they have to say."

Footsteps clambered and more light swung over the deck to search. Catherine went to the rail and looked for Gaspard and for Samuel, who was already haunted by rivers enough. Pulse sluggish from the cold, she rubbed her hands together and fought her rising dread.

Water streamed from Catherine's dress and hair, puddling at her feet. Somehow a blanket now covered her. Except for the growing tightness in her chest, she had no measure of how much time had passed as she watched and waited.

"Go get them." The words burst from her as she clutched the arm nearest hers. "Get in a flatboat and find them."

"No need, there they are." A light snapped over the bobbing barrel, then found Samuel and Gaspard lunging from it toward the sloop.

Catherine turned and sank to the deck, hugging her knees to her chest. The ladder creaked as both men scaled it. By the time they had been heaved over the edge, she had recovered enough to greet them each with a welcoming hug.

"You made it," she said, voice serrated from the ordeal. "We did it."

"Nearly." Samuel turned to a redcoat officer and stood at attention, soaking wet and winded as he was. "Sir, we have urgent intelligence to report."

"Not here," replied the officer. "Follow me. But do wring out a bit first, won't you? Then meet me belowdecks, the three of you. Let's see what kind of fish we netted tonight."

Catherine translated for Gaspard. Both he and Samuel stood shivering until a sailor handed them each a blanket to match hers. The wind drove the chill even deeper. After briskly rubbing their legs with the blankets, Catherine, Samuel, and Gaspard were taken down a narrow set of steps that was more like a ladder than stairs, then into a small, dimly lit cabin.

The officer from the deck stood behind a desk. "I'm Captain Hugh Watkins, and this is my ship. Sit, for you're about to collapse as it is." As they complied, he tented his fingers before his belted waist. "Who are you, and what news do you bring?"

Samuel gave his name, rank, and regiment, along with a brief history of his capture and captivity. "Sir, with all due respect to General Wolfe's previous attempts to attack Quebec, I may know how to finally make it stick. What you need is an access point, and if we can attack before the water freezes, you don't need to wait until spring."

Catherine quietly translated this for Gaspard.

Watkins narrowed one eye. "Curious timing. Ah, young lady, do I understand that this red-haired fellow does not speak English? Then leave off your translating. A deserter he may be, but who is to say he's not a spy? In fact, I'd rather he wait outside. Clooney!"

A sailor stepped inside the cabin and saluted.

"Clooney, you will take the Canadian to the galleys for some victuals. I daresay he won't refuse them, judging by the looks of him. A wet rat would weigh more."

Catherine explained to Gaspard as he was being removed from the cabin that he'd have a chance to eat. The door clicked closed behind them.

Watkins circled back to his desk and sat, drumming his fingers atop its polished surface.

Samuel leaned forward, water dripping down

the side of his face. "You said my timing is curious. How so?"

"Wolfe has planned another attack. For tomorrow."

Surprise flared over Samuel's face. He leaned back in the chair and clutched its arms. "Where will you breach the city's defenses?"

Cringing, Watkins made a seam of his lips before responding. "He won't say. He only says to be ready at a moment's notice."

"That's—" But Samuel caught himself before voicing the ridicule written on his face. "I hear the general has been ill."

Watkins laced his hands behind his head. "You heard correctly. Some say he wants a last jab at the French because he believes he'll die before spring. But he refuses to tell even his leaders what the plan is."

Catherine looked at Samuel. "Perhaps if he knew what you do . . ." She allowed the thought to drift and snag Watkins' interest.

"I don't expect I could see Wolfe myself," Samuel said, "but what I have to share can be heard only by your most trusted men."

"On with it, man, or dawn will be upon us and we'll miss our chance," Watkins said, his voice taking on a more authoritative tone.

"The French generals suspect we are going farther north to lay waste to the country and to destroy the ships and craft we find there. From what we learned in Montreal and at Cap-Rouge, General Montcalm insists that the bulk of the British army is still below Quebec."

Watkins' expression did not change. "So far, this is nothing extraordinary."

Samuel pressed on. "There are three obstacles between Wolfe and the city. First, the Quebec Promontory is its own geographical defense—but the French are so certain of this that it's barely manned at all. Second, the city wall stretches across the east end of the promontory, and third, Montcalm's army will not be moved. But a landing at Anse-au-Foulon is the solution to all three. The Foulon road is rugged, but if it can be scaled in secret, you'll overwhelm the outposts at the top."

Watkins unrolled a map on his desk, weighted the corners with a snuffbox and timepiece, and hovered above the lines and curves.

Samuel rose. "Sir, at Montreal I met another British soldier who had spent months imprisoned here in Quebec. He reported that Quebec's principal defense on the land side is a wall of masonry only three or four feet thick. It was designed to deflect small arms and can hold out for only a matter of days. Bring the fight to the Plains of Abraham using Anse-au-Foulon as your access point, and victory will be all but yours."

The ship rocked and creaked. Watkins planted

his feet wide and crossed his arms. Then, stroking his chin, his attention swiveled from Samuel to Catherine. "And why are you here? Do you have something to add?"

"My name is Catherine Duval, and I served as his guide," she began. "But we chanced upon more information at Cap-Rouge that will prove critical to your plan. You'll think it hard to believe, but Samuel and Gaspard can confirm it."

Eyes round and unblinking, Watkins was hooked. As she told him what they had learned at Cap-Rouge about the wheat convoy, red blotches mottled his neck.

"Let me see if I understand correctly," he said. "The fleet of bateaux carrying the wheat for Montcalm's army is six miles distant at Cap-Rouge. Their plan is to sneak it by, under our very noses, the night of the twelfth." He consulted his timepiece. "By Jove, we are a few hours into the twelfth right now. So they mean to come tonight. And our attack is planned for the following morning, the thirteenth. But in order to keep quiet, all the French lookouts along the shores have been instructed *not* to challenge the vessels. To just let them go by unquestioned."

"Precisely." Samuel folded his blanket and set it on the chair. "Seems like a fine time to move British flatboats, doesn't it? On the one night they won't be challenged?"

A knock sounded on the door, and Clooney

brought Gaspard back in. "Come morning, I'm going home, aren't I?" he asked Catherine as soon as he saw her. "I'm so close. I can't wait any longer. Will you ask them?"

Before she could respond, Watkins cleared his throat. "I'd like for the deserter to confirm the story. Clooney, you understand French, don't you? Stay and translate what this man says. Mademoiselle Duval, you just rest."

She sat back in her chair and watched, unperturbed that Watkins didn't trust her translation. With such a story, he was right to exercise caution. Let Gaspard and Clooney tell the officer exactly what they'd already said.

At the end of it, Watkins seemed interested but not satisfied. "The river will get crowded, don't you think? If both French bateaux and British flatboats take to it on the same night, headed for nearly the same spot?"

Silence hung thick in the room. Gaspard blinked too quickly, and his hands began to shake. If Watkins didn't know that he suffered from lack of drink, he might assume Gaspard was nervous. Or lying.

But Watkins pinned his attention to the map, measuring with ruler and squinted eye. The river was wide, but that was no guarantee the bateaux would keep to their own courses. Even if the lookouts didn't challenge any vessels, the bateaux pilots were bound to realize there were far more boats on the river than their own number. No, it would never work to all travel at once.

"If it helps," she ventured, "the plan from CapRouge is to start by ten o'clock. The British could stagger their launch times with that."

"Better yet," Samuel said, "cancel the order from Cadet for that wheat. Just don't tell the lookouts the plan has changed. The bateaux will stay at Cap-Rouge, and the British flatboats will glide right on by."

Catherine scanned the faces in the room. "Can you do that? Forge an order and deliver it in time without arousing suspicion?"

For the first time since they'd arrived, a small smile curled Watkins' lips. "This is the Royal Navy, my dear. You'd be surprised just what we can do. I'll go to General Wolfe myself. Crane, we'll get some rations in you, as well, and then you and Fontaine will come with me. Mademoiselle, our ships are not suited to accommodate a woman. I'll have Clooney give you a bite to eat and row you across to our camp at Point Lévis. You can stay with the nurses until it's safe for you to go home."

At the door, Samuel turned back and squeezed Catherine's hand. "Thank you," he said.

And then he was gone.

CHAPTER TWENTY-SEVEN

When morning came, Catherine awakened to white canvas walls billowing around her. She'd been delivered before dawn to the quarters of a woman named Eleanor, who was the head nurse at the hospital here at the camp. Eleanor wasn't present now, however, leaving Catherine alone with her thoughts. Samuel and Gaspard were foremost among them, but she couldn't guess where they were or whether she'd see them again. As for what General Wolfe had decided to do, she supposed that would be clear soon enough.

The tent flap snapped in a breeze, and sunlight flashed onto the faded quilt over her legs. She felt for the knife sheath about her neck and found a white cotton nightdress. Then she remembered that she'd lost her sister's knife in the river. Her hand went to her head and stroked down to the end of her hair. Unbound, it stopped at her shoulders, where yesterday it had gone to her knees. She'd been so focused on other things last night on the sloop that she hadn't fully registered until now what the river had taken from her.

She rose slowly and picked up a hand mirror from atop a folding table. The ends of her hair fell crookedly over her shoulders. Spying a sewing kit in one of the crates, she borrowed the scissors and trimmed the strands into a straight line. Cutting her hair the first time had not been a symbolic act, and neither was this. But as Catherine stood in a British camp on French soil, she could not help but sense that she had cut more than just her braid.

Rain fell on the roof of the tent until the pattern sounded like the gentle rush of a river. A glance at the empty cots reminded Catherine that outside this small space, women were working. She quickly dressed in the gown Eleanor had loaned her, though the English style, like the French, had several steps and layers. All were front-lacing, however, which told her that Eleanor likely got along without a maid. The chemise and petticoats were worn thin but clean. The gown was a russet-colored round gown, the very color of a Canadian autumn, to which Catherine added a sensible lawn fichu. She did not bother to pin the lace cuffs inside the elbow-length sleeves. She was sure she looked like a changeling, neither French nor Mohawk, especially with her hair so altered, and still not quite English either.

She tailed and twisted her hair until it began to coil, then flipped it upside down and pinned it to her head. To her surprise, she found herself praying as naturally as she breathed. *Creator God, create in me a clean heart, one that shows loyalty to You above armies and empires and allies.* In truth, she did not know what that meant, but she asked God to show her that, too.

The ground trembled beneath her. Cannon fire drowned out the purring of the rain. Between the roars, musketry rattled and popped.

The battle was here, now. Confusion shuddered through her. It was too early, wasn't it?

Her gaze landed upon an apron folded neatly inside a crate. Without hesitating, she unfurled the faintly stained linen and tied it about her waist. Let others do the fighting. Catherine would join the women nursing in the hospital. She would serve the suffering, regardless of their cause.

When she stepped out of the tent, it was as one entering a different world. Situated on a wedge of land on the south shore of the St. Lawrence River, Point Lévis was stuffed with white tents and bristling with batteries, which pounded Quebec's Lower Town. Only twelve hundred yards of river separated the cannons from the city. British ships arrived from the east, soldiers poured onto the beach and reloaded onto waiting landing craft pointed west, and the Union Jack flew high above them all. Flatboats arrived from the west, and wounded soldiers were carried off them. It was that stream of broken men that Catherine followed into a church.

Beneath a soaring ceiling, whose columns

converged to point to heaven, rough planks had been laid atop the backs of the pews, and several severely injured men lay atop them. Other soldiers sat in the aisles, backs against the wall. More than twenty white-capped, aproned women worked among them. Catherine shuffled through drifts of sawdust that had been thrown over the stone floor.

"Hello?" A woman scurried toward her. The brown calico gown beneath her apron matched her chestnut hair. "You must be Catherine, Eleanor's new roommate. I'm Josephine. We wondered when you'd finally wake."

"Finally?" It could not have been more than four hours since Catherine had gone to sleep.

Josephine tucked a loose tendril of hair into her cap. "You slept an entire day away. We were afraid you might have fallen ill. But now that you're here, we could use your help. Do you mind?"

Understanding dawned. She'd had so little sleep since leaving Montreal, rowing at night as they had been, and so little food to fuel the journey, that her body had finally surrendered to the toll. Today was September thirteenth. Either the French or the British had sailed downstream last night, and she had slept right through it. Quickly she regained her bearings as Josephine awaited her response. "Of course I'll help."

"Very good. Most of the patients who were here yesterday have been moved to a tent in the rear of camp to make room for more. This church will overflow with soldiers before the day is out." She beckoned for Catherine to follow her to the front of the church. Near the altar, she gave Catherine a basket of rags and a bucket of water. "The officers will be treated by naval surgeons on the ships, but the rest—and prisoners—will come here. At least those who can be moved."

"What do I do?"

"Bind what is torn. Give water to those who thirst. Our work is simple but requires an even disposition, which I have no doubt you possess." Josephine bent to scoop up her own supplies. "Should you have any questions, any of these women will answer them if they can. We all have the same aim." Thunder rattled. "Eleanor has gone off with the Royal Artillery, so we shall say a special prayer for her."

Rain sprayed in where windows had shattered in their casings. "Gone where?" But Catherine's question was swallowed in a cry for water.

A tug on her skirt turned her head toward the voice. An outstretched hand rose from a soldier sitting near her feet. Kneeling, she filled a gourd dipper with water from the bucket and brought it to his lips. As he drank, a fresh bandage about his arm caught her attention.

"Have you just come in this morning?" she asked.

"I have." He licked the moisture from his lips. "If that lady Eleanor has gone with the Royal Artillery, it means she's gone to the Plains of Abraham. The heights to the west of Quebec."

Catherine gave him another drink. "The heights! Is that where the battle is?"

"Aye, 'tis where it will be." He leaned back his head. "What you hear out there is mere skirmishing. The true ball has yet to open. And I've already been taken out of it, just when the fight was about to begin." He muttered a curse.

Excitement kindled inside her, for wasn't this the very idea Samuel had brought just in time? "Please, tell me how it was accomplished."

A crooked smile split his angular face. "Either careful planning or a generous dose of luck. Or Providence, if you'd rather. We who were waiting at Saint-Nicolas for days finally got orders to drop down in boats last night after dark and slip past the French lookouts. Turns out there was to be a convoy of bateaux carrying grain down the river last night, a whole slew of them. The French had told the outposts and lookouts to let them by without challenge. For some reason, the order for provisions was canceled, but the order to let vessels pass unmolested was not. And it was us who took their place!"

Catherine stared at him, almost afraid to believe it. "You're certain?"

"Would I jest of such a thing with the Holy Virgin looking down on me?" He pointed to a statue of Mary. "Never."

Samuel had done it. He had delivered the intelligence he meant to, and General Wolfe had seen the value of it. Now all that remained was the battle for Quebec.

Astounded, she shuffled to the next soldier and let him drink. "Were you there, too?"

"I was." Water dribbled from the corner of his mouth. "We landed at Anse-au-Foulon half an hour before daybreak and scaled the cliffs. Found a rugged road for the artillery, and even the sailors lent a hand. The French are laying down fire on us as we get into place. That's what you hear. The battle has yet to begin in earnest."

And that was where Eleanor had gone. How brave she was, or how foolish. The thought struck Catherine that the same might be said of her.

Standing, she moved to another soldier, and then the next. All were thirsty, but only a few had not already been bandaged by the other women so expertly tending their needs. There were hundreds of such women in this camp, ready to take their shifts.

And only one on the heights.

Catherine drifted toward the open door and stood on the church steps, peering through silver stripes of rain. Gunsmoke added to the clouds west of the city, while ships moved in and out of Point Lévis. Her heart drummed a reveille against her ribs.

Josephine was soon beside her, empty bucket in hand. "It doesn't seem fitting, does it? All of us here, and all the men who most need us beyond our reach. What do you think, Catherine?"

"I think your friend Eleanor had the right idea. And I think I'll follow suit."

Josephine's eyes shone. She stood a few inches shorter than Catherine, and her figure was slightly rounder, but what she lacked in stature was clearly more than compensated for with spirit. "I was thinking the very same. The other ladies have the church well in hand, and they won't miss the two of us. Let's go where we might do the most good." She pointed to a flatboat full of soldiers, readying to leave for battle. "There's our ride."

How brave they were, or how foolish.

Catherine's determination had not wavered as she and Josephine rode across the river in the landing craft. Nor did it flag when the wheels of her wooden cart full of nursing supplies kept sinking in the muddy Foulon road.

The rain tapered to a mist as she and Josephine rolled their cargo through tall, thin grass and white clover to the eastern fringe of Sillery Woods. It was west of the Plains and out of the way until they could be of some use. Eleanor was already there, fists on her hips, when they arrived. Her face and hands were rosy, no doubt from a summer spent without the bother of a parasol.

"What, no wounded yet?" Josephine asked.

"No fresh injuries, at least." Eleanor smoothed her apron over a blue-and-tan plaid dress. A ruffled cap topped her blond hair, which was streaked with auburn. "Those wounded earlier were already sent off to Point Lévis. Once the battle is over, men will carry the wounded down the hill and onto the ships. Surgeons will see to those they can. Our job is simply to stop the bleeding and revive those who need it with spirits." Jugs of alcohol stood in the carts, ready to be wheeled out onto the field.

The redcoats had formed six tidy blocks across the field, the line stretching a thousand yards, or near it, as far as Catherine could tell. Their muskets were silent, their ranks still. She could not see the French lines from where she stood but could hear their musket fire, could taste the saltpeter in the damp air. A group of sailors emerged from the Foulon road and pushed cannons into place behind the British lines, struggling in and out of furrows more than a foot deep. From the woods alongside the battlefield, militia and native warriors waited, ready to attack from places unseen. Their war cries and whoops raised the hair on Catherine's neck.

As if no chills rolled over her, Eleanor sent Catherine an appraising glance. "Are you certain this is where you want to be?"

"I aim to help where I can, no matter the cut or color of the soldiers' cloth." Before she realized she was doing it, she looked for Samuel on the field. He was a provincial, not a redcoat, but he was certainly near the battle. Could he fight? Would he?

"Her French will be valuable to us, Eleanor, should we come across wounded from the other side." Josephine retied her apron strings behind her waist.

"Indeed. I'm afraid my French lessons never quite took." Eleanor's gaze riveted on the sailors, who, rather than returning to their ships, were brandishing cutlasses and sticks, or nothing at all, eager to join the soldiers for the fight. "We're glad to have you, Catherine, whatever draws you to our side."

Catherine thanked her, ready for the attention to shift elsewhere.

The sky cleared. French drummers beat out their staccato call to charge, and each note tapped hard on Catherine's chest. But she was blind back here at the rear, or might as well be, and the suspense was unbearable.

Gathering her skirts in one hand, she climbed the maple tree behind her.

Eleanor cheered her on. "That dress will be ruined by day's end, anyhow. Tell us, what do you see?"

Bark pressed into Catherine's palm as she watched the action unfold, amazed. "The French are charging, running down the western slopes of the buttes just outside Quebec's Upper Town." Their white uniforms spilled downhill like a wave of rushing water. But the ground was uneven, with heavy bush and tall wheat in the way. "Their lines are breaking apart."

"Already?" Josephine asked.

Cries of "*Vive le roi!*" carried on the wind, along with the near-constant clamor of their native allies. Catherine waited a moment to see if the ranks would close up. Instead, they seperated further. "They are in three groups now, moving in different directions over the terrain, and at different speeds."

In the distance, the battery at Point Lévis bombarded Lower Town, and batteries in the city shot back.

"How many are there?" Josephine called up. "Can you estimate?"

The booming cannons rattled the leaves in her

tree. Catherine squinted, counting a group of men, then multiplying the number as necessary. "One group is roughly five hundred soldiers, and the other is slightly less. The third is about the size of the first two put together, so nearly two thousand all told. Montcalm has lost control of his men. They are in a mad dash as individuals, not at all like a unit under command." Meanwhile, the English watched and waited. "At the right end of a line of British grenadiers, atop a small hill, there is a redcoat with a spyglass, standing alone with two men."

"That'll be General Wolfe," Eleanor supplied. "Dressed like an average officer, I'd wager, but he's the man in charge of it all. What else is happening?"

The French rushed up to within a hundred and thirty yards of the English line, halted, and opened fire without a command to do so—or at least without a command Catherine had heard. All across the promontory, sparks flew and powder exploded. Thousands of .69-caliber balls streaked out of silver muzzles and across the empty space—and fell to the ground before traveling halfway to the enemy.

Eleanor remained staunch and unmoved. Josephine covered her ears at first, then spun to face Catherine, questions in her eyes.

Catherine leaned forward, studying the lines. "The French are firing from too far away! The balls drop before they hit the British!" But now they were moving forward until they were only thirty to forty yards away. "Here it comes—"

Her sentence was cut off by the first real volley to do any damage. Balls hit their marks in British chests, arms, and throats. At the north flank, Canadian militia and native warriors used muskets and tomahawks and terror.

The British, at last, fired back. The noise was horrendous, a rattling roar Catherine felt through her entire body. Pain throbbed inside her skull with the force of a hammer blow. She peered through it, saw French soldiers and militia felled by English enemy. One man clutched at the crimson stream arcing from his thigh just before his thumb was blown from his hand. Another soldier's knee gave way, and then his white coat bloomed red over his stomach. Six-pound cannons launched round shot at the French. When a soldier's arm was torn away, Catherine could watch no more.

Neither could she leave her perch and wait blindly for what came next. If the British fell back, the women would need to move. Between the light infantry and the grenadiers, a pond of standing rainwater winked at Catherine, and there she fixed her gaze. The water shook and rippled. An Englishman was slain by a warrior and fell into it. Soon the water turned red.

Minutes passed like this. Josephine and Eleanor stuffed their apron pockets with bandages and tied long-handled dippers at their waists. Jugs of spirits sat at their feet, ready to be poured into those who needed them most. But beyond this, they could only wait.

The French line approached, and the British gunners switched from round shot to grapeshot, spraying masses of oversized musket balls at their advance. The French absorbed three or four more volleys into their ranks. Black-powder smoke swirled in boiling clouds above the fray.

"What do you see?" Josephine balled a wrinkled handkerchief in her hand.

"The smoke grows too thick to see much of anything," Catherine replied. "The hill is empty," she added. "Your general is gone—I see bayonets poking up through the smoke."

"He's leading a charge," Eleanor guessed.

The smoke began to clear, revealing the incredible sight of the main body of the French turning back. It could not have been more than twenty minutes of gunfire, and they were running away, back to Quebec. Some of their wounded were left on the field.

Out of nowhere, it seemed, men in kilts and bonnets rushed forward, shrieking in Gaelic, pursuing the fugitive French.

Even Eleanor cringed. "That'll be the Scots.

The Highlanders are fearsome creatures with those claymores."

Claymores, Catherine guessed, were the yard-long, basket-hilted broadswords they brandished as they chased like fire across the field. With a fury that sounded born of hell, they struck men down, dividing limb and head from body, as they swept up the buttes and toward the walls of Quebec.

All was mayhem. Militia and native warriors mingled with the Scots, and gunners left their artillery to charge with bayonets. Grass turned to jelly beneath their feet, and the clover, once white, was stained red. The line of battle was at low tide, leaving hundreds of wounded behind.

Stomach reeling from the violence she'd just witnessed, Catherine slid back down the tree and looked from Eleanor to Josephine. They had not seen what she had from her vantage point in the tree. Their minds were not yet filled with gore. With a pang of sympathy for the shock they would soon encounter, she told them what they were eager to hear.

"It's time to do what we can."

CHAPTER TWENTY-EIGHT

Naïvely, Catherine had hoped the worst was over when the fighting moved away, toward the city walls. But this was worse than the battle by far. Above the Plains of Abraham, smoke thinned in air that still tasted of gunpowder. War cries and *huzzahs* and *vive le rois* faded, replaced by the moans of men laid waste. One of them had been the British General Wolfe, whose body had been carried away not one hour after the battle began.

Eleanor blanched at the sight, and Josephine gasped, but both women had rallied, redoubling their efforts on the field. The loss of their leader seemed to light a fire behind Eleanor's eyes, while Josephine worked through a veil of tears.

Catherine did not cry, though her gut rebelled at the brokenness she bent to touch. She supposed that later, these recollections would fill her nightmares and she'd come near to drowning in this misery. But for now, she set her jaw and worked.

As the only woman on the field who spoke French, she made the soldiers in white her priority, along with Canadian militia, focusing on one man, one wound, at a time. No matter where they were injured or how, they all had a gaunt quality in common. Cheekbones jutted beneath eyes too large, and teeth were too prominent for the face. Collarbones made shelves beneath jackets too big for their frames.

These were the men for whom she had harvested the grain around Montreal. The wheat convoy had been for them. The convoy that was canceled, that allowed the British to pass undetected. It struck Catherine as incredibly cruel that they'd had to face an army with hollow stomachs. Though she had wanted to help Samuel end the war, she had never wanted men to starve.

Neither had she wanted this, a carpet of human suffering. And she had played a part in rolling it out. This was the cost of helping Samuel. But she had no time to feel anything but the gravel in her stomach. She certainly had no time to wonder where Samuel was.

Kneeling in blood-soaked grass, Catherine looked first at a soldier's face. "Bonjour, my name is Catherine," she always began, "and I'm here to help you."

Some faces broke with relief at her very presence, while some stared right through her or groaned through gritted teeth, the tendons of their neck tight. What were strips of linen against torn flesh and tissue? What were words of comfort when a man's lifeblood poured from a severed limb, or brandy for a spirit already collapsed?

And yet Catherine refused to stop tending them, even if all she could offer was dignity.

"It was a rout!" one cried, bleeding from his side and thigh. "All is lost. We shall lose Quebec. After all the hunger, all the bombing, we shall still lose her. We ran from the fight."

"Not you." Catherine threaded a bandage beneath his leg, then wrapped and bound it. "You didn't run, did you? I see it took more than one ball to bring you down, and neither is in your back. You fought brave and true."

"You are Canadian?" he rasped, eyelids fluttering. His color was fading quickly.

"From Montreal, or near it." She pressed a folded cloth to his side and watched the white give way to red.

"Then I'm sorry we have not done better for you. Please . . . forgive us." He exhaled a rattling breath. His last.

Catherine corked her emotion, for uncounted numbers awaited. She moved to the next and the next, with bandages, brandy, and absolution. The hem of her russet gown grew heavy and glistened with blood. Her apron was smeared with it, her hands freckled. Strands of hair fell from their pins, and she pushed them back with the inside of her wrist.

The sound of heaving caught her attention.

Twenty yards away, Josephine bent at the waist, hands on her knees, and retched into the sodden grass. At her feet was a body in scarlet uniform which no longer possessed a head.

Gut twisting, Catherine began walking toward her, but Josephine straightened, one hand to her mouth, the other high in the air, palm out. "I'm all right now, Catherine, thank you." Her voice trembled. "I won't have you tending me when there are men still on the field." With unsteady gait, she skirted the body and knelt by a man who might still need aid.

The firefight grew louder, though it remained out of sight past the buttes. By now Catherine recognized the sound of grapeshot being blown from cannons and the quake of the earth in response.

She whirled back toward the wounded and set her course for a soldier whose blue-cuffed hand lifted in the air from where he lay. Sunlight gleamed on his buttons.

"Bonjour, my name is Catherine," she told him as she knelt by his side, "and I'm here to help you."

His grey-white breeches were slick with congealed blood where a ball had entered his thigh. Another ball, or grapeshot, had taken off two fingers of his left hand. Muscling back a gag, she bandaged the wound in his thigh first. She noted from the exit wound that the ball had gone fully through it, then proceeded to bind up his hand.

"Catherine?" The officer was shaking, his pupils small beneath the open sky. She doubted his body registered yet the magnitude of his pain. "Catherine Duval?"

She bent his arm at the elbow so his injured hand was aloft, and supported it at the wrist. Then she again took in his face.

"Captain Moreau." Recognition sparked a tumult of emotions, none of which were practical for the moment. She poured brandy into a dipper and helped him drink.

"Ah, Catherine. It has come to this. I was so certain the harvest would be here in time. If our men had eaten, they may not have collapsed. How can starving men fight? And why would they fight for an empire that doesn't feed them?"

She shook her head, at a loss. She tugged her apron to cover her knees, and it tore in a thread-bare spot.

"Everything I thought I knew, I now doubt. Except for this. I knew I'd find you here." With his good hand, he caught her wrist. "And the prisoner you set free." His skin was damp and waxy, his hold a clammy pinch.

"Have you seen him?" As soon as she asked, she knew she'd made a mistake.

A smile creased his face, pushing folds of skin toward sagging ears. "I didn't need to. Word arrived from Cap-Rouge to put me on alert. I know he's here. I knew it even before you confirmed it. He is a spy and will be treated as such. And you are the woman who helped him." His speech was halting, his voice like a saw through wood. Though he paused for breath between phrases and sentences, his meaning was undiminished. "What do you suppose they will do with you, the woman who made possible this subterfuge? May this defeat of your army hang about your neck to the end of your days."

From his face and voice, she believed more than ever what Gaspard had said. Moreau had ordered the burning of the barn with Samuel inside. But she had no desire to stay long enough to hear him confirm or deny the report, or anything else he might say.

Wresting from his grip, Catherine stood. The sun was high overhead, her shadow barely present.

"And so you leave me here to die," he said. "Convenient solution."

Ringing filled her ears. The fighting, she realized, had stopped. "I do not leave you to die. Others will come for your care." She swept a glance up the buttes and across the field.

"No matter. Should I die, others are already looking for you and Samuel Crane. You will not be difficult to find."

Chest tightening, Catherine turned her back and walked away.

• • •

The English had won the battle, but the French still held Quebec. On the Plains of Abraham, looting had been quick to begin. In search of coin, unemployed weapons, and mementos of battle, soldiers and militia alike swooped in to pick over bodies and field.

British soldiers still on their feet loaded their wounded onto handbarrows and rolled them over the furrowed field and down the muddy road. The injured cried out with every jostle, all the way down to the temporary hospital on the beach at Anse-au-Foulon, where they awaited transport to Point Lévis. French wounded, and some English, were delivered to the convent's hôpital-général, which lay northwest of Quebec's walls and about half a mile west of the buttes. It sat on the south bank of the Saint-Charles River, just out of range of the batteries coming from Point Lévis, yet still close enough to house civilian refugees and wounded alike.

Josephine had returned to camp at Point Lévis, and Eleanor had been called to embalm General Wolfe's body before it was shipped to London, but Catherine stayed at the convent and served alongside Sisters in grey habits and white wimples. How spotless, how clean they looked to her, while her own dress and apron were a blend of stiff and sodden. With blood and brandy beneath her fingernails, she pumped fresh water from a well outside the hospital, back aching from bending over the wounded. Yet she was grateful to be of use, whether drawing water or translating for patients or nuns as necessary.

Finished at the pump, Catherine hoisted her buckets and turned back toward the hospital, focus locked on the uneven ground at her feet. When water sloshed over the bucket rims and onto her dress, she slowed her pace.

"Catherine."

She glanced up, then halted. Samuel stood not five paces before her. His clothes were filthy, but he was whole. Relief pushed through every part of her. "Where did you come from? Did you fight?" She scanned him for any sign of injury.

"I offered—quite forcefully, I might add—but the officers wouldn't allow it. Their own men were trained so well, they mistrusted whether I could keep up, especially with my weak shoulder, and there weren't rifles enough to go around as it was. If I'd had our muskets, I'd have at least given them to the cause, but we lost them in the river."

She lowered her buckets to the ground and wiped her palms on her tattered apron. "How did you find me?"

"When I didn't see you at Point Lévis, someone told me a few women had come to the field.

It was the sort of thing you would do. I figured the nearby convent had turned hospital, and so it has, and here you are." He stepped closer, reaching out. For a moment Catherine thought he would embrace her or take her hand. But he only cupped her elbow for a moment, his callused fingers brushing her skin. "It's over, Catherine. At least our part in it. We did it. The battle is won. It's only a matter of time before Quebec buckles beneath the new siege. Once it does, the rest of the nation must follow. The war on this continent cannot last long now."

All the energy Catherine had mustered for this day—and for the weeks leading up to it—fled her body all at once. A stone bench beckoned from beneath a tree, and she went to it, bringing her buckets with her. Sitting, she lowered her head into her hands.

Cannons boomed, and the ground trembled beneath her feet. Samuel's presence was warm beside her, but she didn't look at him. Artillery fire resounded and shuddered through her, an echo to her thudding pulse. This was her doing, hers and his, at least in part if not entirely. Would she have played this role if anyone but him had asked it of her? Could she still justify her actions when she was marked by the blood of her countrymen? These were questions she could not, or would not, answer.

Another blast reverberated in the distance, and

Catherine could well imagine smoke and fire and toppling stones. "Does Gaspard know?" she asked. Deserter though he was, she wondered how he would feel about the defeat of the army he'd left, especially since he'd played a more critical role than he first intended. Whatever his response, she felt confident she'd be able to relate.

Leaning against the maple at his back, Samuel stretched out his legs, crossing an ankle over the other. "It's likely, although I haven't seen him today."

It was better this way, sitting side by side rather than face-to-face. Catherine didn't want him to read her expression—or misread it. It was all she could do to comprehend the magnitude of today's battle and siege. "All he really wanted was to go home. Have they released him?"

"They detained him during the battle, but I imagine they'll release him soon, at the latest when the siege breaks and we occupy Quebec."

A bittersweet smile cracked Catherine's dry lips. "I'd like to see him before I leave, but I'm anxious to return home, too."

"Don't rush away." Samuel sat up straighter, angling to search her face. "The river is crawling with retreating French and pursuing British. Stay until the way is safer. I'm attaching to one of the regiments here, but when I'm off duty,

I'll build you a new canoe. Besides, you need to rest."

Held up against her need to see how Joseph fared, the delays sounded like excuses to her ears. And yet she agreed to stay.

The unbinding from Samuel Crane had already begun, however, for the mission that had brought them together was complete. Good-bye was all that was left.

CHAPTER TWENTY-NINE

A yellow-grey haze hovered over the siege-battered city, an echo of the fog in Catherine's mind. She'd agreed to stay a little longer before returning to Montreal, but if Samuel thought the wait would ease her exhaustion, he'd been mistaken. How could she rest when the nuns were vastly overwhelmed by patients? Whether she was motivated by goodwill or guilt, Catherine didn't examine. Instead she occupied herself with drawing water and boiling it, bandaging wounds, and bringing drink to the thirsty.

Artillery fire rumbled the ground. Smoke clouded the air. When the pump outside the hospital brought a mere trickle, Catherine carried her buckets to the shore of the Saint-Charles River. While the St. Lawrence was a fairly straight channel, the Saint-Charles turned back on itself, changing its course over and again.

How well she understood. Now that the battle was over, her thoughts looped from this war to the peace that must follow, from doubt to resignation over her actions, and from parting with Samuel to reunion with Thankful and her siblings. This was the direction she drifted as she filled the buckets from the river.

One of the tales Bright Star had told while Strong Wind and Gabriel argued outside was about three sisters. It was a story that belonged to the People, she'd said, and so it was especially important. According to the tale, three sisters lived in a field a very long time ago, before Strong Wind was born. The youngest of the girls couldn't walk yet, so she crawled along the ground, wearing green. The middle sister was restless, never content to stay in one spot. *"Like me!"* Catherine had laughed. She wore a yellow dress and ran this way and that across the field. The eldest sister stood straight and tall, with long silky hair. *"They all loved each other very much, but it was the eldest sister who kept the younger two together,"* Bright Star had explained.

One day in late summer, a boy visited the field, and the youngest sister disappeared. The other two sisters mourned. The boy returned later, and the middle sister disappeared. The eldest sister sighed for her siblings night and day until her hair dried and tangled in the wind, but she did not bow down. Still, no one heard her.

"Hurry up!" Catherine had always urged at that point, even though she knew it was a story about green beans and squash and corn. *"It's too sad. Get to the good part!"*

Bright Star had tapped her on the nose and called her impatient. But she went on just the same. The boy finally heard the eldest sister crying and took her in his arms to carry her to his home. There, she was astounded to find her younger sisters waiting for her. *"And from that day to this, the three sisters were never separated again. That's like us. We'll be together even if the moon and sun never face each other,"* she'd said, glancing outside toward Strong Wind and Gabriel.

Joseph had scrunched his small nose. *"But I'm not a girl, and we're not vegetables."*

Bright Star laughed. *"You are right, little brother. But am I not the eldest sister just the same, and responsible for both you and Catherine Stands-Apart?"*

The recollection stung. Catherine was still the sister darting near and far, pulling against vines that sought to hold her. In a few days she'd leave Quebec for a reunion with her siblings. She only prayed it would be a happy one.

Cannons roared, jerking her from her reverie. The ground quaked, the river trembled, and Catherine scooped a handful of water to her parched lips. Then, pails of water in hand, she headed back to patients who awaited the same.

A redcoat stood guard outside the hospital, which now operated under British control. As he let her in, all thoughts of Thankful, Bright Star, and Joseph moved to the back of her mind.

The air was as humid here as it was outside, due to the damp stone walls and floors. In this chamber, beds were arranged along both walls, each with a curtain to provide privacy to the patient within. Most, however, kept them open to allow a breeze. Two columns of cots had been set up end to end in the wide middle aisle to accommodate the influx from yesterday's battle. Women refugees from Quebec threaded between patients in search of husbands, sons, or fathers. Their distress was obvious at finding British wounded in their midst. Handkerchiefs scented with lavender could not mask the smell of ruined flesh.

"Pardon me." Catherine pushed between a wigged woman in silk and a peasant in threadbare linen, both looking for their men. Sisters in black and grey moved between the cots, many of them having come from convents inside Quebec.

"Mademoiselle, if you please!" Dr. Simmons, a surgeon with the British army, beckoned to Catherine from the far end of the chamber. If there were French doctors for French troops, they'd fallen back inside the city's walls. "These men have been waiting too long."

A breeze bitter with saltpeter swept the room. Catherine barely registered the color of the uniforms she passed as she shifted between the stone wall and a row of wounded. This convent, she'd learned, had received soldiers ill with smallpox and typhus who'd arrived at Quebec on French troopships throughout the war. *"French patients, we are accustomed to,"* one nun had told her yesterday. *"Battle wounds and British soldiers and surgeons, we are not."*

Perspiration bloomed beneath Catherine's arms and across her chest and back. Uneven flagstones rose and dipped beneath her steps. "Water, soldier?" Helping him drink, she saw past his mangled limb and thought of Bright Star and Thankful doing the same for Joseph. The notion put resolve where there might have been repulsion. What she couldn't do for her brother, she would do for these men until it was time to go home.

When she moved to the next patient, it was recognition that rolled her stomach.

"Bonjour. We meet again," Pierre Moreau rasped. His wounded leg and hand had been treated and bandaged. Whiskers sketched charcoal over his jaw, contrasting with his parchment-pale complexion.

"Bonjour, Captain Moreau. It would appear you've been well tended." She felt the urge to either flee from him or justify her actions. She did neither.

"Never trust appearances, Catherine. A lesson you taught me too well." His tone was sour as vinegar but weakened by blood loss. She had nothing to fear from him now.

On the other side of Moreau from Catherine, Dr. Simmons returned to the narrow aisle to treat the patient opposite him. A rolling cart held a tray of knives, scissors, needle, sutures, ligatures, a roll of bandages, and a bowl of wet plaster compound.

"Will you drink?" Catherine lifted the dipper.

"Water?" Moreau laughed. "Have you nothing stronger, for the love of all that is holy?" He glanced at the neighboring patient, who was being dosed with brandy by a nun called Sister Anne-Marie. "What he's having will suit, but a lot of it. Enough to make even a sailor drop. But you can't do that for me, and I wager you wouldn't even if you had the power. You enjoy seeing me suffer. Admit it." Thick black eyebrows pinched together above his nose, and colorless lips cinched tight, so that his face was pleated and creased.

"I do not." But it did not surprise her that he thought so.

"Why did you do it? How could you prevent your own army from getting food? But you did more than that, if I don't miss my mark. You passed through Cap-Rouge. You knew the plan." The captain's eyes took on an eerie shine to match the sheen of his brow. "You must have reported it to Wolfe. Every French and Canadian soldier here ought to place their blame on you alone."

Her mouth turned dry as starched cloth.

"Mademoiselle." From the opposite aisle, Sister Anne-Marie spoke low but firmly. "Many thirst. Do you mind?"

At her gentle reprimand, Catherine turned to move on and found Samuel threading toward her, wearing a fresh set of clothes. "I brought someone to see you," he said.

Gaspard appeared from behind him, raising a hand in greeting. He, too, was clean and freshly shaved. "Bonjour, mademoiselle." His tentative smile looked brave but unconvincing. His gaze bounced from her to the sea of wounded in which they stood. "I hear you may be taking your leave from us—"

"Gaspard Fontaine?" The cot squeaked behind Catherine as Moreau shifted. "And Samuel Crane! You brought both spy and deserter to the capital? Arrest these men!" he roared. "Arrest this half-breed woman!"

His French words were clearly lost on the British surgeon and soldiers in the chamber, and Catherine didn't translate.

"It's over, Moreau," Gaspard told him. "The British run the place now, and it's only a matter of time before they take the city, too. Those who can do the arresting think us heroes."

Samuel's steely tone cut straight to the point.

"Go back to France. There is nothing left on this continent for you to do." For the captain could not fight without the fingers he'd lost.

A shard of laughter burst from Moreau. "Return after defeat! Return less of a man than the one they sent off with cheers! Because of you." With a primal growl, Moreau lunged with his good arm and grabbed a knife from Dr. Simmons' cart. Light flashed on its blade as he dove toward Catherine.

Nuns screamed, men shouted, and the tip of the knife pierced through fabric to flesh. As Catherine twisted away from Moreau, the blade went no deeper but slashed a vertical line up her side toward her arm. Skin separated beneath her dress. Throwing herself from Moreau's reach, she tripped on a flagstone and crashed against a stone windowsill, catching a rib on the ledge.

Behind her, she heard Dr. Simmons subduing Moreau, heard the knife clatter to the floor. Gaspard unleashed a string of furied French at his former captain. Samuel caught Catherine from behind, holding her up when she wanted to sink down. She squeezed her eyes shut against the searing pain that blazed her skin, her bone. She would cry out if she could but breathe.

Pain held her captive.

As there was no brandy to spare for civilians, Catherine had felt every plunge and pull of the

471

needle four days ago when Dr. Simmons had stitched her skin in a six-inch line below her right arm. It was an agony she felt she deserved to suffer, for because of her, Joseph had endured this much and worse. So had hundreds upon hundreds of British and French soldiers.

She could not lie flat, for it put too much pressure on the rib the doctor suspected was cracked from her impact with the windowsill. Lying on either side or on her stomach was out of the question, so she'd spent the night in a straight back chair in the women's wing of the hospital. The gown and underthings she'd borrowed from Eleanor were ruined, but Sister Anne-Marie had persuaded a refugee woman staying in the convent to donate a new set and then helped Catherine dress. The corset was not laced as tightly as usual but still offered a degree of support. But donning the blue muslin gown had sent flaming arrows through Catherine's sides, and sweat had filmed her body.

Her memory scrolled back to the endurance test she had willingly done as a child, running barefoot over live coals. But she'd been able to breathe through that suffering, and the ordeal was finished in seconds. This time, drawing air made it worse, and Dr. Simmons said the pain could last weeks.

Weeks! She'd planned to stay a few days, no more. She felt stranded and woefully idle, for she couldn't even stay on her feet very long, let alone carry water or bend over patients in need. Instead, she sat in the corridor outside the main chamber where the soldiers were nursed. Thus out of the way, she proved neither help nor nuisance. She burned with pent-up frustration.

Footsteps sounded. Slowly, Catherine turned her head toward the noise. Samuel and Gaspard marched down the corridor toward her. As they neared, Samuel took off his tricorne hat and placed it over his chest.

"What did the doctor say?" Gaspard knelt on the cool, dark stones, face clean and shining beneath its freckles, his hair tidy in its queue. He pulled his toque from his head and crushed it in one hand.

She pulled in a shallow sip of air. "He said to do nothing. Sit still and do nothing, and allow the body to heal." Her tone betrayed her aggravation. Moreau had been moved to a different hospital, and here she sat, unmoved. "I cannot haul water. And I certainly cannot row or paddle."

Crossing his arms, Samuel leaned his back against the wall opposite her. "How long until you recover?"

That depended on a few things, which she did not have the energy to spell out. "At least three weeks before I can paddle back to Montreal." She ground out the words, still unable to reconcile herself to the truth of them, though her body confirmed it. "Even then, I won't be at full strength."

Gaspard put his head in his hands. When he looked up again, his grey eyes looked darker than she remembered. "I know there's a fire in your belly to get home, Catherine. I can't help but think that if I hadn't walked into the hospital when I did, you'd be able to. It doesn't seem right. It makes no sense that this should happen to you, when you've done so much to get us here."

"Maybe it does." She inhaled and winced at the stab to her rib. "I've had some time to think, and I wonder if this is part of God's plan. For if ever an injury was designed that could keep me from traveling, I have sustained it. With stitches on one side and a cracked rib on the other, I'm forced to stay and observe the consequences of bringing the two of you to British lines when all I want is to get back to my family." If there was a lesson to be learned while she was bound to this chair by her wounds, she prayed she could divine it quickly and be on her way.

Samuel bridged the gap between them and bent on one knee before her. "Catherine, the same God who allowed this to happen to you could have caused any number of things to delay us on our journey north. Yet we arrived just in time for our intelligence to be useful. I don't think your injury is His judgment. If He really didn't want Wolfe to know what we did, He could have stopped us with a thunderstorm."

She absorbed this, but remained ill at ease.

A murmuring in the hospital chamber swelled to a commotion. Gaspard pushed himself to his feet and leaned a hip against the wall, arms crossed. "Redcoat. With a parchment. He looks ready to share some news."

Samuel rose and stood behind him but didn't block Catherine's view.

"Quebec has surrendered," the officer began, and the British patients burst into an uproar of cheers.

"No!" cried one of the French. "What of the militia in the city? Did they not take up arms and fight?"

The officer reading the announcement lowered the parchment to reply. "They did not. Against their orders, the Canadians of the garrison would not fight. They heard drumbeats and believed we were about to storm, and laid down their arms rather than die for a cause clearly lost. I do not exaggerate, sir, when I tell you this. It may have been mutiny, but it was also good sense that they did not allow themselves to be massacred in vain. The sacrifice of their lives would not have delayed the capture of the city by an hour."

Gaspard glanced over his shoulder at Catherine,

the tip of his nose pink with emotion. "They chose their families over king and colony. I would have done the same."

Samuel nudged him with an elbow. "You did."

Catherine looked beyond them. The Sisters remained stoic, while several women who had fled Quebec months ago displayed a mixture of defeat and relief. Their homes were rubble, but perhaps their men still lived.

The rest of the announcement followed in English, and while someone in the main chamber translated for the French soldiers, Catherine explained the terms to Gaspard.

"The garrison is to receive the honors of war," she told him. "Canadians will remain in undisturbed possession of their property, provided they surrender their weapons."

"What property?" one patient cried out. "Piles of brick and stone inside the city, or the smoldering farms burned along the river?"

The British officer continued without responding, and Catherine kept up the translation. "The British will not compel Canadians to leave the colony nor punish those who served in the militia. Canadians may freely practice their religion and protect the personnel and property of the Catholic church."

Gaspard's eyebrows arched high, his gaze flicking between Catherine and the officer. When she held a hand to her corseted middle and took a searing breath, he leaned closer to hear.

"The French will turn over Quebec's artillery and munitions. French wounded and those who care for them will not become prisoners of war."

His announcement complete, the British officer left. Gaspard and Samuel each took one of Catherine's hands, and she stood, though it pained her, for this was not news to be borne sitting down. Samuel's expression held quiet triumph. Gaspard's was more difficult to read. She could only imagine the feeling inside the ruined city, or the triumph and celebration in camp at Point Lévis.

"Now," she whispered. "Now it's over."

Samuel's smile was subdued. "The terms are as favorable for the conquered as any could wish," he said. "Now the British will take charge of restoring the city and feeding the people."

Pressure began to build behind Catherine's rib from the effort of standing. She let it. "No more battle, no more siege, no more burning and destruction." Spoken quietly within the convent walls, her words were as much prayer as they were prediction.

Gaspard's eyes shone with emotion. "I'm going home. Today. Right now. Thank you." He kissed her hand, and she eased back into her seat, thanking him for his role on the journey.

"Your parents will rejoice to see you, especially

on a day like this," she added, but sensed a shift in Gaspard.

Bowing his head, he twisted the toque in his hands. "I wish I could bring Augustin with me. He is the one they mourn."

"You are still their miracle child, Gaspard." Catherine smiled up at him. "And perhaps a prodigal returning home?"

He chuckled but didn't deny it.

"I'm glad for you." Samuel gave Gaspard's hand a hearty shake. "I'm genuinely glad you can be with your parents again. Not all of us are so lucky."

Gaspard hooked a thumb into his waistband. "Thank you for bringing me home. Especially considering the small matter of me lighting that barn on fire with you in it."

" 'Twas a little thing, was it?" A wry grin softening his tone, Samuel punched Gaspard's uninjured arm. "And yet, ironically, it opened the door that got us all here."

A smile flared across Gaspard's face. "*Voilà!* Even when I'm misbehaving—on orders, mind you—it's really for everyone's good." Still grinning, he settled his toque back on his head. "Au revoir, Samuel. Au revoir, Catherine."

With a catch in her voice, she returned the farewell and watched him hurry away, knowing she'd never see him again.

"Gaspard will go home, and I must stay." She

straightened her backbone to relieve the pinch she felt. "Once I can bear to stand and walk around, I will see how Quebec fares under British control. I will see what our actions have wrought."

"Our actions would mean nothing without Wolfe's army," Samuel countered, gesturing toward the field beyond the convent with his tricorne in his hand. "Remember, you heard yourself from Watkins that the battle would have happened whether we arrived in time to affect the outcome or not. Wolfe already planned to attack. The battle on the Plains lasted all of fifteen minutes before the French retreated. Had a different site been chosen, had it not been a surprise attack, the fighting would have dragged out much longer and more men would have died."

The reminder took root in Catherine, lifting at least some of the burden she felt. "Thank you. I do need to remember that."

He tugged his hat back on his head. "I understand you feel conflicted now, but I hope soon you'll be proud of what we've done."

"Proud?" she asked, wracked by a punishing pain. "Right now I'd much rather be at peace."

CHAPTER THIRTY

October 1759

It had been the longest three weeks of Catherine's life.

After Quebec's surrender, her rib troubled her less, so she walked some every day. Outside the convent grounds, she saw hundreds of British cattle brought from Boston now grazing the Plains of Abraham, ready to feed the conquering army. Inside the hôpital-général, when nuns scraped and swept between beds and cots, Catherine volunteered to sprinkle vinegar on the floor in their wake.

Murmurs followed her. Word traveled quickly among patients, refugees, and nuns until everyone knew at least one version of Catherine's role in the battle. Wounded British congratulated her, and Sister Anne-Marie's reserved manner didn't alter, but a chill spread from the rest of them.

On September 22, the atmosphere in the convent had grown brittle with the news that the former Quebec garrison had boarded four British transports that would carry them all back to France. Pierre Moreau was among them.

Catherine expected to breathe easier, then. Instead, the pain in her rib had intensified so sharply that she could no longer leave her chair for more than fifteen minutes at a time. Her stitches pulled and itched unbearably, and yet the doctor called all of this normal.

"There are many kinds of hurt," Dr. Simmons had told her. "What you're describing now is the hurt of healing. When the body knits itself back together, it's a kind of magic no surgeon can reproduce. But there is pain in the process. It will pass. Healing comes with a price, and I'm afraid the price is pain. Beyond that, however, is wholeness."

The British doctor could not have known how often she would bring his words to mind. During breathless spells holding tight to her chair, yes, but more than that. The reports Samuel brought from Quebec every few days were disheartening. Five hundred thirty-five houses had burned down during the siege, and the rest were greatly damaged. In Lower Town, hardest hit by the batteries across the river at Point Lévis, the rubble from smashed buildings had made the streets impassable until British soldiers cleared them. Quebec residents were allowed to come home, but what was there to come home to? Houses that weren't ruined were liable to be broken into and robbed by plundering soldiers despite severe penalties for doing so, even death.

The city was hurting, but Catherine prayed that it was on its way to healing.

Today she was visiting what was left of Quebec to see it for herself, Samuel beside her. She tugged her cape tighter about her shoulders, grateful for another layer atop her gown and for the silk hood that covered her ears. Autumn was fully upon them, and the sun, though bright, no longer held much warmth.

"I don't know this place," she murmured. When she'd been here last, Lower Town had swirled with commerce and life. Now, instead of merchants and shoppers going about their trade, armed redcoats patrolled the ruins against soldiers bent on looting. Shingles brightly painted and hung to advertise wares lay in splinters on the ground. Narrow streets that had been shadowed by shops and apartments were now scoured with glaring light in their absence and unprotected from the bitter wind. The town was raw and exposed, and Catherine felt the same.

"It will be rebuilt." Samuel cocked his head toward a pair of soldiers boarding up glassless windows on a building with half a roof. "Carpenters—like myself—and masons within the ranks are working every day to restore what is broken."

Catherine nudged a small shattered teapot with the toe of her shoe. "Restore what is broken?" Pieces of tiny saucers and cups lay scattered over soot-stained shards of mahogany. The broken face of a doll in a silk dress stared up at her with one eye. What a rude interruption some little girl had suffered during her tea party.

"Or we begin anew, of course, where necessary. But the immediate need is simply to put roofs together to shelter those of us who will stay here for the winter. Myself included." Samuel's face and frame had lost the gaunt edges of hunger after weeks of British provisions. But she doubted he would look so hearty and hale after a Canadian winter in this hollowed-out shell of a town.

Her gut twisted as they came to the Place-Royale. Drilling redcoats marched in formation past roofless buildings. The walls that remained were perforated by shot. Some cannonballs remained embedded in the stone.

"Watch your step." Samuel guided her around a hole in the plaza big enough to be a horse pond. "Some shot danced around here a while before finally exploding."

Circling the cavity, she peered at what was left of the church. Named Notre-Dame-des-Victoires for the French victories against the British in decades past, its spire had been shattered, its roof and stone walls a pile of ruins, a monument of defeat. Slowly, she swiveled to take in the jagged remnants all around her. "So much loss," she whispered.

"You and I didn't cause this, Catherine. We stopped it. Without the battle that prompted surrender, the battering of Quebec, especially its Lower Town, would have continued."

Catherine slid him a grateful glance. His words were a salve to her ragged conscience. She must remember this the next time guilt threatened to entwine her. She must banish misgivings with this truth.

Two grenadiers warmed themselves at a fire in the stone courtyard, brass buttons and buckles flashing. A trio of ladies in tattered gowns but perfect coiffures laughed at something they said.

A faint smile tipped Samuel's lips. "Did I tell you that Brigadier General Murray issued an order forbidding any more of his soldiers from marrying Canadian women? Seems the ladies are quite willing to overlook past offenses."

"How forgiving they are." Catherine watched the couples for a moment before adding, "Or perhaps it's simply that many eligible Canadian bachelors did not survive their militia service." She climbed the pockmarked steps that led inside the church.

Samuel followed and doffed his hat. With no roof remaining to catch it, sunlight fell through the rafters and glinted on his golden hair in a way that almost resembled a halo. She saw what he once was to her with fondness, but not longing.

"How like an angel you once seemed to me," she told him. "You were my rescuer, just as you said. And I was yours."

Surprise flicked over his features as he regarded her. "What do you suppose we are now?"

She strolled past piles of shattered window glass glittering on the floor. "Two people trying to bring order from chaos, yet held steadfast by a God who loved us before we loved Him. When I look at you now, I see neither angel nor demon, but an old friend with whom I must part ways."

A ridge formed between his eyes as he offered her a smile. "I see the same."

Understanding threaded between them, both a drawing together and a purposeful sliding away. Catherine broke his gaze, a small act of the distancing that would soon be complete and entire.

A wide swath of the church floor yawned open where shells had exploded, wood planks jagged like teeth around a gaping mouth. Most of the pews had been smashed in the blast or used as firewood. Maple leaves somersaulted across her path, landing in a bronze and burgundy drift against an overturned bench. She turned it right side up and brushed it off with her hand. "Shall we sit?"

They did.

Slowly, Samuel spun his hat in his hands. "You'll want to be going home, then."

She pleated the folds of her cape on her lap. "As soon as possible. I don't belong here. Is a canoe ready for me to take?" As much as she wanted to leave, she'd been steeling herself for the physical toll of the journey.

A cold wind riffled through Samuel's hair and brought a faint pink to his nose and ears. "It is. I know you're anxious to return to your family. There's a British sloop heading upstream tomorrow morning. The captain has agreed to take you and your canoe as close as he can get to Trois-Rivières. He'll give you rations for the rest of the journey, which you'll have to manage on your own. Would that suit?"

Relief washed over her. "It would suit me very well." Paddling upstream would test her stamina and her three-week-old wounds severely. She doubted she'd have much energy left to forage for food.

"It will cut your travel time by half and protect you for the most contested stretch of the river. French troops who retreated after the battle are still camped between here and there, with a large group near the mouth of the Jacques-Cartier River."

Seeing Cap-Rouge in her mind, she drew a fortifying breath and felt only the slightest twinge. "Whatever happened to all that wheat, Samuel? All the grain from Montreal. Where is it now?"

He shifted on the bench. "I don't know for certain. Some say that as the Quebec garrison laid down their arms in surrender, Monsieur Cadet was still desperately trying to get provisions to the city. He was too late, of course, and I hear that what he brought was soggy and rotten."

Dismay crawled over Catherine's skin. "But the majority of it was edible." The pleading in her tone surprised her. "Please say it wasn't all wasted."

Small lines bracketed Samuel's mouth. "I reckon you were in too much pain to notice, but two days after Moreau attacked you, the heavens opened up, Catherine. Torrents of rain, high winds. The wheat was still in transit in open bateaux, with only burlap sacks and wooden barrels to protect it."

"Then it was ruined!" Her stomach rolled at the magnitude of the loss. "All that food. It never reached the soldiers. Montreal will go hungry another year for nothing." A groan rose from the depths of her spirit. Trapping a sob in her chest, she let tears roll silently down her cheeks. She lifted her face to the open sky and whispered, "Lord, how long until we have peace?"

Samuel clapped his hat over one knee and leaned forward, clenching his hands together. "I am sorry. Truly." From the courtyard behind them, the grenadiers laughed with the staccato burst of musketry.

Catherine tasted the smoke in the air from their cookfire. "Will the British army feed the residents here with their provisions?" The British Royal Navy had already been landing food for their garrison in addition to the cattle she'd seen on the fields.

"Not as an official policy, no." Shadows layered Samuel's expression. "A couple dozen soldiers are helping harvest the wheat in surrounding fields here, whatever can be found this late in the season, but British rations must be distributed to the military. Even so, soldiers have been trading their food with residents already." He glanced at her. "You understand."

A rueful smile curled her lips. Of course she did. The ankle-length, fur-lined cape and silk hood he'd brought her were his to give because he'd traded his food to get them.

Quiet enveloped them as they sat side by side. There was little left to say. Pressing a hand to the fluttering in her stomach, she asked where and when to meet the sloop in the morning, adding that there was no need for him to see her off, for she hated drawn-out farewells.

"So this is good-bye, then." Samuel stood and helped her do the same. A muscle worked in his jaw. "To say thank you seems so insufficient. So incomplete. I can't repay you."

She smiled into his sun-bronzed face. "If I've learned anything from you, it's that life is about far more than equal exchange." She paused to master herself. "I'm so glad I knew you, Sam. You gave me hope and love when I needed it most, and more confidence than I knew I could possess."

He swallowed. "And you have been more to me than words can say. Those years we had together—" He paused as if gathering his thoughts from a distant place and time. "We were kids when we met. I was shattered and lost, but you helped shape me into the man I am. For that, and for these last few weeks, I'm grateful."

The crack in his voice sent bittersweet memories washing through her. "After you left, I was so hurt," she said, "that I wished I'd never met you. But what a loss that would have been. I love all the things you were to me. I love that you do the right thing." The admission was a release, for her and for him. Tears rolled down her cheek, and she dashed them away.

His lips parted in obvious surprise. "Thank you," he whispered. "I cannot tell you what it means to hear you say that."

"You don't have to. I know."

Samuel shifted his feet, and dust clouded the tops of his boots. "I once told you to find a husband to bring you the happiness you deserve. That was ill phrased. I wish for you all the happiness and peace that life and God can offer, Catie, whether or not you marry."

She tucked a loose strand of hair back inside her hood. "And I wish you the same, with Lydia, Joel, and Molly."

Lines fanned from his brimming eyes to match his wavering smile. "Could I—if it wouldn't hurt—" Samuel dropped his gaze to the hat in one callused hand, then looked back up at her. Without another word, he opened his arms.

Swallowing a swell of emotion, she stepped into his embrace and felt it wrap gently around her one last time.

Then she let him go.

CHAPTER THIRTY-ONE

It was not weakness of body that shuddered through Catherine as she pushed southwest on the St. Lawrence River. Before she'd parted ways with the sloop downstream of Trois-Rivières this morning, one of the laundresses on board had helped her bind her ribs, the constriction a necessary support. Gone was the freedom of movement afforded by the buckskin dress she'd lost. But this was not what hindered her breath.

Dark rumors had swirled about the docks where she'd disembarked. Stories too horrible to be believed. She'd heard tales like this before.

Some time after Catherine moved from Kahnawake to live with her father, he told her about a man who skipped observing Lent seven years in a row and turned into a *loup-garou*, a werewolf forced to wander the countryside alone for the rest of his life. There was only one cure. Someone who had known the werewolf as a man had to recognize him and draw his blood. Catherine came to think of Gabriel as the *loup-garou*, cursed to meanness and isolation. She'd convinced herself she could save him, for she remembered the merry papa he'd once been. *"But will you draw his blood?"* Joseph had asked, and her heart sank. He would do it himself to save her, he'd said, but he harbored no memories of Gabriel being kind.

Later, Catherine had been trimming her father's fingernails for him and accidentally cut close enough to the quick that he'd bled. She apologized profusely, but to her astonishment, he chuckled and wiped the drop away with his thumb. *"Ah, child,"* he said, eyes crinkling, and kissed the top of her head. *"I daresay I've had worse cuts than this."* Her gaze dropped to his shortened arm, then back to the rare smile on his face. *"Come now, clean me up, for you're the only one who can."*

She'd broken the curse, she told herself. The papa she remembered and loved was back.

But his good humor didn't last. Catherine hadn't cured him of himself after all. *"Some stories don't end the way we want them to,"* Bright Star had replied when Catherine told her.

The river widened, and Catherine glided onto Lac Saint-Pierre. As far as she could see, the surface was covered with snow geese gathered for their annual migration. Then a wave of the honking birds took flight. More rose up after them by the thousands. Tens of thousands. They lifted in clouds and in lines, layering to blot out the sun. The squawking magnified to an impossible scale, buffeting her ears. Still she paddled beneath a sky turned dark with black-tipped wings.

How she envied the geese their effortless speed. By the time she reached the end of the lake, her ears still rang with their noise, and her spirit still felt shadowed, though daylight had returned.

The story that haunted her now was the news that there had been a raid at Odanak just yesterday morning by an entire band of men who might as well be *loups-garous*. *"Only a few escaped,"* she'd heard.

At last Catherine turned onto the Saint-François River and paddled toward Odanak. Nerves taut, she scanned the shoreline. Her siblings and Thankful ought to be home by now. But if Joseph's convalescence had dragged on, they might have remained in Odanak, as Catherine had tarried at Quebec.

Miles passed. The air began to smell and taste of smoke. The bindings about her ribs forced her breath to remain unnaturally calm.

A canoe floated ahead of her, caught between the shore and an uprooted tree that had fallen into the river. Pulse throbbing, she steered for it. "Hello?" she called. "Is someone there?"

Catherine pulled alongside and peered in. Two adults and a child were bent forward, bullet holes in their backs, their blood dark puddles beneath them.

"Bright Star!" she cried, jerking away from the Abenaki bodies. "Joseph! Thankful!" The names of those most precious to her tore from her lips with a force that stabbed her rib. Sweat covered her in an instant. Slashing her paddle through the river, she scanned all around her, searching and praying she would not find them.

A woman's body was splayed on the shore as if she had just climbed out on the other side. A gash through her Abenaki tunic was the size of a tomahawk blade. Catherine's stomach emptied, and she could not fill her lungs. Fear and horror turned her hollow.

She clawed off her hood and cape, leaving them in her canoe when she beached it on the low-lying terrace that led to the settlement. Her skirts in one hand, she stumbled up the slope to a village all but razed to the ground. The wooden palisades were gone, the roads piled with ash and cinders. Wampum beads mixed with melted silver. Every house had been torched save the three that had been used to store corn. Bodies were strewn facedown in the streets, cut down by bayonet or tomahawk and left without their scalps.

"Bright Star! Joseph! Thankful!" She called their names again and again, like Hail Marys on an endless string of rosary beads. She was gasping, tripping, shaking.

Catherine's chest burned, but her hands and

limbs were shaking with cold. She felt no pain in her rib or stitched-up cut. The sun stood still as she combed through Odanak for the living or for the remains of those she loved. After finding a broken pipe stem that had once belonged to Fawn, she dropped to her knees and wept, for she could not muster the air to scream.

Sluicing the tears from her face, she summoned her memory. What had she heard this morning? That American rangers had done this, led by Robert Rogers, on General Amherst's orders. That the carnage was reprisal for all the native raids launched from Odanak on New England for decades. Or was it in retaliation for the mistreatment of the two British officers and six Stockbridge Mohicans the Abenaki had called spies? Whatever the reason, the rangers had attacked before dawn and massacred all but twenty captives—

Captives. Bright Star and Joseph might be among them. Thankful might have been spared because of her heritage. Her thoughts spun until she forced herself to focus on the fact that there were survivors. She searched her soul for some promise she might offer up to God so that her loved ones would be among them.

But that was folly, an old trading habit. God was not to be bargained with. She had nothing to entice Him, for she possessed nothing He needed. Yet He loved her, and that was what she clung to. With empty hands, she begged that Bright Star, Joseph, and Thankful were safe. But the question trailing her prayers grew harder to ignore. If she could not bend God's will to hers, could she possibly bow to His?

A howling gust of wind kicked up a cloud of dust. Coughing, she pushed herself up from the ground. Such a wind would have lifted the scalps on the hundreds of poles around this town. Now it stirred the ashes of the Abenaki who had taken them or condoned it.

Her shadow lengthened as she stood there, until finally she realized time had passed without her. Still dazed by the destruction, she walked back to her canoe. She would travel no farther tonight and had no appetite for her rations, but her cape would be her blanket while she rested in one of the houses still standing.

Stiffly, she scooped up the garment from the bottom of her canoe, then folded it over her arm and trod up the sloping shore. Soft ground cushioned her steps, and the air was fresher here among the pines that fringed the banks. This was a better resting place than one of the store-houses. It was not unlike the one Bright Star had found for those two French lookouts. There was even a willow tree a short distance away from the river, boughs bending as though to comfort. She drew near it.

And stopped.

A bed of rocks mounded the earth at the base of the trunk. The rectangular shape stretched as wide as a man and as long. A grave, carefully made, the way Bright Star had taught Catherine to do.

Her spirit reeled back even as her feet slowly carried her to the grave's edge. There was carving on the wide trunk behind it.

Joseph Many Feathers
Slain protecting his sisters
4 Oct. 1759
WE LIVE

Unable to breathe, Catherine dropped the cape, fingers flying over the buttons on her bodice to unfasten them. Tears blinded her, and sobs struggled to break free. If she could not get air, she would drown in her grief. Nearly frantic, she peeled down her sleeves and bodice, ripped out the pins that held the bindings in place around her torso. She unwound the strips with shaking hands until she stood panting in chemise and skirts.

A keening erupted from her unbound lungs with such force, her mother's people would have been ashamed. They would have admonished her to endure it with dignity, like the eldest sister in Bright Star's story, the one who mourned the loss of her siblings without bowing down.

But Catherine was not Strong Wind or her people. She was fully and wholly herself, and right now she felt every inch a river rapid raging with her own tears. She gave herself up to their release. Without thought for her rib, she threw herself down on Joseph's grave and wept. If she was a river, he was the rocky bed beneath her.

Pain rushed in where she'd been hollowed out by the sight of Odanak's ruins. The aching rib and lungs were nothing compared to the loss that filled her now. This was her Joseph, the son whom no father had claimed, the brother who had bridged the gap between sisters, and chosen not a wife to protect, but them.

Darkness fell, and the stones grew cool, but Catherine did not forsake her hard bed. After rebinding her ribs, she refastened her bodice and pulled her cape to cover her and her brother both. The sharp edges of Joseph's stony mantle pushed into her body.

Wind sang through the willow, a lullaby. The river lapped at its bank, steady as a heartbeat. Eventually, sleep carried her away. In her dreams, she saw her brother whole and healthy, many feathers in his hair. She heard him say, *"You live,"* and then woke with a stabbing pain beside his grave.

CHAPTER THIRTY-TWO

Dawn lanced through the willow tree and the pines that flanked it. The act of sitting up punished Catherine for her hours of paddling and for her unabashed mourning the night before. But now it was dread for the living that consumed her.

Bright Star and Thankful had been alive to bury Joseph, but what had happened to them after that? Fresh worries stabbed as a slew of possibilities leapt to mind. Were they hurt? Had they been captured? Were they too terrified to move? Catherine needed to leave. They could need her help, even now.

Groaning, she pressed her hands to her temples. What would Joseph's death mean to Bright Star, who had already lost so many? Whatever fragile ground she and her sister had gained of late, surely it wasn't strong enough to hold the weight of their brother's death. Bright Star might never forgive her, and Catherine would understand why.

Her thoughts shifted violently to Thankful and to the parting assurances that she would be safe. What havoc had the massacre wreaked in Thankful's heart and soul?

Wincing, she stood, bracing her rib with one hand. She would push through any pain to find them, even if they had no desire to see her. Let them hate her, if it soothed them. Let them blame her for their stay in Odanak. *But please,* she prayed, *let them be safe.*

Leaves shivered and dropped from their branches, sprinkling gold over the stones and earth. Twigs crunched behind Catherine. Turning, she cried out in surprise.

"Catherine?" Thankful dropped a bouquet of sunflowers, new lines on her face aging her beyond her sixteen summers. Blond hair loose over her shoulders, she still wore a simple French gown beneath a woolen cloak, a fashion that might have saved her life.

Relief and sorrow shuddered through Catherine at the sight of her friend's haunted face. "I'm sorry," she rasped. Vision blurring, she ran toward Thankful on unsteady legs. "I'm so sorry. I cannot say how much. This would never have—"

Thankful closed the remaining distance between them, hair streaming behind her, and captured Catherine to herself. "You're here. You're . . ." But her words disappeared into sobs.

Ignoring the pain to her rib, Catherine squeezed the girl's thin shoulders, rocking from side to side as tears rolled down her face. The smell of fire clung to Thankful's clothing.

"Bright Star's coming," Thankful whispered, then pulled back.

Catherine lifted her gaze and saw her sister twenty yards away. Wind ruffled the fox fur mantle on Bright Star's shoulders and the ribbons binding her braids. She was looking at their brother's grave, her face a mask, a defense, a wall unbreachable.

Grief and guilt forged a blade in Catherine's throat. The rangers had wielded knife and gun, but it was she who had led her loved ones here. Releasing Thankful, she stepped into her sister's line of vision.

The instant Bright Star saw Catherine, her eyes flared. She broke into a run. Nearly tripping over her skirts, Catherine raced to meet her, halting only when Bright Star seized her in an embrace so fierce, it sent fire searing from her rib. Catherine cried out in terrible pain and ferocious joy.

"Sister." Bright Star used the name she hadn't called Catherine since they were girls. "My sister, you've returned to me. To us. Thank God you've come home at last."

"But too late," Catherine choked out, crying onto Bright Star's shoulder. *Too late, too late.* The words pounded against her skull as grief crashed over her afresh. "I'm sorry Joseph was killed. I'm sorry you were there to witness it. None of you would have been here if it wasn't for me."

Bright Star's hand stroked the back of Catherine's head. "Stop this talk. You have lost a brother, too."

They stood there long enough for Catherine's tears to cease and for her sister's to begin. Bright Star cried at last.

When at length they released each other, Catherine bent with the pain in her rib.

"You're hurt?" Bright Star steadied her by the elbow, and Thankful took her other hand.

Catherine grimaced, wishing she could dismiss such a trivial thing. A moment passed before she could draw breath to explain. "I was injured the day after the battle and couldn't travel until now, otherwise I would have come weeks ago." Her hair had come loose from its pins and whipped about her neck.

Bright Star hooked a shoulder-length strand behind Catherine's ear but said nothing of its shorter length. "Injured how?"

"I met Pierre Moreau in the hospital. He attacked me with a surgeon's knife, and when I lunged away from him, I cracked my rib on a windowsill. He is gone now," she added. "Sailed back to France with the rest of the Quebec garrison."

Anger pinched Bright Star's face. "I never trusted him. And Gaspard Fontaine?"

"Proved a friend." A small smile flickered over Catherine's lips.

"I'm so sorry Captain Moreau hurt you," Thankful said. She bowed her head, and her hair fell like a curtain over half her face. "Was he upset because your mission was successful?"

"Yes, he was. It was." But she didn't want to speak of Quebec. "I arrived yesterday evening and went through the village looking for you. How did I miss you?"

Bright Star sat on the ground, gesturing for the others to do the same. "Yesterday afternoon we finished laying the last stones on Joseph's grave. In the evening, we were foraging in the woods, since the raiders took all the corn they didn't burn. Then we slept in an empty storehouse. You must have come when we were out."

Catherine gazed toward the river. "Shall we bury the others, as well?"

"We met a few Abenaki who also escaped. They are on their way back and will bury their own people according to their own customs."

Inhaling slowly, Catherine nodded, then let out a breath. Questions burned on her tongue, but she held them back, wary of pushing too hard. She allowed the quiet to possess a few moments, waiting to see if either Bright Star or Thankful would speak.

They did not.

"Will you tell me what happened, or will it hurt too much?" Catherine tilted her head toward the village, encompassing the whole of ruined Odanak in the gesture.

Thankful gathered her sunflowers, then placed all but one on Joseph's grave. This she clutched in her lap. She pinned a dull gaze to the tree trunk, to the letters that spelled *WE LIVE*. "They came before dawn, those Rangers. It was the day after a wedding celebration that lasted far into the night, so most of the people here were deep in their dreams when it began." She pleated a petal with her fingers, a chore without purpose unless to distract herself from her own tale. "They came like banshees, Catherine. With tomahawks and bayonets and bullets, screaming about Fort William Henry and revenge."

Catherine had heard of Fort William Henry. Vastly outnumbered, the British had surrendered after a French siege to the fort. The French general Montcalm had lost control of his native allies, who murdered and scalped sick and wounded provincials by the score, if not by the hundreds.

Thankful's soft voice continued. "The Rangers were mad with bloodlust, ripping doors off hinges, killing families in their beds. It was dark, but we heard the screams of women and children. I hear them now." She pinched the petal in half and creased it, then folded it back on itself. "I don't know if I will ever stop hearing children being killed." Another fold, crease, pinch, crease, until the pace grew frantic.

Catherine's eyes closed for a moment to hold back tears. "Oh, Thankful." Words failed her. She could no more string them together in her mind than push them across her tongue.

Thankful plucked a petal from the flower's center and ripped it to tiny pieces. "Many times over the last several years, I have wished the Abenaki people could experience the same terror I did, the same terror they inflicted upon hundreds of New England families. And then . . ." Her voice trailed away, and she tore more petals until they splattered her apron with sunshine. Tears slid down her cheeks and met beneath her chin. "That wish came true—but not until after I had lived with them, eaten their food, slept beneath their roofs. Fawn behaved like a grandmother toward us, or at least how I suppose a grandmother might be. I didn't understand her most of the time, but I understood she was trying to help us."

The urge to protect her surged in Catherine. "Say no more, Thankful, if you'd rather not. I'm sorry I—"

"Catherine, stop. No more apologies, please." Tone gentle, Bright Star met her gaze not with censure, but compassion. "This isn't about you and what you could have or should have done. We will sit here at the foot of our brother's grave while we can. We will say our piece, each one of us, even if it makes us uncomfortable."

Warmth flushed across Catherine's cheeks at the idea that she might have silenced Thankful for her own sake, to ease the weight of her guilt. Biting her tongue, she pulled her cape closer and waited.

Brushing the petals from her lap, Thankful wound a strand of her hair in a ringlet around her finger. "Being at Odanak was the right hard thing for me to do, just as you said it would be. I won't say that I befriended all the Abenaki, but I ceased to view them as monsters. I saw them as people, with flaws just like anybody else. But I never grew used to living beneath the flags of so many scalps. Then the Rangers harvested their own. . . ."

"You saw this?" Catherine whispered.

"Heard it." A pinecone dropped from a tree several yards distant, and Thankful startled. Composure crumbling, she looked away.

Catherine held herself back from rushing to fill the silence. Instead they sat in grief together, the whistling wind the only sound.

"I will say no more," Thankful said at last. Clasping her hands barely disguised their shaking. "I cannot."

"You were brave," Bright Star told her. "You still are. What is that psalm I heard you whispering?"

Thankful's eyebrow lifted. "'Weeping may endure for a night, but joy cometh in the morning.'

But the night, you see, can last a very long time."

"This I know." Bright Star stood and helped Thankful up, then Catherine. "I am practiced at burying the ones I love, and yet each death carves new runnels in my heart. I don't pretend to know what it is to live inside your skin, Thankful. But I do know that however far off the sun is, morning is on the way." Like a hen gathering her chicks, Bright Star put her arms around their shoulders. "And I know that sisters help us see the light a little faster."

They said good-bye to Joseph and turned their steps away. The fact that Thankful's hands hadn't stopped shaking wasn't lost on Catherine, but no one spoke of it. Worry settled like a yoke on Catherine's shoulders.

As they walked, she touched her sister's elbow. "I have questions," Catherine murmured, "about our brother." She still hadn't heard exactly how Joseph met his end or how Bright Star and Thankful had escaped.

A sad smile curved Bright Star's lips. "I know you do. He fought infection in his shattered leg for weeks before gangrene set in. Had he lived, he would have lost his leg to amputation in order to save his life."

Thankful slowed her pace, dropping several steps behind them. It was obvious this was a story she didn't want to hear.

"Then the raid happened," Catherine prompted.

"As soon as we heard the screams on the other side of town, he was adamant that he would stay and fight and not slow down our escape. But this is where I will be your big sister and carry the rest of the story for you, locked safe inside me. Remember Joseph as he lived, not the manner of his death."

"But—"

"It is my turn to be adamant. He died. We are alive. So let us live." Green ribbons danced in the wind at the ends of her braids.

Catherine's eyelids turned hot and sticky at the conviction in her voice.

Pausing, Bright Star angled and held out a hand to bring Thankful into the fold. "I have a thing to say to both of you. I have been alive for many years without living. I absorbed the deaths of those in my family very deeply. Pieces of myself were buried in each grave, and I believe this is normal to an extent. But I allowed grief to whittle me further and further, until I was more shell than soul. It is right to mourn what has been taken from us. What is not right is that I didn't let myself grow in new ways until Catherine began bringing me on the river with her. I had been alive but refusing to live, and that was wrong."

Tears lined Catherine's lashes. She'd observed this in Bright Star, and yet she'd done the same thing in the years after Samuel disappeared. They had been two sisters at odds, so quick to judge the other and failing to see their own twin flaws.

Bright Star veered away from the Saint-François River, leading Catherine and Thankful to a smaller creek similar to the one that flowed behind their trading post. This one coursed down a gentle slope, cascading over slabs of rock plastered with fallen leaves. Mist surrounded a waist-high waterfall.

"I have a story for you." Bright Star's smile flared so wide and free, it was as if Catherine was seeing her true sister for the first time in years. "It is the story of us, and we are writing it even now."

Thankful pushed her hair behind her shoulder, tilting her head to listen.

"It is the custom of the People, when a family member dies, to replace the lost loved one with another," Bright Star began. "We ransom and adopt a captive, and that former captive is given a new name and becomes part of the family forever, regardless of the past. It is the pleasure of the adopting family to do this thing, not because of anything the captive has done, but because we are eager to love completely and are confident that love will heal the wounds of the past. Thankful, my sister ransomed you, not in place of anyone she had lost, but simply because she wanted you for who you are. Your name remains what it has always been."

"Unless—" Thankful hesitated, then began again. "Unless you were the lost sister, and I the replacement for you."

Catherine frowned. "No. You both know how I feel about this practice of replacing people. It cannot be done. No one can stand in for another."

Bright Star held up a hand. "And I agree with you. Allow me to finish, and I think you will agree with me, too." She slipped off her moccasins and waded into the water. "All of us have been ransomed by the Great Good God. Jesus died, and we became God's children. He died, and so we live. The black robes have a practice where a new Christian is taken into the water, baptized, and afterward, the person is clean in Christ. The People have a similar tradition with the captives they adopt into the tribe. They scrub them clean, washing away the white blood, so that afterward they are new and completely part of the family."

A bow of color glistened in the waterfall's spray. On the bank behind Bright Star, birch trees stood tall and straight, their trunks white as snow geese, their leaves like countless candle flames. "Both customs wash away the old and begin something new," she continued. "A new start. A new family. This is what I want for us. Today I allow myself the sorrows for loved ones lost, but wash away the bitterness that has held me back from living my own life." She held her cupped hands in the falling water and laved it over her face.

Catherine watched in awe, pulse thrumming. This was the sister she longed to know. A woman with wisdom and grace and humility, who had been refined by life's trials, not eaten away by them. It was as if Bright Star had been buried beneath an ocean of too many hard years, and she was finally coming to the surface.

Unprompted, Thankful hoisted the hem of her skirts and stepped into the creek.

Smiling, Bright Star held her hands beneath the falls again and wiped the soot and tears from the young woman's face. "Thankful. Today I do not scour away your heritage or your name. But if I can wash away your fears, this I do. I clear away all doubt that you belong here with Catherine and with myself. Today I call you my sister, though you remain Thankful Winslet through and through. You are loved and cherished for who you are. You are enough. You are part of a family once more."

Releasing her skirts, Thankful held her hands to the falling stream, then washed her own face and neck. With creek water streaming down her face, she hugged Bright Star and said, "Thank you. Today I am your sister, and Catherine's."

A hardness, formed by years of tension, lost its grip within Catherine. Autumn's splendor unfurled on the hills beyond them. Wind sighed, the creek riffled, and the sun rose higher to shine upon three women set apart from the world of war, if only for the moment. They were sisters, this was sanctuary, and she reveled in what God had done.

The water chilled Catherine's feet as she joined them. It grounded her to the moment, stones and sand beneath her soles.

Cupping more water in her hands, Bright Star looked deeply, honestly, into Catherine's eyes. "Today I wash away the years and hard feelings that have separated us. I rinse away any judgments I have uttered. I want to be your sister fully and without holding back. You were named Catherine Stands-Apart, but today I rename you Catherine Goes-Between, for you go between places and peoples, and serve them both. This is not your weakness, but a strength. The Great Good God went between for us." With water running down her arms and dripping from her elbows, she washed Catherine's face. "Do you accept this name?"

"I do." Taking Bright Star's hand and Thankful's, Catherine closed her eyes and lifted her face to the sun. She was not just clean, but restored.

CHAPTER THIRTY-THREE

When at last they reached Gabriel's home, Bright Star wasn't ready to carry on to Kahnawake quite yet and chose to accompany Catherine and Thankful to the house.

As she walked up the slope to the front porch, Catherine felt a familiar squeeze around her chest, a constriction she couldn't blame on her bindings. After being away from her father for more than a month, the idea of shaping her days to please him felt like trying to fit into a gown she'd outgrown.

Walking beside her, Thankful seemed as fleeting and thin as a shadow. Her hands still had not stopped their trembling except when busy at a task. Pulling her cloak tighter about her, she whispered, "I feel as though I've been ransomed all over again. The memories of my childhood terror were unlocked by that Odanak raid. I wonder if they will haunt me as they did when I was seven."

"You are not a child this time," Bright Star told her. "You're not alone."

But wariness hung in the air.

The front door opened before Catherine's hand touched the latch.

"I've been waiting for you." Gabriel's greeting held no warmth. His hair was unkempt, face unshaven. His empty sleeve was unpinned and dangled by his sagging trousers. If he was surprised to see both of his daughters, his expression did not reveal it. His glare was for Catherine alone.

She had not remembered how small he was, nor how small he made her feel. "Papa." In all the time she'd had to imagine this moment, she could never picture how it would go. She clasped her hands. They were chapped and raw as a fishwife's. "We're cold."

Smoke rose and divided, curling up from the pipe in his hand. So he'd found a way to light it without her. "You left me."

But he stood aside, and all three women filed in. It was the first time Bright Star had ever entered the house, yet her gaze didn't wander from Gabriel.

Fire crackled from the parlor hearth, and they went to it. Thankful warmed her hands, back turned to the man who had never understood her purpose in his household. Bright Star stood shoulder to shoulder with Catherine.

"I came back," she told her father. "I have gone on trips before, and I have always come home to you. I see you managed fine without us."

Flames hissed and popped behind the grate. At last, he regarded Bright Star. He pursed his lips around the pipe stem, then puffed into the space between them. "Does she speak?"

Indignation licked through Catherine. Here was his firstborn child, in the same room as him for the first time in more than fifteen years, and this was how he addressed her.

"When she wants to." Bright Star crossed her arms and stared down her nose at Gabriel, matching his glint with her own.

Gabriel grunted. He did not ask where they had been, or how they fared, or if they might care to eat or sit down.

"There has been a battle," Catherine told him, though she supposed he'd already learned about it.

"Oui, Quebec is lost, and no doubt in the spring, the British will come for Montreal." He waved the pipe through the air, putting talk of war behind them without asking what she knew. "When you disappeared, I figured you'd taken Samuel Crane to safety. That didn't trouble me much, to be honest, for I didn't want him dead any more than you did. I'll never get the money back I spent for his ransom, though."

Catherine listened as if from far away. Two empires raged in war, men were dying, women being widowed, and Gabriel Duval's chief concern was the protection of his own interests.

His voice grated on. "What surprised me was that you'd spirited away the key to the trading post, and when the porters returned from their trip to Schenectady, whoever had the key helped themselves to payment for their troubles."

"And left all the trade goods inside," Catherine added, thoughts spooling back to the days before they'd left. "That was the arrangement."

"No." The word exploded from him, and Thankful stiffened. "They did not. Aside from one barrel of oysters, no other British goods from that trip were delivered. All those furs must have brought a small fortune, certainly enough to see us through the winter. We have none of it."

Catherine untied her cape and draped it over her arm. "Then there has been a mistake. My instructions were to deliver a barrel of oysters to Yvette Trudeau in Montreal, and stock the rest of the goods inside the trading post." She turned to her sister. "Do you know anything about this?"

"Your instructions were the same words I passed along." Bright Star's lips flicked up on one side. "But if they became confused somehow, the porters may have delivered the one barrel of oysters here, so Monsieur Duval would not go hungry, and taken the rest to Madame Trudeau."

Thankful spun away from the fire to listen. Warmth had returned the color to her cheeks.

Catherine's eyes rounded. "A mistake, then."

"Yes, but not one that bothers me," Bright Star whispered in Mohawk. "Although if you ask Madame Trudeau, I'm sure she'd return the goods."

Sparks showered from crumbling logs turning grey with ash. "What did she say?" Gabriel set his pipe in a bowl on the table and put his hand behind his ear. "What did that savage say?"

"She is your daughter," Catherine hissed. "Every bit as much as I am."

Thankful's countenance clouded, and she sank into an armchair and pulled an unfinished piece of knitting from the basket on the floor. The work transformed her fingers from shaking to purposeful and smoothed away the brackets around her mouth.

In the silence, noises amplified—the clicking of Thankful's needles, the ticking of the clock, the pop and crack of flame.

Gabriel stared between all three of them. "I see one daughter here, though she seems to have forgotten her loyalties." Turning, he drew a book from the walnut tea table. "Look familiar?"

Recognition darted through Catherine at the sight of Monsieur Trudeau's ledger book. It seemed that years had passed since she had gone through it with an eye to help Yvette understand the business she'd inherited from her late husband. "You went through my things?"

"You must have known I might, or you

wouldn't have hidden this as well as you did. But in vain. I read all your notes, tucked so neatly into the pages. How very helpful of you, how kind of you to resurrect our competition by teaching that widow how to trade, and with whom, and when and where."

Catherine reached out to take the ledger from him. He pushed past her and, holding the book open under his shortened arm, ripped the pages from the binding and threw them into the fire.

"No, don't!" She lunged for it, but Bright Star held her back. The pages blackened and curled. The record of an entire career in trade crumbled into ash. Dazed by Gabriel's selfishness, she watched the destruction long enough for her face to grow burning hot.

"You are a traitor," Gabriel said. "To me."

The words were live coals heaped upon Catherine's chest. After all she had done with Samuel to affect the battle at Quebec, her father's accusations landed here, on a gesture of goodwill toward a harmless milliner. At least if he'd chastised her for helping the British, he would have shown some patriotism. But her father's allegiance was to himself alone.

"I did not betray you." Catherine kept her voice cool, though fury boiled inside. "I was helping a widow in need, a good woman who has shown me nothing but kindness. I fully intended to keep running your trade for you. She was no threat, trust me."

Gabriel's eyes narrowed into slits of disapproval. "I will never trust you again. You play two sides of the same game. You always have. Speaking of which, where is Samuel now? The man I paid for—twice. Where is he?"

Breath pushed in and out of Catherine, pulsing against her ribs. It crossed her mind that she could tell her father that Joseph had been killed in a brutal raid, and still Gabriel would care more about the captive he'd paid for than the death of Strong Wind's son. She would not prove it by speaking her brother's name here.

"Well?" Gabriel shouted, shoulders hunching up with mounting tension. "Where is Samuel Crane?"

Catherine looked at her father and saw twenty-five years of striving to please him, of trying to be enough. Over and over again, she'd tried to save the *loup-garou* from himself and failed. "He is gone. Free of you." Those last words broke loose a bond inside her.

She could be free of him, too.

Cursing, Gabriel picked up the porcelain teapot from the table and hurled it against the wall. It shattered with a crash a foot from Thankful's head. She screamed, and Bright Star stepped in front of her to shield her, exuding strength and protection like an atmosphere.

"We're leaving. For good." Catherine swung her cape back over her shoulders and tied a quick knot at her neck.

Gabriel blanched. "You can't be serious. I need you here. This is your home!" An odd mixture of anger and fear crawled across his face. Veins throbbed across his temple and neck.

"No. It *was* my home. I thought my love would be enough to bring back the papa I once knew. I was wrong."

"For pity's sake, girl—"

"Pity?" she repeated. "It was for pity's sake I left my siblings and came to live with you. It was for pity's sake I stayed. You've had my pity all these years, and in truth, you have it still. But you shall not have me nor Thankful beneath your roof anymore. You've proven you can live without us."

"You can't just leave the house, the post. You have nothing without me. Where will you possibly go?" But as soon as he asked, understanding filtered into his eyes. He knew.

So did she.

With his protests in her ears, and Bright Star and Thankful at her side, she put Gabriel, and that pain, behind her.

Outside, Bright Star squeezed Catherine's shoulder. "You did the right hard thing. I'm proud of you." She kissed Catherine's forehead, a comfort that was both sisterly and maternal, a pouring of water into places of her heart that had been dust-dry for years.

"Thank you." Thankful exhaled deeply, an act that seemed to push the last several minutes, or longer, far away. "I couldn't bear another moment in that house. I know you loved your father, though, and I'm sorry your relationship came to this."

A small smile tugged Catherine's mouth. "Someone very wise once reminded me that some stories don't end the way we want them to. But only when one story ends can another begin."

Bright Star's eyes misted as she took Catherine's hand and Thankful's. "Then I will take my new beginning with you."

EPILOGUE

Montreal, Quebec
October 1761

Two Years Later

"You're in luck, sir." Catherine smiled at her customer as she handed him the three large beaver pelts he'd asked for. "These are the last of our current stock."

The British officer ran his hand over the dense, soft fur with a murmur of approval. "Out of furs already? Either you didn't have many to begin with, or business has been good for you."

Lacing her hands before her sprigged coral gown, she told him it was the latter. "Since the hostilities ended last year, trade has been very good indeed." With Montreal's capitulation in September of 1760, the war—at least on this continent—was over. The trappers moved freely once more, and Catherine collected furs at Lachine as she had for years. Only now she sold them from inside this establishment within Montreal, just as the late Monsieur Trudeau had. Yvette had turned the trading post entirely over to Catherine's control and legally made her a partner. She had also updated her will so that upon her passing, the business would be solely Catherine's.

Sergeant Huntington scanned the shop. Several women browsed the opposite half of the store, which held all the bonnets and hats a woman could wish for, in styles both French and English. While Yvette hosted a wealthy patron at the tea table with her usual charm and grace, Thankful displayed her latest millinery creations to interested shoppers.

Thankful was made for this work. Not only was she talented enough to create the fashions, but her upswept blond hair—thick and shining now that she had enough to eat—made her a stunning model. Because she could also speak English, British soldiers came to her when shopping for the women in their lives.

One young Englishman came shopping for hats more than anyone else. They were for his sister, he said, but the flush in his cheeks and the stammer in his voice when he was near Thankful suggested he actually came for another reason. Eventually Catherine expected him to outright court Thankful, or try. At eighteen years of age, she was certainly old enough for a suitor. Some day she might choose to marry and begin her own family, but for now, Catherine and Yvette both cherished the time they still had with her.

The sergeant turned back to Catherine. "I suppose it didn't hurt that so many Montreal merchants moved back to France when your country surrendered."

She straightened the cameo pendant at her neck. "I understand why they didn't want to stay, and I wish them all the best, especially since the war still rages in Europe. But you're correct, we did inherit some of their customers and have gained new ones like you."

"It's a good thing you speak our language, for so many of us are hopeless with French. But tell me, mademoiselle, do you find yourself conflicted, doing business with your conquerors?"

The word surprised her. "I don't feel conquered, sergeant. We suffered through a war that I never would have asked for. But we're on the other side of it now. We have food, we are safe—no longer under threat of raid, or siege, or battle. Most of the refugees who filled this city have found their way back to their own homes or those of relatives. I'm doing work I enjoy, and I'm surrounded by the people I love. You won the fight for this country, and yet, in these simple ways, I feel victorious."

Huntington smiled, though he didn't look entirely convinced. "An interesting view of victory, to be sure, especially coming from you. As a businesswoman and one who conducts good trades, I would have thought you'd have a more logical definition." He straightened the tricorne on his white powdered wig. "I'm grateful to do business with you, in any case. Shall we?" He paid her for the furs, and she wrapped them in paper and tied the package with string.

"Until next time," she said with an amused smile.

With a touch to the brim of his hat, he bade her good day. The bell above the door jingled as he left.

Catherine recorded Sergeant Huntington's sale in the ledger book she had started when she and Thankful moved in with Yvette. Then, indulging in a rare idle moment, she watched the people passing by on the street outside the window. After the solitude of her former home on the opposite bank of the river, she sometimes tired of the city. But for the most part she thrived on the robust business the people brought through her doors. It was so different from her first time living in Montreal that the two experiences defied comparison. As a child at Madame Bonneville's school, Catherine was an outcast. Now she was at the center of activity.

Bright Star passed the window, stooped beneath a bundle on her back, tumpline across her brow. Catherine hastened to meet her at the door.

"This is the last of them." Bright Star patted the bale on her back. "They got wet in last night's rain."

Catherine escorted her to the back room of the shop and held the fifty-pound bundle while Bright Star eased out from under the strap. "These are all from Kahnawake families?" Catherine guessed.

"Yes." Bright Star rubbed at the mark left on her forehead by the tumpline, then pushed a fist against the small of her back. "Here, let's spread them out to dry. I'm sure Yvette and Thankful wouldn't appreciate the animal smell mixing with their patrons' perfumes."

Chuckling, Catherine cut the rope and unwrapped the furs. "This is good timing, Bright Star. Did you notice my shelves are bare? I sold the last of the beaver pelts just before you arrived." Her fingers sank into the top pelt as she moved it to dry on a rack.

Nodding her approval, Bright Star did the same. "Here is fox, wolf, and some beaver. They took a while treating the skins, or I would have had them to you sooner."

Together they spread out each fur until the back room was covered with a lush carpet of grey, orange, and brown. "Still coming for dinner on Sunday?" Catherine asked.

"I wouldn't miss it. And believe it or not, neither would Gabriel." Bright Star's lips slanted into a smile. "Do you know what Yvette's cook will make for us yet?"

"Roasted goose and apples, salad greens, fresh white bread."

Bright Star raised an eyebrow. "He'll love that. Last week he talked about that clove-and-cinnamon-spiced pork pie all the way home."

"The *tourtière*?" Catherine opened two windows to permit a breeze. "That's a favorite of Yvette's, too."

Dinner had become a weekly tradition, and a hard-earned one at that. Unwilling to completely abandon Gabriel, Catherine had brought him food regularly, and after each visit had gone to Kahnawake to see her sister. But once the trading post and millinery shop were doing well enough that Yvette could hire a cook, she insisted that Catherine invite Gabriel to dine with them there. Several months later, he finally agreed. No less astounding, Bright Star volunteered to bring him. For the past year, Gabriel and Bright Star had shared every Sunday dinner with Yvette, Catherine, and Thankful. Bright Star still didn't call Gabriel her father and most likely never would. The small kindnesses she showed him were for Catherine's sake.

"How is Papa, really?" Catherine asked Bright Star, for even though Gabriel came for Sunday dinners, he still gave cagey answers meant to spark guilt. *"You'd know how I am if you were around more,"* was a favorite line of his. But she felt no hint of regret for her decision to move away. Living and working with Yvette had been the absolute right thing to do for all of them. Thankful's hands, which shook so much after the raid at Odanak, were calm and steady when she worked millinery. In time, the trembling had subsided even when her hands were at rest. For Catherine, this new beginning allowed her to fulfill her potential while nurturing relationships with her family in healthier ways. She kept in touch with her father, but his happiness was his own responsibility. The freedom in that realization gave her wings.

A gust of cool wind stirred the room, ruffling the furs about them. "Gabriel is fine," Bright Star said. "He hired a couple British soldiers stationed at Fort St. Louis who were looking to make extra money during their off-duty hours. They chop firewood and fill in chinks in the mortar between the stones. It's day labor, a very simple arrangement, but it's good for everyone. Despite what he would have you think, his needs are well met. Between his hired help, the Sunday dinners, and you coming to check on him once a week with a basket of food, you need not worry that he's neglected."

"Thank you." Catherine grasped her sister's hand and squeezed.

In the front room, the bell chimed over the door as more patrons left, hopefully with hatboxes in hand.

"It's almost closing time," Catherine told Bright Star. "Stay a moment, if you can, while I get your payment. I know Thankful will want to see you."

"And I want to see both my sisters. And the woman who loves to mother them." Brushing loose tufts of fur from her deerskin dress, Bright Star flashed a smile.

When Catherine and Thankful had first moved in with Yvette, their stories about Bright Star stirred the older woman until she offered her home to Bright Star, too. Catherine had extended the invitation, but Bright Star had turned it down. *"Remember how hard it was for you to live in Montreal when you were only a child?"* she'd said gently. *"I am a woman grown. I cannot fit there, and I have no wish to try. My place is with the People, but I promise you this: We will continue to work together, and I will see more of you from now on than I ever did when you lived less than two miles away."* It was a promise she had kept.

When Catherine and Bright Star returned to the front of the store, the last customer was just leaving. Yvette locked the door and turned to greet Bright Star, arms outstretched. "Ma chère! What a delight to see you!"

Thankful placed a *Closed* sign in the window display and whisked over to buss Bright Star's cheek. With all the animation of youth, she regaled her with stories from the day's work, tugging laughter from Bright Star's lips. Quietly, Catherine watched the three of them together.

Because of their string of victories in 1759—the fall of Quebec chief among them—the British called it their *Annus Mirabilis,* or Year of Miracles. But right here in this store, Catherine stood looking at hers. Thankful had risen above her terrors. Yvette had found new life and joy after nearly losing everything. And Bright Star had surfaced from the sorrows that had drowned her, emerging a loving sister again. Two years after Joseph was killed at Odanak, she and Catherine were closer than they'd ever been, his death the bridge he had tried to build between them during his life. Miracles, indeed.

Yvette swept out of the room, likely to call for fresh tea. As Thankful and Bright Star conversed, Catherine withdrew payment for the Kahnawake furs but didn't want to interrupt them just yet. Pulling a pin from the coil about her head, she let her braid fall against the lace trim at her shoulder and gazed through the many-paned window.

Outside, scarlet maple leaves fluttered to the ground. Nibbling pastries, cherub-cheeked children held fast to mothers hurrying home.

A dog ran by, chasing a squirrel. Even horses had returned to the city, stamping their horse-shoe seals upon the roads. And there were men in Montreal once more, those who had survived, returned from the militia and reunited with their families. Life still wasn't easy under the new regime, but hunger no longer haunted their eyes.

A smile unfurled on Catherine's face as she saw a father pass by with his young daughter riding his shoulders, his son skipping at his side, holding his mother's hand. It brought to mind another father, far away from here, in a colony called Massachusetts. When she thought of Samuel, which wasn't often these days, this was how she saw him in her mind, in the context of his family. Lydia, Joel, Molly. At last, he was where he belonged.

And so was she.

AUTHOR'S NOTE

Before I began researching for this book, my knowledge of the French and Indian War was limited to George Washington's role in it and legends made famous by the classic novel and movie *The Last of the Mohicans*. But the French and Indian War, as we call it in the United States, was part of a much larger conflict called the Seven Years' War, which involved the Americas, Europe, Africa, and India. For this reason, some historians call it the first world war.

Between Two Shores centers on just one slice of the action, but an extremely pivotal one. Most of the characters are purely fictional, but they are all inspired by the experiences of real people, from the Kahnawake Mohawk to the British captives living in New France to the Canadian militiamen and French soldiers and sailors. The heroine, Catherine Duval, took shape in my mind when I learned that women, from both Montreal and Kahnawake, were involved in the international fur trade between New France and Albany, New York. They were strong, intelligent, and remarkably independent.

Samuel Crane and Thankful Winslet were

both inspired by true stories of British colonists captured by Abenaki and Mohawk warriors and ransomed by French colonists. For further reading on this subject, see *The Unredeemed Captive: A Family Story from Early America* by John Demos and *Captive Histories: English, French, and Native Narratives of the 1704 Deerfield Raid*, edited by Evan Haefeli and Kevin Sweeney. For more about the practice of using captured British or American soldiers to meet the labor shortage in Canada, see *Hodges' Scout: A Lost Patrol of the French and Indian War* by Len Travers.

Supplying the French and Canadian army with food truly was a struggle of epic proportions. Governor-General Vaudreuil spoke for New France when he said, "Of all our enemies, famine is the most fearsome." Several details of the wheat harvest on the Montreal Plain in August 1759 as I presented them in this novel come straight from history:

- Women, children, and old men were called into service to harvest and send the wheat to Quebec.
- Several bateaux loaded with wheat were damaged when they ran aground trying to escape Holmes' squadrons and needed to be repaired at Cap-Rouge.
- The French did notify their lookouts that

533

a convoy of bateaux would carry the wheat to Quebec by river the night of September 12, 1759. The lookouts were ordered not to challenge them.

- The order for the wheat convoy that was to take place September 12 was canceled, but no one informed the lookouts. Historians haven't discovered why the convoy was canceled or postponed.

- A French deserter was the one who informed the British about the wheat convoy and that the lookouts were to let them pass.

- Joseph-Michel Cadet, the Quebec butcher who rose to become the purveyor general for New France, was still trying to get wheat into the city while Quebec was formally surrendering.

- After Quebec surrendered in September 1759, Montreal capitulated one year later, ending hostilities in North America. But it wasn't until 1763 that the Treaty of Paris was signed, officially concluding the Seven Years' War.

For a fascinating study of the battle for Quebec, I heartily recommend *Northern Armageddon: The Battle of the Plains of Abraham and the Making of the American Revolution* by D. Peter

MacLeod. In this volume, I learned not just about the major players like Amherst, Montcalm, and Wolfe, but also of the more than five hundred women who accompanied Wolfe's army to Quebec. One of them was thirty-six-year-old Eleanor Job, wife of a Royal Artillery gunner. She served as head nurse of the British field hospital, nursed on the battlefield, and embalmed General Wolfe's body. I'm also indebted to MacLeod for his book entitled *The Canadian Iroquois and the Seven Years' War*, which provided much-needed context for the role of the Kahnawake Mohawk, among other native nations.

The raid on Odanak headed by Robert Rogers and his rangers was a historical event, as well. The subject is addressed in context and detail in *White Devil: A True Story of War, Savagery, and Vengeance in Colonial America* by Stephen Brumwell.

In *Between Two Shores*, Joseph Many Feathers expresses doubt about the Mohawk alliance with the French for reasons stemming from actual historical events. In the summer of 1760, less than a year after the fall of Quebec, the Kahnawake Mohawk decided it was time to end their French alliance. Viewing themselves as free agents, they helped the British navigate the Lachine Rapids on their way to seize Montreal in what proved to be a quick and relatively bloodless campaign.

While this novel is full of history, I hope it also brings to mind how God views you. He loves you without you earning that love. You were lost, captive to sin, and He ransomed you with Jesus. You are ransomed, redeemed, set free, and loved. You belong.

ACKNOWLEDGMENTS

This book was made stronger because of the help of the following people:

Ann-Margret Hovsepian, my dear friend and fellow author who lives in Montreal and hosted me for a weekend of on-site research, which took us from Kahnawake to Montreal's stunning museums and north to Quebec City. Her help continued when I had follow-up questions for her about the weather, nature, and geography in and surrounding Montreal. (If you get a chance to visit the city, don't miss museums Pointe-à-Callière and Château Ramezay!)

The staff at Kanien'kehá:ka Onkwawén:na Raotitióhkwa Language and Cultural Center in Kahnawake, Mohawk Nation Territory. The reading room offered a goldmine of resources, and Teiowí:sonte Thomas Deer kept up a robust correspondence with me well after my trip ended as I fact-checked details and cultural nuances.

Katia Garon, our tour guide in Quebec City, who gamely answered all my obscure questions.

Author Lori Benton, whose award-winning novels of frontier America have included the

Mohawk culture with respect and sensitivity. Lori read over my work in its less-than-polished state, keeping an eye out for any faux pas I might have made.

A multitude of medical and health professionals who answered questions related to physical injury, including Scott Lockard, Linda Attaway, Elaine Cooper, Anne Reed Love, Doug and Caroline Keiser, and countless friends who chimed in with ideas and personal experiences. Special thanks to Jennifer Major, my brother Jason Falck, and Dr. Rob Keyes.

Everlasting thanks to Matthew Miller, our church's missionary to Siberia, who was home on furlough during the writing of this novel. Sadly, he broke his rib while home. Amazingly, he answered all my questions about what exactly that felt like and how the recovery process went so I could model Catherine's experience on his. When I told Matt I wanted to know if a person could paddle a canoe three weeks after breaking a rib, he decided to try. With permission from his doctor, three weeks exactly after his injury, he loaded and unloaded a kayak himself and paddled it alone so he could tell me how it went. I promise I didn't force him to. Yes, he was sore afterward, but he did it. Now that's research!

I am also incredibly grateful for my agent, Tim Beals of Credo Communications, and for my editors, Dave Long and Jessica Barnes, for believing in this story and helping me shape it into something worth printing.

Many people have prayed for me during the creation of this book, and I'm thankful for each one. Special thanks to Susie Finkbeiner, whose gift of encouragement knows no bounds.

I'm blessed by my parents, Peter and Pixie Falck, for watching the kids and sometimes giving my family food; my husband, Rob, for supporting me and my work even when that means cereal for dinner; and my children, Elsa and Ethan, who have become quite encouraging little people. It can be challenging having a writer in the family. You all handle it with grace and good humor, and I am so grateful for that.

Thank you to The Pie Lady of Gladbrook, Iowa, for baking and selling delicious pies suitable for every stage of the writing process, and thanks to Tea Cellar in Cedar Falls for supplying the best teas ever and a lovely place to write and edit.

Most importantly, thank you, Lord, for being a ransom, for redeeming Your children and calling us Your own.

DISCUSSION QUESTIONS

1. In the prologue, Catherine makes a choice to live with her father, and that choice was interpreted by her sister as a personal rejection. Can you think of a time when you were forced to choose between two valuable things? What was the result?

2. For years, Catherine tries to earn her father's love by supplying the practical help he needs. How have you noticed people trying to win approval in your own family or community?

3. When Catherine was a pupil at Madame Bonneville's School for Young Ladies, the ladies in charge tried to scrub and train the "savage" out of her. Have you ever felt that you had to deny who you are, or part of who you are, in order to please someone else? How so?

4. As a trader, Catherine's philosophy is that an equal trade is always the best answer. But when is that untrue?

5. When Samuel Crane tries to explain to Catherine his perspective on love, he says that love is greater when need is not part of the equation. What role do you think need plays in love?

6. The relationship between Catherine and Bright Star is complicated by grudges and grief. Catherine felt her sister was an impenetrable wall at times. Have you had a family member or friend who was also difficult to reach? If so, what has worked in connecting with that person?

7. At the end of the book, it is a revelation to Catherine that she is not responsible for Gabriel's happiness, so she is finally able to put some healthy boundaries in place. Have you had the experience of others relying on you to make them happy? How have you coped with that?

8. Samuel reminds Catherine that life is about more than just the two of them and their happily-ever-after. When have you had to set aside your own desire for a greater purpose? Did you freely make the choice, or do you feel it was made for you?

9. After the battle on the Plains of Abraham, Catherine wrestles with guilt, even though the battle would have happened even if she had not brought Samuel to Quebec. Do you tend to struggle with guilt even when the blame is not yours alone? How do you deal with that?

10. Catherine fears that Joseph's death will be the final shattering to her relationship with Bright Star, and yet Bright Star shocks her with forgiveness and acceptance. When have you been surprised by grace?

About the Author

Jocelyn Green inspires faith and courage as the award-winning and bestselling author of numerous fiction and nonfiction books, including Christy Award–winning *The Mark of the King*; *A Refuge Assured*; *Free to Lean: Making Peace with Your Lopsided Life*; and *The 5 Love Languages Military Edition*, which she coauthored with bestselling author Dr. Gary Chapman. She graduated from Taylor University in Upland, Indiana, with a BA in English, concentration in writing. She loves Mexican food, Broadway musicals, strawberry-rhubarb pie, the color red, and reading with a cup of tea. Jocelyn lives with her husband, Rob, their two children, and two cats in Cedar Falls, Iowa. Visit her at www.jocelyngreen.com.

Center Point Large Print
600 Brooks Road / PO Box 1
Thorndike, ME 04986-0001 USA

(207) 568-3717

US & Canada:
1 800 929-9108
www.centerpointlargeprint.com